T0095368

Germania

Robert Chipley

iUniverse, Inc.
New York   Bloomington

Germania

iUniverse books may be ordered through booksellers or by contacting:

iUniverse
1663 Liberty Drive
Bloomington, IN 47403
www.iuniverse.com
1-800-Authors (1-800-288-4677)

ISBN: 978-1-4401-5425-6 (pbk)
ISBN: 978-1-4401-5426-3 (cloth)
ISBN: 978-1-4401-5427-0 (ebook)

Library of Congress Control Number: 2009931839

Printed in the United States of America

iUniverse rev. date: 7/23/09

A Note to the Reader

The S-bahn and the U-bahn are the train systems in Berlin; the former is mostly elevated or surface while the latter is mostly underground. The German word for "street" is "*Strasse*," or, in German spelling, "*Straße*," and is often tacked on to the name of the street to make a single word, e.g., Scharnhorststrasse.

Joseph Goebbels, Nazi propaganda minister, kept voluminous diaries that stopped only in early April 1945. A copy on glass plates lay for many years unrecognized in the archives in Moscow. The death of Hermann Goering is documented in the book *The Mystery of Hermann Goering's Suicide*, by Ben E. Swearingen. I found it in the stacks of the Georgetown University Library. While adapting from it, I have remained true to the spirit of its findings.

Most importantly, I first became aware of the remarkable structure featured in chapter 14 from the book *The Ghosts of Berlin*, by Brian Ladd. Only the fact that it really exists makes it believable. It is pictured in *Von Berlin nach Germania*, by Hans J. Reichardt and Wolfgang Schäche, a study of Albert Speer's plans to destroy Berlin and replace it with the Nazi capital. On a trip to Berlin I sought it out, and it is much as I describe it.

CHAPTER 1

A Death on the Frontier

"Herr Doktor Klug? Or should I call you Herr Leutnant Klug? Or perhaps just Comrade will do?" These words were addressed to a man in a tan raincoat by a thin blonde woman who had fallen into step beside him.

It was a chilly day in early spring. A light rain was falling, and gray clouds swept across the sky. The two were just stepping into the sheltered walkway beside the Grand Hotel on the broad boulevard Unter den Linden in the eastern part of Berlin. To one direction lay the Brandenburg Gate, and behind it the western part of the city with the Victory Column a few blocks beyond. To the other direction lay the former Marx-Engels-Platz, with its statues of the two heroes of socialism, one standing and one seated, still gazing out over a vast but now empty public square where thousands of citizens of a state that no longer existed had once gathered to pay them homage. A stream of cars and yellow double-decker buses passed by in either direction.

"Excuse me?" The man stopped and turned toward her. He was perhaps forty, tall and slender, with wide-set, light blue eyes and pale skin stretched taut over high cheekbones, a strong jaw, and a straight nose. His thick, ash-blond hair was combed straight back and carefully trimmed above the ears.

"I've been watching you, Herr Leutnant. You haven't noticed me?"

"Why should you be watching me?"

He looked at her closely. She was perhaps a few years younger than he, but it was hard to tell. Her cheeks were sunken and gray, and her lips were white and pinched. Beneath her almost translucent skin one could see little blue lines of veins branching across her face, ending on one side in a large bruise below the eye. A few droplets of water fell from her hair onto the collar of her shabby brown coat, which one thin hand clasped closed. Her shoes were faded and worn, and her slacks were thin at the knees. There was nothing familiar about her at all. By this point they had moved beneath one of the arches and stood next to a cement planter in which grew a tired evergreen, brown and dead at the top with only a few green needles on its lower branches. The noise of traffic and construction across the street made their conversation entirely private.

"Why indeed? With a past like yours, can't you imagine one? But you surprise me, Herr Leutnant. I'd have expected you to be more alert. A man who formerly watched other people. It was your career, wasn't it? Have you forgotten so much?"

"You're quite mistaken, Fräulein. I watch no one. As for my career, I am a translator and interpreter. I have no other."

"Oh, yes. A translator and interpreter." Coming from her, the words sounded quite different. "How learned and intellectual you must be. Do you suppose the people around us know what sort of man walks among them? Those workers up there on the scaffolding? That man just opposite on the motorcycle? But they don't know you the way I do, Herr Leutnant. Herr Leutnant Klug, Christian name Hans, formerly of the border troops of the German Democratic Republic. I've been watching you since yesterday. That pamphlet slipped under your door—it was I who put it there! The person you bumped into at the elevator—that was me! And today, I've had you in my sights since the moment you left your flat. At times I was close enough to spit on you! How your talents have slipped! Your former superiors would be quite disgusted with you!"

"Fräulein, I do not expect anyone to follow me. What do you want?"

"What do you think I want? To stick a knife in you? To watch you die right here at my feet? Oh, I'd like that just fine, Herr Leutnant.

After all, you stole my life from me! It's what you deserve! But no, not today. There's something else I want. You and I have something to discuss."

"That seems unlikely, Fräulein."

"Unlikely, is it? I think not! Oh, I've often imagined what I'd say to you when first we met, but now when I look at you, I can't think of any of it. I thought you'd look hard. I thought I'd be able to read your life in your face. But there's nothing there at all. You're like everyone else. You're ordinary." She gave him a mocking and contemptuous smile.

"I'm sorry to disappoint you."

"Let me come to the point, Herr Leutnant. Tell me, is your memory good? Heinz Kalmbach: do you remember him?"

"That name means nothing to me."

"Think back, Herr Leutnant. Blond. Slight. His ears stuck out. People made fun of him for that. You still don't recall? Of course you met him only once, and you saw him alive for only a few seconds."

"Fräulein, this is pointless. I know no Heinz Kalmbach. If you will excuse me, I have important business to attend to." This was true; he had been called that very morning to interpret at a meeting at the Grand Hotel between two American businessmen and representatives of a German auto firm. It was scheduled, in fact, to begin in only a few minutes.

"I warn you, Herr Leutnant, hear me out! Pointless, is it? Then let me ask you this: how does it feel to kill someone? To see a gaping hole in his chest that you put there? To watch him writhe and pour out his blood on the ground? Do you feel regret? Or are you proud? After all, wasn't that what you were out there for? To kill people?"

"If you are referring to the state frontier, Fräulein, I was there to do my duty and nothing else."

"Oh, your duty. How noble! And what does that include? Shooting children? Do you know where I grew up? Schierke. The loveliest little town in the Harz Mountains. You must have gone through it many times. We used to see the border troops every day, on their way to their posts. Heinz was our neighbor. Little Heinz; I loved him from the time we were ten. We were lovers at fifteen. What a child he was! Do you know he never weighed more than sixty kilos? And so harmless, so without malice. He'd have had none even for the man who killed him!"

With that, she transfixed him with a look of pure hatred, one unlike any he had ever seen before.

"Oh, yes, Herr Leutnant," Now the words cascaded out of her, as though she'd said them over many times. "He learned very early what life in our Republic was like. Do you know what made him decide to flee? He'd just turned eighteen. The next month he had orders to report to the army. That would have killed him! Escape to the West was the one chance he had! But that was a crime, wasn't it? Worse than murder, worse than rape! I tried to talk him out of it. I begged him, in fact! A boy in our village had tried the year before. They brought his body in the back of a truck and made his mother look at it. Do you know what they said to her? 'Comrade, here is your son. You have failed in your socialist duty to educate him.' The swine! How frightened I was! But his courage gave me courage. I asked to go with him. I thought we could have a life together, far away. Do you know where I was when I heard the shots? In the forest, right where the death strip began. Not one hundred meters from the West. I could almost hear life going on over there!"

She stopped and wiped the raindrops from her brow. Her voice grew low and hoarse.

"He was to go first, and I was to follow. It was foggy that night. You were extra alert on nights like that, like a predator stalking its prey! We thought we'd been so careful. We had a rope ladder and we'd practiced climbing every wall in the district. And we'd been out near the frontier. Oh, it wasn't easy, getting close, but we were careful! We saw where the patrols went. And when we got close to the border, we found just where the watchtowers were. We chose a spot halfway between two and lay in the woods for hours, timing the patrols on the death strip. Sometimes it was a soldier driving an open vehicle with an officer in the back; sometimes one on a motorcycle and another in the sidecar; sometimes two men on foot with a dog. One like that had just gone by that night. It was just past three. A wind had come up. We heard the distant voices of the guards. Heinz was to go first. We waited for two minutes and then he kissed me and ran. Why did they turn back, just as he reached the fence? Was it me? Did I trip a sensor? Suddenly a dog was barking. Sirens were blaring. The guards were running back. A vehicle came speeding out of the mist. I heard shouts. And then a shot. Then shouting and more shots. Was it you who pulled the trigger? Was it you who shot him down? I got up on my knees. I looked, but I couldn't see. But I knew it was over. I knew he was dead."

"Whatever you experienced, I regret, Fräulein, but it has nothing to do with me."

"Nothing to do with you? You filthy swine, it has everything to do with you! What do you think came into my hands, not one week ago? A report of that night; your report, Herr Leutnant. It's all there: the time, the rain, the fog—everything but his name. To you he was just 'the subject.' 'The subject this, the subject that.' 'The subject was detected in the free-fire zone. The subject attempted to scale the outer defenses. The subject ignored the order to halt. The patrol was forced to take measures to neutralize the subject.' What do you think I should do with it? Give it to the state prosecutor? What would happen then? You'd be in the tabloids. They love stories like that! 'Neutralize the subject!' Can you imagine what they'd do with that? You'd be a marked man! Decent Germans would spit on you! People are settling the debts of the past, Herr Leutnant. Sooner or later they'll get to you! Your life won't be worth a *pfennig*! You'll be dragged out and killed just the way you killed Heinz!" Unfortunately what she said bore some truth. Only a month before, a former border guard who had shot an escapee at the Wall had been attacked on the street by a gang of thugs and beaten into a coma.

"Fräulein, come to the point. What do you want?"

"You owe me something, Herr Leutnant; reparations, one might call it. The Jews got them. I lost as much as they did. Why shouldn't I get them, too? And who is there to give them but you?"

"So you compare yourself to the Jews? And that's what you want from me? Reparations?"

"What is a life worth, Herr Leutnant? A hundred thousand euros? In cash? Does it make up for what you did to me?" At this he looked her in the eyes, while she stared back, equally hard. She was no longer just a sickly blonde in a ratty brown coat. She was small, contemptible, greedy, and dangerous.

"And that's the price you put on your dead lover's head? A hundred thousand euros? Whatever happened to Heinz Kalmbach, it's more your fault than mine. You could have stopped him, and because you didn't, I had to. You knew the laws of the time. I was sworn to uphold them. You and this Kalmbach were fools. And what makes you think I have that kind of money? What a ridiculous sum."

"Ridiculous, is it? You'd best find it, Herr Leutnant. I shall give you until precisely three tomorrow afternoon. Hear me well! Bring it to the flea market near the Tiergarten, to the tenth booth on the right aisle on the side closest to the S-bahn station. There is a bin at the back. In it you will find a box of woodcuts with views of the city. Stand next to it and pretend to look through them. Bring the money in hundred euro notes, wrapped in clear plastic, in ten packages of one hundred notes each. Put them in a shopping bag, and when I stand beside you, hold it open so I can look inside. Then we will make a trade. You shall hand me the bag, and I shall hand you the report. If you try to cheat me, I shall denounce you on the spot! And if you don't appear, I shall go straight to the authorities! Do as I say or suffer the consequences!" And with one last look, full in the face, she turned and walked away.

Hans watched her as she disappeared down the Friedrichstrasse toward the entrance to the Stadtmitte U-bahn station, stepping out into the street where the sidewalk was blocked by construction. In a way he'd expected her, or someone like her, years before. The past had finally laid a cold hand on his shoulder.

CHAPTER 2

Mrs. Laibstein

With its fine restaurants, expensive shops, and luxurious suites, the Grand Hotel had become the fulcrum of international business in the new Berlin. Once one entered it, the language in the air became English. The only German one heard came from the staff, set apart from the guests not only by their scraping, servile manner, but also by their degrading little livery with the seal of the hotel on the coat pocket. At just past two, the lobby was filled with people from all over the world. Amid ordinary, well-dressed Westerners scattered about among the potted palms, there were Indian women in saris and Arab men in white robes. At the foot of the grand staircase stood a beautiful Asian woman in a sable coat with an equally sleek male companion. As Hans passed by her, she turned and looked him over, from head to foot—whether with admiration or contempt, it was impossible to say.

Upstairs, the two Americans were already waiting in a small conference room: one was a dark little fellow with a twitch, and the other an older man with heavy features, slicked-back gray hair, and deep bags under the eyes, wearing cowboy boots and a shiny suit. Three Germans, two men and a woman, were there, too, as was Hans's colleague, a somewhat eccentric, balding middle-aged man in a worn, brown sweater and rumpled slacks who had grown up in New York but had lived many years in Berlin. Everyone was seated around an inlaid oak table that was covered with glass. The older American was slouched in his chair, with one foot propped rudely on a coffee table, cleaning his nails with a penknife. The other was looking at his watch: Hans was five minutes late.

The meeting began with greetings and introductions all around, followed by an exchange of documents. Then came a long statement by the Germans and a shorter one by the Americans, each side expressing great respect and trust for the other, doubtless felt by neither.

At last, the discussions began. The topic was importing German auto parts into the U.S.; everyone, especially the Americans, planned to get rich from it, since German parts were so much better than the shoddy ones made in America and would therefore be snapped up in an instant. As they spoke, a waiter in a white coat moved among them, serving coffee and cakes, but Hans and his colleague had no time for such amenities which in any case weren't meant for them—the work was far too demanding. It followed the usual pattern; Hans translated from English to German, no more than half a sentence behind the speaker, trying as best he could to match the cadence of the speaker's voice, while his colleague, who in every way sounded like an American, translated the other way around.

But this day Hans couldn't concentrate; his mind was elsewhere; there was no denying this little extortionist had seriously upset him. There were dozens of technical terms and it was hard to avoid mistakes, despite the fact he had reviewed a dictionary of such words that very morning. Once in the middle of a sentence he lost his grip entirely on what the dark little man had said and his colleague had to come to his aid. At that the American in the shiny suit made a sour face; it was clear that he regarded interpreters as no more than trained dogs performing a trick. How typical it was of Americans to sneer at people when it was they who deserved to be sneered at. As for German, clearly no American would ever learn more than a few garbled phrases, uttered in a repellant accent. They had no ear for it; they didn't see language as an intellectual structure; to them it was no more than a collection of words. In general, it seemed as though in America people of lesser ability could rise to heights that in Germany would have been quite impossible to them. But in contrast, as time went on, more and more Germans were learning English, which meant competition among interpreters for the little business that was left was getting fierce; the day would come when no one would need them at all. But what would that matter to someone sitting out his days in prison?

In an hour the meeting drew to a close. The Americans and the two German men turned their backs on the interpreters, shook hands with one another in silence, and left the room. The German woman, brought along for just such a purpose, now counted out to Hans and his colleague his respective fee: two hundred euros, in cash. His colleague stuffed the money down under his sweater and into his shirt, then remarked in English that Hans hadn't seemed quite himself that day and inquired after his health. At last he, too, drifted away and was gone.

Outside, Hans stood a moment by the planter where the woman had approached him. This ordinary little object, half-filled with cigarette butts and its cement edges crumbling into dust, marked a spot where his life had very likely changed forever. Scarcely aware how he got there, he found himself what seemed a moment later at the Friedrichstrasse S-bahn station, where, borne up to the platform by the rush of commuters, he arrived just as a train rolled into the station, brakes screeching. As it pulled out again in the direction of the Alexanderplatz, filled with tired-looking people on their way to shabby suburbs to the east, he looked out with a weary gaze over a city getting uglier and worse by the day. As the capital of a just state, Berlin had been orderly, neat, and clean. Banners had hung from public buildings, extolling brotherhood and solidarity with the distant oppressed of the earth.

But now the oppressed of the earth weren't distant at all. Refugees from the endless ethnic wars in the East brought about by the collapse of socialism were everywhere—Rumanians, Russians, Albanians, Gypsies, Bosnians—dirty, starving, coughing, and spitting into the gutters, sitting on filthy blankets or cardboard on the sidewalks, surrounded by their children, all of them with their hands perpetually outstretched. They seemed scarcely human. Wherever one turned, one saw them. They lurked under bridges, selling contraband cigarettes. They pilfered from merchants and snatched purses and cameras from tourists. In warm weather, they prostituted themselves behind bushes in the park. They rooted through the trash at trash dumps or knocked over garbage cans and foraged in the mess they made, like stray dogs. They cooked their meals over open fires in empty lots and defecated in the street between parked cars. They built shacks for themselves out of packing crates, stuffing rags and bits of wood into the cracks, and every winter, a few died of the cold. The new state did nothing for them but drive them relentlessly from one place to another. They had brought down on themselves the hatred of half of Germany, as was evident from the graffiti, angry smears of red and black, all over the city: "Foreigners out—Germany for the Germans!" "Our Fatherland has become a cesspool for the filth of Europe!" "Our grandfathers were right!"

There were posters, too—the walls were plastered thick with them—many from a neo-fascist group, the Aryan People's Party, which got more and more votes in every election and already had one or two representatives in provincial parliaments. "Stand Up for a New Germany!" read one. In black gothic letters across the bottom it read, "German men aged Fifteen to Twenty-five—Can You Prove Aryan Descent? Then Join the Aryan Youth!" Yet another showed a little blonde girl with bowed head, laying a wreath on a soldier's tombstone that bore the words "He met the hero's death on the Eastern Front." Its caption read, "Remember! March 8 is Heroes' Memorial Day! Teach Your Children to Honor Our Sacred Dead!" There was no doubt the fascists were back. The new Germany had given them the courage to show their faces and swagger about.

As for the Jews, who were moving to Berlin from the East in ever-growing numbers, only an unfathomable stubbornness could have drawn them to such a place as the capital of a unified Germany. Their few places of worship were under constant guard, not even the few Jews who visited from abroad could get through the door. Of course nowadays swastikas were everywhere, scratched into the window frames on the trains, scrawled on advertising pillars, and painted on the sides of buildings. There was even one on the statue of the grieving mother by Käthe Kollwitz at the square in the workers' district of Prenzlauer Berg. No one did anything about them, and every day there were more. In all of Germany, there wasn't enough paint to blot them out.

At the Greifswalder Strasse station, Hans got off the train and walked toward the decaying blocks of flats where he lived. These lay behind a park once named for Ernst Thälmann, a Communist hero martyred by the Hitlerites. Once tended by gardeners from spring to fall, now it was hardly a park at all. The gardeners were gone, and their flowerbeds had gone to weeds. Instead of grass, there were patches of bare ground, muddy and rutted. Instead of raked, gravel paths with trimmed edges, the walkways were littered with cans and broken glass.

As for the flats, they were just one more sign of how the city was falling apart. Once the best in the capital and open only to party members, now many of the residents came from abroad. Too many of them were ethnic Germans repatriated from the East; a swinish, drunken lot far worse than any non-Germans. They beat their wives and screamed curses at one another any time of day or night. Sometimes one found them in the halls, asleep in their own vomit.

In his own block, there were a number of Russian Jews, as well, a notably better class of people who were quiet and kept to themselves despite the indignities visited on them. Hans, who knew Russian after years of study from earliest school right up through University, had struck up a friendship with two of them—a mathematics professor and his daughter—who lived two doors down. Driven from his Moscow post by anti-Semites, the professor now eked out a living correcting papers for instructors at the technical university while his daughter, a graduate engineer, waited on tables in a restaurant catering to their co-religionists, a fact that had already brought it a brick through the window. The mathematician was a man in his fifties, with a thin, deeply lined face, a pock-marked complexion, and dark circles under his eyes. The young woman, however, no more than twenty-five, was utterly lovely. She had gray, almond-shaped eyes, a straight nose, thin lips, and thick, dark hair that stood out in every direction at least twenty centimeters from her head. No German girl had anything like it. She was lively and good-natured, and when she smiled, her eyes narrowed, giving her an almost feline look—the effect was quite dazzling. There was no denying that an attraction had existed between the two of them ever since their first chance encounter in the hall. Now, gradually, he had grown closer to these people. He sometimes drank tea with the professor in the afternoons or played chess with him in the evenings, and three mornings a week, for an hour or so, he tutored the daughter in German. She had nothing to pay him with—not that he would have taken anything—but she brought him delicacies from the restaurant and, occasionally, a Russian book. Gradually she had entered more and more into his thoughts, and now he found not an hour of the day went by that he didn't think of her.

There was some evidence she liked him, as well. One day she knocked on his door and told him she had borrowed a car from a countryman for the day; she wondered if he might like to accompany her and her father on an excursion into the countryside. Another day she had accepted his invitation to her and her father to have coffee and cake in the revolving restaurant at the top of the television tower. A photographer had taken a picture of the three of them, and Hans had pinned it to the wall near his writing table. He found, somewhat to his dismay, that she was a very direct young woman. One day he had casually mentioned that he'd once been married. With a look like she was laughing at him, she had buried him under a barrage of questions. What was she like? Why did they part? Why had he married her in the first place? What, exactly, had he done for a living in the old days? Finally he had deflected her questions with a smile. "Let's not talk about me, Sonja Davidovna," he had said. "Let's talk about you." At that, she had changed the topic altogether.

As for her father, he may have been brilliant, like many of his race, but in some ways he was a fool. When people on the streets called him a dirty Yid, he seemed not to hear. To him, the SS runes painted on the door of their flat was a childish prank. As Hans had helped the two of them scrape them off, shaking his head in anger and disgust, he tried to reason with the man. "Herr Professor, it pains me to say this, because I greatly value my friendship with you and your daughter, but the new Germany is no place for you. You must believe me. You and your daughter should settle elsewhere. No Jew will ever make a life for himself here."

But Professor Eisenberg—his name had branded him as much as did his appearance—had merely smiled and said, "Herr Doktor, why should I not try, when there are people in Germany like you?"

Wearily, Hans entered the lobby of his building and rode up in the elevator. But getting home and simply closing his door on the rest of the city offered no relief from the decay overtaking Berlin—quite the opposite, in fact—his flat was falling apart, too. Plaster was flaking from the walls, and cracks and water-stains patterned the ceiling. The beige carpet had worn through in several places, revealing crumbling, brown linoleum. Hot water was sporadic, and in the winter, the heating system gave out such tepid puffs of air that in the evenings he had to sit wrapped in his coat. The building was teeming with vermin. At night when he turned on the light, hoards of roaches came pouring out of the sink. When he lay in bed he could often hear a mouse skittering across the floor.

As for the pamphlet this loathsome woman had put under his door, he fished it out of the trash, where he had thrown it with hardly a glance. On the cover was a fallen knight, laid out on a bier, while a robed woman, with bowed head, lay a wreath at his feet. Below, in the heavy Gothic script so favored by the Nazis that it had virtually disappeared from modern Germany, were the words, "Give to the Memorial for German War Dead." On the inside, framed with the figures of men in the uniform of every branch of the Nazi war machine, was text that read:

"Why does Germany have no memorial to those who gave their lives for the sacred cause of our race? We owe it to our fallen comrades to set this right! Contribute to the Memorial for German War Dead! We are assembling the names of all those of German blood who fell defending the Reich. Special honor will be paid to the winners of the Knight's Cross, the most important decoration in the history of the Aryan tribes of man. Our work will some day be the basis for a great memorial to be built in our sacred capital when we have taken back our role as the leader of the cultured world. Lesser countries have their memorials. Even Japan has one to honor its fallen heroes. Why should not Germany?

"You can help! We need the contributions of good Germans everywhere to carry on our work. Because the Fatherland is not yet in our hands, we cannot openly collect funds at home. Send your contributions to The Committee to Honor the German War Dead, P.O. Box 445, Lynchburg, Virginia, 22555, U.S.A. Stand with us and some day Germany will be ours!"

Setting the pamphlet aside, he stared at the pile of papers on his desk, next to which was a stained teacup and an opened English-German dictionary. What he had told the woman was true—that he was a translator and interpreter. Once, though, he had been much more. Once he would have been among those who hunted down the antisocial elements who disseminated trash such as this. But when the state had fallen, his life lost all meaning. Instead of political analysis, he now did mere translations, many of them articles from the American press, which then appeared in newspapers all over Germany. Among those he was working on now was one from the *Washington Post*, a muddled and intellectually slack paper written largely for the political class and those who served it, where what was little more than light entertainment for idle minds passed itself off as serious analysis and was circulated as such around the world. This piece was typical. By a reactionary columnist—a tepid little sour-faced man in glasses and a bowtie whose picture appeared framed by the tripe he wrote, it was entitled "Germany and America: an Alliance for Peace," it was little more than a mass of lies, exaggerations, repetition, and cheap rhetorical tricks. Hans had translated many like it; German newspapers had an unlimited appetite for such trash. How painful it was that all that remained of his career was his command of American English. How degrading that, instead of using it to fight the enemies of the working class, now he, too, served this rapacious and contemptible culture whose tentacles stretched throughout the world and corrupted whatever they touched.

The great irony was that learning English hadn't even been his choice. His facility with Russian had come to the attention of someone, somewhere, and that person had decided that if Hans were to learn English, he might be of even greater use to the state. Since the Ministry for State Security, the Stasi, sponsored his studies, he really had no alternative but to do as they bid. And so the best student and winner of several prizes in Slavic Studies at Humboldt University in Berlin had one day abruptly switched to English, to his own disgust and to the mystification of everyone else. At first his mind rejected it like the body rejects a pathogen. Russian was so structured and elegant: from the form of a noun or an adjective, one always knew just where a word belonged. But English wasn't like that at all. As an engine of commerce and efficiency, it was stripped down; it was, in fact, so smooth and slippery, there was nothing to hold onto. A noun had one form and a plural, and that was it—there was no telling by looking at it what role it played in a sentence. Its grammar was so arbitrary that it scarcely seemed to have one at all. Because it had sprung from the mouths of the most rabid kind of imperialists, it was a language that had grown in a haphazard fashion, like a cancer, sucking up and corrupting words from the tongues of conquered peoples because it was too lazy to make up a word of its own. Just as those who spoke it had robbed from others the riches of their lands, they had pillaged their languages, too, so that learning it was like learning two or three languages. But under the influence of his teachers, an American couple, Jews from New York, Hans had soon begun to absorb it in a way that surprised him. Sometimes it had seemed like English was seeping into his brain, taking it over. Every new word he learned went into a cement blockhouse somewhere in his head, where it was protected forever.

Because of his teachers, what angered him most about this wretched woman was her talk of Jews and their supposed compensation. What right did this little parasite have to compare herself with people who had really suffered? Besides, the professor and his wife, the Laibsteins, had neither asked for nor received a *pfennig*. It was sad to think of these good people, who existed only in memory and in the picture of them he had hung over his bed—she, a short, wizened creature with dark little eyes, a sharp chin, and thick, frizzy hair that seemed to him just perfect for scouring out a pot, but a highly gifted musician who had been a violinist with the German State Opera, and he, a professor at Humboldt University, a sallow and bent little man with a concave chest and tufts of gray hair around a bare scalp, brilliant, kind, and saintly, born in Berlin of immigrants from Poland but sent to relatives in America at the age of seven while his parents stayed behind to be shipped off to die at Treblinka. But when Jew-baiting racists had lynched the Rosenbergs, he had fled from fascism once more, this time back to a just and progressive German state, bringing his American wife. Hans had liked him from the beginning—he was the only thing that made learning English bearable. As his most promising student, Leibstein began to invite Hans to his apartment in a quiet street near the university for evenings of conversation. With his wife it was different. She avoided Hans. In a sneering tone she called him "little Siegfried" and laughed from the other room whenever she heard him make a mistake. But childless and cut off from her own, she gradually succumbed to his efforts to court her, until finally she had taken him into their home, where he had become like a son.

At home they spoke only English—hers refined and educated, his in an accent from the streets of the Bronx. While Laibstein had taught Hans vocabulary and sentence structure, it was she who had critiqued his accent relentlessly and mockingly, making him repeat the same words and phrases over and over while looking at the position of his lips and tongue in a mirror, helping him at last through hours of this tedious practice to master the "ch" and "th," the "w," the "r"—sounds on which German tongues so often come to grief. When her work was done, she'd presented him, her greatest achievement, to visiting American progressives as a fellow American, and they had believed her. These visitors were mostly Jews themselves, with names like Cohen, Shapiro, and Bernstein, but that wasn't anything they ever referred to, at least not in front of Hans. Their relatives who had died in the camps were victims of fascism and nothing more. At first Hans couldn't imagine why this was, but in time it grew clear. They were ashamed that millions of people had wanted them dead.

As for the Laibsteins and their guests, it was hard to say whether or not they were typical Jews, but Hans suspected they were. They had ideals, they loved mankind, and they were ready to sacrifice all for the lowest and most wretched of their fellow man without regard to what tribe he belonged. How different that was from Germans! In the German soul, there was no space for anything transcendent. It was petty, suspicious, shabby, and small. It stared at other peoples and, suspecting it was inferior, hated them all.

Now the Laibsteins both lay in the Jewish cemetery at Weissensee, a short tram ride away. Hans had watched as their coffins were lowered into the ground, a scant ten days apart, while both times an old rabbi with food stains on his shirt and crumbs of a roll in his beard muttered prayers in Hebrew, a language that meant nothing to them. She had died first, wracked with ovarian cancer, right as the frontiers of the state collapsed. As a screaming mob ran through the streets outside the clinic where she lay, she heard instead the pounding on the pavement of marching boots. She had clutched Hans's hand and said, "My darling boy! You must protect us! You must promise me you won't join them! You mustn't let them take us away!"

Although he had promised as he mopped her brow with a cloth, each day her suffering and her fear had grown more acute, until there remained only one way to bring her relief. And so Hans had gone to a Stasi physician and bought ten morphine pills for fifty marks apiece. He had given them to Laibstein, who had carefully ground them up between the bowls of two spoons and mixed them into a pudding, which he fed to her, tears streaming down his face. As her life ebbed away, Hans could see that Laibstein's was ebbing away as well. Already someone from the American embassy had come to the university, asking questions about him; it was clear he'd soon be dismissed.

On an evening only a few days later, Laibstein had come to his flat, carrying a briefcase; he claimed he was going to Leipzig to visit a friend, and he wanted to leave Hans a few items for safekeeping. Among them were his wedding ring and his wife's, a gold watch, a sealed envelope that turned out to have a thousand American dollars in it, and some photographs of his family. He'd sat there, at that very table, spreading the pictures before them, pointing out various people and telling Hans who they were: this man was a tailor, that one ran the dairy, a third was the rabbi, and here was the village doctor, his own grandfather, an old man in a worn black coat. Then, with a handshake, he was gone. And when he had gotten home, he had spread newspapers on the floor, put towels on the sofa, opened the veins in his wrists, and lay down to die.

Now Laibstein and his whole family were gone from the earth. His grandparents, his uncles, his aunts, his cousins, and everyone who had stayed behind in the little stetl in Poland—they had all been herded into the ghetto at Lodz and marched one day by a German police unit into the woods, forced to dig their own graves, and shot. These photographs were the only record they had ever lived at all. They had ended like countless other nameless Jews: dark, pinched faces with angular noses and jaws, peering from their rags and filth at their torturers from behind the ghetto wall. Laibstein's photos showed them in happier days: men in black hats with full beards and sidelocks, draped in prayer shawls and bent over scrolls, fulfilling some ancient compulsion of their race; young boys in yarmulkas reading from holy texts; tables with candles, piled high with food. It was wrong that he, from the people who had killed them, should have ended up with these sad and fading mementos. They were people he didn't understand—not their traditions, not their lives. Still, he could look at the photographs and feel for them a bond and a sympathy; they were at least human beings, however strange and different. They weren't like the photographs of his own family, given to him by his aunt, of his father, a student at a special Nazi school, in his Hitler Youth uniform, standing before a banner with the words "Believe, Obey, Fight!"; and of his grandfather, a Knight's Cross winner and officer in the SS Death's Head Division who had fallen in the East. Both were blond and Aryan, with grim lips, pale skin, hair like his own, and icy blue eyes, like light shining through a glacier.

As to this creature who'd accosted him on the street, what choice did he have but to pay her? But where was the money to come from? As a translator and interpreter, he earned perhaps seven hundred euros a week, rarely more. His existing assets were certainly not nearly enough. Perhaps now was the time to take stock of them.

Going into the bedroom and stooping to his knees, he withdrew a metal box from beneath the floor of the wardrobe. The box was about thirty centimeters by twenty and no more than ten centimeters deep. Opening it, he added to the few hundred euros in cash it contained the notes he'd gotten today, but still, altogether, it totaled less than a thousand. He then looked at his account at the savings bank, which had a balance of a mere two thousand. In the box, too, were Laibstein's watch and rings and money, worth altogether no more than another four thousand, even if he could bear to part with them. There also were the only relics he had kept from his former life. One was a document, in Russian, signed by Premier Chernenko, which read "By your selfless act, you have forever sealed the friendship between the peoples of the German Democratic Republic and the Soviet Union; I hereby declare you to be an honorary citizen of the USSR and confer upon you the rank of colonel in the KGB." Another was a pistol of Czech manufacture issued to him by State Security, along with a handful of bullets that rattled around in the bottom of the box—all highly illegal to have. The last item was a polished, dark mahogany presentation case lined with velvet, and inside was the highest order the Republic awarded, Hero of the German Democratic Republic, with the seal of the state, in gold, circled with diamonds and a silk ribbon in the colors of the national flag. It was worth at least twenty-thousand euros, or to a collector, perhaps much more—only a handful had ever existed. Of course selling it, or even merely possessing it, would open him to questions as to why he had it in the first place, so not only was it was worth nothing, it was a positive danger. But tucked into the corner of the case was a card, and on it a name and telephone number. He took it out, replaced the box beneath the wardrobe, went to the phone, and dialed the number.

The phone rang six or seven times before someone answered. "Beckmann here," it said. Years later, the voice was still familiar.

"Herr Beckmann. This is Hans Klug."

"Herr Doktor Klug! You are not someone I expected to hear from again. What, may I ask, has brought you out of the shadows?"

"An urgent matter, Herr Beckmann. I must speak to you in person at once."

"At once? I'm sorry, Herr Doktor, but that won't be possible. I'm about to leave for my shift. How about tomorrow, first thing?"

"Tomorrow will be too late, Herr Beckmann."

"I see. Well, for you, Herr Doktor, perhaps I can make an exception. I have a break at three a.m. Come to the Prenzlauer Berg S-bahn station and rap on the bars to the gate. If I can, I will come up and talk to you. Not the best place, perhaps, but it will have to do. But I won't have much time!"

"I understand, Herr Beckmann. I will be there."

As he hung up, Hans looked at the cracked plastic clock on the wall. It was already past six. Low on the horizon the sun shone forth from beneath a bank of clouds. Tomorrow would be bright and clear, but the evening promised to be long and wearisome. After a meal of sausage, a stale roll, an apple, and a glass of cold tea, he took forth from his small collection of CDs Mahler's last symphony—a mere fragment; a grim piece reeking of death. It had been a present from Frau Laibstein. She had introduced him to that composer whose music had been much played by German orchestras since the end of the war, as if by doing so they could somehow help make up for what they had done to the Jews. As he put on the earphones and listened to it, he thought of her strange, beautiful face and peculiar little smile and of how everything had changed for the worse since she had departed life. Toward the end of the piece—Mahler had time to complete only the first movement before he died—came one massive, shattering chord, a stroke of doom: the world collapsing into ruin.

CHAPTER 3

In the Service of the State

Late that night Hans lay awake on his bed as the minutes ticked away, thinking of the little towns near the frontier he used to pass through in his days in the border troops. What dark, barren places they had been. Most of the buildings were boarded up; no one had lived in them for years—their residents had been removed from the border zone decades before. The few people left hardly ever stirred about. Most were old and infirm, and it was hard to say what they did there or why they had stayed behind. There was no normal traffic. One never saw a car, nor even a bicycle, on the roads. And almost never, even early in the evening, were there any lights. No one grew anything. There were no flowers in the courtyards, and there were no crops in the fields. In fact, there were no fields—mostly there was unbroken, gloomy forest.

The town of Schierke, it was true, had been an exception. The state had kept it open, despite its nearness to the frontier. That was only because it lay just below the highest point in the Harz Mountains, which had some interest as the scene of the Walpurgisnacht. Worshippers of Goethe came to it from every town in Germany, east and west, even though the peak itself lay right on the frontier and had been closed to visitors for forty years. But for border troops, it was strictly forbidden to wander the few streets of Schierke or mix in any way with its inhabitants—they saw the town only from the back of a truck on their way to and from their posts. On off-duty days, they had to content themselves with Magdeburg, a hundred kilometers distant, a town dismally gray and decrepit, with ruins and rubble still left from the war.

Yet serving on the border was an honor and a trust open only to the few. Even an ordinary soldier had to be recommended for it. To be an officer, one had to have shown the proper socialist attitude from one's earliest years; that for example one had taken a leadership role in the Free German Youth; that further one had to have read the texts of the great thinkers of socialism and could pass an examination; and one had to present oneself as a candidate for party membership. Only then might one be deemed worthy to defend the borders of the peasants' and workers' state from its enemies, both at home and abroad.

Mostly life on the frontier was boring. One drove along the corrugated concrete road a few meters inside the fence, or one sat in a watchtower, scanning the death strip and the edge of the forest with binoculars in either direction, hoping and expecting to see nothing. On occasion, a patrol would go by on the other side. These were the federal police in their green uniforms—slack-looking fellows, who lounged against their vehicles, smoking, then sometimes as a provocation, urinating against the border posts which marked the frontier or even squatting down, pointing their buttocks toward the east and defecating in plain view, wadding up the paper and throwing it over the fence.

As for Kalmbach, a common soldier had shot him, not Hans. It had merely been the last in a whole series of unfortunate events, though in Kalmbach's case, he certainly got what was coming to him. The soldier, Müller, was a quiet fellow, the sort who kept to himself. Life in the army didn't seem entirely to suit him, and he was often in violation of some little regulation which Hans, as his superior, had learned to overlook—he was a fraction of a second late to parade, or there was a missing button on his tunic, or a speck of mud from a patrol could still be detected on his boots. He came from a collective farm near Cottbus, and his one joy in military life was that he was good with the dogs. His favorite was a bitch named Queenie whom he was always brushing and grooming and giving some little treat he'd saved from the mess hall. On patrols they were scarcely ever apart, and it was this that had led to Kalmbach's death.

As for tripping a sensor, the woman was right: that was just what they had done, the fools. Did they think they could just walk right up to the border and climb over the fence? Sitting in his watchtower, Hans had known for twenty minutes that someone or something was out there. Finally, when nothing moved, he'd sent out a foot patrol, consisting of Müller, Queenie, and another man, to pass by the spot in hopes of luring whoever it was out of the woods. Border jumpers were a stupid lot, and that seemed in general what they were waiting for. Hans and his sergeant, a man named Grabowski, had then driven in their vehicle to a spot some three hundred meters distant, where they had stopped the engine and switched the lights off, waiting for a signal from the foot patrol, which had been told to double back after a hundred meters.

At last, when the signal had come, the fog had delayed them, and they had driven off the track and spun their wheels in the sand for a moment. Müller, his partner, and Queenie had arrived back at the spot perhaps half a minute before, which was long enough for Queenie to back Kalmbach up against the fence and sink her teeth into his calf. It was long enough, too, for Kalmback to strike at her madly with an iron pipe and smash in her head. Müller had, to this point, shown remarkable forbearance, and it was only after the second blow that he had shot Kalmbach, just once, through the chest. By the time Hans was out of the car, Müller was already standing over the man, his weapon pointed down, as though the man might somehow rise to his feet and run away. "You filthy swine, look what you've done!" he was shouting.

His partner, reluctant to come near, kept saying in a low voice, "Leave him alone, Karl, he's done for."

But this only set Müller off the more. "What about Queenie?" he had shouted. "Isn't she done for, too?"

And it was true. Both the dog and the man were pathetic sights. The man, slight and blond—whether his ears stuck out or not Hans didn't remember—lay on his back, his mouth gaping like a fish. Blood bubbled up through his lips, and he was spitting it out in a fine spray. A dark stain was spreading over his shirt, as though he'd spilled some soup. He was putting his hands over it, as if he could hide what had happened to him. Queenie was even worse. One eyeball was a bloody pulp, and the other hung useless out of its socket. Her muzzle had been crushed, and broken teeth lay on her tongue. Through the blood and gore in her throat, she was whimpering and whining in a way that went right to the heart, until finally Müller could stand it no longer. Putting the barrel of his weapon to her ear, he blew the rest of her head away. Then he turned and emptied the magazine in a great burst into the dying man's midriff, nearly cutting him in two and splattering blood, intestines, and dirt in every direction. At last he had dropped his weapon and sunk to his knees, his face in his hands. Hans, at first struck dumb by this sight, finally recovered enough to order Grabowski to call for a truck. The minutes dragged by while Müller barely moved. When it finally came, he revived a bit and began to shout and rave anew: the idea that the man's remains should ride back in the same truck with Queenie sent him into a rage.

And so, after the first truck had departed with Müller and Queenie, who was covered by Müller's greatcoat, Hans had to send for another to tend to the disgusting business of removing what was left of Kalmbach. Two privates had spread a plastic sheet on the ground and then, using a shovel and a rake, had put on top of it as much of the man as they could find before closing it up. Even after that there were other things that had to be looked after, which took nearly to dawn. First, a new patrol had to be called out to relieve them, then the local police had to be summoned to the barracks to take charge of the remains, which none of them could look at without gagging. Of course it was left to Hans to write a report. There was no point in setting down the exact circumstances and possibly exposing Müller to difficulties, so he had said only that the subject was armed and that the patrol had been forced to shoot. There had been a hearing from which Müller, at Hans's recommendation, had been excused. The board had asked a few questions but no one had wanted to delve too deeply into the matter—the report and Hans's word were enough to settle it. The commandant of the border troops sent to each a letter of commendation, stating he had done his duty under difficult circumstances, a copy of which was placed in his file. At Hans's request, the flag was flown at half-staff for a day for Queenie, and she was buried behind the barracks while the bugler played "Arisen from the Ruins" and an honor guard fired a salute over her grave. Afterward, everyone involved in the incident was given a month's extra pay and three weeks' leave and then transferred. Sergeant Grabowski was sent to the border with Poland, which no one ever tried to cross in either direction. Hans went to a desk job in Berlin, where he'd done his first work for State Security. Müller's partner, who had only a few weeks to serve anyway, was allowed to go home for good. Müller—if there was truly a victim in the whole affair, it was he—spent a few weeks in a sanatorium on the Baltic, and then went home as well. Hans had never heard anything of any of them again.

So this wretched, scheming, bloodsucking, Jew-baiting little fascist leech held at least four lives in her hands. If only she'd died on the frontier herself! Why hadn't they looked for her on the spot, as procedures required? Why hadn't they at least fired a few dozen rounds into the woods? With any luck, one might have started her from her lair and given them a clear shot at her. Then this whole business would never have come up! Now Müller might well be brought before a magistrate, and this time the truth would come out for sure. Reliving it would unhinge him for good. Sergeant Grabowski would end up there, too, as would the other man, whatever his name was—Hans couldn't even remember what he looked like. Worst, all three might justifiably blame their misfortunes on him.

As for Hans, this would be just the start. Soon enough, his career at State Security would come under the lens. That would make his current troubles seem like nothing. His main task had been to gather intelligence about staff at the American Embassy, which was thoroughly bugged and spied upon. But that had meant more than just reading intercepted mail and listening to telephone conversations. Some of it had been a nasty business. His linguistic abilities meant that State Security could use him in special ways. Two cases in particular had upset him: one was that of a sergeant—a black man—attached to the embassy guard. He was estranged from his wife, he drank too much, he had an East German girlfriend who informed on him to the Stasi, and he occasionally shared drugs with her. At Hans's instruction, she arranged for the man to sell a small amount of cocaine to a Stasi agent, in a place where the transaction could be watched. Hans then had the man arrested and taken to a police station, where he himself conducted the interrogation. The man had wept like a child and rocked back and forth in his chair. After telling the man it was his duty either to prosecute him under the severe drug laws of the Republic or to turn the evidence over to the American authorities, Hans had persuaded him to begin photographing documents from the embassy safe. This the man had done for several months, until finally, he had come under suspicion, and rather than face arrest, he had shot himself. Of course it was inevitable that some people would get ground up in the struggle between clashing ideologies, but it wasn't pleasant to be part of the process.

The other case was far worse. It involved an American security expert called to West Berlin to look into a bombing at a club frequented by American enlisted men. State Security feared what he might find out. Through an agent highly placed in the U.S. State Department, they learned the man would arrive at Tegel Airport as an ordinary tourist, expecting to be met by an American military officer in civilian clothes. The real officer was intercepted—someone had followed him into the rest room and stuck a needle in him. Instead, the man was met by Hans. Hans had prepared for days for the role. He'd read the latest American magazines and newspapers, even the comics. He'd practiced small talk with Mrs. Leibstein, who had no idea what he was up to. He'd had his hair cut short, and he wore American clothes and American shoes that hurt his feet. The security expert, despite his profession, had been thoroughly deceived. He was a stuffy little man with a briefcase and glasses he kept wiping with a pocket handkerchief. They had chatted about opera in the car. The man was quite knowledgeable and Hans had liked him; in fact, to put the man at ease, Hans had suggested that they go together to the opera that very night. At a prearranged spot, the driver had suddenly spun around in his seat and immobilized the man with a stun gun. At the next block, he'd pulled over to the curb, letting Hans out while another man got in. Hans had made his way back to the East through the Friedrichstrasse border crossing, but the man—he had probably crossed through the Wall as a passenger in the trunk of a taxi—had never been heard of again. It wouldn't take much: a few carelessly handled files would do the trick, and the case would be opened again. Then the Americans, a vengeful people, would get into the act, and the German government would do nothing to protect him. Manacled and drugged, he'd be flown to the United States as a trophy, where the world's most expert torturers would exact on him a terrible revenge.

At two-thirty, having slept not at all, he arose from his rumpled bed and warmed some tea in an open pan. At the first faint sign of steam, he poured it into a cup and started to drink it, pacing slowly back and forth. With the last bitter swallow, he walked to the window and looked down at the desolate Greifswalder Strasse and at the trolley tracks that ran down its center. Near the bench where the little parasite had sat in wait for him stood two youths under a flickering streetlight. One of them handed something to the other, who slipped it inside his coat and strolled away. From down the hall came a drunken shout, a woman's scream, and the slamming of a door. Wearily Hans turned away, then pulled on his clothes and went out the door.

At this time of night, the streets of the former capital of the German Democratic Republic were nearly deserted. A night bus went by, empty save the driver. Then came a man on a bicycle, emerging from the mist rising from the street and disappearing into it again down the block. A little farther away, on a traffic island, a group of gypsies stood, warming themselves around a fire in a barrel. In a few more minutes— it was less than two kilometers away—he was tapping on the locked door of the Prenzlauerallee S-bahn station. The place was eerie, silent, and depressing. After a few minutes with no signs of life, he began to tap a bit louder and call out in a low voice, "Herr Beckmann! Herr Beckmann!" At last from the depths of the station came a man, walking slowly up the steps from the platform, wearing a work jacket and a cap. In the streetlight Hans could see the smoke rising from his cigarette.

The man leaned forward and stared at him through the glass before opening the door and ushering him inside. The intervening years had taken a toll. Vigorous and confident when Hans had seen him last, his shoulders were now slumped, his eyes were hooded and tired, and his face was deeply lined. When he spoke, it was in a voice that was flat and dull.

"Herr Doktor. Tell me. What is it that brings you out in the middle of the night?"

"I wish to make a report."

"What sort of report?"

"I wish to report an incident of extortion."

The man took a long last drag on his cigarette, then stubbed it out and dropped it in the trash. He had turned to the side and continued to stand that way while he spoke, as though he were talking to someone else. "Why do you come to me?" he said.

"State documents are involved."

"State documents? May I remind the Herr Doktor that the state he refers to no longer exists? Besides, what do you think I can do about it? I have no authority. My days of ordering people about are over. I push a broom."

"I could go to prison, Comrade."

"So could we all, Herr Doktor."

"How is it that someone has found me, Comrade Supervisor? This is unforgiveable! I thought all files relating to me had been destroyed!"

"Time did not always permit us to be as thorough as we wished."

"If one exists, others might also. Suppose a certain case were to come to light? You know to what I refer. That could prove highly unpleasant. Many people could be dragged into it. Comrade Supervisor, my instructions were that if such matters were ever to come up, I was to report them to you. That is what I am doing. Yet you seem to lack interest. What am I to think?"

The man was silent for a moment. Then, in the same flat tone, he said, "You may tell me the circumstances, if you wish."

"Very well. A woman approached me on the street. A sickly little blonde in a brown coat. She has a report of mine."

"About what, Herr Doktor?"

"A death on the frontier."

"I seem to recall such an incident in your career. The details, however, escape me. Where and when did it occur?"

"Near Schierke, in the Wernigerode District. On 14 March 1983. The man's name was Heinz Kalmbach. This woman claims to have been his lover. She says she was waiting in the woods for him to cross, and then she planned to cross, too."

"But you prevented him."

"It was my duty, Comrade."

"Of course. The report on this Kalmbach: you've seen it?"

"No. But she quoted from it quite exactly."

"And she proposes to sell it to you."

"Yes."

"How much does she want?"

"A hundred thousand euros."

"Of course you don't have that sort of money."

"Hardly, Comrade."

"When are you to come up with it?"

"That's the problem. By this afternoon at three."

"Scarcely twelve hours off."

"Yes."

"Difficult. But there are measures we might take. Perhaps you could point her out to us. Perhaps we could send someone to remove her permanently from the streets."

"No, Comrade. She's going to meet me in the flea market near the Tiergarten S-bahn station, in full view of thousands of people."

"Tell me, Herr Doktor, have you ever considered going abroad? We have friends there, you know. It might be just the thing! A new climate, a new country, a new identity, a chance to begin all over again! With your talent for languages, it would hardly even matter where! You'd be at home in no time! We could arrange it, you know. You could be on a plane before noon!"

"I do not wish to leave Germany, Comrade Supervisor."

"Isn't that a bit unreasonable, Herr Doktor? Why are you making this report to me, if you intend to do nothing to help yourself? Just what is it you want me to do?"

"I want you to find me the money, Comrade Supervisor. It's to be in one-hundred-euro notes, wrapped in plastic in packages of a hundred notes each. I want you to send me someone who knows every corner of Berlin. I propose that once I have given her the money, the two of us together will track her down and get it back." To Hans, this was the only thing that made sense. In a way, it was just finishing what the woman and her lover had started on the frontier years ago.

"A hundred thousand euros is rather a lot. Suppose you fail?"

"Do you doubt my abilities, Comrade Supervisor?"

"My doubts are not the issue, Herr Doktor. I must convince others. Do you think I have that sort of money just sitting around the house? If so, I would gladly give it to you! But I've never seen such a sum in my entire life, nor do I expect to."

"Perhaps it might have some bearing if I were to demonstrate to you that there is an ideological aspect to this affair. This woman is a distributor of dangerous fascist literature, undoubtedly imported from the United States. Here is a pamphlet she claims to have put under my door." With that Hans handed it to the man, who peered at it in the faint light a moment and stuck it in his pocket.

"This could possibly play a role, Herr Doktor. Meanwhile, I will report to others what you have reported to me. I make no guarantees as to their response. As for yourself, you had best get some rest! Whatever the day may bring, you will have to be ready for it." With this, he shook hands with Hans once more, let him out onto the street, and disappeared back into the dark.

CHAPTER 4

The Flea Market

Shortly before ten, Hans was awakened from a fitful doze he had fallen into what seemed like only minutes before. At first it was hard to tell what had roused him, but as the objects he had last seen at dawn came back into focus, he became aware of a persistent but barely audible knocking at the door. Still buttoning his shirt, he opened it to find a man carrying a small canvas bag. The man was perhaps forty-five, solidly built, but not very tall; he wore a leather jacket and held a cap in his hand. He was clean-shaven and had short, brown hair intermixed with gray. His eyes were hidden behind reflective sunglasses. His skin was pasty white, as though it rarely saw the sun, and on his right cheek was a small scar. He gave a slight nod and rapidly glanced up and down the hall.

"Herr Doktor Klug?" he said in a low voice.

"Yes?"

"I am Breitbach. A colleague has asked me to drop by. May I come in?"

"Please do."

Once inside, he looked around critically. "Herr Doktor," he said, still in the same low tone, "you recognize that I must take precautions. You must prove to me who you are."

"Perhaps I might ask you to do the same."

"There is no need for that! I am Inspector Breitbach, formerly of

State Security. I bring you something that will be proof enough. You, however, Herr Doktor, must oblige me."

"My personal identity card? Will that do?"

"If you'll pardon the suggestion, I require something a bit more basic. I'm told you have an identifying mark on your chest. May I see it?"

"I don't disrobe for strangers."

"But today you must make an exception. Those are my instructions!"

This was, to Hans, a matter of some sensitivity. In truth, he did have such a mark. It was a scar, just inside the right nipple, large and vertical, some seven centimeters long. It had rough edges and at the center, where a section of rib had been removed, there was a depression. It was ugly and something that not only repelled him but caused him embarrassment. Whenever he dressed or undressed, he never went near a mirror. Any situation in which he would have to expose it—going to the beach or a public pool or sunbathing in the park—he avoided. But now, reluctantly, he narrowed his eyes to slits, undid the lower buttons of his shirt, lifted it to the level of his neck, and quickly lowered it.

The man gave a low whistle. "A handsome souvenir! Does it cause you pain?"

"Not often." Other than a slight ache brought on by the destruction of some of the muscle, it had never really hurt much after the surgeons at the Soviet military hospital outside Berlin had set to work on him. The blinding light and their little snatches of conversation were with him still:

"This guy is a mess!"

"What do they expect us to do? Raise the dead?"

"Who is he, anyway? Not even Brezhnev got this kind of attention. Every fucking doctor in Potsdam is here working on him."

"Some Fritz. Didn't you hear him muttering? German! It sounds like a pig grunting."

"Look, pay attention and don't screw this up! The old man himself is right outside. When was the last time he turned up for anybody? Shit! He wouldn't do that for his wife!"

"Yeah? Well a hundred rubles says this one doesn't make it past dawn."

"That's a hundred rubles you don't want, Karpov. He croaks, and you'll be doing hemorrhoid operations in Siberia!" Then the voices, the lights, and the whole world had faded away.

When he awoke, hours or even days later, he was in a large and pleasant room, filled with flowers, with sunlight flickering through foliage on the trees. Through the window he could see a lake, and on the opposite shore, a grove of birches, their leaves just beginning to turn gold. As he tried to sit up to get a better look, he realized that something was holding him back. He was, in fact, strapped to the bed, and there were thin tubes in his arms and a thicker one in his chest. At his bedside was a nurse, smiling and mopping his brow. She turned out to be only one of the round-the-clock nurses who changed shifts but never left. As he got to know them, he quickly developed a favorite: a young woman from near Sevastopol, no more than twenty, who held his hand, fed him, emptied his bedpan, and washed him gently with a soft cloth. She was sweet and good-natured and pleased when he first spoke to her in Russian. When she took out the tube in his chest, sponged away the discharge, and put it back in, there was no pain but something worse: an obscene tickling that still made him writhe whenever he thought of it. And always when she performed this task, there was a slight look of distaste on her pretty face. Once they'd gotten to know each other a bit, she'd told him about her fiancé, her parents, and her village. When in a few weeks he at last had begun to revive and the tubes were gone, she sometimes put her hand beneath the covers and hummed to him a peasant song while gazing deep into his eyes and touching him in a way that made him want to stay there with her forever.

Breitbach, meanwhile, had turned the bag upside down and was shaking its contents out onto the table. "Here it is, Herr Doktor. A hundred thousand euros. Wrapped just the way you asked. Quite a wad of paper, isn't it? You must sign for it, of course. From the moment you do, it's your responsibility, not mine. You understand that, I hope."

"Perfectly, Herr Inspector." With that, Hans signed the receipt Breitbach had shoved toward him while Breitbach looked on. This done, Breitbach himself signed it as a witness, folded it up, and put it in his pocket. Then he gave a little sigh of relief and smiled.

"Your little friend. You're meeting her at the Tiergarten flea market, I'm told."

"Yes."

"The perfect place for someone extorting money from a good comrade. It's crawling with fascists! A regular Nazi bazaar! If you want to buy Hitler's undescended left testicle, someone there will sell it to you!"

"You know the place, then."

"Of course! I drive a taxi! That's my job in the new Germany! I know every street, every alley, every building in Berlin! I'm given to understand you asked for someone with just my talents! And by the way, we know who she is. Ingeborg Mohr, that's her name. At the time of the little incident she recounted to you, the police held her for a few days in connection with this Kalmbach. Turns out you did the world a favor. Kalmbach was a social misfit and a criminal! He'd beaten an old woman in his village within an inch of her life and stolen the money her sister had brought her from the West. That's why he was trying to flee—whatever else she may have told you is a pile of shit! The police had been looking for him for three days!"

"How did she get her hands on my report?"

"Hard to say. We think it was stolen, along with a great many other files, by a clerk, now dead, who worked at the archives of the border troops at Potsdam. Such material has been floating around for years. Sometimes it falls into the hands of someone who can use it. As to who gave it to her, perhaps we'll have the chance to ask! Tell me: where precisely are you to meet her?"

"In the tenth stall on the right aisle on the side closest to the S-bahn station."

"Herr Doktor, we must develop a plan. Once you have delivered the money, we will follow her and get it back. Tell me, can you drive a car?"

"Yes, Inspector. I had one, in the old days, until it broke down."

"A Trabi, no doubt."

"Yes, a Trabi."

"There were many fine things about the Republic, but its ability to make cars was not one of them. You must arrive at the S-bahn station at least an hour in advance. There is a small parking lot between the station and the flea market. I will be waiting there next to a car I will have parked there. We will greet each other and shake hands, and I will use that opportunity to give you the key. Then you might wander around in the market a bit to get a feel for the place. Shortly before the appointed time, I will take up a position where I can keep that booth in view. Once the woman has contacted you, you must do as she instructs. If she tells you to stay there for ten minutes, then stay for ten minutes! When she leaves, I will keep her in sight. It's my guess that with all that money, she'll head right for home, like a fox taking a rabbit to its den. Getting it back shouldn't be too difficult! I have brought you a cellular phone to keep in contact. As soon as you can, you must get into the car and wait for me to call. To reach me, just push this button right here."

"Very well, Herr Inspector." Hans took the phone the man handed to him—it was no bigger than the palm of his hand—and slipped it into his pocket.

"You've done well to come to us, Comrade," the man went on, "but if I might be allowed to remark, you might keep this place a bit more tidy."

It was true. There was a bit of dust on the floor, while the shirt Hans had worn two days before still lay draped over a chair in the living room. As for the kitchen, at least a dozen dirty dishes lay piled in the sink.

"How I live is hardly your business, Herr Inspector."

"I beg to differ, Comrade. It is our duty to instruct one another. A good socialist is not content to live in unclean conditions. A good socialist does not relax his discipline. But you're not like the rest of us, are you? An intellectual. A student of languages. A private docent at the University. Oh, and yes, of course, let's not forget: an intelligence officer formerly with the American section at State Security."

"You know quite a bit about me, Herr Inspector."

"I don't take up my old profession for just anyone. Your reputation precedes you, Herr Doktor! Your former colleagues quite hold you in awe! I wish to state that I find it a great honor to work with you." With that, he solemnly shook Hans's hand, gave a stiff little bow, and turned to the door.

~

Shortly before two, Hans walked down from the platform of the Tiergarten S-bahn station, carrying with him the money in a shopping bag from the Karstadt department store. As he reached the bottom stair, he could see Breitbach, a few paces away, standing in a parking lot next to a gray VW. Breitbach walked up to meet him, smiling, and clapped him on the shoulder, and as they shook hands, passed him the key.

Though the flea market was a tradition in western Berlin, Hans had never before gone near it. It was in a part of the city he generally avoided, just as he did nearly all parts of western Berlin. One of its many unappealing features was that the boulevard on which it was located was named to commemorate a day, 17 June 1953, on which misguided workers, stirred up by fascist provocateurs in the pay of the West, had staged an abortive uprising in Democratic Berlin. Every time he looked at a street sign there, he was reminded which side in the struggle between ideologies had won and which had lost.

The day was sunny and warm—the warmest, in fact, of the spring so far. At this time of day, there were hundreds, if not thousands, of people about. Once one penetrated the flea market, one could hardly make one's way down the aisles between the booths. Some were tourists and others were ordinary Berliners looking for a bargain, but all too many were dangerous-looking youths with shaved heads, chains hanging from their belts, and heavy boots with metal-tipped toes. They hung around together in groups of three or four; they pushed other people out of their way; they were loud and profane, and several were drunk.

The flea market itself was a series of makeshift booths of wood and aluminum tubing covered over with canvas, set up and taken down each weekend, where all kinds of junk were offered for sale. There were sentimental paintings of dogs and cats and little blond children. There were forest landscapes in the Mecklenburg Lake District and scenes along the shores of the Baltic. There were pictures of the Charlottenburg Palace and the royal residences at Potsdam. There were trays of cheap rings and earrings, some quite grotesque—one was a mausoleum, beneath which dangled a skull and crossbones. There were assortments of stamps, coins, and obsolete paper money from every country on earth. There were piles of comic books and CDs, pirated DVDs of every movie of the past two decades, cheap and gaudy clothes, cameras and lenses, miniature television sets and phones, and video and audio equipment—no doubt much of it stolen. From the little Hans knew of the place, it was disreputable and disorderly, filled with thieves and pickpockets and criminal in other ways, too. For one, it was known as a marketplace for pornography of the most appalling kind. Hans had once read in Berlin's progressive newspaper about a child molester selling obscene videos out of a knapsack behind one of the booths. A reporter had bought a few and their covers had been displayed on the front page. Showing young boys in provocative poses, they had titles like *Karl and Peter Go to the Beach, Building Young Bodies for a New Germany*, and *Behind the Scenes at a Summer Youth Festival.*

As bad as any of this, mixed in among all the other trash, were relics from the Third Reich. Despite the fact that the law making it illegal to display Nazi artifacts had never been repealed, it seemed that more and more nowadays, people were dragging such stuff out of their attics and openly putting it up for sale. There were Nazi uniforms, helmets, and battle flags. There were ceremonial swords and daggers. There were collar insignia of the Waffen-SS and Death's Head insignia for a cap. There were orders and decorations in glass cases—service medals for the French campaign, Iron Crosses, and decorations for mothers who had borne seven or more children for the Fatherland. There were military passbooks and signed oaths to the Führer. And everywhere were books and pamphlets of fascist propaganda, some from the Third Reich, but many from the Aryan People's Party and other such groups. They bore titles like *World Jewry and Its Lies about Germany, Heroes of Stalingrad,* and *The National Socialist Struggle to Save the West.*

One booth had been set up by the Aryan People's Party to recruit new members. A sign at the entrance read "Are you of Aryan descent? Then you are eligible to join the Aryan People's Party! It is the only party that represents your interests!" Inside a couple of middle-aged men who looked to be ordinary workers were sitting at tables, filling out applications. At the center was a glass-covered case, around which several people had gathered. Hans made his way among them and looked down. In it was a copy of *Mein Kampf,* signed by the Führer and inscribed, "To Rudolf Pfister, a loyal comrade in our struggle: 29 October 1930. Together we will take back Germany!" On either side, as a sort of honor guard, stood a skinhead armed with a baseball bat and wearing the armband of the Aryan Youth. In a nearby booth were a few souvenirs from the Holocaust: scrip and aluminum coins issued by the Reich for use in the ghettos and concentration camps; a ragged overcoat on which was sewn a yellow Star of David; a passport stamped with a "J," for a gaunt, ill-kempt, grim-looking man named Erich Israel Goldfarb; a poster giving a key to the armband colors worn by various classes of prisoners at concentration camps; a book on the model camp at Theresienstadt called *The Führer Builds the Jews a Village*; and last, a commemorative album issued by the Wehrmacht and given to the soldiers who had taken part in the destruction of the Warsaw ghetto, after the Jews trapped inside, at last laying aside their numb disbelief at what was happening to them, had taken up arms and struck back at the fascist beast.

Just before three, Hans sought out the meeting place. As he approached it, he saw that Breitbach had made his way to a food stand a few paces away, where he stood at the counter, the brim of his cap pulled low over his eyes. Next to him was a cup of coffee, and he was eating fried potatoes with a little wooden fork, dipping them into mayonnaise.

The booth Hans entered seemed to specialize in books, magazines, and newspapers from the Third Reich and little else. Wrapped in clear plastic and laid out on the folding tables were issues of the Nazi Party newspaper, The *Folkish Observer*, several of the wartime periodicals of the Waffen-SS, *The Black Corps*, and Goebbels's weekly publication, *Das Reich*, plus song books from the Hitler Youth and the League of German Girls. Amidst the usual copies of *Mein Kampf* and *The Myth of the Twentieth Century* was a boxed set of two volumes from the Institute of Racial Science, the first called *Physical Attributes of the Aryan* and the second *Physical Attributes of the Jew*. The bin at the back had prints of scenes of Berlin, all right, but not of a Berlin that had ever existed. Marked with the seal of the Berlin Academy of Arts and dated 1944, they showed the city, reborn from the ruins as Germania, as it would appear in the year 1960. Though there were several dozen, there seemed to be at least ten that were different. One showed the massive Hall of the German People, where a hundred and fifty thousand racial comrades could gather to listen to the rantings of their leader. Another showed the monument to the Victory over Bolshevism, with two German soldiers, bayonets at the ready, protecting a woman and child from a band of ragged, hairy, half-human brutes who approached them with upraised clubs and rocks. Yet another showed the North-South Axis, and on it, the Great Arch, onto which were inscribed the names of the honored dead who had fallen in the Nazi war of conquest, with the nearby Obelisk of the Heroes, bearing on it the names of the eight thousand greatest warriors of all: the winners of the Knight's Cross.

As he looked through them, a low voice behind him said "Very good, Herr Leutnant. You have come! I knew you would! Have you brought what I asked for?" It was the woman, dressed just as she had been the day before. In her hand she held an envelope.

"Yes. And you. Do you have the report?"

"First show me the money! Then we'll talk about the report!" Hans opened the bag and tilted it toward her. She peered in and stepped back.

"Is it all there?"

"It's all there."

"What if I should take out one package at random and open it up? What would I find?"

"Exactly what you're looking for. Try it and see, if you like."

"No, Herr Leutnant. You're too smart to try to cheat me. And you're afraid, too, aren't you? Say it! Tell me you're afraid! Tell me or you get nothing!"

Hans did have a curious feeling, but it wasn't fear; it was more like disgust.

"All right," he said. "I'm afraid."

"Of course you are! Here, then, take it, damn you! But listen closely and do exactly as I say! There's a train just pulling out of the station up ahead. Do you see it? Wait until you see two more pull out in the same direction. Do not move from this spot until then! A friend of mine has his eyes on you this very moment! Good-bye, Herr Leutnant. Life is changing for us both today. Mine is getting better, and yours is getting worse. Some day may you pay for your crimes and rot in hell!" Then she turned and left, the bag clutched under her arm. The whole process had taken no more than two minutes. He watched as she pushed her way into the crowd until it swallowed her up. When he looked to the spot where he had last seen Breitbach, Breitbach was gone.

Glancing up occasionally at the train station, Hans continued to look through the prints, hardly seeing them. In a few minutes, the proprietor, who had been bargaining with a customer, came over to him. He was a short man with a wispy little moustache, one drooping eyelid over a very bloodshot eye, and bald, save for a few long blond hairs combed across his skull. His pot belly bulged beneath a sweat shirt with a Maltese Cross, and below, in gothic letters, were the words "Proud to be German."

"You seem to like my little prints," he said. "Shall I show you my favorite? It's the best of the lot. In most sets it's missing! I don't show it to everyone, but you look like a good racial comrade. If you like it, I can give it to you at a good price."

Unlocking a small tin cabinet below the bin, he carefully removed a print in the same style as the others, and holding it gently by the edges, showed it to Hans. It was easy to see why it wasn't out with the rest. Depicting a serpent coiled around a beautiful woman, it showed the eternal flame at the Shrine to the Victims of World Jewry. The inscription at the base read "It is Germany's sacred task to avenge the crimes that the Jew has perpetrated against mankind. The new Aryan man will be born from the fires that consume the ancient enemy who seeks to destroy him."

"Nice. Is it genuine?"

"Of course! They're all genuine! Germania! Capital of the world! Pity it doesn't exist! If it did, instead of living in this cesspool full of foreign trash, you and I would be members of the race that ruled the world!"

"A pity indeed. It's very handsome. How much?"

"A hundred euros. I guarantee you won't see another like it for years." The price was ridiculous, but buying it might serve a purpose.

"I like this one, too," said Hans. "The one of the Great Arch. My own grandfather fell on the Eastern Front. I've always felt that Germany had forgotten him. His name would have been inscribed there with the others. How much for the two together?"

"For you, a hundred and forty euros. I can't go any lower than that.

But I feel it's my duty as a German to get these items into the hands of those who will cherish and preserve them."

"All right, I'll take them."

The man smiled. "A wise choice!" he said. His teeth were yellow, and his lower incisors were no more than stubs.

Hans opened his wallet and counted out seven twenty-euro notes. "By the way, the little blonde who came over to me," he said. "Have you seen her before?"

"Sure! Lots of times! What did she want?"

"Nothing, really. She had some sad story to tell. Who is she?"

"A little whore, that's who. She used to work the Kleist-Park—I used to see her back when I had a newsstand there. I even tried her out myself a couple of times. The fucking business can't be going too well for her these days. Did you take a good look at her? She looks like she'll be dead in six months! Heroin, that's why. She's always trying to raise money for the next fix. A few weeks ago, she turned up here and sold me a couple of items—from 'a friend,' that's what she said. Probably more like a customer! They weren't bad! One was a shoulder-patch from the Führer's personal bodyguard—you don't see those every day. She said she could get me more stuff, even better. She even showed me a photograph of one of them. A Golden Party Badge! She claimed it had belonged to Hermann Goering! Pretty damned nice! I was all set to buy it—we even agreed on a price—but then the little bitch screwed me over and sold it to some damned American. Some bastard who was always showing up here, grabbing all the best stuff. Those fuckers have all the fucking money in the world! They're just like their damned soldiers at the end of the war—a bunch of fucking magpies! If you want to know where half the stuff from the Third Reich is, look for it over there!"

"How about the friend who got her the stuff? Was he an American?"

"God knows. He could have been. She came by here with somebody one day, that might have been him. Big, mean-looking fucker in a leather jacket. She did all the talking. He just stood there and didn't say a word."

"So she's around pretty often?"

"Yeah, every damned weekend, passing out leaflets. She didn't happen to mention anything to you about the Treasure of the Jews, did she?" The man gave a nasty smile.

"Treasure of the Jews?"

"Yeah. A week or two ago she came in here, just as I was packing up. All jumpy and scratching herself. Looked like she really needed a fix! Said she was sorry about the Golden Party Badge, but that she'd make it up to me. If I could just lend her a little money—five hundred euros—in a little while she'd pay me back twenty-fold, or more! Pretty soon she was going to be rich! When I asked her how, at first she wouldn't say, but then she started in about how that she and her friend were going to find the Treasure of the Jews. Piles and piles of gold and diamonds, buried by the SS under the streets of Berlin. She'd give me a whole handful of it, for just five hundred euros! All they needed was some damned key or something, and her friend knew right where to get it! Yeah, right! Stories about the Treasure of the Jews have been around for years. Did she think I was going to fall for that crap? I told her to get the fuck out of here and not come back. I was surprised to see her in here today!"

Over the man's shoulder Hans could see that a second train had pulled into the station. Meanwhile, a customer was standing at the man's elbow, holding an item. Shaking the man's hand by way of farewell, Hans put the prints into the envelope with the report and pushed his way back into the crowd.

In the parking lot, Hans unlocked the car, got in, and pulled the report out of the envelope. It was the original, there was no doubt about that. On paper already yellowing at the edges, it bore the seal of the Republic and the heading "Border Troops of the GDR." Below was the text he had typed himself, and there, at the bottom of the page, was his name, rank, and signature, followed by that of his commanding officer. The report itself was no more than a few terse paragraphs in a neutral and bureaucratic tone. Here were the names of the others on the patrol: Grabowski, Müller, and Henning. Here were the references to the subject, a man about twenty years old, detected in the highest security zone of the frontier, in violation of Paragraph 22 of Act 77, the law for the protection of the borders of the state. Here were the words the woman had quoted to him: "The subject attempted to scale the outer defenses. The subject was armed and attacked a member of the patrol. In accordance with regulations and in fulfillment of our duty, we were forced to take measures to neutralize the subject." Of course there was a reason he hadn't used Kalmbach's name—he hadn't even known it until yesterday. It was state policy that border troops were not to be told the identity of those they had shot. Still, the woman was right, such language wouldn't look good in the changed conditions under which Germans lived today, though such an idea hadn't even remotely occurred to him when he had composed it. Attached to the report was a clipping of an article from a West German newspaper from the nearby border town of Bad Harzburg. It read "The inner-German border claimed another victim Thursday night, when a man was shot dead by GDR troops while trying to cross the frontier near Elend. From materials gathered at the scene, Lower Saxony police have tentatively identified the victim as Heinz Kalmbach, nineteen, of Schierke. On Sunday a local group of citizens from Bad Harzburg conducted a memorial service and laid a wreath across from the spot where Kalmbach fell. The federal government has sent a protest to the GDR Ministry of the Interior in East Berlin."

Hans put them back in the envelope and stuck it in the pocket of his coat. The article was something he'd known nothing about. As for the man's identity, it was quite apparent how they had found out who he was. Before attempting to scale the fence, the man had thrown a bundle over to the other side; no doubt it contained not only his identification but the money he had stolen. Just as the truck with Kalmbach's body was departing, a police patrol had pulled up on the other side, attracted by the shots and the commotion. One of their number had retrieved the bundle, despite the fact that that by doing so he was violating the territorial limits of the GDR, which extended ten meters beyond the fence. This patrol had also attempted to photograph the scene, which Hans had counteracted by training a spotlight on them from his vehicle. In fact, the two sides had exchanged beams of light for the better part of an hour. Of course this meant that his own report was matched by one from the other side, plus witnesses, which made the situation all the worse.

At that moment, the phone in his pocket began to ring. He opened it and put it to his ear.

"Our little bird is leading me quite a chase," came Breitbach's voice.

"First she gets on the S-bahn and rides two stops to the Lehrter Bahnhof station. Then she buys a bouquet of flowers in the arcade and walks up to the Invalidenstrasse. Two minutes later, along comes some guy on a motorcycle and pulls up right next to her. She gets in the sidecar, and shit, off they go! I thought that was the last I'd see of her! But no, after a block they turn up the Scharnhorststrasse—the one that dead-ends at the army hospital. The only other thing up that way is the cemetery where the Prussians used to plant their generals. That's where they are right now, out by some grave toward the back, practically right next to where the Wall used to be. She put the flowers on it and now the two of them are just standing there, looking around, like they're waiting for somebody. The guy's carrying a long box—he's got it propped up against the gravestone. He seems real nervous—he keeps looking at his watch and then at the front gate. And here I am on my damned knees, peeking at them around the edge of a tombstone, pretending to pray! When they take off, we're going to lose them sure as hell, unless you get over here fast! Just park at the end of the Scharnhorststrasse and wait for them. When they come by, keep your head down. Next time this phone rings, it'll mean they're on their way."

Starting the car, Hans made his way through a fresh crowd of people coming down from the train. Just as he had pulled into the Scharnhorststrasse and had turned around, the phone rang again, and a few seconds later the motorcycle roared by out onto the Invalidenstrasse, heading east. Looking up after it went by, he could see Ingeborg Mohr, low in the sidecar, one hand on her hair, blowing in the wind. As he headed after them, he could see that a block ahead the cycle had turned onto the Chausseestrasse and then veered off onto the Oranienburger Strasse, where in the middle of the first block it slowed down, pulled across the sidewalk, and drove down an alley between two abandoned buildings.

Heading up a side street that angled into the Oranienburger Strasse from the left, Hans parked and then walked back to the spot where they had disappeared. This was the part of town where the Jews had once lived, and the city's main synagogue was only a block or two down the street. Depopulated by the Nazis and neglected by the German Democratic Republic, it was only now that the buildings were being fixed up. One of the two buildings at the alley was no more than a shell.

From the street one could look up through the empty window frames and see the sky. The other, however, looked sound. Once a department store, it had, up to a few weeks ago, housed a colony of artists and street people. One day, in a pre-dawn raid, the police had driven them all out. Now the front was covered with scaffolding, and attached to it was a sign that read "Building for a New Berlin: A Project of the Berlin Redevelopment Corporation."

Hans walked down the alley, sticking close to the wall, at one point stepping into the shadows of a doorway. From there he had a good view. Behind the buildings lay a field of rubble, stretching an entire block to a high wall that cut off the view from the street beyond. At the center was a crater, half-filled with water, made by a bomb dropped on the city some sixty years before. Around its edge grew clumps of reeds, while on its surface was a green scum. Evidence of renovation was all around. Heavy equipment had been moved in, and there were portable toilets for the workers and a trailer for the foreman. A metal chute for debris stretched up the back of the building, right to the top. It emptied into a dumpster on the back of a truck.

The motorcycle was parked at the back entrance, and next to it stood the man and Ingeborg Mohr. He had her by the collar and was shaking her. She was trying to break free, still clutching the bag. As Hans watched, the man raised his fist and hit her in the face, knocking her to her knees. Then he jerked her up, twisted her arm behind her, and with one hand, pushed her into the building, carrying the box in the other. Hans took out the phone and called Breitbach. A second into the ring, Breitbach answered.

"Where are you?" came his voice. There were sounds of traffic in the background.

"On the Oranienburger Strasse, in an alley next to that former artists' colony."

"The place they're fixing up? I know it well! Our friends, though. What are they up to?"

"They just went inside the building. They don't seem to be getting along. The guy just hit her and then marched her through the door. He's still got that box. Should I go after them?"

"No! Just wait where you are! This is a sensitive matter, Herr Doktor. I have my orders. I must carry them out. I'm already out on the Invalidenstrasse, no more than a kilometer away. I can make it on foot in ten minutes. I'd take a cab, but every damned cabbie in Berlin knows me."

Hans hung up. The minutes dragged on. A man ducked into the alley from the street, urinated against the wall, and then moved on. A flock of pigeons flew over and landed on the gutted building. Finally, closer to fifteen minutes than ten, Breitbach came walking down the alley. Hans stepped out of the shadows to meet him. Together, without a word, they walked past the cycle and into the building.

Just inside was a corridor littered with paper, bottles, and chunks of cement. Propped against the wall were toilet bowls, urinals, and sinks—most cracked and discolored. Ahead was an elevator shaft with the door chained shut, and beyond that, the stairs. With Breitbach in the lead, they started up, pausing at each floor, listening, then looking into the rooms on either side. Occasionally the plaster crunched beneath their feet and a breeze blew up a cloud of dust behind them. Graffiti in Turkish, German, and English covered the walls. They listened for voices, but heard nothing.

At last they reached the top. From the end of the passageway came a faint ray of light through an opening to the side where there had once been a door. It seemed to Hans that there were faint noises coming from inside it. Signaling for Hans to stop, Breitbach took from his jacket a small flashlight and a pistol. Then he stepped back, knocking over a bottle that had been leaning against the wall. It rolled down the stairs and smashed on the landing. The faint noises kept on.

Peering around the doorframe, they could see before them a large room filled with upended tables, broken chairs, and piles of plaster. The only light came through a window facing the side of another building. At the center something moved. It was a figure, floating in the air, in a strange, slow dance. Breitbach shined his light on it, and the beam fell on the contorted face of Ingeborg Mohr, her tongue protruding and her eyes rolled upwards. Her hands were tied behind her back, and her feet twitched spasmodically, a few centimeters off the floor. Around her neck was a cord thrown over a pipe in the crumbling ceiling, its other end tied to a metal bracket set into the wall. On her chest was a crudely lettered cardboard sign with the words "I am a filthy sow. I betrayed the Fatherland!"

Breitbach switched off the light and stepped cautiously into the room, with Hans a step behind.

In the shadows at the far end of the room something moved. It was the man, now in the field gray shirt and trousers of a Nazi soldier, the chevrons of a sergeant on the flaps of his collar. The helmet he wore bore the runes of the SS. He stepped forward and lifted something to his shoulder—Hans could make out the barrels of a shotgun. At that moment he threw himself forward, knocking Breitbach to the ground and falling beside him, just as there were two flashes of light and two explosions. The wall behind them disintegrated into a shower of plaster and dust. The man broke open the gun, took two more shells from the pack around his waist, and shoved them into the chamber with a loud click.

Breitbach raised his revolver, fired once past the man and shouted, "Police! Drop it, or I'll shoot you dead!" At this, the man lowered to a crouch, turned and leapt over a pile of rubble to the door at the other end, where he whirled around and fired again, this time hitting Ingeborg Mohr and setting her swinging back and forth like a pendulum. They could hear his footsteps as he ran onto the landing and down the stairs. Hans moved quickly to a window on the landing and looked out, just as the man emerged from the door, ripping off the shirt and the helmet and throwing them and the shotgun into the sidecar. A few seconds later came the roar of the engine, which soon faded into the distance.

Breitbach had stood up, looking himself over and dusting off his trousers.

"That son of a bitch!" he said. "Quick work, comrade! Getting shot by a fascist dressed for carnival is not the way I want to exit the world! Don't worry, he's not coming back. He thinks half the police in Berlin are after him. I almost wish they were! As for all the noise, let's just hope no one figures out where it came from."

Ingeborg Mohr, meanwhile, had stopped her dance. A minute before she might still have been alive, but now she was quite clearly dead. Along with the cord around her neck, a blast of pellets had caught her square in the midriff, ripping through her coat and tearing up her flesh—but since apparently her heart had stopped before it hit her, there was little blood. With her exertions over, her face had relaxed a bit, but that did little to improve her appearance. Her eyes had popped out like boiled eggs, and mucus below her nostrils had formed a glistening trail across her lips where it mixed with saliva and dribbled down her chin. On her face where the man had hit her was a bloody bruise.

Breitbach, who seemed ready for everything, took a knife from his pocket and cut the cord at the bracket. With a hiss it whipped around the pipe, and Ingeborg fell to the floor, face down. With his foot, Breitbach turned her over and then knelt beside her, first emptying her pockets, finding only a package of cigarettes, a few coins, and a personal identity card, which he shoved in his coat. Then he reached down inside her shirt and into her bra, pulling forth a few banknotes and a scrap of paper, which he held up and shined the light on. It was a telephone number, the first part of which was an international code. Sticking this in his coat as well, he unbuttoned the cuffs of her blouse and rolled up her sleeves.

"See?" he said, shining his light on her arms. "No wonder she wanted money! Needle tracks. Never used to see those in Democratic Berlin. Welcome to a reunited Germany! As for that fascist bastard, I can see just what he did. First he tied her up and put a blindfold on her—there it is, right on the floor. Then he asked her some questions. See those spots on her face and neck? Cigarette burns—and there's the butt on the ground! Then he put this cord around her neck and just before he hoisted her up, he pulled off the blindfold, so she could see what was happening to her! He'd probably planned this for days, the swine! We got here not thirty seconds later! As for the sign, it's what SS execution squads used to put on people they hanged from lampposts at the end of the war."

Breitbach got up. Then, walking around the room and shining his light into the corners, he suddenly stopped. "Here's the box that gun was in. And over here is your shopping bag, Comrade. Empty, of course. Damn! How am I going to go back to my superiors with *this* story? At least he saved me the trouble of shooting her."

"That's what you were planning to do? Shoot her?"

"Of course! And him, too, if I had to. Those were my orders! Do you think we should let people like that run around on the streets? But let's look around a little. Looks like this was their little camp for the weekend. Not much of a housekeeper, was she, Herr Doktor? Reminds me of you. What a mess!"

It was true. The place was complete squalor. On the floor were a few empty cans, a half-eaten Turkish sandwich still wrapped in greasy paper, some candy wrappers, and at least a dozen empty beer bottles. Near the back wall under the window were two sleeping bags, one with a rip in it and the stuffing coming out. On top of it were two filthy pillows. There were a few clothes—some in paper bags, others just tossed on the floor. Next to the sleeping bags was a wooden crate. On top of that were a syringe, a length of rubber tubing, a candle, and a blackened spoon. Taped to the side of the crate next to the sleeping bags, just at eye level, was a postcard of the Hotel Heinrich Heine, Schierke, GDR, and next to that, a photo of a skinny blond teenager with ears that stuck out—Heinz Kalmbach. Breitbach ripped those off the crate and put them in his pocket, too.

Near the clothes a few pamphlets lay strewn on the floor. Some were like the one the woman had slipped under Hans's door, but others were anti-Semitic propaganda of the most depraved kind. Hans picked one up and looked at it. On the cover was the caricature of a hump-backed, hook-nosed creature with dollar bills sticking out of every pocket and the words "Germans! Defend yourselves against the Jew! The Jew is back and his numbers are growing! He will pollute our sacred land and make you his slave! Did our fathers and grandfathers really kill six million of these demons? If so, they only did what had to be done! The cleansing flames of the crematoria consumed the racial trash of Europe!"

Breitbach had picked one up and was looking at it, too. "Look at this crap!" he said. "It's disgusting! Anybody who passes it out deserves to end up like she did, hanged like a dog! What a filthy mess Germany has become! Back in the Republic, we'd have put her away for good! But the question, now, Herr Doktor, is what do we do with her? You talked to her on the street two times in the last twenty-four hours. Suppose someone noticed you?"

"I know for a fact someone did."

"Then it won't do for them to find her with a rope around her neck. What do you suggest we do with her?"

Hans thought a moment. "We might throw her down the rubble chute."

"Congratulations, Herr Doktor! An excellent idea! Then we might send a few things down on top of her, and with any luck on Monday or Tuesday, they'll haul her off to the dump, before she really starts to stink! Look, there's no mess, not even a drop of blood on the floor. The workmen won't notice a thing, especially if we clean up some of the junk they threw around. It's perfect! And by the time they find her, if they ever do, there'll be no way to figure out where she came from. Here, Herr Doktor. You take her feet, and I'll take her shoulders."

Lifting her up—it was surprising how light she was—they carried her out the door and over to the chute. Breitbach steered her headfirst into the opening while Hans held tight to her ankles. Then he let go. There was a banging as she fell from floor to floor, and a satisfying thud as she hit the bottom. Gathering up the shotgun casings, the sleeping bags, the clothes, the wooden crate, the needles, the beer bottles, and the leaflets—Breitbach saved one or two as samples—they dropped them in after her. Last, Breitbach picked up the sign that had hung from her neck, folded it, and put it in his coat. Cautiously, they looked around the edge of a window that faced the street and stood there, watching. A few cars and trucks went by, along with a few people on bicycles and a woman on foot with two small children. Then came a police car, which cruised by slowly and disappeared down the block. It was as though nothing had happened.

In the courtyard, they paused for a moment before going out into the alley.

"Our Nazi friend," said Breitbach, "did you get any kind of look at him?"

"No. How about you?"

"Just for a few seconds. He's blond, in his forties, maybe. A crude-looking brute. Walks with a slight limp. Didn't seem to slow him down much, did it? He's got a chest like an ape and a neck like an ox. Looks like a weight-lifter."

"You think he's an American?"

"He's a German just as sure as you are yourself, Herr Doktor. Of course they've got all kinds of people over there, don't they? By the way, where is the car?"

"Over on the Auguststrasse, just up the block."

"Good. You might oblige me by driving it back to where you got it. I shall go by S-bahn and meet you there. Of course you must give me that report this woman sold to you; I'll have to show it to account for all that money we've lost. Then I'll drive you home in my cab and use that time to debrief you."

"Very well."

They shook hands. Hans waited until Breitbach had turned the corner and disappeared from sight. Then he walked out to the street, crossed it, and headed up the Auguststrasse. How glad he would be if today were the last time he would have to see this man. But he knew just how unlikely that was.

---------------------------- CHAPTER 5 ----------------------------

Arisen from the Ashes

Three days later Hans sat at an outside table at the Opera Café, having a coffee. Set back from Unter den Linden, the café offered a fine view across the historic avenue, with the New Watch just opposite, flanked by the armory on one side and a corner of Humboldt University on the other. Save for the great increase in traffic, the scene before him looked much as it had in the old days. It was almost possible to pretend that nothing had changed. Often in his university days he had sat there with Mrs. Laibstein, listening as she talked about her childhood and youth in New York—her own father had been a professor of composition at the Julliard and a distinguished scholar of Haydn—and what it was like to grow up in a household surrounded by the greatest art man has produced. Sometimes during those conversations it seemed to Hans that she regretted leaving it all behind. Perhaps the reason she had worked so hard to turn him into an American was that she missed her countrymen and wanted to create one of her own. Whatever the case, the moments spent there with her were among his life's most pleasant memories, and often, in times of strife and uncertainty, he had sought it out.

The day had started bright and pleasant, and in honor of the greatly improved weather, the outdoor portion of the café had been opened for the first time that year. But only a few minutes before, a stiff breeze had come up, driving the other patrons inside. High above, white clouds raced across the sky. For the moment at least, the upsets of the past few days seemed equally far away. It was almost as though life might begin anew. He had just come from a session at the Grand Hotel, one that had gone far better than the last. This time his colleague hadn't shown up at all, and the entire burden had fallen on him. But he had been more than equal to the task. It had seemed as though there were reservoirs of English words and phrases in his brain that he'd suddenly been able to tap—they had welled up and bubbled out at just the right times and in just the right combinations. One American, a high official with the board of trade of an important manufacturing center in the Middle West, had asked for his card. There was even talk of interpreting at a large international trade conference to be held in Berlin a few weeks hence. As he poured the last few cold drops from the porcelain canister into his cup, however, he became aware that someone was approaching his table. He saw that it was Breitbach, cap in hand, giving tentative little nods of greeting, as though he weren't quite sure Hans would remember him. As soon as he caught Hans's eye, he began to speak. It was jarring and unpleasant to see him in this place of refuge.

"Herr Doktor, how fortunate to find you here! I spotted you from my cab, just as I was dropping off a fare! This saves me the trouble of paying you a visit! May I join you?"

"If you must, Herr Breitbach." At this Breitbach sat down. It was quite apparent that the coolness of Hans's greeting didn't bother him a bit. The sun glinted ominously off his close-cropped skull.

"Back at work, are you?" he said, putting his cap on the table, smiling pleasantly, and waving away the waiter who had come over to him. "Everything all right?"

"Everything is fine."

"Then there's nothing more to disturb you, I trust."

"Not for the moment."

"'Not for the moment.' Well put! But after all, what could there be? Our little friend is no longer a problem, thanks to an unknown benefactor. There won't even be any awkward investigations where you might be involved—you and I have seen to that! Incidentally, I went by that construction site on the Oranienburger Strasse earlier today and peeked out in back—and do you know what? That dumpster is already gone! Oh, of course, there's a little matter of Nazis running around in the streets of Berlin, killing people, but we shouldn't let that bother us, should we? And then there's that hundred thousand euros which, as I recall, you signed for, but having it go astray was hardly your fault, I can attest to that! Still, it's rather a lot! Too bad such a sum has to fall into the hands of that fascist, don't you think? God knows what he'll use it for! Even though, you understand, no one holds you responsible in this whole unfortunate business, perhaps there's something you could do to make up for it."

"I see, Herr Breitbach. Then I take it this little visit is not entirely social."

"Very perceptive of you, Herr Doktor! We do have in mind, in fact, a little matter where you might lend a hand. Of course it's nothing like what we've just been through, you can be sure of that! You're educated, Herr Doktor. You know foreign languages. German, that's always been good enough for me! I can't imagine why the whole world doesn't speak it! When I hear those Turkish fellows, or even Americans, they always seem to me to be gibbering like apes in the zoo! Nonetheless, they persist in it, and that's why we need people like you."

"So you wish something translated."

"Something like that, Herr Doktor. A colleague of mine who has heard of your linguistic talents would like to consult with you. Someone who, how shall I put it, doesn't get out much. And since he is quite unwilling to come to us, we must go to him! Of course I've told him how busy you are, with your translating business and all, but I can't very well refuse him! That little debriefing we had on the ride back to your flat, my colleague found it quite fascinating! Goering's Golden Party Badge, a box with a shotgun in it, the Treasure of the Jews—what next? And by the way, I went back the following day and checked the grave where that creature laid the flowers—and do you know what? Another Goering connection! It was of the Luftwaffe Ace Colonel Mölders, one of Goering's favorites, and a holder of the Knight's Cross with Oak Leaves, Swords, and Diamonds, the highest decoration for bravery that our beloved Führer gave out! He's buried right next to the Luftwaffe General Ernst Udet, a friend of Goering's from the First World War. Goering used to visit those graves to leave flowers himself—there's even a photo of him doing it! As for my colleague, he's very eager to meet you. Might you do me the favor of accompanying me to pay him a visit?"

"Right now?"

"No time like the present, Herr Doktor!"

"Where do you propose we go?"

"Not far, but into a different world! You'll see my own little home in the process. He lives with me, after a fashion. Now if you will be so kind as to walk over and wait by the curb, I shall pick you up directly! You might wave your arm a bit when you see me, just like an ordinary fare! But please, Herr Doktor. Smile! Look as though you're glad to see me!"

A few minutes later, Hans found himself in the back of Breitbach's cab, riding once more down the Invalidenstrasse. Breitbach, who suddenly no longer seemed at all eager to talk, had given his entire attention to driving. As he did so, he kept up a tuneless little whistling that quite grated on the nerves. Turning onto the Bernauer Strasse, they went past a remnant of the Wall, protected by fencing from souvenir-hunters who would have long since chipped it to bits. Though it was only late March, the weather over the last few days had been quite mild, and trees all about were showing the first slight signs of spring. On the western side of the street, daffodils had already appeared in the window boxes of the apartment buildings, while in the open area on the opposite side, two Turkish youths in shorts and T-shirts, swarthy fellows with shocks of black hair, were kicking a ball back and forth across what had once been the free-fire zone.

Shortly after the S-bahn station, Breitbach took an abrupt turn into the East and drove into a neighborhood that lay just inside the former frontier.

Here, on the Rheinsberger Strasse, within a block of where the anti-fascist defense wall had once stood, a few of the buildings were still pockmarked with bullet holes from the last days of the war. On this side there were no Turks; they hadn't lived in the East in the old days and showed no inclination to do so now. In fact, the only person in sight was a bent old pensioner walking an old and equally decrepit dog. Breitbach, who had slowed to avoid a hole in the pavement, now turned and proceeded halfway up the block, where he pulled into a courtyard of an old building with a crumbling facade. Parking by the remains of an ancient Trabi from which the wheels and doors had been removed, he jumped from the car and opened the door for Hans with a flourish. At the entrance to the building, Hans paused for a moment to read the brass plates, one above the other, that announced the names of the tenants. One was Klaus-Peter Breitbach, identified below his name as the building manager. Another was a doctor named Pritzger, a graduate of Humboldt University, currently associated with the Polyclinic, his hours of consultation Mondays through Thursdays from two to five. The third showed a cat sleeping before a tile oven, beneath which were the words "Association of Friends of Cats of Eastern Germany." Breitbach noted his interest.

"A cozy little building, Herr Doktor," he said. "Pritzger's half-deaf and he's blind as a bat. I doubt he even has one patient a week, and the cat people moved out years ago. God, how it used to stink in here! The top three floors haven't been occupied since 1961, when the state put up the anti-fascist defense wall and moved the tenants out! But when it came down, some squatters tried to move in—after they saw me, they changed their minds! Of course the former owner turned up and tried to cause trouble for me, but my dear colleague whom you're about to meet came up with his asking price, and now I own the whole place, free and clear—the wonders of capitalism! So I've got it nearly all to myself. It's the safest, most out-of-the-way little nook in all Berlin!"

Inside the front door, which Breitbach opened with a large and heavy key typical of the older buildings in the city, a skylight cast a faint gray over the black-and-white checkered tile floor and the marble staircase. But instead of heading up, Breitbach walked behind the staircase to a door at the ground level. This took a minute to open, since it had two locks and a deadbolt, each with a separate key. Once he'd swung it open, it proved to be fortified on the inside with metal plates that lined the door from top to bottom. Ushering Hans through, he swung it shut behind them and again went through the ceremony of locking all the locks. Inside was a short flight of steps, leading down, so that the floor of the room they soon entered lay at least a meter and a half below the level of the ground. Wiping his feet carefully on a mat by the entrance, and with a little nod and hand gestures encouraging Hans to do the same, Breitbach took Hans's jacket and hung it on a coat rack, saying as he did so, "You see, Herr Doktor? Nothing out of order, nothing out of place. That's my motto! It should be yours, as well!"

The room was quite tidy and neat, if rather gloomy. The only light came from three windows high in one wall, all of which had thick bars. Through two of them one could see only the sky, and through one, only the upper branches of a tree. Other than its curious placement, it seemed what might have been a typical middle class living room left from another age. There was a deep carpet on the floor, and the furniture was heavy, dark, and old, of a sort that hadn't been made in Germany since before the war. There was a sofa with a brocade pattern, and nearby, an ornate floor lamp with a fringed shade stood next to an overstuffed chair. On the wall was a large and murky oil painting, the subject of which it was hard to make out. It looked, perhaps, like a ship in a storm. In one corner was an upright piano, and on top of it, in heavy silver frames, a collection of family photographs, all from the distant past. It was very quiet, and there were no signs of anyone else about. That, in fact, was a bit unnerving.

"This person we've come to see," said Hans, "is he out?"

"Oh, no, he's not out! What an amusing idea! He's never out! You must be patient, Herr Doktor! It's a bit of work to get to him, but it's well worth the effort! You'll soon find out there's a whole other world beneath the streets of Berlin. If you'll oblige me for a moment by just stepping into my sleeping chamber. You must of course agree, Herr Doktor, not to reveal anything you are about to see. Few others have gotten this far. It's a measure of our trust in you that you're here at all!"

The side room they now entered was even darker and more gloomy than the one they had left behind, since the windows were heavily draped. Breitbach flipped on a light, revealing a wardrobe in the corner, a marble basin with a mirror over it, and a brass bed with a featherbed on top, fluffed up and without a single wrinkle. Next to that was a bedside table, on which were a goose-necked lamp, a book, a pair of reading glasses, and an automatic pistol.

"Expecting trouble, Herr Breitbach?"

"I always expect trouble, Herr Doktor! If more people had expected trouble in 1989, our Republic might still exist!"

On the wall just over the head of the bed was a picture of Comrade

Director Erich Mielke, sitting at his desk, and behind him the seal of the Ministry of State Security, with its emblem as the sword and shield of socialism. Removing the picture and reverently laying it face down on the pillow, Breitbach pulled the bed forward from the wall. When it was far enough out, he walked behind it, removed the section of panel where the picture had hung, and closed a circuit-breaker concealed behind it. At that point a motor began to whir, and a section of the wall perhaps two meters wide slowly swung inward, revealing a cement staircase leading down into darkness. A cool but musty breeze blew suddenly into the room. Mounted over the stairs was a faded wooden sign marked with a swastika and the seal of the Reich Ministry of Defense. On it were the words "Notice! Entry only for those with written permission from the Führer! Violators will be shot!"

"What is this place, Herr Breitbach?"

"Well you might ask, Herr Doktor! Oh, this isn't a building like others. Some of the Führer's closest personal staff once lived here—his valet had this very flat! After the great air raids of November 1943, the whole street was cordoned off, with all the residents expelled and SS control posts at either end. It's reinforced concrete and thirty meters below the ground! Even a direct hit would have caused barely a tremor! Our beloved Führer himself came here—think of that! That little Austrian embodiment of Teutonic virtue stood on the very spot you're standing now! Many of the top Nazis came down these stairs, running for their lives! But once they got deep down into the ground and left ordinary citizens behind, life wasn't bad at all! There was a fully staffed kitchen. There were stocks of French brandy and champagne, plenty of coffee, tea, and chocolate, jars of preserves, potted meats, tins of caviar, tobacco, a plentiful supply of flour, sugar, and leavening for baking bread and cakes—all of life's little luxuries that no one else in Germany had seen in years! When we found it in 1981, a few of those things were still left. Of course we had to redo all the wiring and install this door—most of the work I did myself. Oh, the authorities would love to know about this place. But we kept it a secret ever since we found it, even from most of our own top leaders!"

Breitbach flipped a switch, and on came a line of lights, each consisting of a naked bulb set into the roof of the passageway and covered with a little metal cage—they stretched down the stairs and almost out of sight. As they started down, Hans noticed that drops of water had formed on the ceiling. There were patches of slime on the walls and puddles underfoot in the depressions at the center of the stairs. With each step down, the air grew more dank and sour.

At the bottom they reached a long corridor, arched at the top and lit in a similar fashion, with several abrupt turns and an occasional metal door to the side. Breitbach pushed one open and shined in his flashlight. The beam fell on a row of blackened, wooden bunks and the remains of mattresses, of which only rusty springs were left. In the center of the room was a decrepit table with some ancient and dusty bottles on it, surrounded by a few chairs. Painted on the wall was a huge swastika, and over it the words, "Our belief in Germany's final victory is unshakeable! We will never surrender! *Sieg heil!*" On the opposite wall was a framed picture of the Führer in half profile, grim-lipped and intent, in military uniform with the iron cross on the pocket of his tunic.

"See, Herr Doktor, the first highlight of our little tour! This is the barracks for the detachment of SS, thirty of them, the elite and most fanatical of the Death's Head Division, brought here in the last weeks of the war to guard the bunker. In that corner we found quite an arsenal: machine guns, thousands of rounds of ammunition, grenades, mortars, even a couple of rockets! Hard duty down here, under the ground, wouldn't you think? But life was good, at least compared to life up on the street! They had special rations and an exercise room. There were plenty of books and magazines. There was a phonograph and a bunch of Zarah Leander and Hans Albers records. There were pinups of Ilse Werner and Brigitte Horney and other stars of the day. There was even a movie projector and a good supply of films. Of course by the time the Russians arrived, they'd all cleared out, but before they left, they rounded up the whole kitchen staff and the orderlies and shot them, in a room right across the corridor—we found the remains of twenty people there, each with a hole in the back of the skull! The SS died, too, up on the streets, shot down like dogs by the brave soldiers of the Red Army! There's evidence, by the way, that someone lived here for a while right after the war. We found a newspaper dated in January 1946 and empty cans of food from the American army. Perhaps it was a last

SS man, hiding out. But come ahead, Herr Doktor. Here's the very last line of defense."

At the end of the corridor were two reinforced cement alcoves for guards, built into the wall on either side. In each was a seat and a narrow vertical slit at eye level and another at chest level for the muzzle of a machine gun, pointing down the passageway. Just beyond was a heavy steel door, which Breitbach, with some effort, rolled aside on a track fitted into the floor and ceiling. This revealed an ordinary wooden door, much like that to Breitbach's flat, on which Breitbach knocked discreetly, calling out "Comrade, it is us!" He waited a moment before pushing it open.

They stepped into a large well-lit room, at least ten meters on a side; in the wall opposite was an open door leading to a passageway beyond. Here the air was suddenly better; there was the constant low hum of a fan and even a slight draft. The ceiling was low, perhaps fifty centimeters above the top of Hans's head. Both it and the walls were painted a bright white. On a wooden table just by the entrance were a few potted geraniums and an amaryllis under a plant light, and a white orchid in full bloom. From a bracket in the wall, also under a light, hung a basket of ferns. On a platform below, a miniature pine tree grew in a bed of rocks, next to which were a small trowel, a tiny pair of clipping shears, and a green spray bottle. Nearby was an aquarium, with a few rooted aquatic plants and a little underwater castle, around which swam a pair of angelfish. The floor was covered with Persian rugs, and one side was completely lined with bookcases. On one shelf was a bust of Karl Marx, and on the wall above, flanking the banner of the German Democratic Republic, hung portraits of the socialist martyrs Rosa Luxemburg and Karl Liebknecht, murdered by the Berlin police in 1919 and thrown in a canal only a few blocks away. In the opposite corner, in a leather upholstered chair under an old-fashioned floor lamp with brass legs, sat an old man, perhaps seventy, dressed in a blue housecoat and slippers. Next to him was a table with several books and a pile of papers, and on the other side, another chair. The old man rose slowly while nodding to them both and said, "Ah, Breitbach! It must be day on the surface of the world!"

"Yes, Comrade," said Breitbach. "Bright and sunny!"

"I see you have brought us a visitor from up above! This is indeed a special occasion!"

"I knew you'd be pleased, Herr Director. This is Dr. Klug. Dr. Klug, I have the honor of presenting you to Comrade Otto Wiehle, Director of the State Archives of the German Democratic Republic."

Hans bowed slightly and shook the old man's hand. Everyone of course had heard of Comrade Wiehle, a high party official who had disappeared, along with a large number of documents under his care, only a day or two after the Wall had fallen. Nowadays, whenever the papers mentioned him, which was not often, they always stated that he had fled abroad, to Cuba or the Middle East. No one ever expected to see him alive again.

"Dr. Klug! I'm very honored to meet you!" said Comrade Wiehle, with a polite little nod. "You may wonder, Comrade, that Comrade Breitbach uses my official title as though it still applied! Up there the Republic may be gone, but down here it still exists! No one has relieved me of my duties, and until they do, I shall continue to exercise them. No doubt you are surprised to see me!"

"I am, Comrade Director."

"Of course! I'm among the most wanted men in all Germany! But please, sit down. We have much to discuss. Perhaps Comrade Breitbach will bring us some tea." At this, Breitbach, who had been hovering behind the Director's chair, stepped through the door at the back, closing it softly. The Director sat down, as did Hans, and then continued.

"You're a talented man, I understand. An interpreter!"

"Yes, Comrade Director."

"Breitbach speaks highly of you. He tells me that, among other things, you saved his life. Lucky for me, since I'd be lost without him! He does everything for me. He cooks for me. He does my laundry. He brings me medication. He buys me little treats. He even cuts my hair! A good and loyal comrade, of which few such remain! There is one disturbing little event of the past few days, which I should mention, just to get it out of the way. He tells me that he delivered to you the sum of a hundred thousand euros and that he personally witnessed you giving it to a nasty little extortionist at a flea market, but that it has somehow gone astray. He says it was not entirely your fault and that even he might be partly to blame. A hundred thousand euros! Rather a heavy blow for our dilapidated little treasury."

"I greatly regret it, Comrade Director."

"I'm sure you do, Comrade Klug, as do we all! Well, no matter, perhaps there is some way you can make amends. Perhaps you can even get a part of it back. I have full faith in your abilities to do so. After all, you're the former Deputy Chief of the American Section of the Department for the Surveillance of Suspicious Persons, a high position for someone so young. One of the most promising young men in the entire Ministry of State Security. Your qualifications are impressive! They say among other things that your English is flawless, that you speak it without an accent, that even Americans take you for one of their own. How can that be? I spent several years in the Soviet Union, yet no one ever took me for a Russian."

"I had excellent teachers, Comrade."

"Ah, yes, I know. The Laibsteins. That Laibstein was a clever fellow. I met him once or twice. A Jew, as I recall."

"Yes, Comrade Director."

"A fascinating people, the Jews. The most talented of the tribes of man! I quite admire them. But they express man's deepest doubts about himself. Freud. Schoenberg. Kafka. Einstein. Wittgenstein. Even Karl Marx! Every little twist and turn in modern man's path, there's a Jew there, pointing out the new direction. As for Laibstein, they tell me you were his star pupil. But it wasn't just the language you learned. You learned American ways, as well! You learned to eat without gagging their disgusting food—even a horrible paste they make from peanuts; to understand their foolish games; to listen to their depraved music; to watch their coarse entertainments and pretend they were part of your youth. What was that crude and witless show that has so molded the American mind? *I Love Lucy*! I recall reading about it in the party newspaper! This Lucy was always breaking things that could not easily be replaced, yet Americans found that funny! How typical of their character—antisocial and destructive! Laibstein used all his tricks and more to turn you into an American, didn't he? Do you know, in State Security, what they called you? 'The American.' Is that what you are? An American?"

"No, Comrade. I'm not an American."

"Yet you know them so well!"

"Only as a behaviorist knows a colony of rats, Comrade Director. I studied America to serve the state and the cause of socialism."

"Well said! Perhaps you can serve that cause again, Comrade."

"Perhaps, Comrade Director."

"Comrade Klug," said the old man as he leaned forward, touching the tips of his fingers together and looking at Hans intently over the little cage they formed, "I wish to know what sort of man you are. Tell me, how do you entertain yourself? Do you often go to the West?"

"No, Comrade Director."

"So you've not been to Hamburg? Or Cologne? Or Munich?"

"Never, Comrade Director."

"Strange. You've the chance to travel, yet you don't take it. What's the matter? Don't you like it over there? Have you no faith in the new Germany?"

"None at all, Comrade Director."

"Of course not! Why should you? The new Germany is the destroyer of peace in Europe! Germany has once again become the fulcrum on which world history turns! Germany once wreaked havoc on the world and brought mankind to disaster. Unchecked it will do so again! Breitbach tells me, by the way, that Berlin is much changed since I saw it last. He says that everywhere, hideous new buildings have sprung up. He says that, according to those who know, the Potsdamer Platz resembles a shopping mall in America! And he says our Antifascist Defense Barricade—the so-called Wall—is gone altogether. Is that true?"

"All but a few meters left as a sort of monument, Comrade."

"Intended as a mockery, no doubt! He says that at the Brandenburg Gate there's not even a line left on the pavement. Is that true, too?"

"Yes, Comrade Director." In fact it had been true for several years.

"Tell me, Herr Doktor, what did you think of the so-called Wall?"

"It was a historic necessity, Comrade."

"Exactly! It stabilized Europe! It was the greatest structure of modern times! Greater even than the pyramids of old. Rather than memorializing the dead, it gave hope to the living. It didn't show the failure of socialism—it showed the bankruptcy of capitalism! It kept back the tides of filth and protected the good! To our youth, it was like a stern but loving parent. It said, 'Stay, help us to build socialism!' As for those who tried to violate our frontier, they were social parasites! Whoever turned his back on his state and his people deserved whatever he got!"

"I agree, Comrade."

"Of course you do! These are upsetting times, Comrade Klug. The new night of mankind! Is it just another stage in history? One Marx didn't foresee? The resurgence of capitalism? The return of fascism? Yes! That's exactly what it is! Comrade, the end of socialism has cast a shadow over the world. And it leaves an ideological gap, one which fascism seeks to fill!"

At this moment Breitbach reemerged through the door, carrying a tray with a china teapot, two cups and saucers, and two little cakes on a silver platter. He obligingly set the service on the table between the two chairs and then stepped back. The Director poured two cups, lifted one to his lips, and took a sip.

"Comrade," he said, reflectively, "there is no doubt that the Americans are mixed up in the entire unsavory affair of this little extortionist. As proof, Inspector Breitbach has obliged us by calling that telephone number found on her person. It turns out, just as I suspected, to be a number in the United States. He has made a recording of the reply, quite apparently an answering machine. Inspector, will you play it for us?"

At this, Breitbach put a small tape machine onto the table between them and pressed a button. First came two rings and a click, and then the voice of a man, speaking in English, emerged. "You have reached the voice mail box of Dr. John Prober, at the New Light Bible College," it said. "I am unable to answer your call at this time. Please leave a message after the tone." The voice was hard and suspicious. At the end of the recording came a long beep, followed by silence.

"Did you understand that?"

"Yes, Comrade Director."

"Prober. That is the man speaking, I take it. We are quite familiar with that name," said the Director. "Further, we have checked the code for this telephone number. It is in America, in the state of Virginia. That is where this Prober lives, where he teaches at that whatever-it's-called religious school. This man is a dangerous neo-fascist! We have identified him as the source of much of the propaganda being imported into Germany today, including that pamphlet put under your door! He has unleashed on us a stream of filth! He is well known as one of the associates of this Aryan People's Party, and in fact has placed advertisements in its disreputable little journal, a copy of which Breitbach has bought for us at a newsstand which sells such trash under the counter."

At this point he took from the papers on the table beside him a publication and held it up, "Take this with you, Herr Doktor! Read it at your leisure! But let me point out to you in particular this notice in the back." The Director handed it to him, open to the back cover, on which there was an advertisement circled in red, with the title "German Heroes' Project." Hans took it and read.

"A substantial cash reward is offered for information leading to the recovery of the icon of the Siegfried League," it read. "This important relic of the German past has been missing since 1945. We are at present seeking this and other items for an important collection. Top prices are paid and no questions asked! Among the items wanted are any relating to the top leadership of the Third Reich and all materials relating to winners of the Knight's Cross. You can deal with us in full confidence. All communications will be kept strictly confidential." On the last line was the name "The German Heroes' Project, Dr. John Prober, Director," with a phone number and a post office box in Roanoke, Virginia, U.S.A.

"That phone number," said the Director, leaning over and putting his finger on it, "is the very one found on that woman Mohr, the one we called! Why did she have it? Quite apparently she had something to sell to this Prober. Was it to him that she sold the Golden Party Badge the dealer at the flea market told you about? Quite likely, don't you think?"

"Yes, Comrade Director."

"And why were she and this man on the motorcycle out in that cemetery at those graves? The graves of two winners of the Knight's Cross, one with Oak Leaves, Swords and Diamonds? It's sinister! Other tributes have been laid there as well, you know. And not just by Hermann Goering. In 1976, when the cemetery lay within the border zone and the Anti-fascist Defense Wall cut off access to it from the

West, an unknown person threw a wreath over from the other side with a ribbon reading "German Hero, Rest in Peace." Below the words was the figure of Siegfried, slaying the serpent, and the legend "I serve the German Volk." Precisely the motto of the Siegfried League that so enthralls this man Prober! The Siegfried League! Tell me, Herr Doktor, do you know what it is?"

"No, Comrade Director."

"It is the organization founded by Hitler to keep his ideas alive after the defeat! Herr Doktor, we are coming to the point of this little meeting. Let me begin by making a few remarks. Will you allow that?"

"Certainly, Comrade Director."

"Comrade Klug, I have had little to do down here but study and think. And in my own poor way, I have stumbled on some truths. Marx teaches us that history is an orderly process, replacing one stage of society with another, as the human spirit matures. But something has happened to derail it! Do you know what that is? It's your friends, the Americans! They're a disruptive force in history! Cultural mongrels with no sense of higher purpose! Do you know what America is? A writhing mass of seething vitality, a maelstrom filled with monstrous and rapacious creatures, sucking the life blood from the world, devouring all who come near it, in pointless existence! And purposelessness and disorder is what America has given to Germany and to the world! But even worse, it has blown on the dwindling embers of fascism until they are rising into a flame! Do you know something is being born up there? A monster! The spawn of a Nazi whore by a Yankee pimp! I can hear its birth cries. I can feel it taking shape. It will cast a shadow over the world. Do you know what it is? Germania! The heart and soul of the German Reich! The Führer's Dream! The spirit of Hitler is alive in Germany, Doktor Klug! From his grave, he directs the rebuilding of Berlin, the new Capital of the World! All the ill-gotten riches of the earth are flowing here. Capitalists from every corner of the planet are gathering above us. And the essence of capitalism is fascism. Fascism is metamorphosing itself into something that fits this degenerate modern age. It is emerging stronger and more vital than ever. This Aryan People's Party is only one manifestation of it. Oh, Breitbach occasionally tells me what's going on up there, but I'd know it anyway.

I have no television. I have no radio. I read no papers. I can feel the pull of history without distraction!"

At this point he got up from his chair in great excitement and began to pace back and forth, the untied sash of his robe trailing on the floor.

"Fascism!" he said, and he spat the word out as though it had produced a vile taste in his mouth. "The worst doctrine ever to spring from the sickest recesses of the brain of man! At its very core is a monstrous lie. That the driving force of history is not class struggle but racial struggle! That while the various tribes of man fight one another for ascendancy, the Jew stands to one side, waiting to grab the crown of victory from the exhausted winner! That the Jew is a demon, plotting to enslave mankind! Are we supposed to believe these poor people closed up their little shops at night and then went home to plot the destruction of Germany? What nonsense! Yet six million of them died for this delusion! And there are people who would finish the job and kill the rest! These swine make a hero of the most disgusting man who ever lived. Shall I tell you about the great German Führer, the embodiment of the spirit of our race? Oh, yes, I know all about him. I have made a study of him and his last days! I have had access to materials that no one else alive has ever seen! He was an ugly, shriveled little man with greasy hair and gray skin who, at the end of his life, shook like a leaf! The whole right side of his body was in a constant tremor!" At this moment, before going on, he mocked the maladies of the dictator by reducing his pace to a limp and spasmodically jerking his left hand and arm.

"His personal habits were degenerate! He stayed up nearly to dawn and then lay in bed until well past noon! His favorite foods were sweets and chocolate and his teeth were rotting right out of his head—they were a disgusting brownish-yellow mass, covered with fillings and bridges! You could smell his breath from five paces away. His intestines were constantly rumbling, and nearly every sentence he uttered was punctuated by a fart! He had horrible, light eyes, the eyes of a wolf and a madman, that followed one around the room wherever one went. He was fixated on his bowels and had an enema at least three times a week. His personal physician, a filthy, disreputable quack named Morell, wrote in his medical log that his star patient's lower intestines were so weak he could barely pass a stool the size of a grape! When worried, he would suck his fingers and stare into space, for minutes on end! He showed, in fact, all the heightened irritability of an advanced syphilitic! Whenever anyone disagreed with him, even on the most trivial matter, he would throw a screaming fit! He ended his life living where he belonged, in the sewers beneath Berlin, a cringing, depraved, cornered little rat! He sent four million German boys to their deaths and then didn't have the courage to face death himself! Oh, yes, Herr Doktor, I know this for a fact!"

The Director had paused at the far end of the bookcase and now supported himself a moment on one of the shelves. Then he continued to pace.

"Yet the fascists want to resurrect this monster! They want to breath life into his perverted ideas and let them loose upon the earth again! Already they are marching in the streets! Oh, yes, this farcical Aryan People's Party—a collection of clowns and misfits, just like the original Nazis—their leader, Fritz Westermarck, is a strutting little puppet just like Hitler—they think they can again lead a sheep-like, stupid people back down into the pit, and perhaps they're right! But let me tell you something, Doktor Klug ..." At this point he was almost shouting. "... it is I who have set myself against them. How can I fight them? I can tell the truth! Twelve years! I've been in this room twelve years! Twelve years without the sun! Twelve years without seeing a bird or a tree! Twelve years without the warmth of a summer breeze! And here I shall stay until my work is done! Herr Doktor, we are living in the new night of mankind, where lies and distortions have driven underground those of us who speak the truth. I have a sacred mission! It is to conserve the socialist view of the past. I am like one of the scholars in the Dark Ages who kept the spark of culture alive. I am gathering the materials to construct my Museum of the Historical Imperative, which will demonstrate conclusively the truths that Marx taught us. It will show how Germany strayed from the path of history and led mankind toward disaster. At its center will be an exhibit of the horrors of fascism. I have many of its documents and relics. I shall display them as a warning to mankind. The Aryan People's Party would pay a fortune for them! Even at this moment they are buying up whatever they can find! Theirs is the so-called 'important collection' that swine Prober is talking about!

Oh, yes, they have trashy little items like that Golden Party Badge, and they're willing to buy all sorts of junk of no historical value, but what they are really searching for is the greatest relic of all, the decree in which Hitler ordered the destruction of the Jews! The revisionists claim it was never Hitler's intent, that the proof he ordered it is lacking, that it was all the work of overzealous underlings, but they know as well as I that this decree exists! If they find it, they will suppress it, but I will show it to the world! I know it exists and I know where it is! The Black Vault! The secret place where Hitler and Goebbels stored the relics of their movement!"

With this, he sat down again, rearranging his robe and taking a sip of tea and bite of cake. Then he sat silent. When he spoke again, his voice was calm.

"Let me tell you, Herr Doktor, about the Black Vault. By 1943, the Führer had largely disappeared from public view. What was he doing? Using the appointment logs of the Reich's Chancellery, I have attempted to localize him for every minute of the day. There are many times when he cannot be accounted for at all. Where was he? I think I know! Brooding and depressed, he had retreated to his private quarters to plan the future of his movement in the face of Germany's crushing and total defeat. I quote from the secret diary of Joseph Goebbels, kept in parallel with the voluminous official diaries he kept as Reichsminister of Propaganda; it was the twisted little doctor's intent to put it in the Black Vault, but in the confusion of the last days it fell behind a cabinet in the Führer's bunker, where it was swept up with a great many other items and shipped off to Moscow. I myself found it in a corner of the Red Army archives where it had lain unrecognized for thirteen years. I was able to smuggle it out undetected. Only Breitbach, and now you, even know it exists!"

He picked up from the table a worn, leather-bound journal, with scraps of paper between the pages to mark places. Opening to the first, he began to read.

"'March 18, 1944: The Führer speaks much of our historic tasks. First among them is the total destruction of Jewry. Only then will Aryan man be safe. And only then will Germania arise from the ashes of Berlin!' And here is one from late December, 1944, when the armies of the Reich were crumbling on all fronts. 'The Führer sees only too clearly that we, the Cleansers of the Human Race, will be reviled as monsters, and that our great work is in danger of being undone. He is making provisions that it be carried on.'"

The Director cleared his throat and continued. "On January 30, 1945, with the Red Army at the borders of East Prussia and the Anglo Americans massing on the Rhine, Goebbels writes the following: 'Today is the twelfth anniversary of the historic day on which we seized the reins of power! To mark the occasion, the Führer called together several of his most intimate circle—Reichsführer-SS Himmler, Reichsmarshall Goering, Staatssekretär Bormann, and me—and announced he is creating a new movement. It shall be called the Siegfried League. It is to be secret—not even its name shall be known beyond a few! The time has come, said the Führer, to adopt the cabalistic scheming of International Jewry—we must learn to be as secretive and as devious as the Jew. We must create an International Aryan Conspiracy to promote our agenda, just as the Jew, generations ago, created one to promote his own. The Siegfried League will keep our ideals alive until the world is ready for them once more. Central to our struggle are the sacred relics of our movement. We will conceal them until the day they can emerge to rekindle the flame of our ideas in a new generation. A special place—a vault dark and secret—has been built in a place our enemies will never find. The Führer has made us swear to carry out our responsibilities and to put aside any differences we have had with one another—God knows there have been enough of those! He is giving Reichsmarschall Goering a last chance to redeem himself—his failures to make the Luftwaffe an effective fighting machine may well have cost us the war! Each of us is to have his own task: that of Reichsführer-SS Himmler is to find from among the ranks of the SS the perfect hero to guard the Black Vault; that of Staatssekretär Bormann is to assemble the funds to launch our movement anew; mine is to have an icon made containing the key to the Black Vault and, at the proper moment, in the company of the hero, to escort the relics there. That of Reichsmarschall Goering is to help our hero elude capture so that he may live to fulfill his sacred mission.'"

The Director paused again and looked at Hans intently.

"You see, Herr Doktor?" he said. "The Siegfried League is like a virus that defies detection, lying in wait for the right moment to reinfect the world. Does this vault with its poisonous contents exist? Yes! Hear what Goebbels says of it. 'The Führer has shown me the items to be placed in the Black Vault. The sacred banner from the 1923 massacre at the Freiherrnhalle, soaked in the blood of the martyrs. The historic documents of our struggle against World Jewry. The draft of the Law for the Protection of German Blood and German Honor in the Führer's own hand. The original text of the Nuremberg Racial Laws, with the Führer's notations. And most important, the Führer's historic decree to Reichsführer-SS Himmler commanding him to deal with the Jews as they would have dealt with us! This vault shall be the last refuge of the holiest relics of our cause!'

"And here is what Goebbels writes a few days later.

"I have presented to the Führer the icon of the Siegfried League. He is very moved! It holds the key to the perpetuation of our struggle! Made by Hermann Kretz, a winner of the Reichs Arts Prize, and fitted to a lock by a master locksmith, Karl Grimm, it shows Siegfried beheading the serpent of World Jewry—the hilt of his sword bears the swastika and on the head of the serpent is the six-pointed star, the sign of the Jew! On his shield are the words, "I serve the German Volk!" It is a beautiful piece of German craftsmanship!'"

The Director paused and looked up.

"The question is, Comrade Klug, what did Hitler do with this icon? The twisted little doctor tells us that, too. Here is what he says on March 29, 1945: 'In a secret search over many weeks, Reichsführer-SS Himmler has been seeking the most heroic living racial comrade to guard the sacred relics of our cause. He must have shed blood for the Fatherland. He must be racially pure, fanatically devoted to our cause, and a holder of the Knight's Cross. At last the Reichsführer has found him! He is coming to Berlin from his unit at the front. We eagerly await his arrival.'"

The Director adjusted his glasses and read on.

"'April 9, 1945. Our German hero is here at last. What a splendid fellow! His name is Gottfried Lenz. A strapping lad from Munich, he's the son of a welder, a party member since 1929, who raised him in the best National Socialist traditions. Barely twenty-one, he is simple, clean, noble, blond, and the perfect Aryan. His heroic act defies belief. When a horde of Bolshevik tanks and infantry assaulted his artillery battery, he remained at his post, firing constantly, while his brave comrades fell all around him, until only he remained. Using in turn the weapons he had taken from the hands of his dead comrades, he held the enemy at bay during the day, while at night he crept from his battery and brought back ammunition from the destroyed batteries all around him. When our troops recaptured the position two days later, they found this lad, a bullet through the lung, with Russian dead in heaps before him. He had singlehandedly destroyed five Russian tanks and killed nearly one hundred Bolshevik infantry! For this incredible deed he was recommended for the Knight's Cross with the Golden Oak Leaves, only the second ever awarded. Brought to a clinic, he passed in and out of the shadow of death for many days, but his unshakeable belief in the Führer allowed him to recover and return to his unit! Just as the hand of Providence shielded our Führer from the plotters' bomb, it has shielded this lad to take up his task.'" The Director turned to the next mark and read on.

"'April 20: the Führer's birthday. Tonight our hero accompanied us to the vault, the most holy place in all the Reich. We left at the stroke of midnight—it is the first time the Führer has left the bunker in many days! In a moving torchlight ceremony deep beneath the earth, the Führer entrusted to him the icon, and he swore an oath to serve our cause to his dying breath. The Führer presented him, too, with a dagger, the symbol of the sword Notung, forged by Siegfried to slay the dragon. The hero will accompany us to the sanctuary once more to perform a sacred task, and then he will take up his duties as guardian of the treasures of the Siegfried League! We will take every measure to assure he succeeds! Like the helmet that made Siegfried invisible, he, too, shall be invisible! His military records now show he died of wounds and his parents have already been told of his death. It is cruel, but they are enduring no more than countless other German families have endured. They take strength in the belief they have sacrificed a son for Führer, Volk, and the Fatherland! We have given him a new name and papers showing he is a worker in an essential industry, wounded in a bombing attack and exempt from military service. His true identity will be known only to the five of us! In these last difficult days he has spent many hours with the Führer. The Führer loves him like a son! He knows now that our movement will live on in this youth and that some day, the racial community will rise again.'" At this point the Director closed the notebook and laid it back on the table.

"Save one last entry," he said, "here Goebbels' secret diaries come to an end. But there is evidence that that last trip to the sanctuary did take place. On the evening of April 30, 1945, an unmarked truck left the bunker beneath the Reich's Chancellery, preceded by two SS on motorcycles. Seen by several witnesses, it disappeared into the night. It is clear to me what was in it. The sacred relics of the leader who embodied the will of the German Volk! They were on their way to the Black Vault."

The Director took a last sip of tea and closed his eyes for a moment before speaking again.

"Now, Herr Doktor, let us review what happened to the five members of the Siegfried League. Hitler: dead by his own hand in his bunker on April 30, 1945; his body taken to the courtyard of the Reich's Chancellery, where it was soaked in gasoline and burned to ash. Goebbels: poisoned his wife and children and shot himself on the following day. Bormann: killed fleeing the bunker; his skull was found buried near the site many years later. Himmler: captured by the British, he bit into a cyanide capsule mounted in his bridgework and died on May 23, 1945. Goering: condemned to the gallows at Nuremberg; but he cheated the hangman! Someone slipped him a cyanide capsule, though he was under constant guard. The night he was to be hanged, when they came for him, they found him dead in his cell! Of the five, only he survived the war—he lived nearly a year and a half longer than any of the others! Is it possible that this bloated braggart went all those months without once mentioning the task entrusted to him? Of course not! In the days before he died, he boasted to an American army psychiatrist, a Jew as fate would have it, that he had helped Hitler outwit his enemies, that because of him Hitler's ideas would live on and some day emerge again to rule the world! He even mentioned the Siegfried League and a secret place beneath Berlin. Everyone regarded it as a cynical maneuver to avoid the rope, and for many years, the allies suppressed any mention of it; but it finally got out and became a legend in neo-fascist circles. An American even wrote about it in a book! Oh, our friend Prober has heard about the Black Vault, of that you can be sure! He believes in it as fully as I do! I have spent years looking for it.

I have street maps of Berlin, the way it was in 1945. I traced possible routes that truck with its SS escort might have taken, through the only part of the city still in fascist hands! The spot can be no farther than three kilometers from the bunker. Let me show you, Herr Doktor." From beneath the table he took a map and spread it on the floor before them. Marked in red was a large circle, enclosing many blocks.

"Here is Berlin as it is today. Within this circle, centered on the bunker behind the Reich's Chancellery, is the spot where the Black Vault must lie. As you see, it includes much of the Mitte district in our part of Berlin and the Tiergarten and Kreuzberg districts in the West. Over the years, I took many soundings in buildings and under the streets of Berlin-Mitte. That is how I found this place! No excavation in our part of Berlin was allowed to proceed until I had examined the site! Of course the West was closed to me—it is my belief the vault must lie there, in some section of the city little touched since the end of the war!"

"Comrade Director, what of this woman's talk of the Treasure of the Jews?"

"The gold and jewels plundered from the dead of Auschwitz? Yes! It, too, is in the Black Vault! If the fascists find it, they will use it to spew poison throughout the world. Even worse is how they plan to use the relics. They intend the Black Vault to be the womb for Germany's rebirth! It is there they will put their fulcrum to move the world! We must find it before they do! If we fail, fascism will be born anew from the belly of Berlin!"

"Was Ingeborg Mohr's death related to the Siegfried League?"

"Of course! And she is not the first to die at the end of a rope. Many years ago I had a promising young colleague at the archives in Potsdam. His name was Walter Jahn. I asked him to look into this matter of the Siegfried League, right after I had recovered Goebbels's secret diaries and read them through. Here is his report!" Taking a file from the pile of papers, he began to read.

"'On January 14, 1959, I interviewed Frau Heidi Grimm of the Wedding district of Berlin. In February 1945, her husband, Karl, a master locksmith, was visited by two SS officers. They requested him to construct a special lock and key and to put the latter into a decoration they had brought with them. They remained while he did so. Then they took him away. He was never seen again! I spoke next to Frau Trude Kretz, whose husband Hermann had likewise received a visit from two SS officers with a commission to make that decoration. Frau Kretz furnished an exact description of it. Tipped off that the SS planned to detain him when they picked up the icon, Kretz went into hiding. But in 1948, a German-speaking American soldier, a military policeman, came to his flat and arrested him for black-marketeering. He went off with this soldier and never returned. All attempts to locate him through the American authorities were in vain there was no record of his arrest.'"

The Director kept the open file on his lap and looked up.

"Jahn was a talented man. I decided he should continue the search for the icon. His cover was to become a dealer in Third Reich medals and decorations and to write a catalogue of them. We thought in this way we might flush the icon out. Since trade in such items was prohibited in the GDR, I arranged for Jahn to carry on his search abroad. Crossing to the West and asking for asylum as a political refugee, he emigrated to America, to Washington, DC, where he opened a shop. He took with him his wife, a pretty young thing—she was my secretary. To get him started, I gave him several objects taken from the state collections. He was quite successful, but for many years he encountered not a single mention of the Siegfried League, though he continued to send me reports through a courier. We had both given up any hope of success. But nearly sixteen years after he had gone to America, he sent me a report of only a few lines."

Taking a paper from the folder, he began to read.

"'October 3, 1975. Honored Comrade Director! I write to tell you I have purchased a decoration of great interest—the *Pour le Merite*, the very one given to Hermann Goering as a flying ace in World War One. And this has led to something of far greater interest—to someone offering to sell me Goering's Golden Party Badge. And more importantly has given me a photograph proving the icon of the Siegfried League exists. I am enclosing it herewith. I ask that you have delivered to me as quickly as possible a hundred thousand dollars in cash. I hope to obtain the icon shortly and to return to the GDR, leaving this wretched land behind me forever!'"

With this, the Director handed Hans a photograph. It was of a little girl, dressed in a white gown, holding out the icon in one hand, and in the other, a Star of David on a gold chain. The icon—all its details were clearly visible—matched exactly that described by Goebbels. Behind the child was a mantle on which stood a porcelain figure of a woman, in eighteenth-century dress, with a high, powdered wig and a parasol. On the wall behind, a small, black curtain had been drawn aside to reveal a framed photograph of Hitler, looking bent and old, standing next to a young SS man, his hand on the young man's shoulder.

The Director went on.

"Who gave him this photograph? We never found that out. Of course we delivered the money to Comrade Jahn through our operative. But no more than a week later, Jahn was murdered in his shop! Hanged, just like this woman! And with a sign around his neck that read, 'I am a swine. I betrayed the German People.' His safe was open and everything in it was gone—including, we presume, our hundred thousand dollars and the Golden Party Badge."

"Didn't the police investigate it?"

"Oh, yes, the clowns! But they totally bungled it! All they ever found out is that two men had come to his house, late at night. His wife was the only person left alive who saw them. This whole business and the subsequent investigation—the fools suspected her!—drove her over the edge, and she ended up in an institution where the insane in America's capital are locked away and forgotten—it's called St. Elizabeth's—and there she remains to this day. Since then, not one new fact about this case has come forth! But even the little we have has helped me to focus my thoughts, Where did this hero go, after the fall of Berlin? I thought for years that, if he had even survived, he had buried the icon or thrown it into the Spree. This photograph was the first sign he did not. I now believe he took it to America, where it has been ever since! He married there, and the little girl in the photograph is his child! But where does the Star of David come from? Do you know what I think? It is from the Treasure of the Jews!"

"Until three days ago, I believed the Siegfried League had disappeared. Its last act was to murder Walter Jahn, thirty years ago! Oh, I can understand the death way back then. The German hero himself would still have been up to such a deed. But now he is old, if he is alive at all! Has he sent someone else to carry on his work? Is it that man on the motorcycle? Why, after so long, did Goering's Golden Party Badge suddenly turn up? It can only have come from the men who murdered Jahn. And this man on the motorcycle—does he really know where the icon of the Siegfried League is? I must find out! And to do so, Herr Doktor, I must call on the services of a loyal comrade such as yourself! Before we come to your role, let me give you a little tour."

While Breitbach cleared the tea service, the Director arose and led Hans through the door at the back of the room and into a corridor. On either side were other doors. The Director opened one and turned on the light. In it were metal shelves, filled with books, files and boxes.

"You see before you, Herr Doktor, the contents of the bunker where the Führer spent the last days of his life. I've inherited, so to speak, his personal effects. See those books? His personal library, taken from his bedside table. And what do we find? Goethe? Schiller? Kleist? Fontane? No, none of the greats of German literature! It's an accumulation of utter trash! A Wild West novel by Karl May, the sort read by teenage boys! A book on astrology and the occult! A popular book on vegetarianism! Hofnagel's *Ten Point Program to Train Your Dog*! And of course a book he had with him at all times—a collection of Richard Wagner's ludicrous anti-Semitic scribblings. And here, his personal medicine cabinet." The Director pointed at a collection of dusty bottles and tubes.

"See? Laxatives. Antacids. An enema bag. Hemorrhoid cream. Salve to kill the pain in his rotting teeth. And look here:" With this, he picked up an ancient piece of cloth from which protruded a band of crumbling elastic. "A hernia belt! I have many of his clothes, as well, in those boxes. His underwear, his socks, his shoes, his shirts. All I lack is he, himself! Think how that vile Fritz Westermarck would like to put on these rags and strut about! And besides this, I have many of the papers of the Reich's Chancellery, those not burned in the final days—the Nazis plans for the future!"

Walking to the next room, the Director opened the door and turned on the light. The walls were covered with graphs and maps, and in the center was the model of a concentration camp, with barracks for the guards, the commandant's quarters under the swastika flag, and a railroad track leading to a station platform at the front gate. From this a path led through a garden and past a fountain to a red brick building—each brick was clearly delineated—with two smokestacks at the top. The whole camp was enclosed by a double electrified fence, and spaced along its perimeter were little wooden guard towers.

"Herr Doktor, consider for a moment," said the Director, "if Germany had won the war. The crimes of Auschwitz would have been but the prelude to monstrous crimes on an even greater scale. Here, on the wall, are graphs that the Institute for Racial Studies prepared for the Führer of the Jewish populations in Europe, the Americas, and elsewhere, as of 1939. They are color-coded as to the number of Jews in each country. Note how Germany is a light rose color but Poland is a solid red! See how Norway and Ireland are nearly white! The next set of maps shows so-called Jew-free areas as of 1943 and projected at two year intervals beyond. Note how the white area spreads until it covers first Europe and then the entire globe! You see, Herr Doktor, the goal was to eliminate every Jew on earth by 1949, by the Führer's sixtieth birthday. On that day the whole world was to be declared Jew-free! But with eleven million Jews spread out over the globe, this required careful planning. A commission was appointed, of bankers, lawyers, academicians, industrialists, efficiency experts, police officials, and high SS officers. First, Jews were to be criminalized and declared international outlaws. All the powers of the state were to be devoted to hunting them down. A bounty was to be placed on their heads— anyone who denounced a Jew to the authorities was to receive a reward. For anyone helping a Jew, he and his entire family were to share the Jew's fate!"

The Director turned to the model.

"The efficiency of the death camps was to be greatly improved. This model was built to the specifications of an expert in industrial design, Professor Friedrichs of the University of Göttingen. A great admirer of Henry Ford, he had studied American production techniques and had been to America to witness them firsthand. Killing Jews was to be an industrial enterprise, like any other. There were to be no more mobs of weeping women and screaming children awaiting their turn to die. At the unloading platform, camp personnel dressed as Red Cross workers were to give each new arrival a warm drink, containing a sedative. Each was given a copy of the camp rules and told to read it.

"After a short and orderly march to this large brick building, the victims were to be told to turn in their clothes and that after showering, they would be issued camp uniforms. Once they had disrobed, victims were directed into a large tiled shower room, with ten centimeters of water on the floor; at either end was an electrical plate, wired to deliver a massive electrical charge—the equivalent of a bolt of lightning—when a switch was thrown. Experiments indicated that two minutes at full voltage would kill up to 250 people in each cycle. This was a method far superior to the poison gas used at Auschwitz. There was no blood, no excrement! Death was instantaneous and clean!

"After the current was turned off, workers would push the corpses into a chute that emptied onto a conveyor belt. As each corpse passed by, other workers with rubber gloves would search its body cavities for valuables, while others down the line would extract gold bridgework and fillings. At the end the conveyor belt would dump each corpse into another chute leading directly to the flames! From the moment of arrival to the moment of incineration, no more than half an hour would elapse. At full capacity, each camp would be able to process five thousand Jews a day. That meant they could finish the job well within two years! It was a brilliantly designed closed system, with the burning corpses fueling the dynamos that ran the killing chamber! Each Jew that burned furnished the power to kill another Jew! And now, Herr Doktor, let me show you what was to arise from these crimes!"

They reentered the corridor and passed by a room to the side. Through the open door Hans could see workbenches, vises, clamps, chisels, power tools, sanders and polishers, little bottles of paint and miniature brushes arranged in racks, and cabinets. In the corner were blocks of wood and sheets of plywood. At the far end of the passage was a final door, which the Director pushed open. He turned on a switch and powerful lights lit the room.

It was dazzling. The room was large; the walls were painted bright white and the ceiling a light blue, like the sky. Occupying most of the room was an elevated platform, waist-high, some ten meters on a side. On it was a miniature city, perfect in every detail. There were grand buildings in neoclassical style and wide boulevards lined with streetlights; there were canals and little bridges, some with vehicles crossing them.

"Do you know what you see before you, Herr Doktor?"

"No, Comrade Director."

"It is Germania! The Utopia Hitler planned to build with the riches he had plundered from the Jews. The cultural and administrative center of a world totally controlled by Aryans! On the corpse of the last Jew, this new Athens was to arise! See here, Herr Doktor, I am building it to scale from Albert Speer's original plans from 1940, with changes by Hitler in 1944. I have followed them exactly! It is nearly complete! The Great Hall—I am working on it now—will go right here. And the Hall of Heroes, here." Taking up a pointer, he indicated two empty spaces at the city's center.

"Herr Doktor," he said, "allow me to give you a little tour. Save the Brandenburg Gate and the Victory Column ..." At this he touched each in turn. "you will see here very little of present-day Berlin. This is the East-West Axis ..." Here he pointed at a wide boulevard cutting through the center of the city. "... replacing much of the present Unter den Linden. The building just here is the Ministry of Propaganda and Enlightenment. It was to exercise total control over everything printed, seen, or heard throughout the world. This is the Racial Institute; the attached building was to house the greatest collection of human remains ever assembled. One floor was to be given over to skulls alone—over a hundred thousand of them—each labeled, measured, and classified by race. Here is Hitler's residence, the Führer-Palais, and near it, the new Reich's Chancellery, flanked by the Headquarters of the Gestapo and the High Command of the SS. Here, radiating from the spot where the Great Hall will be placed, is the North-South Axis, with a railroad terminal at either end. And far from the center of government, at the site where the main synagogue on the Oranienburger Strasse now stands, is the Center for the Study of World Jewry. In it were to be displays showing the evils of the Jew and how Aryan man so narrowly escaped his clutches. It would house the world's only library of Jewish works, open only to scholars doing research on the crimes of Jewry."

The Director stretched his hands out toward the city.

"And who was to live here," he said, "in this earthly paradise? One million of the racial elect, selected for their strength and beauty and measured to assure their features met the Aryan ideal. Racially deserving youth were to be recruited and brought here from all over the globe. Those who wished to sire or bear children could do so only after a rigorous examination. Unsanctioned pregnancies were to be terminated as soon as discovered! At birth all infants were to be examined by a panel of physicians; any with a defect, even if slight, was to be killed."

"But what of the rest of humanity, Comrade Director?"

"The lower races? They were to exist only to serve their Aryan masters. Only a few would ever see Germania. They would enter it, under guard, to see to its sanitation. Sterilized and regimented, they were to live in the concentration camp at Sachsenhausen, at the city's furthest outskirts. In the countryside nearby, there were to be small enclosures of people of the lesser races, allowed to breed under the supervision of scientists from the Racial Institute, maintained for experimental and medical research. Those with interesting physical defects were to be nurtured and studied, until there was nothing left to learn from them alive; then they were to be sacrificed and dissected, and their remains placed in the Institute collections.

"As for the rest of the world, elsewhere there were to be native reserves, where others of the slave-peoples would live, using only primitive technology. They were to be left to speak their own base tongues, but only German would be allowed to be written, and only by a racial comrade. An Academy for the Purity of the German Language was to research the origins of each word—those not meeting rigorous standards were to be banned from public use and purged from the dictionaries.

"And what, Herr Doktor, were the happy citizens of this marvelous city to do all day? Their energies were to be devoted to physical culture and the arts. Here, for example, is the House of German Music. But what was to be performed there? Bruckner's soporific symphonies! Simple-minded choral works by Carl Orff, glorifying the Führer! Endless and sterile regurgitations of Wagner!

"And how were these citizens to end their lives? The Führer taught that, save for heroes, the death of the individual is a non-event; only the life of the race matters! Upon death ordinary citizens were to be reduced to ash and used to fertilize a huge garden on the edge of the city—the Garden of the Ancestors of the Aryan Folk. This was to be a place of tranquil beauty for families to come to remember their forbears.

"But for heroes, it was different. They alone were immortal. They were the racial saints! Here, at the end of the North-South Axis, is the Great Arch, engraved on it the names of all those who fell in battle for the Aryan cause. Here, in this park nearby, is the most sacred place in Germania—the Tomb of Heroes. Frederick the Great, Bismarck, Hindenberg were all to be dug up and brought here. In the inner core of the monument, with an honor guard of SS, was to be the simple sarcophagus of the First Warrior Against the Serpent of Jewry, Adolf Hitler! Only the purest could enter and gaze on it."

The Director put down the pointer and stood a moment in silence. Then, turning off the light, he led Hans back through the corridors to the first room, where he again sat down, motioning to Hans to do the same.

"Now, Herr Doktor," he said, "we come to your role. The mission I have in mind for you is one only a hero who has shed blood for Germany can take up. Your bravery and quick action show you are such a hero! Only you are worthy of a task on which the future of all Germany depends!" At that point he picked up the long, official commendation with which the state had awarded Hans his decoration and began to read.

As he droned on, Hans's mind began to wander. To him, his act of heroism seemed little enough. There had been an important meeting in Potsdam involving Comrade Chebrikoff, the head of the KGB, Comrades Mielke and Honecker and Chernenko, successor to Brezhnev. Comrade Honecker's usual interpreter had suddenly taken ill, so at Comrade Mielke's recommendation, Hans had been brought from his desk at State Security and pressed into service. For some reason, Comrade Chernenko had delayed the opening of the meeting. This gave Hans the opportunity to get to know his partner, the Russian interpreter, Natasha Ivanovna Tartikoff. A wispy blonde with a broad face, she was charming, bright, and helpful. Over coffee, she had told him some of Comrade Chernenko's favorite phrases and how they might best be rendered into German. As the meeting began, Hans sat by Mielke and Honecker and interpreted to them in a low voice whenever the Russians were speaking; the young Russian woman did likewise for Chernenko and Chebrikoff. Comrades Mielke and Honecker, though both old men by then, were alert, but Comrade Chernenko seemed barely to be listening. He was sick and frail. He sat on the sofa, sucking a pastel and fiddling with his watch chain. The material was highly sensitive. The subject was an amendment to a secret protocol on the terms of cooperation between the Stasi and the KGB. Bad blood had arisen between them. Those in the Stasi felt the KGB had misled them, concealed important information and worse, taken credit for information that agents in the Stasi had risked their lives to get. Those in the KGB regarded the Stasi as upstarts who, without constant support and guidance from Moscow, would have been as bumbling and ineffective as their counterparts in the West.

Comrade Chebrikoff presented the KGB case in short, crisp sentences while Comrade Mielke rambled on about Stasi grievances for fully half an hour. Despite the fact that both Natasha Ivanovna and Hans had toned down the remarks in translation, it was quite apparent that Comrade Chebrikoff was getting angry, and even Comrade Chernenko showed signs of agitation. The meeting had ended on a sour note, with Comrade Chebrikoff demanding in a loud voice that the Stasi complainers be disciplined and Comrade Mielke refusing to do so.

Afterward, a photographer had come in to take pictures of the group. The old men sat sullenly in their places, avoiding one another's gaze. As for the photographer, there was something strange about him that no one but Hans seemed to notice. He took a long time to set up his equipment; he kept dropping things; he kept giving little nods and giggling nervously; there were beads of sweat on his brow. A few minutes into the session, after arranging everyone carefully and telling them not to move, he had reached deep into his bags of equipment and pulled out a pistol. Shouting "Freedom for Armenia!" he had begun to fire at Chebrikoff and Chernenko. At the first shot Hans had thrown himself forward, taking the third or fourth in the chest but knocking the man over on his back. Feeling the life ebbing out of him, he twisted the gun around in the man's hand and shot him through the throat. Strangely enough, the only one he had really thought of at the moment was the Russian girl. Chernenko, Chebrikoff, Mielke, and Honecker were unhurt—they sat gaping stupidly—but the young interpreter was slumped on the divan, her eyes glazed over, her mouth open, a hole in her chest. Even as his own blood mixed with the photographer's and congealed on the floor, and the objects in the room began to fade, he knew she was dead.

Days later, as he lay in the clinic, Hans found out his act had changed everything. He awoke one day to find Comrades Mielke and Chebrikoff standing over him, each holding a bouquet of flowers. Chebrikoff, in fact, had patted his forehead and called him "my brave boy." And then he had slipped again into the haze.

Meanwhile, the Director was concluding his reading, apparently adding his own remarks. "You became at that moment a legend at State Security," he was saying. "It is you, alone, who restored peace between the feuding brother agencies." It was true, of course, that he had saved Chernenko from death—not that it mattered, for the man was dead a few weeks later, anyway—but more importantly, he had saved Chebrikoff, a man who forgot neither his friends nor his enemies. Chebrikoff had been greatly impressed with the quick action of a Stasi agent and had changed his mind completely. "If we had just a dozen like him," he was reported to have said, "we would bring the West to its knees!"

Laying the commendation aside, the Director again pulled the photograph from the papers by his chair and handed it to Hans.

"Comrade, fix this photograph in your mind!" he said. "Study the little girl and that spot. She is perhaps ten or eleven in this photograph, so she is in her late thirties by now. You must find her! You must stand where she stands! By whatever means necessary, you must get that icon and bring it to me! Perhaps you will find it by talking to Mrs. Jahn. Perhaps you will find it by following this Prober. What is this 'important collection' he is making? Where does his money come from? Perhaps he will lead you to the man on the motorcycle."

Hans examined it closely. The little girl's blonde braids fell to her shoulders. Her cheekbones were high and her chin was sharp. The porcelain woman on the mantle wore a tall white wig, while at the edge of her skirt stood a little terrier on its hind legs.

"In four days," said the Director, taking it back, "you will leave for America. Breitbach will call for you at ten and drive you to the airport. You will use the weekend to acclimate and to change your appearance. Those people do not look like us. You must become as much like one of them as you can! Breitbach will provide you with an American passport and a driver's license from the state of Ohio. Your new name is John Hunter. They tell me this is English for Hans Jäger. How appropriate! You are from the city of Columbus, a gigantic administrative center in the steppes of the Middle West, and Breitbach will bring you a street plan and some picture postcards showing typical scenes of that place. You must think of an identity for yourself. You might be a wealthy layabout, or a stock speculator and swindler. America is full of such types! You must not pretend to know no German, though if you should ever be forced to speak it, you might make some typically stupid American mistakes—misuse of the conditional, improper placement of the verb, the wrong gender for a noun—ridiculous things like that! But when you get to Washington, you must be very careful. It is a city made dangerous by poverty and suffering!"

"Yes, Comrade Director."

"Then you accept this mission?"

"I do, Comrade." A sense of duty and purpose—gone for so long—came flooding back to him. His comrades had come to his aid in an hour of need, and now he would come to theirs.

"Do you swear, with Comrade Breitbach as our witness, never to reveal what you have heard here today, nor the existence of this place?"

"Yes, I swear."

"Do you swear to serve loyally and without question the cause of socialism and the brotherhood of man?"

"I do so swear."

"And will you fight fascism to your dying breath?"

"Yes, Comrade, to my dying breath!"

"This oath shall override any subsequent oaths you may need to take to attain this goal. As Marxists, we know the truth and pursue its fulfillment. But remember! A lie that serves the historical imperative is not a lie. It becomes a part of the truth itself! Now, stand before me and receive my blessing." Hans arose and turned to face him.

"You are a citizen of the German Democratic Republic. Never forget that."

"I will not, Comrade Minister."

"Keep this in mind! You have the authority to act in the name of the state. In the name of socialism, you must not shrink from applying the harsh hand of justice to all those who deserve it!"

"Yes, Comrade."

"Remember, Comrade Klug. You are in a brotherhood! State Security is not dead. It is not dead in Germany, and it is not dead even in America." The Director embraced Hans and kissed him on both cheeks. Then he spoke again.

"Now, go forth, hero! You are the embodiment of the historic imperative! You will redeem the crimes of the German people! You will help us find the rotten heart of fascism and together we will rip it from the breast of Berlin!"

Breitbach, meanwhile, had wheeled in a little cart; on it were three long-stemmed glasses on a clean, white cloth, a corkscrew, and a silver bucket of ice in which sat a dark green bottle with a faded label.

"Breitbach! Open the champagne! It is French, Herr Doktor, vintage 1923, from Goebbels' private stock—the last one left!" Breitbach uncorked the bottle and poured some of its contents into each glass. Despite its age, it bubbled up right to the top.

"Comrades!" said the Director, rising from his chair, "let us drink to the Republic! As long as we live, so shall it!" Together they faced the banner of the Republic, lifted their glasses high and sang the national anthem of their defunct land, "Arisen from the Ashes," and the words of the great socialist poet, Johannes Becher, rang through the room.

CHAPTER 6

Aunt Rosa

Three days later, Hans found himself high over the North Atlantic, on his way to a country he had never expected to go to and had never wanted to see. Looking around, he felt that in some ways he had gotten there already; it was an American carrier, and everyone on board seemed to be American. Although during his days in the border troops he had occasionally flown along the frontier in a helicopter, this was only his second trip by plane: once before, when the Republic had still existed, he had flown to Moscow for a ceremony held in his honor, stayed a few days to be shown the city, and had flown home. Now, nothing about the experience seemed familiar: not the carts full of cans and bottles that came clattering down the aisle; not the adjustable jets of air in the panel over one's head; not the buttons that turned on the lights or called the steward; not the lever that allowed one to tilt one's seat back into the lap of the person behind.

Of course that earlier flight had been on a Soviet military aircraft, with only a dozen or so passengers. He had been with a Russian general and a high official of State Security who also spoke Russian. The three of them had sat up front, a curtain dividing them from the others, and had talked, joked, and sipped vodka the entire trip. But this time he knew no one and felt totally isolated, a feeling made worse by the landscape below. For the first three hours there had been nothing but clouds and water, but now an icy, barren, rocky coastline had suddenly appeared, while further inland, snow-capped summits emerged from the mist. He felt as though he had been plucked from the midst of life and put into the sky with only the double pane of a window to keep him from being sucked out into the void.

Next to him sat a middle-aged man reading a bible with a worn leather cover on which was embossed a golden cross. When the steward brought the man his meal, he had bowed his head and muttered something over it. After dinner, when Hans had fallen into a light doze, the man suddenly nudged him in the side with his elbow. Hans opened his eyes with a start to find the man staring at him, his finger pushed against a passage in his book marked in red. In a deep and sonorous voice, as though he were addressing a great multitude, he said, "The country that turns from God will perish in flames! So is it written and so shall it occur!" Then he turned back to his reading and didn't speak for the rest of the trip.

Now thoroughly awake, Hans once more patted the pocket of his jacket and felt the folder that Breitbach had handed him on the way to the airport. In it were an American passport with a photograph he'd had taken in a shop on the Kurfürstendamm, his airline ticket to New York with a continuation to Washington, an Ohio driver's license with the same photo, only smaller, on it, and a credit card, all in the name of John Hunter.

"That icon," Breitbach had said, "it's a fantasy of his. You want to know what I think? You can forget about it! The money—that's what's important. I'm counting on you to get it back. By the way, Herr Doktor, do you know what I heard on the street since we last met? Seems that last Saturday a prostitute was seen leaving the Savignyplatz on the back of a motorcycle. A witness described the driver as a thick-necked brute with a limp! On Sunday they found her in the Grunewald, hanging by the neck from a tree. She'd been beaten and burned on the face with a cigarette. Apparently our friend picked her up right after he left us— like a beast, driven from its meal, that right away seeks out another!"

Besides the passport, Breitbach had given him a wallet with a few twenty-dollar bills, a five and several ones—one of which had been torn in two and taped back together, and a change purse with a few quarters and a dime in it. As Breitbach opened the trunk of his cab at the airport and got out a worn brown suitcase that Hans was seeing for the first time, he said, "Well, Herr Doktor, you're on your own. Off to America! I wouldn't trade places with you for a million euros. And by the way, there are two other sets of identification in the lining of the suitcase, in a different names, should you suddenly need them. You never know! And there's a phone number there as well, in case you need to reach me. The order of the last four digits is reversed—don't forget that!" Then he had pulled up behind another cab, and when Hans looked back as he entered the terminal, Breitbach was already opening the door to another fare.

In the briefcase he had stuck below the seat in front of him, Hans had put several items to look at during the trip. He pulled them out and put them on his foldout tray. One was a pamphlet on his supposed native city, about which he knew nothing. Called *This is Columbus*, it had somehow been dug up by Breitbach, who was quite resourceful, though it seemed to date from several years before. According to it, Columbus was not only the important governmental nerve center for a leading state, but a city with many parks, a fine zoo, an excellent school system, a distinguished art museum displaying the works of talented Ohio artists, and a world-renowned university, where one could study anything, from nuclear physics to managing a golf course. It was hard to imagine why anyone would want to live anywhere else. Breitbach had also found a couple of picture postcards from the city, though they were useless to communicate what the place was like. Two showed only motels, and another showed a shoe store. There was one, though, of the state capitol. There was also a map of Washington, DC and its surroundings, which sprawled into two adjoining states. It showed a confusing mass of densely packed numbered and lettered streets with avenues named for the states cutting diagonally across them and a huge ring-road, like the one Hitler had built around Berlin, enclosing the city. On it Hans had marked the location of a cheap motel not far from the airport. It was called the Iwo Jima Inn and was once favored by agents of the Republic many years before. He had even called from a telecom office in Berlin to make a reservation in the name of his new identity and to get directions on how to get there.

Putting the map aside, he again picked up the copy of the publication the Director had given him. Called *New Studies in German History*, it was an odious little publication, fit only to be placed beneath a defecating dog. He paged through it and looked at the articles. One was a flattering profile of SS-General Theodor Eicke, founder of the Death's Head Division of the Waffen-SS and architect of the concentration camp system—in reality a thoroughly depraved and degenerate lout. Another put forth as fact the manufactured evidence that Poland had first attacked Germany, rather than the other way around. Then came an article on the Russian soldier, his strengths and weaknesses. According to it, the Russian had grown up in cold, rain, and mud, to which he was impervious. Brutal and ignorant, he preferred to fight in a mass and showed no enterprise or individual initiative. Guided by a cruel and perverted doctrine that had totally laid hold of his primitive mind, his fanaticism and robot-like nature made him a formidable enemy. Yet still, figures on casualties from both sides showed that it took four of these creatures to bring down a single soldier of the Reich.

Another was on the Hitler Youth—according to the author, the most successful youth movement the world has ever seen. It took youth's natural idealism and turned it to a purpose. Through its songs, rituals, and rallies, it forged a thousand wills into a single will. It instilled in its members a fierce courage and an iron discipline. Now a new movement, the Aryan Youth, had come along to take its place. In structure it was alike. In beliefs it was identical. From its ranks would come a cadre of leaders who would think with one mind and speak with one voice. And some day it would rule the world.

The last article was the most offensive of all. Written by the party's leader, Fritz Westermarck, it set forth as the defining event of the twentieth century the battle waged by the noble People of the North against the treacherous People of the East—an uncreative and unproductive folk who in a cultural sense do nothing but occupy space. In contrast, the People of the North, the Aryans, are the source of all that is good in mankind. Their art, music, literature, and science have spread throughout the globe, and only they give meaning to human existence. Take them away and all that remains is the dance of apes.

According to Westermarck, there had arisen in Europe a demon ideology, communism, invented by the Jew to make himself master of the earth. Foolish and easily deceived, the People of the East were the first to be seduced by it. As an antidote, there came forth in Germany a movement of renewal among the People of the North, led by a figure of great strength and vision. Under his direction a whole people rose, cleansed itself, and put aside shame and defeat. But according to Westermarck, the Jew looked on in alarm, for the leader of this movement saw through the Jew and divined his purpose. And so, to destroy this leader and scatter his followers, the Jew had incited the peoples of the earth to rise up and attack them. Besieged on all sides, the People of the North fought back with such courage that their deeds will be celebrated as long as mankind exists.

Hans turned again to the back cover, with Prober's notice. How was he to approach a man like this? In all probability the only way was to offer him something he wanted. When he had looked at it back in his flat, it had given him an idea. And so, two days before, he had taken the train to Oranienburg, the town just north of Berlin where he had grown up, to pay a visit to his Aunt Rosa. Aunt Rosa was someone he hadn't seen in years. Even as a child he rarely saw her. Hans's mother saw scant reason to keep up with her first husband's family, about which hung the unfortunate odor of fascism. He had been raised by his stepfather, a fine man, filled with socialist ideals. A leader in the Free German Youth, he had done much to set his little stepson on the right road in life. By contrast, his own father was, from the little he had heard of him, a solitary and brooding man, given to outbursts of rage. Ill-fitted for life in a socialist society, he had died suddenly only a few weeks after Hans had been born.

His Aunt Rosa had, for many years, held a minor post in the Transport Ministry, but now she kept a little shop in the center of town, a short walk from the train station. Hans walked up to the main street, where he waited to cross. Nowadays the traffic in Oranienburg was nearly as bad as in Berlin. In the days of his childhood, besides the trucks full of Russian soldiers, about all one saw were occasional buses of tourists from other socialist countries, on their way to visit the infamous Sachsenhausen Concentration Camp only a kilometer away, where the fascists had starved, beaten, and murdered tens of thousands of innocent people.

Aunt Rosa's shop was tucked away in the middle of a block that was otherwise mostly flats. On the, window in gold lettering outlined in black trim, were the words, "Meissner's Groceries." Behind the glass appeared some bags of flour and sugar and a few cans of cooking oil, all formed into pyramids. A bell jingled as he opened the door. Inside it was dark and musty. He winced as he recalled their conversation.

"Aunt Rosa."

"Oh, it's you." The old woman—she must have been on the far side of her sixties—showed no interest, and in fact didn't move from the little stool on which she sat behind the counter, bent over a cup of tea. In a long, dark dress with a kerchief over her head and a white knit shawl around her shoulders, she looked like a figure from three generations before.

"Yes, Aunt Rosa, it's me."

"I thought of you recently. A week or two ago a woman came out here looking for you. She was asking around at your mother's old house if anyone knew you, and someone sent her here."

"Really. Who was she?"

"Oh, I don't know. A funny, tired-looking little creature, as pale as a dead fish. She said she knew you from your army days. One of your little tarts, I expect. She came up here with a man on a motorcycle. He didn't even come in—he just sat outside and ran his motor."

"So you didn't see him."

"No. What difference does it make?"

"Did you tell her where I was?"

"Of course! Why shouldn't I? She was perfectly nice. She even bought a bottle of beer and a sausage!"

"I see. And how are you doing?"

"Not so well. Can't you see for yourself? Look at this place! It's empty! I haven't had a customer all day! Even the people who live next door don't come here. The big chains take all the business. There's one two corners down—you must have gone right by it. Packed to overflowing, wasn't it? Why would people come here when they can go there? They're run by Jews, all of them. I knew the Jews would be back, just as soon as they saw there was a little money to be made."

"Really? I've heard they're owned by rich Germans from the West."

"Nonsense! Those are only the front people! Behind every one of them is a Jew! You can take my word on it!" The old lady set her jaw and stared at him. It was hopeless to continue this line of conversation.

"When was the last time we met?" he said.

"When your mother died, wasn't it? That was quite a while back. Not that she would have invited me to her funeral, if she'd been able. I wouldn't even have been there, if I hadn't read about it in the newspaper! You came up with your wife. I remember her well. A pretty little thing with blonde hair and a pert little nose. A regular decent German girl, not like that black creature from the jungle you brought up here once in your university days. My God, that was a shock! Your grandfather would have turned you out of the house! I'd half a mind to do it myself! What was your wife's name again? Monika, wasn't it?"

"Marianne."

"Marianne, that was it! But you split up, I hear. A pity! Have you heard from her recently?"

"No, not for a while." Nor did he expect to, ever again. She had moved to Dortmund, remarried, and as time went on, Hans thought of her less and less, and in fact, knew nothing about her now. Perhaps she had a child. Perhaps she was dead. Like so many, her devotion to socialism had proved to be mere words, and as soon as the state collapsed, her beliefs had melted away.

"So you've no one else?"

"Not at present."

"Well, then, what do you do with yourself, now that you're no longer making a living spying on your neighbors?"

"I translate. I help foreigners who want to invest in Germany."

"You do, do you? Is that what you're doing out here today? Helping foreigners?" Hans hadn't recalled just how shrill and unpleasant the old woman's voice was.

"No. I came to see you."

"Why?" She rose from her stool, hobbled past him and began to dust the pyramid of cans in the front window, meanwhile leaning forward and looking both directions down the empty sidewalk.

"I've been thinking a lot about my life. Everything has changed for me, Aunt Rosa. My education and my work blinded me to the truth. Now I've had a chance to think things through and I want to find out who I am. I want to understand my heritage as a German. I was wondering if you might have anything of my father's or my grandfather's that would help me."

"So you've come to your senses at last, have you? That's quite an about-face! I never thought I'd live to see the day. When you turned eighteen I gave you some photos. Do you still have them? I thought at the time you might throw them away!"

"No, I didn't throw them away. In fact I look at them often. In a way they're the reason I've come out to see you today."

"I don't know whether to believe you or not. But what choice do I have? At any rate, assuming you're telling the truth, I do have two other items I might give you. God knows, they're of no use to an old woman. One of these days I'll be gone myself, so it's just as well I get rid of them now. After all, you're the last one of us left! In some ways they are our family's greatest treasures. Do you promise to take care of them?"

"Yes, Aunt Rosa, I promise."

With that, she put down her dust rag and went through a door behind the counter into a back room where she rummaged around for a few minutes, emerging at last with a packet of letters and a large, brown portfolio held closed with a string. Untying it, she withdrew first a certificate and a family tree, both on parchment, both with the eagle and swastika seal of the Third Reich on the top.

"This proves you spring from the purest German blood," she said. "It shows our ancestry, going from your father back more than eight generations, to 1725. See here? Nothing but good names—German, Christian names! Not a Jew or a Polack in the whole bunch! And this is the SS Suitability Certificate, showing your grandfather met the strict racial requirements to join. Everyone had to have one, down to the lowest private. Those men were the finest flower of our race!" Next, she took from the depths of the portfolio a small cedar box, which she held up and looked at for a second before handing it to him.

"This is the most precious relic of all. It's what sets our family high above others. Open it!"

Hans undid the little brass hook and lifted the lid. Inside, on a bed of velvet, was a black Maltese Cross, edged in gold, on a red ribbon; at the center, flanked with swords and oak leaves, was a swastika. It lay before him, a glimmering object, like an evil charm.

"It was awarded posthumously to your grandfather—one of the highest grades of the Knight's Cross!" said the old woman. "It is your inheritance. Do you want it?"

"Yes, very much. It's beautiful."

"I had to hide it all these years. The authorities would have confiscated it, the swine! They'd have sold it to some Westerner and pocketed the money for themselves! Once the wall came down, I could have sold it myself for thousands of marks. There are very few of them, you know! But I saved it for you! The Führer himself touched this medal—think of that! I well remember the ceremony where the Führer presented it to your father, in honor of your fallen grandfather's heroic deeds! How proud your father looked, in his Hitler Youth uniform! I was there myself, a girl of no more than eight! They sent a military vehicle up from Berlin with the Führer's personal standard and two SS officers to bring us down to the Reich's Chancellery! My mother braided my hair, and I wore my best dress. That day, I was the perfect picture of German girlhood! I handed the Führer a bouquet of flowers, and he patted me on the head! How kind and gentle he was! The poor man—he looked so old and gray. How he suffered for his people! I shall always remember that moment as the proudest of my life."

"What did Grandfather do to win it?"

"Oh, I don't know, I've forgotten, but it was something very brave! The important thing is that he served Germany! He should be a model for you! You should take your name back. Meissner, that's what it ought to be! It's a name that belongs to heroes and patriots! You shouldn't walk around the rest of your life with the name of some turncoat scum who served the Bolsheviks!"

"Perhaps I will, Aunt Rosa."

"Let me read you something. It might help you make up your mind! It's from your grandfather's letters to your grandmother. Your mother threw them out when your father died. I had to rescue them from the trash! I plan to keep them until the very end. They're in a little table by my bed. When I'm laid out in my casket, you can take them, but not before! There is a passage here that applies directly to you! It is in the last letter my mother ever received from him." After smoothing out a creased and yellowing sheet of paper she had taken from among the packet, she withdrew a pair of glasses from the pocket of her dress and began to read.

"My dearest Christiana. My unit is being transferred once again, I know not where. The fighting recently has been very hard and bitter. We have lost many good men, and many of us shall follow them! It is a noble path, and I have no fear to walk it. Should I die in battle, in the company of my comrades until the very last minute, then this will be the ultimate fulfillment of my life. I have but one wish—to serve my Führer and my Fatherland! It is I and my comrades who are fighting to defend Western Civilization from the Asiatic hordes who threaten to swarm, like a plague of locusts, over all of Europe! I die happy in the knowledge that my sacrifice guarantees renewed life for our Volk and that our blood that flows together in the veins of our Aryan son will some day flow in those of his son, as well. Of one thing I feel sure—our blood will engender a new hero, strong and noble, who will be among the sacred few who redeem Germany! Should you, my darling German wife, be saddened at my death, then take a walk in the countryside near our home and behold the greenery of our German spring! See how new life bursts forth from our sacred soil, nourished by the sacrifice of thousands of its sons. Then you will understand that no price is too high to preserve our sacred Reich!" She folded the letter and put it back with the others. There were tears in the corners of her eyes.

"Do you have what it takes to fulfill his prophesy? Heroic times will come again! Germany is awakening! Just remember, even though your mother was weak and soft, your father and your grandfather were as hard as Krupp steel! You must be worthy of them!"

"I will do my best, Aunt Rosa."

"Then embrace me, my child. Perhaps this is the last time we will meet!"

Hans put his arms around her. Her neck was bony and her shoulders frail and brittle, and as she kissed him, her lips felt dry and rough against his cheek. Then she had turned and gone back to her stool behind the counter, and he had left, taking with him the papers and the box with his grandfather's Knight's Cross.

That evening and the following, he had brooded over his aunt, his father, and his grandfather, and what they were like. Their ideas and entire lives were monstrous and ignorant. How were they any better than the criminals who had been tried and hanged at Nuremberg? And what had made them that way? Obviously Germany was full of such people, even today, and now they had a sinister new banner to flock to. Was there something of them in him, as well? If he hadn't known and loved the Laibsteins, could he have shoved them into the gas chamber and thought he was doing the world a favor?

To dispel such thoughts, that very morning, before Breitbach had driven him out to the airport, he had taken the tram the few blocks up to Weissensee and walked along the Herbert-Baum-Strasse to the Jewish Cemetery, where more culture, learning, and refinement had been buried than anywhere else in Berlin. Since covering one's head was one of their customs, he had brought along a knit hat, which he put on as he walked through the front gate and past the urn of ashes of victims from the concentration camps. Going to the new section where there were even a few fresh graves dug since the Laibsteins had died, he found the stone that he himself had helped erect for them.

He remembered back to the dark days when he had come twice to this same spot, and when for the second time he had sought out the old Hungarian rabbi, to perform again a service for the dead. The rabbi had expressed surprise at seeing him and had said, "What? Back so soon? Where's the old man?"

"Dead, Rabbi. He killed himself."

"Dear, dear. A pity. But it doesn't surprise me. He had that look in his eyes. He didn't want to live. I saw many like him at Auschwitz. They didn't want to live, either. Musselmen, we called them. The evil of the world had robbed them of their strength. Some of them threw themselves on the outer fence and were shot down by the guards. If that old man had been there, he'd have been one of them."

"I'd like to put up a headstone for them, Rabbi. Is there an inscription I could have put on it?"

"Yes, my son. I shall choose something suitable. A psalm, perhaps. These were not religious people, but they deserve to be commemorated for the good they did in life and for the sufferings they endured. There is a member of our community who does such work. I will contact him. If you care to contribute to it, that would be a kindness."

"Of course, Rabbi," he had said, and had pulled from his wallet a thousand marks. And as he had turned to go, the rabbi had put his hand on Hans's shoulder and said "You're a good boy. When I asked the old man who you were, he said you were his son. But look at you! You're no Jew. You're a German! So it's not true, is it?"

"No, Rabbi, it's not true."

"Well, no matter. Go forth into the world with his blessing, and with mine!"

When he stood once more before the headstone, his head bowed, he rededicated himself to his teachers and to the brotherhood of man. He had respected and revered Laibstein, but it struck him that perhaps Laibstein's wife was the person he had loved most in his life, more even than his own mother, and that whatever finer feelings he might have acquired in life, had come from her. Finding a small stone along the path, he placed it on top of the grave marker—that was another Jewish custom—and said aloud, "I will remain true to my oath to you. Whatever happens, I will never betray you, not to the last second of my life!"

CHAPTER 7

America

At home he had made the last preparations before leaving. First, there were things in the refrigerator that would surely go bad during his absence—some sausage and the cheese—so he threw them out. Then he had straightened up his papers and made a few calls cancelling his engagements. What if the authorities were to search his apartment while he was gone? It was certainly possible. If they did, how long would it take them to find that box beneath the wardrobe? Ten minutes at the most—and that only if there were just one of them. It was quite apparent that that was a stupid place to leave it, though in looking around the flat, he could think of no other. With that, he pulled it out, and, putting into it the photographs from the Laibsteins, walked down the hall and knocked on the Eisenbergs' door. From inside came the sound of footsteps and a slight cough, and in a moment the professor's lovely daughter stood before him.

"Sonja Davidovna," he said, "I need to have a few words with you."

"Certainly, Herr Doktor," she said. "Please come in. I only regret that my father is at the university. He will be sorry to have missed your visit."

With a slight smile, she stood aside for him to enter. He took a chair in the living room, one identical in its floor plan to that in his own flat, but a great deal cleaner and more pleasant. It was in every way the room of cultured and educated people. On the wall was the reproduction of an Old Master that hung in the Hermitage; in a corner stood a cello and a music stand, and on it, sheet music of sonatas by Bach. There was a carved wooden chess set on the dining room table and a bookcase with the complete works of Chekhov and volumes by Gogol, Turgenev, and Lermontov. On the sideboard was a samovar and several tea glasses in metal holders with scenes of Moscow. The young woman poured him a glass of tea and set it by him. There was something cat-like in the way she moved across the floor. Then she sat down in a chair facing him and leaned forward, her hands folded on her lap.

"Sonja Davidovna, I have a favor to ask of you."

"Herr Doktor," she said, "my father and I are only too happy to be of service to you. What is it that you would like?"

"Simply this. I will be gone for a few days. I don't know quite when I will be back. I would like you to keep the key to my apartment. When I leave tomorrow morning I shall put it under your door. If you would, I also wish you to keep something for me. If anyone—even the authorities—should come asking questions about me, you are not to tell them of it. Will you do this for me?"

"Of course, Herr Doktor."

Continuing to speak to her in Russian so that there could be no possibility of misunderstanding, he said, "If I do not return within a few weeks, or should you hear definitely that I shall not return at all, then you are to dispose of the contents as you see fit and use any money you might find for you and your father to start a life somewhere else." At that point he handed her the box, and she took it, a worried look on her face.

"Herr Doktor Klug, are you in some sort of difficulties?"

"Sonja Davidovna, I'm not what you think I am."

"You're a decent person. That's what I think you are. Are you telling me otherwise?"

"No."

"Where are you going?"

"On a trip. It's quite possible I will be gone only a few days. As for my reasons and destination, I will perhaps discuss this with you in detail at some point, but I cannot do so now. You must understand me."

"I wish you would be frank with me, Herr Doktor."

"One day, if you wish, you will know everything about me you care to know." Then he rose to go.

At the door they stood and faced each other. "Well, good-bye, Sonja Davidovna." He held out his hand, and she took it.

"Good-bye." She looked him in the eye, pursing her lips, as though she expected something more.

The words came out before he could stop them. "Sonja Davidovna," he said, "I wish to say one more thing to you before I go. If I were able to live my life over, I would choose to live it with you."

At that, a look both startled and pleased had passed over her lovely face. Clasping the box to her chest, she had leaned forward and kissed him lightly on the cheek.

Inside the terminal in New York, there were a great many people, crowding and pushing their way into the non-citizens line for passport control. Hans joined the much shorter line for citizens and stepped forward from the white line painted on the floor to the booth when the man inside motioned to him. Recalling his own service at passport control on the Republic's borders with the West, he applied, in reverse, the tips he had learned to recognize those with something to hide. Does the subject avoid looking you in the eye? Does he show signs of agitation? Is he excessively friendly or accommodating? If so, he should be removed from the sight of others and searched thoroughly. He remembered, too, another important point he had learned during intelligence training: should one be asked a question which one can only answer with a lie, recall that every good lie should have in it at least one element of truth.

"You've been out of the country for how long?" The man looked at the passport photo and glanced at Hans.

"Two weeks."

"Business or vacation?"

"A family visit. I went to see an aunt."

"Where?"

"She lives in what used to be East Germany."

"Did you have a good time?"

"Not very. It's pretty dismal over there. I'm glad to be back."

"Then welcome home, sir." The man smiled slightly, stamped the passport, and handed it back to him, with a blue card he had placed inside it; as he did so, he was already turning toward the next person in line.

The customs hall was even more chaotic. Several carousels were spewing forth suitcases, boxes, and bags. An official, a white man with a huge gut and rolls of fat on his neck, had separated a large group of black people to one side, while another, nearly as fat, moved among them with a dog, which sniffed their luggage. The people were docile and quiet. Their children clung to them, while the men pointed out which items they wanted opened and then pawed through the contents. One little girl was weeping; the dog had lingered over the doll she had clasped in her arms, and one of the officials took it away. He had made a slit in its back with a knife and took some of the stuffing between his fingers and held it to his nose. At last Hans's suitcase emerged. For him there was no inspection. Taking his card, an official pointed him down a corridor that opened directly into the terminal.

Within an hour he found himself on the shuttle flight to Washington, and soon enough, it was coming to an end. The plane flew down a river, past a business district with broadcasting towers and a reservoir surrounded by trees, and then, suddenly, there it was: the great imperial city of the West, with a towering, white obelisk, a vast dome in the distance, and other white marble monuments scattered below. For a second the obelisk was reflected in a long, narrow pool, and then the plane passed over two bridges clogged with traffic and abruptly touched down on the runway.

Once in the terminal, Hans stopped at a phone, where he dialed the number Breitbach had given him. A woman answered. She had a slight German accent, but her words were English.

"Mr. Hunter?"

"Yes?"

"Are you at Gate 20 in Reagan National Airport?"

"Yes."

"Please proceed to the main hall of the terminal and turn right. At the sign for 'Metro' and 'Parking,' turn left and take the escalator and then walkway to the parking garage. Once inside, take the stairs to level B-3 and exit to your right. The eighth car in Row 4 is a light gray Honda Accord with Ohio plates. According to the U.S. Department of Transportation, it is one of the five commonest models and colors on the road. On the bumper is a sticker: 'School's Open—Drive Carefully!' The key is taped to the inner side of the front left tire. Try to leave as few fingerprints on the car as possible—a pair of driving gloves are on the dashboard. Beneath the rubber mat on the driver's side is a sealed envelope with further information for you. Should you need further assistance with the car, please call this number again."

Within a few minutes, Hans was feeling for the key and opening the door. On the dashboard was a pair of driving gloves, which he put on. He reached down and found the envelope. Inside was a message that read, "Dear Mr. Hunter, welcome to Washington. Enclosed is the parking garage ticket, which you must present in order to leave this lot, and ten telephone cards, allowing you to make twenty dollars of calls on each. To avoid having your movements traced, use each card only once. When you are finished with the car, please put the key in the ashtray, lock the doors, and call the same number to leave information as to where you have left it. In the glove compartment are local maps, and beneath the passenger seat is a road atlas of the U.S. In the compartment beneath the armrest are funds to cover your expenses; please leave any you have not spent there on your departure. Should you need them, there are two extra sets of license plates and two more bumper stickers in the trunk. Take a few moments to familiarize yourself with the controls of the car. It is a reliable model and should serve you well."

Hans lifted the armrest and found the well beneath it stuffed with cash; a quick count revealed there was at least fifteen thousand dollars, much of it in smaller, used bills. In the ashtray were a couple of toothpicks and the wrapper from a candy bar, and in the drink holder between the seats, an unopened bottle of water. On the front seat was a box of tissues, and on the back seat lay a Columbus newspaper from the previous day. The odometer showed twenty thousand miles, and the gas tank was full.

Soon he had pulled onto a parkway near the river, passing by something he had seen in the newspaper and on propaganda posters a hundred times—the Pentagon. Just beyond it lay a massive military cemetery with identical headstones, set out in lines like crops in a field, stretching from a hill right down to the road. Then came a heroic statue of battlefield soldiers raising the flag, and a minute later, he was in the parking lot of the motel.

The room they gave him stank of a thousand cigarettes. There was a double bed that faced a large mirror and a writing table with a lamp and a chair. Across the front window and above the heating register was a heavy curtain, hung by brass rings from a metal bar. In the corner, on a platform riveted into the wall, was a television. Below that was a small refrigerator, which gave out a distracting hum until he unplugged it. On the bed stand were a clock radio and a phone. He sat on the bed and looked at the time; it was nearly three-thirty. Tired as he was, it was time to begin. Putting the Knight's Cross and the Ahnenpass beside him, he took out a phone card and used it to dial the number Breitbach had taken from the bra of Ingeborg Mohr. The phone rang once, and a man answered.

"John Prober here." It was the same hard, suspicious voice he'd heard under the streets of Berlin.

"Dr. Prober, my name is John Hunter. I understand you're an expert on German military decorations from the Third Reich. I'd like to consult you about one awarded to my grandfather."

"Not just another Iron Cross, is it?"

"No. It's a Knight's Cross with Swords and Oak Leaves."

"Really." The voice showed interest. "Tell me about it."

"I inherited it from my father, along with some photographs and documents. He came over from Germany around 1950. He just died, and I found it up in the attic. I was interested, so I went to the library and looked it up in a book."

"Jahn's catalogue?"

"Yes, that's the one. Now I want to find out whatever I can about my grandfather and I thought maybe you could help me."

"You mentioned documents. What are they?"

"Well, my German's not so good. One is like a family tree and another is like a military pay book, with 'SS' on the front. Another is like a passport. It says something like A … h … n … e … n—it's in that old-time script. It's hard to figure out."

"Ahnenpass! An Ahnenpass is proof of Aryan descent. Anyone

joining the SS had to have one. As for the medal, it's really quite rare. There can't be more than one or two in the whole United States. Your grandfather must have done something extraordinary—only true heroes ever won a decoration like that. Are you interested in selling it? Such items have gone up considerably in value in recent years. We might be prepared to offer you as much as forty thousand dollars for it. In cash."

"Forty thousand? That's quite a bit. But no, I wouldn't feel right selling it. It's part of my heritage. The ideals it represents are in my blood. They're what my grandfather died for. If I have a son, some day I will pass it on to him."

"An excellent answer and one that does you credit! But in our hands it would become part of an important historical collection and be on permanent display. It would inspire not only your son, but other young men like him."

"I might consider lending it to you, under certain circumstances. Would you like to see it?"

"Of course."

"I'm in Washington for a few days. I could drive down to meet you. Would that be convenient?"

"This coming week is rather busy for me. The only day I could fit you in is Monday. Would you be able to get here by two o'clock?"

"Yes, certainly."

"Good. Come to the college. There's a guard at the front gate. I'll leave word to let you through. Mr. Hunter, wasn't it?"

"Yes. Hunter. John Hunter."

"My office is in Jericho Hall, on the lower level. I will meet you there. Please be prompt."

A moment later Hans was calling information and getting the number of St. Elizabeth's Hospital. Soon he was talking to a woman in records.

"I'm looking for a relative of mine," he said. "Mrs. Frieda Jahn. She entered I believe in 1978."

"Just a moment. Could you spell that?" The woman had a deep, rich voice with a Southern accent. Hans spelled it out and waited. He could hear tapping on a keyboard. Then the voice came on again. "She's no longer a patient here," it said.

"No longer there? Where is she?"

"She was discharged three years ago. Our records show that for two years she was an outpatient. She came into the clinic three times a week to get her medication. Her last visit was in September of last year."

"That long ago? What happened then?"

"She stopped coming in. It's not unusual."

"Why was she discharged?"

"There are a lot more people in here than we can take care of."

"Do you have an address for her?"

"Last we knew she had no address."

"What does that mean?"

"That she's probably out on the street."

Hans hung up. What a country. Isn't it the state's job to care for those who can't care for themselves? It seemed the essence of capitalism to throw a sick old woman out to fend for herself. Why was there no record of her for the past seven months? She was probably dead.

Wearily he lifted the battered suitcase onto the bed and opened it. A random assortment of old clothes spilled out—socks with holes in the toes, ragged underwear and shirts, one with a frayed collar and a torn sleeve, a pair of slacks nearly out at the seat—it looked as though Breitbach had grabbed a few handfuls of clothing out of one of the collection bins for the poor along the streets of Berlin. Beneath this mess was a cheap plastic overnight kit with a football helmet on it and the words "Dallas Cowboys." Inside were an unwrapped bar of soap, a razor, a nail clipper, a comb, an opened roll of disintegrating antacid tablets, and an American aspirin bottle in which two or three pills rattled around. Running his fingers along the lining of the suitcase, he came to what felt like an envelope. Ripping out the lining and taking it out, he found in it two more complete sets of identification— passports and driver's licenses with his photo on them and two more credit cards—and the telephone number to reach Breitbach. Putting the phone number in his wallet and the rest aside, he stood before the mirror and saw in it a European man at the threshold of middle age, looking much like any other German on the streets of Berlin. What was it that the Director had said? 'Those people do not look like us. You must become as much like them as you can!' How was he to do that? There was little he could do little about his light blond hair and blue eyes. Apparently it was a rare combination in modern America—hardly anyone he had seen since getting off the plane looked like that. Still, there were things that might help. Leaving the room, he walked up into the commercial district until he found a barbershop—all the barbers in it were Asian—and got a haircut like any American might get. This was at least a start. Tomorrow he could do more. Then, after buying a sandwich and some fruit, he went back to his room.

Shortly before seven, he showered and lay down on the bed, listening to the faint sounds of traffic and the occasional sound of a plane. He thought of Sonja Davidovna and what she was doing at the moment. Since in Berlin it was the middle of the night, she was no doubt asleep. Suddenly every limb felt leaden, and he was overwhelmed by fatigue.

The next morning he turned back to the task of melting into the crowd. He headed for a huge suburban shopping center he had first heard of years before from advertisements in the *Washington Post*. It was near the ring road, surrounded by hectares of parking lots and garages packed with cars. Surprisingly, the shops in it were neither as exclusive nor as well-stocked as those along the Kurfürstendamm in the West or even the Friedrichstrasse in the East. In a department store that bore as its name the German word for a kind of fish—it was the cheapest place he could find—he bought blue jeans, khaki trousers and a blue blazer, a striped blue and maroon necktie, black loafers and a pair of walking shoes, two sports shirts and four dress shirts, a sweater, a raincoat, a lined waterproof jacket, a belt, socks and underwear, and then, on his third trip back from the car, a briefcase and a respectable-looking suitcase; the whole thing came to nearly twelve hundred dollars. Back at the motel he put on some of his new clothes and looked at himself again in the mirror. "I am an American," he said, aloud. "My name is John Hunter. I am from Columbus, Ohio." Then he hung his German clothes in the closet and took the clothing from the old suitcase out to the trash.

The rest of the day he allowed himself to look around the city. Walking to a subway station at a place called Rosslyn, he bought a sandwich and a cup of coffee at a delicatessen, and then sat for a while at a little table supplied for the customers next to the passageway leading to the entrance to the trains, watching the people go by. A few steps away, at an automatic teller, stood a perfect specimen of humanity, such as one sees only a few times in one's life. She had dark hair and eyes and brown skin and wore a long, black coat. Her face was something one might never get tired of, no matter how long one looked at it or how old it became. She was surely no ordinary American—she was too dark for that—but what was she? Lebanese? East Indian? Mexican? He almost wanted to ask. But as he watched, she took the money from the machine, put it in her purse, and disappeared into the crowd.

From the map he could see that Washington's transit system was tiny compared to Berlin's. Once on it, he found it was also more disciplined. No one smoked or ate; there were no stands on the platforms selling candy and magazines; no musicians went from car to car, playing for coins; no one brought a dog onto the trains. It was quiet and fast, and getting off a few stops down the line at a station called Federal Triangle, he soon found himself on a wide boulevard lined with massive buildings, like those planned for Germania, with much the same purpose in mind: to overwhelm the citizen and make him feel powerless in the grip of the state. Traffic was heavy, every bit as bad as on Unter den Linden, but here pedestrians wandered across wherever they pleased, with no regard to the crosswalks or the signals, while the police disregarded them completely. In the street itself were hundreds of bone-jarring holes such as existed only in the most isolated country roads in Germany.

First he walked toward the Washington Monument, where cement barriers blocked access to a parking lot empty save for four armored vehicles with their guns pointed toward the sky. Then he approached the White House from the back, going slowly around to the front. This, the only exception to the fascist architecture, seemed less like a palace for the world's most powerful ruler than the country residence of a wealthy landowner. Surrounded by cement barriers and a high, spiked, iron fence with lights and sensors, it was patrolled by armed guards with dogs, much like the former border between the Republic and the West.

Everywhere was overwhelmed with grime and filth, and every block—even the block where the White House lay—had its assortment of the destitute and the homeless. It seemed as though the city were occupied by a vast army of the dispossessed. Some carried bedrolls on their backs, and others pushed wire carts, piled high with junk.

Some lay on pieces of cardboard on top of heating grates, half asleep, enveloped in a cloud of steam. Still others sat huddled in little odd corners behind shrubbery, covered with filthy blankets. There were street people waiting at stoplights on the largest avenues, walking into the road amidst the stopped cars, knocking on the windows, holding out cups and rattling a few coins inside. They were ominous in their disease and misery. Everywhere he went, hands stretched up at him. Even in the square across from the White House, a black woman sat on the sidewalk with her child, holding a crudely lettered sign saying "I am hungry and my baby is sick." It was a wretched, deteriorating, hellish place, worse even than Berlin.

Even more than in Germany, social structure seemed determined by race. Black people were driving the buses and collecting the trash; brown people were tending the shrubbery and sweeping the floors; yellow people were selling snacks and candy out of trucks parked along the street. And wending their way among their downtrodden and exploited fellow citizens were the whites, well-dressed and well-fed, getting in and out of cabs, talking on cellular phones, blind to everyone not like themselves. One could close one's eyes and still know what the city was like. All around were the sounds of the rigid class structure—the hum of limousines, the clink of glasses at fine restaurants, and behind this an undertone of what made it all possible: the poor shuffling through the streets from their dreary homes to their dreary jobs. After an hour, Hans had had enough, and he went back to his room.

The next day he devoted to preparing for his visit to Prober. First, he needed to find a library. Since it was Sunday, only one at a university was likely to be open. From the map the closest was at Georgetown University, just the other side of the river, an easy walk away. He set out from his room. Up the hill from the motel was a series of low brick apartments, with old cars parked in front. Then came a neighborhood of small houses interspersed with stores and businesses. Soon the little houses had dropped away and there was nothing but tall buildings surrounded by roads, traversed by a skywalk. As he approached the bridge, he could see, up a hill on the other side, the steeples of the university, and in the distance, the spires of a cathedral. He walked out on the bridge. First it passed over a parkway by the river, and then out over the river itself. Few people were around. A young woman jogged by, and then came a man on a bicycle with a backpack. A street person was next, carrying his possessions in a shopping bag. At the center Hans looked down at the water. The current was swift and a tree trunk floated by, bobbing up and down. Just downstream was an island, connected to the Virginia shoreline by a footbridge, and farther down another bridge for cars. At the Georgetown end, the bridge passed over the bed of an old canal, half-filled with water; cans and paper cups lay all around and the end of a supermarket cart stuck up out of the mud. He crossed a busy street, passed a liquor store, and walked up a steep cobblestone street with cars parked into the curb at an angle.

At the library, he looked up Walter Jahn's book. Called *A Catalogue of German Military Decorations and Party Insignia, 1933-1945*, it was in the stacks, on the fourth floor. The stacks—row after row of metal shelves five levels high—were deserted. It seemed like no one was in the building but him. He found the book and carried it to a carrel to sit down. The carrel was dirty. On it was a Styrofoam coffee cup, crumbs of a roll, and a wrapper from a candy bar. Graffiti had been etched into the wood with a ballpoint pen. One said "Jeff gets chicks," to which had been added "with strap-on dicks." Another read "Why is this place crawling with foreigners? Because schools in their countries suck shit."

Thirty years on the shelves had been hard on Jahn's catalogue. The glue of the binding had dried out, and some of the pages had come loose. The layout was simple, and the text was brief. Each page on the right was a plate, with photos of medals, decorations, and insignia, numbered and laid out in rows on a plain background. A few were in color, but most just black- and-white, while on the facing page was a description of each and its value. Most were in the range of ten to fifty dollars, but some were in the hundreds, and a few even in the thousands. One page showed the various grades of the Knight's Cross. The value given for the very lowest—without even the Oak Leaves—was four thousand dollars and that for the Knight's Cross with Oak Leaves and Swords— the one his grandfather had won—was ten thousand dollars—just a quarter what Prober had offered him. For the Knight's Cross with Oak Leaves, Swords, and Diamonds, there was no value given at all. On the next page were various insignia of the Volkssturm, the militia of old men and boys the Nazis had scraped together right at the end. On the very last page, in a black-framed box, was a paragraph entitled, "Icon of the Siegfried League." It read "Insignia of a secret group formed by the top leadership at the end of the war; not pictured; supposedly commissioned by Joseph Goebbels as a gift to the Führer, in 1944 or 1945; said to depict Siegfried, beheading a serpent bearing on its head the Star of David. This decoration is of great historical interest. Anyone knowing its whereabouts is urged to contact the author. A substantial reward is offered for information leading to its discovery."

Hans put the book back on the shelf. The shelves all around were filled with other books about the Third Reich. There were twelve volumes of the collected rantings of the Führer. There were the twenty-seven volumes of Goebbels's official diaries, from his earliest days in the party, heady with success at his power to persuade and delude, to his last, in the bunker, grasping at straws as the Red Army rolled over the Wehrmacht on its way to Berlin. There were biographies of Nazi potentates like Himmler, Hess, and Speer. There was a whole shelf about Goering, one on his mysterious death and another on the grotesque palace, Carinhall, he had built for himself in the woods north of Berlin to house the art he had looted from every country under the Nazi yoke. Hans paged through it. It was full of photographs of paintings, tapestries, and sumptuous furnishings—and of Goering himself: Goering on a sled, his fat body swathed in furs; Goering in full uniform, presenting a medal to Charles Lindbergh; Goering playing with his model train set; Goering sitting on a mechanical horse while the Führer looked on; Goering at Christmas, handing out toy soldiers, tanks, and fighter planes to the children of the poor.

There was one more thing to do to prepare for the trip. In the late afternoon, he found a Laundromat and washed the clothes he had just bought to take the newness out of them. The place was filled with brown people with dark eyes and dark hair; they looked at him as though they had never before seen such a creature in their lives. Everything in the room was in Spanish—the signs on the walls, the instructions on the machines, and the words coming out of the people's mouths. The room was small, and the air was warm and moist—no doubt much like the air in the places these people came from. It was restful to listen to them talk without understanding a word. He was still very tired. The time on the clock on the wall, ten past four, seemed unreal. He sat down on a metal chair and watched the clothes churn around and around in the machine until he nearly forgot where he was.

Next morning he arose and showered yet again—one good thing about America was its limitless supply of hot water—and put on a light blue shirt, khaki pants, and blazer. Wiping the steam off the mirror in the bathroom, he tied his new tie, parted his hair on the side as an American might, and went out to the car. On the map he found again the town of New Jerusalem, which lay near a river, what looked to be a few hours to the south and west.

Leading out of the city to the west was a large road, much like an Autobahn. Down its center ran the tracks for the Metro, punctuated by an occasional station, and planted all along with shrubs and small trees. As Hans drove along, a train went by, going only slightly faster than he was. At the windows sat passengers reading newspapers or gazing out at the road. Soon the tracks were gone. Now besides cars and vans there were heavier vehicles of all kinds and descriptions: open trucks filled with junk, moving along in the slow lane; long-distance vans with license plates of states thousands of kilometers away, creeping up behind him and roaring by; sports utility vehicles with boats on the roofs; huge, square vehicles that were like houses on wheels, complete with curtains in the windows; buses of children on their way back to the provinces after seeing the capital. Amidst the noise and senseless talk on the radio he found at last a Mozart piano concerto. In a few more kilometers, a low ridge of mountains appeared in the distance, and the Mozart faded away.

After driving through a gap in the mountains and crossing a river that wound through the valley, he left the main road and drove out into the countryside. It was a perfect day, bright and clear. Spring was farther along than in Berlin, and the pastures where cattle and horses grazed were an intense green. There were white and red flowering trees in the patches of woods, while a carpet of yellow flowers covered the ground. Swallows with blue backs and long tails, like those at home, skimmed over the fields and swooped in front of the car, while overhead, huge, black birds, unlike any he had ever seen before, circled high in the air on tipped-up wings. There were occasional towns, until finally one was New Jerusalem. It was no more than a few white wooden houses with porches and vines on trellises and a small commercial section with a gas station, a bank, a grocery, and a post office. Beyond that were two churches and a school. In a little park at the town center was a column erected to the soldiers who had fallen serving a cause of conquest and racial imperialism, much like that of Nazi Germany, and before it was a wreath.

Just beyond the town's last outposts lay the college. Around it was a cement wall, perhaps two meters high, into which were set high iron spikes, curving inward and down at the top. At the entrance was a sign, "New Light Bible College—Education Based on Christian Principles," with its seal, an open bible, flanked by a cross with a crown above it and an American flag. Below, in gold letters with black trim, were the words "Jesus is the Light of the World."

Hans pulled into the entrance and up to the guard house. Just ahead of him was a pickup truck with huge tires and tinted glass. On either side of its tailgate was a sticker. One, with crossed rifles, read, "An armed citizenry is the only guarantee against the tyranny of the state"; and the other read, "A true Christian must be ready to give his life for his beliefs." The guard waved the truck through, but held his hand up for Hans to stop. Hans rolled down the window.

The man bent down and leaned forward. He was inches from Hans's face. "Driver's license, please," he said. His voice was low and sinister. At his hip was a pistol, and in the guardhouse behind him, a shotgun was mounted on the wall. Hans handed him the license. The man looked from the picture to Hans and back at the picture and gave it back. He went into the guardhouse and returned with a clipboard.

"Okay," he said, "you're on the list. Just sign here by your name. But watch the time. All visitors have to be off the campus by five o'clock. Jericho Hall is the second building on the right, right up the road. Put this in your window." He gave Hans a visitor's pass and waved him through.

Just beyond the checkpoint stood three large crosses on a little mound. Then came park-like lawns and flowering trees with large pink blossoms, followed by several red brick buildings. Hans pulled into the parking lot of the second one. Several students were walking by. The young men wore dark slacks, white shirts, and dark ties, and the young women wore long-sleeved white blouses and skirts below the knees. He looked at his watch. It was just before two.

The weather had changed greatly from the day before; now it was warm, probably close to 25° C, and the door to the building had been propped open. Just inside was a Directory. The history department and Dr. Prober were downstairs, in a hallway with cinderblock walls, painted a light green. Halfway down the corridor was the door to the departmental office, and outside it was a bulletin board with several notices. One, an advertisement for dried foods, asked, "Are you ready for the chaos which could at any moment erupt in America? Every Christian man should put aside enough to feed his family for a year!" Another read, "On Tuesday evening in the auditorium, Pastor Smith will speak on 'Christianity vs. Islam: the Battle for the Soul of the World.'" Largest of all was a poster showing a scene with well-kept homes and people out mowing their lawns and tending their gardens, while over them crested a huge wave of brown, black, and yellow faces, bursting through a dike marked, "U.S. Immigration Policies." Beneath it were the words "America is being engulfed! Are you going to stand by and see our nation's sacred values swept away by alien people and alien ways? Join the League for Immigration Reform—America for Americans!"

Just beyond was an office. The nameplate by the closed door read, "John Prober, Ph.D., Professor of Modern History." From behind it came the sounds of country music—a woman's nasal voice accompanied by a guitar—but when Hans knocked, the music stopped abruptly, and there came the sound of a chair scraping across the floor. When the door opened, instead of a middle-aged man, before him stood an attractive young woman, dressed much like the ones he had just seen. She had blonde, shoulder-length hair, blue eyes, even features, and a very smooth complexion. There was a slight scent of perfumed soap about her, and he could see that, save for a few light freckles on her cheeks and her nose, there wasn't a mark on her—even her earlobes were unpierced. There was something nice about that, although it made her seem not quite grown up. Behind her on the desk was a computer, and on the screen a card game. She looked him in the eyes and said, "Yes?"

"I'm here to see Dr. Prober."

"Was he expecting you?"

"Yes. We arranged to meet here at two."

"Oh. You must be the man with the Knight's Cross. Dr. Prober said you might turn up. He's very sorry he can't see you today—he had to go out of town, like, real sudden." She let her eyes fall to his feet and then slowly raised them again. Her gaze was cool, but not unfriendly.

"Sudden?"

"Yes. You just missed him. He left an hour ago."

"That's too bad. I really wanted to talk to him. When is he coming back?"

"Not for a few days, probably."

"Looks like I came a long way for nothing." He sighed.

"A long way?"

"Yes. All the way from Columbus."

"Wow. Look. I'm sorry about this. Dr. Prober told me about you. He said you're doing research on your grandfather. Maybe I could help. I'm his research assistant. My name is Astrid Brenner." She abruptly held out her hand.

"I'm John Hunter," he said. He had said it to himself enough times over the past two days that it came out without a pause.

"Look, why don't you come in?"

She opened the door wider and stepped aside for him to enter. Then she walked out in the hall and looked up and down. Back in the room she left the door open a crack. Meanwhile, Hans looked around. The office was windowless, but large. In it were two desks, both with computers. From a vent near the floor came a rush of air and the hum of an air conditioner. On the wall was a sign, in German, with the eagle and swastika on the top. It read "Watch Your Tongue! The Enemy Is Listening!" Near it was a poster showing a young man in black trousers, a khaki shirt, and a black tie with a lightning bolt on it. Behind him, reaching out of the mist, a Hitler Youth in his brown shirt, black tie, black shorts, and swastika armband was passing him a torch. In gothic script were the words, "discipline—loyalty—courage," and beneath them, "Can you prove Aryan ancestry? Then take up your birthright and join the Aryan Youth! We Form an Unbroken Link with Our Racial Brothers in the Past!" Near the door were a couple of filing cabinets, and along the opposite wall, a bookcase, with shelves almost to the ceiling. In it were books by a noted British apologist for Hitler and two copies of *Mein Kampf,* one in English and one in German. There was a book called, *How the Holocaust Lie Serves Jewish Interests* and another called *The Myth of the Six Million*. With them was a book in German by Fritz Westermarck entitled *Talking Sense to Germany*, and another, also in German, called *The Waffen-SS: Soldiers Like Any Others*. On the shelf below were several German grammars and various German-English dictionaries, including one of military terms. It reminded him of his own shelf at home, and in fact contained several of the same books. Over the second desk, which was much larger, hung a photo of Hitler presenting the Knight's Cross to a young Luftwaffe officer, with Hermann Goering, in a white uniform dripping with medals, beaming and leaning forward from the background. Stuck in the corner of the frame was a photo of a grave with a stone inscribed, "Colonel Werner Mölders, 1913–1941." On the grave was a wreath.

Nearly everything in the room, in fact, reeked of the Nazi war machine, even the screen saver that had come up on the young woman's computer—it was a series of images, a few seconds each, of the tanks, planes, flying bombs, and rockets that Germany had loosed upon the world some sixty years before.

There were other signs of Prober's tastes and opinions: on the wall by the door was a map of Germany in the borders of 1937, incorporating the lost territories in the East and giving the German names—Breslau, Stettin, Posen—for towns that for more than two generations had Polish ones. Below was another map showing the farthest extent of German conquest, covering all of Poland, the Ukraine, and parts of western Russia. And on the wall opposite was a recruitment poster for German farmers to settle on lands stolen from Poland and Russia, which the Nazis had christened the Wartegau. Showing a man behind a plow, it read "German farmers! Land is yours for the taking in our new colonies in the East! Labor is cheap, and the land is fertile! Protected by German arms and German justice, you can build a safe and prosperous future for you and your children!"

On the larger desk was a photograph in a silver frame. It showed two men on the balcony of a chalet with a backdrop of snow-capped peaks. The inscription, in German, read, "To my great friend—and a great friend of Germany—John Prober, with all best wishes, Fritz Westermarck."

Meanwhile the young woman had sat down, motioning him to do likewise.

"So you're from Columbus?"

"Yes."

"Is that a nice place?"

"Well, it was, up until a few weeks ago."

"What happened then?"

"My dad died. Funny how you take someone for granted and then suddenly one day they're not there and everything changes. Now I just want to get out of that place. That house, that town, even Ohio. It's like it's lost all meaning for me."

"Gee, that's too bad. You and your dad must have been close."

"We were. He was the only family I ever had. His death was bad enough, but other bad things have happened since. After he died, I started looking around. Turns out, there were things in that house I didn't know about. Stuff he kept in a drawer in his room. Stuff about my mom. She died when I was only two years old. My dad always told me it was cancer. But that wasn't true. She killed herself."

"That's terrible!"

"Yes, I found the police report. One day she took me to a sitter and then came home and turned on the gas. The postman smelled it, but by that time, it was too late. One thing I know for sure—my dad never forgave her. There were no pictures of her in the house, and he never talked about her. In a way, I think it's why this medal is so important to me. I guess I'm looking for something positive in my family, and I was hoping my grandfather could provide it. My dad was very secretive. There was a trunk in the attic he always had a lock on; in fact I don't think he'd opened it since he came over from Germany, after the war. I had to pry it open with a crowbar. This medal was way down at the bottom, with a couple of photographs and some documents. It's got my grandfather's name on it. All my dad ever told me about him was that he was in the German army on the Eastern front and that he died in the war. It got me to thinking. I went to the library and looked up the medal in a book. The book says it was awarded only for exceptional bravery. That's when I called Dr. Prober."

"Do you have it with you right now?"

"Yes."

"Can I see it?"

Hans took the little box out of his briefcase, opened it, and held it forward. She stared at it intently and wrinkled her brow. When she looked up, she had an entirely different look in her eyes.

"Wow, that's the first one I've ever seen!" she said. "Boy, would Dr. Prober ever love to get his hands on it! He collects that kind of stuff, you know. But just a second—I think I can help you. I've got the stories of most of the winners right here in the computer. Dr. Prober has gotten hold of their old German army records and translated most of them. Let's look up your grandfather and see what he did."

"I'd like that. That is if it's not too much trouble."

"Oh, no, it's no trouble at all! You came all this way! Now your grandfather. What was his name?"

Hans hesitated a moment. He was curious. What had his grandfather done? Here was his one chance to find out. Besides, what was the harm in telling the name? There was no chance anyone would ever make the connection between him and that name. The records of the former republic were a chaotic mess. Documents for his name change were buried so deep they'd never be dug out. "Johann Meissner," he said.

"Two *n*s and two *s*s, right? I'm getting pretty good with German names. I've sure entered a lot of them into the computer since last semester. But your name's not Meissner. How come?"

"When my dad came over, he changed his name from Friedrich Meissner to Fred Hunter. I guess he thought his old name was kind of a mouthful. I think he was trying to leave Germany behind. He never did, though. He had an accent to the day he died. Sometimes I think he gave part of it to me."

"Really? It doesn't seem that way to me. If anything, you sound like you come from New York."

She had turned in her chair and was tapping out a few strokes on the keyboard. The Tiger Tank on the screen disappeared and up came the Nazi battle flag with the words, "Welcome to the Database of German Heroes." She tapped in a few more, hit the return, and then entered the name. A second later up came several paragraphs of text.

"Here it is," she said. "Meissner, Johann, of Oranienburg, Gau Brandenburg. Obersturmführer, Death's Head Division. Is that him?"

She so massacred the vowels in the German words they were barely recognizable.

"That's him."

He took a deep breath, not ready for what might come. The young woman promptly began to read from it.

"'Joined the unit Brandenburg as a guard at the Sachsenhausen Concentration Camp on 23 June 1937, where his exemplary conduct soon brought him to the attention of the Camp Commandant. With the beginning of the war, he rose rapidly through the ranks until he was promoted to Obersturmführer on 2 May 1942.' Here's the commendation from his superior officer in the Waffen-SS. It says, 'Obersturmführer Meissner has consistently shown the highest devotion to National Socialist ideals. His zeal in combating partisans and in cleansing the area of Jews has served as a model for us all. As only one example, on 17 October 1942, unmindful of risk to himself, he singlehandedly attacked a hovel where an armed Jew band lay hiding. Though wounded in the leg and under a continual barrage of fire, he crawled forward until he was able to destroy the hovel with a packet charge, resulting in the elimination of twenty-seven dangerous enemies of the Reich. For this act of bravery he was awarded the Knight's Cross to the Iron Cross.' And here's the commendation from SS-General Stroop. 'In May 1943, our division was given the task of decontaminating the Warsaw Ghetto. As a proven Jew-hunter, Obersturmführer Meissner was assigned an entire section, consisting of a block of approximately twenty buildings. The action had gone very well under his capable command, resulting in nineteen dead Jews and no casualties among our troops. But in the last building, a young soldier who had gone in to reconnoiter failed to return; a Jew came out, waving a white flag, offering to release the man in return for safe passage for their women and children to Bolshevik lines. Obersturmführer Meissner drew his revolver, and saying, "No German negotiates with a Jew," he shot the man through the head. This brought a hail of fire from the cowardly Hebrew scum inside. Motioning for his men to take cover, the Obersturmführer burst through the door, his machine-pistol blazing, until one of the Jews, lurking in a door frame, shot him in the back. Though grievously wounded, he continued to advance; his last act on this earth was to detonate a grenade and destroy the Jews as they attacked him. This broke the back of the resistance. No mere Jew could hold out in the face of such valor and devotion! There is no nobler death than to lay down one's life for one's Volk! I recommended that he be posthumously awarded the Oak Leaves and Swords to the Knight's Cross.'"

At hearing this, Hans felt a profound sense of shame. His grandfather was even worse than he'd thought. What would Sonja Davidovna think of him, when his own grandfather was a monster, dripping with the blood of her people? He wished he could die as a German and be reborn as a Jew. Meanwhile the young woman had exited the record and was looking at him with interest.

"Wow!" she said. "Your grandfather was really something!"

"I guess. I have a picture of him. Would you like to see it?"

"Sure!" Hans withdrew the photograph from his briefcase and laid it on the desk. She looked back and forth several times from the picture to him.

"You look like him," she said. "You have his eyes!"

"Maybe so."

"And his nose. You've got that, too!"

"You might be right. I've never thought about it."

"I'll bet you're like him in other ways, too! That's exciting! Dr. Prober says the winners of the Knight's Cross are like the saints and martyrs of early Christianity. They act out of unshakeable inner convictions—that's why he's drawn to them. He thinks we should take them as our models. He says the best of all were in the Waffen-SS, like your grandfather. That they were like the crusaders in the Middle Ages. Maybe that's what you're like, too."

"Maybe. But what's this database, anyway?"

"It's this big project. 'The German Heroes' Project.' That's what Dr. Prober calls it. He says Germany doesn't have a war memorial. He wants to fix that. He says someday Berlin will be rebuilt the way it should have been, and this should be the first monument in it."

"So Dr. Prober is a professor here. What does he teach?"

"He's got this course, 'Race as Destiny: Germany and the Modern World.' I'm taking it this semester."

"Oh? And what does he tell you?"

"Well, here's what we're studying right now." She reached into a book bag on the floor and pulled out a handout. It was a map of the world with a little box inside the borders of each country, showing the numbers of people there of German descent. The legend read, "The Germans have always been a restless people, wandering outside their borders and taking their culture to new places. This illustrates that, of all peoples, Germans have spread out most over the world. But the sacred soil of Germany gave birth to the German spirit and must remain true to it. It is from Germany that Aryan man set out to civilize the world. It is the Holy Land of Western Civilization. With the unity of Germany, we enter a new era in world history."

"Interesting," Hans said and handed it back to her.

"Yeah, kind of. I've just been reading through my notes. There's a big exam coming up. On the exams Dr. Prober likes us to repeat exactly what he said. The more we can repeat, the higher a grade we get. I always make a tape of his lectures, and then I transcribe them, word for word."

"Sounds like you study pretty hard."

"Well, what else is there to do around here? Women can't even leave the campus without permission. And that's hard to get. I'm pretty much stuck here until I graduate."

"Really?"

"They have so many dumb rules. Gosh! You can't do this, you can't do that. Know why I left that door partway open? Because it's against the rules for a man and a woman to be alone together in a room with the door shut. There's a student patrol that goes around looking for stuff like that. If the door was shut with you in here and they caught me, I'd have to go in front of the Elders. They'd skin me alive!"

She shuddered and then gave a little smile. She seemed only too ready to say whatever popped into her head. He thought of another woman he had known—a secretary at the U.S. Embassy to the GDR in Berlin. He'd been assigned to make friends with her and that hadn't been difficult. Lonely and bored, for months she had kept him up-to-date on the comings and goings of everyone in the building. As a reward he had slept with her, even though she was twenty years his senior.

"Dr. Prober's lectures, what sorts of things does he say?"

"Well, here's one thing I just memorized." She stared at the wall and began to recite, in a sing-song voice: "Artistic and scientific development is correlated with the percentage of German blood. In all the greatest works of man, the hand of the German is clearly visible. Think of Beethoven. Think of Goethe. Think of Kant. At the very pinnacle of every field of art and knowledge stands a German! The exact opposite of the German is the Jew. The Jew's brain operates only at the surface, while the German's delves into the myths and mysteries of life and ties everything together in a sacred bond." At that point, she turned back, gave a little shrug, and smiled.

"You think it's true?"

"Who knows? At least Dr. Prober thinks so. So I'd better think so, too, at least until after the exam." She gave a little laugh.

"Why did he go away so suddenly?"

"That's one thing I don't know. Lately he's been hard to keep track of. But whatever it is, it has something to do with a trip he just took to Berlin. A week ago last Friday he went over there, but by Monday he was already back."

"He went all that way for only three days?"

"Yes, and that was his second trip there in a month! The first time he went over to buy something—some special badge Hitler gave just to his best buddies. What was it called again? 'The Golden Party Badge.' It belonged to that fat guy, the one who ran the air force, what was his name again?"

"Hermann Goering?"

"Yeah, that's it. There's a real history to that thing. For years it was missing. Then some guy in Washington came up with it but somebody killed him and it disappeared. Then three weeks ago, all of a sudden, it turned up in Berlin. One of Dr. Prober's contacts over there called him up and he rushed right over and bought it. He was real proud of himself. He even showed it to *me*! I've got to admit, it was kind of pretty! It had this gold swastika with all these rays coming out of it, like the sun. But the trip last week he left like, real sudden. Friday during his class somebody called up and left a message—it was some woman, talking German. I walked back to the office with him, and when he listened to it, he got all upset and said he had to leave right away. While I was booking his flights he started opening files and jamming things in his briefcase."

"Really? Like what?"

"Papers, mostly. But one thing he took was a picture of the fat guy, old what's-his-name, with a shotgun."

"A shotgun?"

"Yeah, a fancy one with all kinds of engraving on it. Then he went running out the door. He had to drive down to Lynchburg for a flight that left for New York in only two hours. It was a rotten day—rain, fog—it's a wonder the plane took off. When he came back on Monday, he was in a really rotten mood." She shook her head.

"Why was that?"

"His connection was late, and he missed some meeting. He called his friend, Mr. Foerster, and said, 'My flight was held up. By the time I got out to the graveyard they were gone. I looked for her everywhere! She's disappeared!' Then he used a bad word. He could get in big trouble for talking that way around here!"

"So after he came back, then what?"

"Oh, he moped around most of the week, like he didn't know what to do with himself, but this morning—it was right after class again—he got another call, but this time he was right here when the phone rang. It set him off even more than the first one. His voice was shaking—I thought he was going to fall apart!" She smiled. But then a shadow passed over her face.

"Hey," she said, "don't tell anybody I told you all this stuff."

"Don't worry, I won't. But Dr. Prober and I, we had an appointment. I drove all the way down here, and suddenly he's not around. You can't blame me for wanting to find out why."

"I guess not."

"So what happened next?"

She went on, a little tentatively. "Well, first he said, 'Who is this?' And then he said, 'I'm sorry, I couldn't get there, the flight was late,' and then, 'Yes, I'll meet you wherever you say.'" She stopped again.

"Was that it?"

"No—then he said, 'Yes, that gun, I want it, but that other thing, you really think you can get it?' And then he said "Yes, it's a lot, but we'll pay. But I'll have to make a stop along the way." Then he gave his cell phone number and told whoever it was to call him the next night. Then he scribbled something on the back of an envelope and shoved it in his pocket. And in a second he was back on the phone again, trying to call his friend Mr. Foerster, up in Washington. But he didn't get through."

"Did he take anything with him this time?"

"Yes. One thing. The last page of that book up there. He asked me to copy it, but the copier was broken. That's always happening. So he just took the book and ripped that page right out of it." She pointed at the shelf with Jahn's catalogue. Hans remembered the last page. It was the page with the icon of the Siegfried League.

"This Mr. Foerster, who's he?"

"Oh, a guy at the American Forum for the Study of Germany. He's assistant Director or something. He and Dr. Prober are good buddies. They must call each other five times a day. They're putting on an exhibit up there with all kinds of relics from the war. You know, stuff like the fat guy's Golden Badge. At the end of the week there's a big reception to open it. A bunch of scholars and professors are coming over from Germany. They printed up this fancy invitation, like it's a wedding or something. It has all this old-time German writing on it. I had to send them all out. Almost forty of them. Want to see one?"

"Sure."

"Can you read German?"

"A little. I took it in high school."

She poked around in a pile and pulled out a card. Hans read it quickly. "The American Forum for the Study of Germany cordially invites you to a reception to inaugurate a new exhibit on Heroes of the Reich. It represents the most significant collection of historical items from the Third Reich ever assembled. The reception will be followed by a dinner and a tour of the exhibit. At dinner, Dr. John Prober, Professor of History at New Light Bible College, will speak on the topic 'Keepers of the Flame—Finding and Preserving Historical Materials from the Third Reich.' Mr. Fritz Westermarck, Leader of the German People's Party, will deliver the keynote address, 'The Hitler Youth: A model for the youth of today.' Guests are advised that we have reserved a block of rooms at the Omni Shoreham Hotel near the Forum."

Hans handed it back to her.

"Could you read it?"

"A word here and there."

Just then the phone rang. She looked at the display. She nodded her head and mouthed the words, "It's him." She picked it up and started to talk.

"No, Dr. Prober," she said, "Mr. Wohl hasn't called yet. Yes, I'll change his reservations. I'll make sure he gets the message. I won't forget." She paused and looked at Hans. "Yes," she said, "the man with the Knight's Cross, he's right here." She handed Hans the phone.

The voice on the phone had the same hard, suspicious tone. In the background were announcements over a loudspeaker.

"Mr. Hunter, I regret I wasn't able to meet with you," said the man. "I've been called away on sudden business."

"So I've been told," said Hans. "But I understand you'll be in Washington at the end of the week. Could we arrange to meet then?"

"No, I won't have time for that. I'm going abroad, probably for several days. I suggest you contact me when I return. Now if you'll excuse me, I've a flight to catch." He sounded suddenly as though meeting Hans no longer mattered to him. The man was fading into the distance, and there was nothing he could do about it. Hans gave the phone back to the young woman. She hung it up, looked in a rolodex, and dialed a number.

"Better do this before I forget," she said. Soon she was talking into the receiver.

"Omni Shoreham?" she said. "I need to change a reservation. It's for Mr. Eberhardt Wohl." She spelled out the name. "Yes. He's arriving tonight instead of tomorrow. He's very particular. He wants a single room on the top floor, away from the street. And I want to leave him a message. Dr. Prober was going to meet him tomorrow at eleven. Would you please let him know that Dr. Prober won't be able make it?"

Eberhardt Wohl; that was a name Hans knew. He was a man who made his living spreading lies and falsehoods about the Republic. Among his books was one that had sold thousands of copies, *Death of a Puppet State: The Last Days of the GDR.* So this was the sort of man coming to Prober's reception. And Westermarck was coming, too. It must be special indeed.

Meanwhile the young woman had hung up. She looked at the clock. She logged off the computer and started to gather up her books.

"I'm sorry, I've got class," she said. "Look, you're a nice man. I'm really sorry about your dad. I hope I helped you."

"You did."

As he stepped to the door, he picked up the frame with the picture of the two men on the balcony of the chalet. "Is one of those guys him?" he said.

"Yes, the one on the left."

"It's kind of hard to see what he looks like." The men in fact were dwarfed by the setting; their faces were half the size of a fingernail.

"He's pretty average-looking. You can't see it there, but his nose is a little off. He was in a car accident last year. He hit the windshield nose-first! He keeps having operations, but they still haven't got it right. And his hair looks blonder now than it did in that picture. I think he dyes it." She gave a little laugh. With that, she closed the door behind them and disappeared down the hall.

Hans headed back to the city. The trip went on hour after weary hour. It gave him a chance to think. The first call Prober had gotten, when he'd run off to Berlin, must have been from Ingeborg Mohr. But the second one—who could have sent him into such a frenzy? The man on the motorcycle, that was apparent. That man kept turning up everywhere. He was the American the dealer at the flea market had seen. He was the one who had sold Prober the Golden Party Badge, with Ingeborg as go-between. Now he had Goering's shotgun besides—that's why he was waiting for Prober in the cemetery when Prober didn't show up—and apparently he even knew where the icon of the Siegfried League was. As for the man and Ingeborg, what had brought them together? Drugs, probably. Besides, she was a prostitute and maybe he was a customer. She set up the meeting in the graveyard, where Prober was supposed to buy the shotgun, but when Prober didn't show up, the man got mad. Her hundred thousand euros were a big temptation. If she couldn't deliver on her promises, what good was she? So he'd killed her and taken the money.

Late that night, Hans sat on the edge of his bed. Everything was going wrong. What were his chances of finding the man on the motorcycle before Prober did? Exactly zero. Wherever the man was, Prober was already there or would be shortly. Soon he would have what he wanted and that would be the end of it. It was hopeless. Perhaps he should just return to Berlin and face the Director empty-handed. He might even offer to pay back the hundred thousand euros a little at a time. That would put him in debt for years to come. This whole trip had been a disaster. What was the likelihood of finding some Nazi trinket more than two generations after the war? The Director—sitting underground for the past twelve years had sent his mind in strange directions. The strangest was Hans as the historical imperative. What a ridiculous notion. History proceeded quite independent of his efforts.

For an hour or so he flipped through the television channels, from police shows to comedies to a basketball game; nothing distracted him. Finally he lay in bed and tried to relax, but there was nothing restful about that room. From outside came the sound of motors being started up, doors being slammed, planes flying low overhead, screeching pipes from a shower in the next unit, and the clunk of cans hitting the chute in the soft drink machine right outside his door. To escape it, he closed his eyes and thought about Sonja Davidovna. What a beautiful young woman. How nice it had been when she had kissed him at her door. How pleasant it would be to marry her, settle down, and forget this mess. Perhaps they might emigrate to a more reasonable country, like Canada or Australia—someplace where no one knew them and everyone would leave them alone. Why not? His old comrades could provide them with papers that would let them go wherever they pleased. Sonja's father was a nice man—he could come, too. Perhaps that would guarantee him a bit of rest in his declining years. Who knows, they might even have a child. A girl would be nice. With any luck it might look more like her than like him. Then, while he and his lovely wife worked, the child's grandfather could stay home and take care of it. Of course, Russian would be the language of the household, but that was all right. And when the child got a bit older, he could invent for himself a past that would satisfy its questions, since children tend not to be too critical where their parents are concerned.

Soon the noise began to fade away, and he fell asleep. He found himself out in the woods, back on the border. It was night, and he was on patrol. Somehow he and his men had become separated. In the distance, a dog barked. A dangerous traitor had escaped from custody and was about to cross to the West. Agents on the other side were waiting for him, standing near their cars and flashing their lights.

Suddenly there was a crackling in the brush, and there was the man, looking up at him, his eyes glowing red in the dark. For a moment they stared at each other. Then the man bolted for the fence and started to climb. As he reached the top, Hans threw himself on him and dragged him back, just as the agents on the other side opened fire.

He woke with a start and looked at the clock: it was a few minutes past two. His heart was beating fast, and there was sweat on his brow. Everything in the room was as he'd left it. The glass of water he had put by his bed was still there. The fan in the register was still blowing, and the curtains still stirred in the faint breeze. A wedge of light from outside still fell on the wall opposite. His mind focused on where he was and what he had to do. Suddenly it was all clear.

Turning on the light, he looked up the American Forum for the Study of Germany in the phone book and found it on his map. Then, putting out his German clothes and shoes to wear the next day, he went back to bed and slept fitfully until dawn.

CHAPTER 8

Heroes of the Reich

The Omni Shoreham was a huge brick building that took up most of a block. On the upper stories, hundreds of windows faced the street. To one side a road led to the parkway that cut through the city. Near it a ramp led into the parking garage. Hans drove down it and parked in a corner at the lowest level. As he got into the elevator, he looked at his watch. It was just ten o'clock.

After checking out the lobby and fixing a few details in his mind—chandeliers hung over Persian rugs and in a side room were glass-doored cabinets filled with vases and patterned china—Hans walked out the front door and headed to a side street toward the Forum. The road led down a hill into a wooded glen. Deeper it went, into a valley, where it curved around, crossed a stream, and started up the other side. This was a beautiful spot, far from the uproar of the city. The sound of traffic was no more than a distant hum. All around were embassies, official residences, and large private homes. The building he sought was as impressive as any. Made of white marble with columns at the front door, it had a green copper roof into which gabled windows were set. On either side of the door were huge magnolia trees, growing so close to the building that their branches clung to the façade like ivy. Arranged up the front stairs were tapered cedars in stone vases mounted on pedestals. A circular hedge of forsythia, in full bloom, lined the front drive. Across the street and all around was dense woodland, with huge trees, just starting to turn green. Hans turned up the drive, walking past a long, black town car. Next to the front door, set into the brick, was a brass plaque that read, "The American Forum for the Study of Germany," and below it, a date: 1946. There was a visitor's bell and a camera mounted over the door.

As Hans rang the bell he read a notice, on the Forum's letterhead, taped to the glass inside the door. It read, "Due to a special event, we will be closed Friday of this week. Normal hours will resume on Monday. We regret any inconvenience." A buzzer sounded, and he pushed open the door.

Just inside was a foyer and a curved balustrade of marble steps, leading to a gallery above. Along the wall of the foyer was a display in glass-topped cases entitled, "The German Contribution to America." Hans stopped a moment to look at it. In the first case was a series of photographs—writers, musicians, policemen, executives, soldiers, scientists—with a sign that read, "Among those of European ancestry, Germans form the largest ethnic group in the United States. By and large, they have intermarried with the descendants of other Northern European peoples, but some 25 million Americans count German lineage on both sides. Better educated and more prosperous than the descendants of other ethnic groups, they play a leading role in the intellectual and creative aspects of American life. They are energetic and industrious. Much of the wealth of this country was created by their hard work and devotion to duty." Next to the text was a map of the United States showing where Germans had settled, with degrees of shading correlated to their percentage in the population. The shading was light in the south and heavy in the Upper Midwest; in the state of Wisconsin it was the heaviest of all. In the next case was a series of photographs of famous Americans of German descent, with biographical notes beneath. There were Nobel prize winners in the sciences, there were actors, poets, military figures, cabinet ministers, and senators; there was even a president. In the next case was a graph showing how trade between Germany and America had grown since the war—it was a line that went straight up. Below it were several textbooks in beginning German and a sign that read, "Why study German? Because it is a world language, growing in importance each year. It is the language of the greatest number of Europeans in the

Common Market. Those who speak it have the highest per capita rate of production in the world. Next to English, it is the world's leading language of commerce and industry."

In the last case was a display of books by scholars affiliated with the Forum. One, showing a voluptuous movie star of the '30s and '40s, was entitled "Zarah Leander and the Ideal of Nordic Womanhood." Another, showing rubble-women loading bricks into a wheelbarrow, was called "Germany's Postwar Economic Miracle: A Defeated People Puts Its Shoulder to the Wheel." Yet a third, with an astronaut in a space suit on the cover, had the title "Werner von Braun: How a German Took America to the Moon."

Just beyond the foyer was a small reception area with a few leather chairs and a low, glass-topped table. Before the double doors leading to the interior of the building sat a receptionist. She was a solid-looking, middle-aged woman with short, gray hair, wearing a white blouse stretched taut over her heavy upper arms. She watched as Hans approached her. He smiled. Speaking slowly and carefully, he said, "Good morning, madam. I am Professor Eberhardt Wohl from Hamburg. I am afraid, how do you say, that I am coming to this place a bit early. Dr. Prober and I, we have intended to meet us here at ten o'clock. He is here, yes?" He had lapsed for the moment back into the accent that Mrs. Leibstein had worked so hard to cure him of, turning his final *d*s into *t*s and swallowing his *r*s.

"I'm sorry, sir, I couldn't tell you." She answered in German. "But perhaps I can find someone who can help. Just a moment." She picked up the phone, dialed two digits, and in a moment began to speak. "Dr. Foerster, a gentleman from Germany is here in the lobby, asking to see Dr. Prober. His name is, uh, sir, what did you say your name was again?"

Hans leaned over and spoke into the receiver she held out to him. "Professor Eberhardt Wohl," he said, enunciating very clearly. "Professor Eberhardt Wohl of Hamburg. I am here to see Dr. Prober."

A minute later, the door to the inner offices opened, and out came a man of perhaps thirty, dressed in a dark, three-piece suit, a light blue shirt with gold cufflinks, a patterned tie, and well-polished black shoes. He had thinning, sandy hair and a neatly trimmed moustache. His skin was pink and ruddy, and there was a scrubbed appearance about him. On his lapel, he wore a pin with crossed American and German flags. Stepping forward and smiling broadly, he shook Hans's hand and began to speak. His German was fluent, but with a slight accent.

"Herr Professor, I am Assistant Director Bruce Foerster. I am so happy to meet you. On behalf of myself and our organization, let me welcome you to Washington. It is a great honor to meet a distinguished scholar such as yourself. You are the first of our honored guests for the reception to arrive. I regret that Dr. Prober has been called away suddenly on important business—he tried to reach you—but if you would be so kind, please step into my office where we might chat a few minutes." As the man turned, Hans caught a faint whiff of cologne.

"Tell me," said the man, once inside the door, "is your hotel satisfactory?"

"Oh, quite. The Omni Shoreham is very nice, and my accommodations are quite luxurious. First class all the way! They even have a desk clerk who speaks German! Though I have come before I was expected, they have found a room for me. As for the city, I have had a chance to look around a few hours, but I have done something quite regrettable and reckless! I have gotten an American haircut! I was quite unable to express to the barber, who appeared to speak English even less well than I do, exactly how I wanted it, and this is the sad result! I fear than when I return home, my wife will not let me into the house!"

The man laughed and nodded his head, then ushered Hans through the door and guided him down the hall, past other offices, to a large and pleasant office in the back, with a view out to a garden that had raked, gravel paths and a wrought-iron bench under an arbor. At the center of this garden was a fountain with water pouring forth from a swan's beak into a basin, and scattered elsewhere amid the ivy were statues of satyrs, water nymphs, a centaur, and other such mythological figures. Beyond a low hedge at the back loomed the trees of the park.

Hans sat down in a chair and turned it slightly toward the window. "This is very pleasant, Herr Dr. Foerster," he said. "You have a wonderful view. Not like my office in Hamburg, with nothing but the roof of an adjoining building to look at!"

"Yes, indeed, it's very nice. There are many birds that bathe in our fountain, and an occasional deer comes to drink."

"Herr Dr. Foerster, let me also remark that I am pleased to be addressed in my own language. You speak it so well that I must conclude you are a fellow countryman."

At this the man smiled again. "No, Herr Professor. In my heart, perhaps, but not in my nationality. I'm an American."

"Really! But your accent is flawless. If anything, I detect a slight trace of Bavaria in your speech."

"You are quite right, Herr Professor." He leaned back and looked at his nails. "I studied at the Ludwigs University in Munich. I spent four enjoyable and fruitful years there. How I long to go back!"

"Ah, yes, a wonderful city—everyone wishes to go back!" said Hans, who had never been within three hundred kilometers of Munich and knew nothing about it save that it must be a dreadful place, full of fat, drunken people speaking a debased and hideous dialect.

"It's an honor to meet a distinguished scholar such as yourself." The man was obviously thrilled to be talking to him.

Hans had a moment of unease but nodded pleasantly. "You are too kind, Herr Foerster."

"If you would be so good, Herr Professor, could I trouble you to autograph your book?" From the desk in front of him he picked up a copy of *Death of a Puppet State: The Fall of the GDR* and handed it to Hans. Hans inscribed it, "To Herr Doktor Bruce Foerster, in pleasant memory of our meeting." He dated it and signed it, "Eberhardt Wohl." He handed it back to the man, who looked at it with satisfaction.

"I was just looking through it this morning," said Foerster. "You mention in the introduction that you have another book planned—a sort of sequel, I imagine—on what became of the leading figures of that government."

"Yes. You'll forgive me, Herr Foerster, but I find it difficult to talk about my work when I'm right in the midst of it."

"I quite understand. Have you looked at the program for our little reception?"

"I have indeed. I note with interest that Herr Westermarck is attending. I look forward to meeting him. A man with interesting ideas!"

"Very! And a bit of a controversial figure! In fact, to avoid attracting attention, he is traveling here under an assumed identity. Very cloak-

and-dagger! He's coming in by car from Toronto tomorrow night. I wasn't sure, at first, of the wisdom of inviting him. But he and Dr. Prober have become good friends. And they have developed such a close working relationship. Besides, Herr Westermarck has often expressed the wish to visit the Forum. We have given him much support through the years."

"Excellent! But this Forum—it seems quite a remarkable institution. Perhaps you could tell me a bit about it."

"Gladly! It was founded soon after the war through contributions from a group of American businessmen representing corporations that had factories in Germany before the war. They wished to find a way to rehabilitate Germany after its defeat and ultimately to reestablish their companies' operations there. For our motto they chose "That Germany might take its rightful place among the nations of the earth." And at last, it has! Of course, we've adjusted our direction in the last few years. Our Director, Mr. Adams, is nearly 80 years old. He doesn't really keep up on our activities. Our board has changed, too. It has become a bit more friendly, shall we say, to trends reemerging in Germany. One of our current goals is to form stronger bonds between right-thinking groups in Germany and the United States. Fortunately, we have the resources to do so. The Forum began with gifts of stock from the founding corporations—among them were Merck, IBM, and Coca-Cola—and the intervening years have been quite kind to our portfolio. They generate an income of several million dollars each year."

"Impressive! And how do you use those resources?"

"Oh, in many ways. We prepare and distribute lesson plans on German history for use in American classrooms. We encourage those of German ancestry to learn the mother tongue and to preserve their heritage. We collect and preserve materials, such as important relics and films, photographs, and documents dealing with National Socialist Germany. We have the largest collection of Third Reich materials outside Germany, along with many historic artifacts and documents from the so-called German Democratic Republic as well. We sponsor film festivals, such as our recent retrospective on German wartime films called 'Cinema in the Service of the State'; academic conferences, such as the meeting last fall called 'The Third Reich in a New Light,' and monthly performances of chamber music. So many Europeans think of our city as an Africanized hellhole, and in some ways I suppose they are right. But there are a few oases of Western culture that stand out, and our concert hall is one of them. Just now we're doing the complete cycle of Beethoven's late string quartets as performed by some of Germany's leading musicians. It's been quite wonderful!"

"I'm sure. But I find your remarks interesting. I wasn't aware, for example, that you had such an extensive collection of materials from the GDR. Other than a few scholars like me, why would anyone want them, after all? What sorts of things do you have?"

"Mostly state records and other official documents. A few relics of the top leadership. For example, we have Erich Honecker's original Communist Party membership card from his days as an agitator in the Saarland. Despite the contempt in which we and most of the rest of the world now hold the GDR and its leaders, we feel it is important to collect and preserve such items."

"Well, I suppose it is. How did you get them?"

"Most came to us during the period of chaos in 1989–90, when former Stasi agents were carting off files by the truckload! Not all of these men, as it turns out, were immune to the appeal of hard, cold cash. We were fortunate enough to have agents on the spot, ready to pay for immediate delivery! As an example, we were able to purchase many materials taken from the GDR military archives in Potsdam, which otherwise might have been destroyed."

"The military archives in Potsdam. Isn't that where the records of the border troops were kept?"

"Yes, indeed it is. Many of their papers have ended up in our collection as well, but I tell you that confidentially. It's rather a sensitive issue."

"I understand. But are they available to researchers?"

"Oh, no, Herr Professor, I regret to say, not for at least twenty-five years. But you're still a youthful man with a long career ahead of you—perhaps you will come back and look at them then! If I am still here, I will show them to you personally! For the present, though, they are kept locked in climate-controlled vaults in the basement."

"I see."

At least one thing was clear: vault or no vault, Prober had gotten hold of the file on the death of Heinz Kalmbach, and no doubt in exchange for her promise to place him in contact with the man on the motorcycle, he had delivered it into the hands of Ingeborg Mohr.

"But what of this exhibit? I presume some of your more interesting materials will be displayed there."

"Yes, indeed! I would be happy to give you a personal tour—a little preview, as it were—if that would interest you."

"It would, very much."

Unlocking a drawer of his desk and taking out a key, the man led the way to an elevator in the back and pressed the button for the top floor. Facing them as it stopped was a set of double doors, which he unlocked and pulled open before switching on the lights. Inside was a gallery with display cases along the walls and interpretive signs above. It smelled of paint, and in fact there was a paint-spattered sheet covering part of the floor.

"Welcome to our secret little place! There's nowhere else like it in the world! Dr. Prober has been working on it for the better part of a year. The whole exhibit is his idea, really. It's not quite done, you understand—we still have a bit to do before the opening ceremonies on Friday. But come, Herr Professor, let us look around! I am very eager to hear your reaction!"

In the room, both at the beginning and near the display cases, was a series of signs, in German, with an English translation below, in smaller type. The first, at the very entrance, bore a text flanked by drawings of Knight's Crosses, which read "Welcome to the Exhibit on Heroes of the Reich. Enter and learn!"

In the first case was a life-sized model of a German soldier of the Waffen-SS as he might have appeared in Russia in 1942. His head was turned back and with raised hand he was motioning to his comrades to follow. He bore a machine gun of the type MG-34, as indicated in an accompanying diagram. There were cartridge belts around his neck, and at his waist were grenades and a canteen.

Behind the glass was a sign that read, "The role of the hero is to provide the myths by which a people can live and by which it can rise above other peoples. Few societies have been as driven by myth and blood sacrifice as was Nazi Germany. Few causes produced as many heroes as did the Nazi cause."

Next to this was a sign that read, "How do we recognize true heroism? It means the willingness to die for a cause, not merely to fight to the death to preserve one's life or the life of one's loved ones. It means mystic dedication and the desire to shed not only another's blood, but one's own. It is seeking out and slaying one's enemy while offering one's breast to his sword."

A few steps on, in a case filled with party badges and military decorations was another sign. Foerster stood aside so that Hans could read it.

"In this exhibit," it said, "you will see medals and decorations and descriptions of heroic acts. You will see also heroic paintings, portraits and photographs of some of Germany's greatest heroes, nearly all of whom fell in the service of the Reich. Mark them well! These men were the fathers and grandfathers of those who live in Germany today."

"These items," said Hans. "Where do they come from?"

"Frankly, Herr Professor, for many, I don't know. One cannot really ask too many questions as to their origin. As the archeologists of the Third Reich, our mission is to preserve materials that might otherwise be lost. Wherever these historical items are, and whoever has them, we must bring them here however we can. Many are not safe in Germany, where various archaic laws make it difficult to put them on display. Besides, in fifty or a hundred years, when scholars from around the world are consulting our collection, what difference will it make where they came from or how we got them?"

"A good point, Herr Dr. Foerster. I quite agree."

In the next room, nearly covering the wall, was an enlarged photograph showing welders working on damaged track at an elevated S-bahn station in Berlin. The sign read, "Devotion to duty inspired the entire German people. Despite the destruction of their homes and the death of their neighbors, workers reported to their posts right up to the end. With the Red Army already occupying its outer suburbs, the telephone exchanges of Berlin continued to operate; it was only with the entry of enemy troops into the buildings themselves that the system collapsed. Transportation workers were particularly heroic. Whenever services were disrupted by the Anglo American terror bombing, within a few hours, these men had the trains and trams running again."

The next room displayed a map showing the farthest extent of the Nazi empire, from the coast of France deep into the heart of Russia.

There was a photograph of Hitler and his generals around a table in their war room, looking down at a battle plan. On the wall opposite hung a large oil painting of a unit of the motorized SS—a phalanx of tanks, armored vehicles and motorcycles—advancing over the steppes, passing the wreckage of a Soviet tank. The caption below it read, "The German army provided the setting in which the hero could perform his acts. Superbly trained and equipped, it was the greatest military force the world has ever seen. Almost to the last, it inflicted over two casualties for every one it sustained. It was truly the instrument of the will of the German people. It is the hero himself who embodies that will and is its greatest expression. The hero feels himself in the grip of a higher purpose. He is transfigured by it. Nothing can stop him, because, should he fall, he passes it on to his comrades. The defeat of National Socialist Germany is like the hero falling in battle, yet in doing so passing that sense of higher purpose on to another generation. Much of this heroic energy survived defeat and lives on in modern Germany, where it lies beneath the surface, ready to be called forth again."

"This painting," said Hans. "It's remarkable. I thought few such works had survived the war."

"In this case I *do* know where it came from," said Foerster, in a reverent tone. "It is one of Dr. Prober's earliest triumphs! He found it in a storage shed on a farm in Bavaria. Of course it had to be cleaned and restored once it had come to this country. We employed one of the finest restorers at the National Art Gallery here in Washington."

Over the next display hung a formal portrait of Hermann Goering, dressed in a white uniform trimmed everywhere with gold and dripping with medals. The caption in the case read, "There were heroes among the top leadership of the National Socialist State. The Führer himself had been decorated twice for valor in the First World War. Reichsmarshall Goering had been a war ace, a member of Baron von Richthofen's Flying Circus; he is credited with shooting down twenty-two enemy aircraft. In the portrait above you, he is wearing around his neck the *Pour le Merite*, Germany's highest decoration granted at the time. As head not only of the Luftwaffe but Director of Germany's five year plans, he was also awarded the highest decoration for distinguished service bestowed by the Party—the Golden Party Badge. The *Pour le Merite* has been missing since the end of the war, but the badge you see in the case before you is the actual decoration awarded to him by the Führer in 1935."

Hans looked down at it. Here was one of the very items that Walter Jahn had died for. "Wonderful!" he said. "Did Dr. Prober find this, too?"

"Yes! And although he is quite silent about the origins of many of his discoveries, again, I do know something about this! He managed to buy it in Berlin earlier this year. It was once in the possession of a man who dealt in such items. It is uncertain where he got it."

"I see."

"Reichsmarschall Goering is, of course, an interesting case," said Foerster. "A brave but flawed man, he was, after Baron von Richthofen, the greatest German aviator of the First World War. Though he had declined, he seemed to regain his powers and put up a gallant defense before the so-called War Crimes Tribunal at Nuremberg. His bearing in the last months of his life was again heroic. It was a great joy to the German people that he was able to die by his own hand rather than by the rope the judges had prepared for him."

Walking ahead, Foerster led him into the next room. On the wall were portraits of two boys in the Hitler Youth and a third portrait, which Hans immediately recognized: the infamous Reinhard Heydrich, one of the prime architects of the murder of the Jews. "Similar to the hero is the martyr," read the sign, "killed because of his beliefs. Among the earliest of the Nazi martyrs were those who fell in the company of the Führer at the Feldherrnhalle in 1923, the so-called 'Munich Putsch.' They were later disinterred and committed, with great solemnity, to a magnificent tomb, later destroyed by the Russians. The standard which they bore in front of them, soaked with the blood of those who fell, was used to sanctify other banners. Like so many other sacred relics of the cause, it disappeared from the Reich's Chancellery in 1945 and has not been seen since." Next to it was a picture of Hitler, in the midst of a great crowd of Storm Troopers, solemnly touching the banner to another banner.

Below the portraits of the Hitler Youth was a text that read, "Here are two martyrs from the early days of the National Socialist struggle to wrest power from the weak and unpopular government that had brought upon Germany the contempt of other nations. On the left is

Herbert Norkus, a Hitler Youth member of only fourteen, struck down while distributing flyers announcing a meeting at which the Führer was to speak. The other is Horst Wessel, who fell bravely during street fights with the communists. His story and the stirring anthem that arose from it inspired a whole generation of German youth."

They stepped to the next case. In it was a military baton of ivory and gold, engraved with the eagle over the swastika and the runes of the SS. Next to it was a series of photographs. The caption read, "The martyr is often the victim of deceit and treachery. Such was the case of Reinhard Heydrich, head of the Reich Security Service, assassinated in the Protectorate of Bohemia and Moravia by British agents in 1942. This series of photographs was taken at his funeral, a great pageant in which the entire top leadership of the state took part. The first photograph shows an honor guard meeting Heydrich's casket at the train from Prague. The second shows his flag-draped casket, lying in state under a canopy in the courtyard of the Reich's Chancellery. At the head of the bier is a satin pillow with Heydrich's decorations on it; note particularly the military baton. The next photo shows the German leader, his head bowed, placing the baton in the casket by Heydrich's side. A moment later he stands at attention, while the honor guard closes the lid. Note the Iron Cross on the breast pocket of the Führer's tunic, a decoration of which he was very proud. It is presumed to have been lost in the bunker along with his other personal effects. The baton in the case before you is the very baton in the photograph. It was stolen by grave robbers when Heydrich's tomb was violated in 1946 and taken to Kiev, where it was only recently recovered from their heirs."

Hans pointed at the baton. "Did Dr. Prober get this, too?" he said.

"Yes, indeed. He had heard rumors of its existence in a village in Ukraine. He went there, made inquiries, and was led by an ethnic German to a miserable hut at the edge of a pig farm. He walked in and saw it right away, mounted over the hearth! The occupant had no idea what it was worth. Dr. Prober was able to obtain it for only a few thousand rubles!"

"The text on the wall is quite penetrating. Did Dr. Prober write it?"

"Yes. Much of it is excerpted from a book he's writing."

"It seems he is a remarkably insightful man."

Between this room and the next was a little alcove, no more than two meters on a side, with a sign labeled, "The Role of the Jew in the Heroic Myth." On the wall was a poster for the infamous 1940 Nazi film *Yid Suess*, with Ferdinand Marian as the scheming moneylender and Werner Krauss as his rabbi, both smirking and rubbing their palms, while behind them a dark, alluring and corrupt-looking young woman leaned forward out the window of a ghetto building. The text next to it read, "How did the Aryan myth of the hero lead to anti-Semitism? It is because the hero requires an anti-hero. The myth must put a face on its enemy. For Nazism, the face was that of the Jew. In the words of a nineteenth-century German philosopher, the Jew was perfect for that role. 'The Jew is different, yet not different,' wrote Christian Gehler (1832–1886), a professor at Tübingen University and friend of Richard Wagner. 'We feel a mystic bond with him. He is both our brother and our betrayer. He sets himself above us, without our consent. He seeks to impose his laws on our conduct. In doing so he seeks not only to codify our behavior but to set limits on the actions of our heroes. Worst, he labels as blasphemy the myths that inspire us. Thus, it is only when we have fought the Jew and vanquished him that our destiny can be played to the end.'"

In the next room, the walls were covered with floor-to-ceiling photographs of the ruins of Berlin—street after street of bombed-out buildings. It was almost like standing amid the rubble itself.

Mounted on one wall was a placard with the text, "Here is the German capital as it appeared in 1945. Over 90 percent of the city had been destroyed by ceaseless Anglo American bombing and the looting and pillaging by the Red Army. These scenes represent the legacy of German heroism. It is quite beautiful, in its way. There is a redemptive power in destruction, for destruction is the prerequisite for creation. As the war came to its conclusion, the number of acts of German heroism increased dramatically until they reached a crescendo in the Battle of Berlin. Mere lads of fourteen, laden with explosives, hurled themselves beneath the treads of Red Army tanks. Why did this happen? It is because the more defeat is certain, the greater the significance of the act of heroism. It contributes to the ruin and destruction, which is its inner goal. The ultimate fulfillment of heroism is death, and the hero knows that the only way to participate fully in death and destruction is to die himself. Far from despairing, the German Führer and his inner circle rejoiced in the destruction of their capital. For they believed that on the ruins of Berlin, a magnificent new capital would arise—Germania! Now, more than sixty years later, a new capital is indeed arising on this soil consecrated by German blood. Berlin is the major city of Europe and dominates the continent. It is one of the great capitals of the world, and every passing year adds to its glory. Yet without the destruction, without the selfless acts of sacrifice made by German youth, would this have ever come to pass?"

Together they turned the corner into the next room. On the wall facing them was a photograph of President Reagan and Chancellor Kohl, together laying a wreath at a monument. Next to it a caption read "Can even former enemies admire Nazi heroism? The answer is yes. A great American, President Ronald Reagan, recognized this when, on May 5, 1985, he laid a wreath at Bittberg Cemetery, where brave soldiers of the Waffen-SS lie interred. If he could honor them, why can't we? Whatever their beliefs, it is hard to deny that these men were heroes. For the act of heroism justifies itself, quite independent of the victory or rightness of its cause. It is defying fate, on behalf of all mankind."

On the next wall, beneath a portrait of a Luftwaffe officer with the Knight's Cross on a ribbon around his neck, was a display with a sign that read, "After the war, the graves of many of these heroes were desecrated. A few, though, lie untouched and undisturbed. Here, in the Invaliden Cemetery in Berlin, is the grave of Colonel Werner Mölders, a great German ace and holder of the Knight's Cross with Swords, Oak Leaves, and Diamonds—one of only twenty-seven such awarded. Next to him is the aviation pioneer Ernst Udet, a hero of the First World War and a comrade of Reichsmarschall Goering. The two died only a few days apart; in fact, Colonel Mölders died when his plane crashed on his way to attend General Udet's funeral. These heroes lie unremarked and unremembered amidst the hustle and bustle of the modern capital. The Great Arch, meant to honor them and all those who fell in the German cause, was never built. But more than just wreaths on their graves, these men deserve a monument to commemorate their sacrifice and there is a growing movement in Germany to construct one for them.

Heroism is part of Germany's cultural legacy. It can give the German people the strength and the courage to take up again the leading role in world history that destiny has assigned them."

Next to the photograph of the two gravestones in Berlin was a pen-and-ink sketch labeled "This depicts the tomb the German leader designed for himself. His tastes were simple. It was to be no more than a simple wooden coffin on a marble bier with an epitaph revealed only to his closest comrades. It was to have been attended by an honor guard of Waffen SS. It is a tomb destined never to be built, for the Führer's remains have never been found."

Next to it was an empty case.

"What is this?" asks Hans.

"This is reserved for the most important decoration of all—the icon of the movement to carry on the Führer's ideals. Dr. Prober has been searching for it for years! Some have even doubted its existence—but not he! I spoke to him just yesterday. I expect him to call again at any moment. He is in contact with someone who can take him right to it. It involves some very delicate negotiations. A large amount of money will change hands. With the financial support of one of our board members, he will soon bring it back! He says it will electrify our guests. He calls it 'the most important historical discovery since the end of the war.' It will remain here only for our opening reception. Then Dr. Prober will take it to Berlin. He says it is the key to unlock a treasure trove of immense historical importance. He says it will make both our careers. I can only guess what it is." The man gave Hans a conspiratorial and self-satisfied smirk.

"Then is he in Germany?"

"No, he is here, in the United States!"

"Do you think he will succeed?"

"Of course! He always succeeds! His ability to locate such material is uncanny."

They stepped into the last room. In it was a sign that read "The GDR: Forty Years of Shame," with a series of photographs of the Berlin Wall, some with guards in the background, peering through binoculars from their watchtowers. "One tragic consequence of the Russian invasion of Germany," read the text, "was the creation of a Soviet puppet state from several of the states of central Germany. This so-called German

Democratic Republic was neither German, nor democratic, nor a republic. It was, rather, a gigantic prison camp, surrounded by walls, mine fields, and barbed wire, its guards drawn from amongst traitors to their country. The large photo in the center shows three soldiers of the border troops as they carry off the body of a young victim shot down at the Wall. Now that the cancer of communism has been cut away, these cowards have crawled back beneath the rocks from whence they came. Yet we must never forget the hundreds of their victims who died while trying to flee oppression and slavery. They bear witness to the desire of the German people for freedom and unity. The tablet bears only the names of those we know about. It is the sacred duty of every German and every lover of freedom throughout the world to honor their sacrifice."

There, facing him, were the names of those who had died trying to flee the state. Among them, with the date of his death, was that of Heinz Kalmbach. How could they include as a martyr a man who was no more than a common thief? Perhaps many of the others were no better. Hans felt a grim wire tighten within him. The hand of fascism had risen from the grave to put together this entire obscene exhibit, glorifying Nazism. How fitting that it should end by denigrating those whose greatest purpose was to destroy it. Now, because of people like this wretched Prober, Germans were again running around painting swastikas on walls and spreading lies about the Jews. Any decent society would have long ago locked him up and this man Foerster, as well. This whole business with the icon of the Siegfried League was just one more stepping-stone that would lead Germany back to fascism. His mouth felt dry, and he involuntarily gave a sigh of disgust which the odious man immediately misinterpreted.

"The exhibit has quite an emotional impact," said Foerster.

"Indeed," said Hans. "But tell me. How do you intend to use it?"

"We will use it to inspire youth, to give them ideals. To train the youth of the future, we must first give them a sense of the past. You see, Herr Professor, we are building our own Aryan youth movement here in America. We have made great progress, but much remains to be done! That is why we are bringing over Herr Westermarck: to advise us! The moment is ripe! Racially aware groups are growing up all across this country. So-called 'hate crimes' are on the rise. Of course, that's only a term coined by the leftist press for what are really no more than expressions of racial consciousness. After all, it is only natural law that one race should seek to rise above another, don't you think? We need a way to harness and direct this power for our own political purposes. We must unify these groups behind a common cause. That is the true function of the exhibit—to inspire, to educate, to recruit!"

Just then a curious sound came forth from the pocket of Foerster's coat. It was a tinny, mechanical rendition of "The Ride of the Valkyries." He reached in, took out a phone, and put it to his ear.

"John!" he said. He gave Hans a smile and a nod. "Then things are going well? Splendid! So you're in Pittsburgh? And Mr. Halwell has put up the funds? Wonderful! He'll find it a good investment. I can't wait to see it! Incidentally, our first guest has arrived. Professor Wohl from Hamburg. He says he was to meet you here at ten o'clock. I've been showing him around a bit. Yes, he's here with me now." In a moment he gave Hans an uneasy look. Then he took the phone from his ear and addressed Hans.

"There seems to be a bit of confusion. Dr. Prober says he has just talked to Professor Wohl from his hotel room, a man with whom he has spoken several times."

"As you can plainly see, he must be mistaken."

Foerster put the phone back to his ear and spoke again. "He's blond with light blue eyes and high cheekbones. He's about 185 centimeters tall. I'd say around forty." Hans could see they were approaching a dangerous moment. He stepped forward, grabbed the phone, and twisted it out of the man's hand. Hissing like a cat, the man reached out suddenly with his other hand and clawed him across the cheek. Hans struck him full in the face with his fist, slamming his head into the display of the guards at the Wall. The glass shattered—the man fell to his knees, his arms over his head, blood pouring from a cut in his scalp.

Hans ran into the hall, the phone still in his hand. He pushed open the fire door and ran down the stairs as an alarm began to sound. The lower door opened to the garden; in four or five bounds he was across it. Leaping the hedge, he crossed the street and ran down the slope into the woods, slipping and sliding on the dead leaves, and grabbing at branches to keep from falling. At the bottom, out of breath, he came to a path along a rocky creek. Behind him he could still hear the alarm, rising and falling, joined by a second. As he moved along the path, the sounds grew fainter. A runner went by him, paused, spat into the creek, and went on.

Leaving the path, Hans stayed near the tree line and walked up the hill and into the garage of the hotel. He walked down the ramp toward the lowest level, stepping behind a pillar when a car went by. Opening the door of his car, he got in and turned on the interior light. He looked at himself in the rearview mirror. On his right cheek was an angry red line. With a little water from the water bottle, he wet a tissue and wiped away the flecks of blood. Then he pulled the trunk release, got out the toolbox and changed the license plates; the new ones were from New Jersey. He put a new bumper sticker over the old one—it had a flag on it and read, "God Bless America."

As he got back in the car, he again heard the beeping little version of the "Ride of the Valkyries." He opened the phone and put it to his ear.

"Yes?"

"Herr Hunter, if that is your name." It was the same tight voice he'd heard the day before, but now the words were German. "You're quite a violent man. You've so brutalized poor Foerster that he's quite incoherent. And you've left us quite a clean-up job to do!" His German was good, but his accent was strange. Hans said nothing. The voice went on. "You turned up at my office, and now here you are again! And just overnight, you've gone from someone who doesn't know a simple word like *Ahnenpass* into a speaker of fluent German! Quite an achievement!" Hans remained silent. The man went on.

"We are looking for you, Herr Hunter. We have a complete description of you. One of our artists is preparing a sketch. We have put it on the Alert Network of the Aryan Youth. A thousand eyes will be looking for you. We will find you, and we will find out who sent you. Be forewarned! We know how to deal with enemies of the Aryan race." Then came a click, and he was gone.

Back at his motel, Hans packed up his things. From the lining of the suitcase he took another driver's license and another credit card— now he was Tom Bradford of Trenton, New Jersey. Then he drove a few blocks to a motel near the bridge over the Potomac. He left his car in the underground garage and took a room. Before he went up to it, he found a payphone in a deserted corner of the lobby. The time had come to call the Director. With another phone card, he dialed the number Breitbach had given him. In two rings Breitbach was there.

"Herr Breitbach!"

"Herr Doktor!" Hans could then hear him saying, "Herr Director, it is Doktor Klug." Then he was back again.

"The Director asks, how is your search going, Herr Doktor?"

"Tell him not well, Herr Breitbach. Tell him I would like to speak to him directly." Hans could hear Breitbach relaying the message to the Director, whose reply was indistinct. A second later, Breitbach came back on.

"He says he has no need to talk to you, Herr Doktor. His faith in you is complete. He has asked me to tell you once more that you are the agent of the historical imperative. He asks, why is it that you are calling?"

"Tell him that I suspect Prober has found Gottfried Lenz and is about to buy the icon."

There was another delay. Faintly in the background he could hear the Director's voice. The words were still indistinct, but the tone was calm and unhurried. Then Breitbach came back on the line.

"The Director says you are not to become discouraged, Herr Doktor."

"Not become discouraged, what does *that* mean? If Prober returns with the icon, how am I to get it? They have seen me. Prober claims he has put my description on something he calls the Alert Network of the Aryan Youth and that hundreds of people are looking for me."

"The Director has faith in your abilities to avoid them. He says you are not to worry. He says Prober will not get the icon."

"And how can he be so sure of that?"

"The Director says that Gottfried Lenz will not sell the icon to Prober. Prober will have to kill him to get it! Gottfried Lenz will never sell the icon, as long as there is breath in his body! He will pass it only to the hero who succeeds him. So it is written, and so it will occur. He will give it only to you."

"Ask him, if you please, Herr Inspector, where such a thing is written?" Again he could hear his question repeated and a faint voice in the background. A few seconds later, Breitbach was relaying the reply.

"He says you will find out when you return."

"Ask the Comrade Director, what am I to do in the meantime?"

"The Director says you must find Mrs. Jahn. She will help you find the icon. It is she who holds the key."

"How am I to do that? For twenty-five years Mrs. Jahn was locked up in an asylum and now she is somewhere out on the streets."

"The Director says there is someone who can help you. The Director will get word to him. He says there is a local street atlas in your car. On page thirty-two, there is a small cross on a road next to a park. At that cross there is a paved path; the path passes over a small bridge. The Director asks, what time is it there?"

"Nearly noon."

"The Director says to be at that bridge at eleven tonight. A man will come walking down the path. The Director says he will greet you in German, and you are to answer in German. Then he will ask you who you are, and you are to answer, 'I am called the American.' He will help you to find Mrs. Jahn."

"And suppose I find her, then what? Why should she tell me anything? This is hopeless."

"The Director says you must say to her, 'I have come from Comrade Wiehle. He sends you his greetings.' And then she will tell you what happened to Jahn."

"But what happened to Jahn was twenty-five years ago."

"The Director says that time doesn't matter. What was there yesterday is there today and will be there tomorrow. The dead leave their secrets behind. They are there for you to read. The Director says you must open your eyes. He says you must never give up!"

Wearily Hans went down to the garage and took the street atlas from beneath the seat. There, on page thirty-two, in a suburb called Vienna, there was a tiny cross, in red ink, wedged between the green of the park and the blue of a road. He closed the map and went up to his room. He lay on the bed for a long time, staring at the ceiling, until he fell into a light sleep.

CHAPTER 9

Pour le Merite

That night, Hans drove out into the suburbs. He passed shopping malls, gas stations, apartment buildings, and townhouses, some built nearly right to the road. There were cars everywhere, even at this hour. Along the way were dozens of traffic lights, and every time he stopped at one, it seemed like the person in the next car was watching him. Soon he came to the town of Vienna and found the road that paralleled the park. Leaving the car in a cul-de-sac filled with big houses and small trees, he crossed to the path. It was paved and ran next to the road. A few meters ahead, it entered a woods and veered down deeper into the park. Looking ahead, just inside the woods, he could see a little footbridge, hidden from the road by a few rows of trees. It led over a creek, in which there was a trickle of water. Beyond that was the beginning of a fitness trail; in the faint light he could see a set of parallel bars. He checked his watch—it was ten to eleven. He stood in the shadows and waited.

The night was clear, and the moon was low in the sky. A cold wind rattled the branches. He turned up his collar and stuck his hands in his pockets. Eleven o'clock came and went. Above he watched the lights of a plane, banking as it turned toward the airport. A few cars passed on the road. Across the street, an upstairs window in one of the houses suddenly went dark. A minute or two later, out of the dark, came a lone man walking a dog. Hans started toward him. In the middle of the bridge, they met.

"Good evening," said the man. His words were German, and his voice was that of an old man.

"Good evening." The dog, a little creature with pale hair, sniffed around the cuffs of his trousers.

"Do we perhaps have an acquaintance in common?" said the man.

"Yes, I think we do."

"What is your name?"

"I am called the American." The lights of a passing car shown through the trees, and for a moment Hans could see the man's face. It was deeply lined, and his hair was sparse and gray.

"The American!" said the man. He offered Hans a gloved hand. "How pleased I am to meet you!" Now his words were English. "You were my benefactor, you know." He unhooked the leash from the dog's collar. It ran ahead and nosed around in the bushes.

"Your benefactor?"

"The Collins case. Surely you recall. I'm told you played a role in it. If so, I owe you a debt, my dear American. It's why I'm out here tonight."

"Yes, I did play a role in it."

"Poor Collins! I've always felt a bit bad about that. A fair and likeable man! But he had the misfortune of standing between me and the job your colleagues thought I should have. We were the two final candidates for the same post—Chief of American espionage against the German Democratic Republic! It was I who sent to your colleagues the time and circumstances of his arrival in Berlin. Of course with him gone, the position was mine. Nice job for a Stasi operative, don't you think? How many secrets did I send to your friends in Berlin through the years? How many evil plots did I stop in their tracks? This bridge is one of my favorite spots. I used to leave little packages beneath it for your colleagues. It became an occasional part of my evening walks. And many times your friends left little sums of money here to repay me for my efforts. But times are different now, aren't they? My chief pleasure nowadays is recalling the triumphs of the past. Of course it was correctly assumed Collins was betrayed by one of his own colleagues.

What a fuss that caused! There were repeated interrogations, even of me. Everyone had to take a lie detector test. Fortunately the laboratories of the GDR synthesized not only chemicals that allowed its athletes to perform superhuman physical feats, but others that allowed prodigious feats of deception as well. One could answer any question and remain totally calm. Still, what happened to Collins, it was a pity. I hope he didn't suffer. I knew his wife and children. For years I brought them little gifts on the holidays. Charming, all of them!" His voice never lost its cheery tone.

"Yes. It was regrettable."

"But my dear American, I understand you're in a bit of a tight spot yourself!"

"I am. John Prober. Do you know the name?"

"Oh yes. A neo-fascist. One of the worst. I understand you did something to annoy him."

"Yes. I had an unpleasant encounter with a colleague of his at the American Forum for the Study of Germany."

"The Forum? A venerable institution! I attended many a lecture and concert there. What can it have to do with all this?"

"It seems it is supporting Prober and his activities. Are you familiar with a board member called Halwell?"

"Charles Halwell? He's a wealthy collector of Third Reich materials. He's from an old Pittsburgh family. A complete fascist. He got in the news a few years ago for paying ten million dollars for one of Hitler's second-rate watercolors. If he's on their board, then things *have* changed."

"How about the Aryan Youth? Prober claims there are thousands of them, and that they're all looking for me. Are there really so many?"

"No, no more than a few hundred—but their numbers are growing. Some day the world is going to have to deal with them. They patrol the streets from time to time, looking for trouble. We've even had a few out here in peaceful Vienna! Their chosen weapon of attack is the sawed-off baseball bat. Brutes and fools, all of them."

"What do they do?"

"Harass black people. Beat up homosexuals. Paint swastikas on homes where Jews live. You must do your best to keep out of their way.

But my dear American, let us turn to why you are here. I'm told you're looking for the widow of Walter Jahn."

"Yes. My superiors in Berlin want me to talk to her. I called the hospital. They discharged her years ago. They think she's out on the streets."

"A hard life! Poor old woman. We've wondered for years what she saw. I suppose that's what you're after. Of course I can't help you directly. I never met her, nor her husband. I dealt with them only through an intermediary. A good comrade. I can put you in touch with her. She will be happy to help you."

"A good comrade?"

"Does that surprise you? There is a small core of us whose beliefs are unchanged. For us, the struggle goes on."

"I will need to see her as soon as possible."

"Of course, my dear American. I will contact her tonight. She will meet you tomorrow morning, and you can make your arrangements. But you need to stay out of the public eye. I know just the spot. The Nature Center at Rock Creek Park. Few people go there. You can reach it on the parkway—it's only a mile or two beyond the zoo. The signs will take you right to it. As for why you are there, you must pretend to be a birdwatcher. I did that for years! I was even forced to learn a bit about the dirty little creatures. You can wander about in the parks and consort with whomever you like, as long as you both have binoculars, all without arousing the slightest suspicion. Just past the building there is a nature trail and a few paces down it, a bench. That is where you will find her. Her name is Ursula. She will be there at ten. I will tell her to wear a dark coat and carry a pair of binoculars. You will wear dark glasses and a blue knit cap and carry binoculars as well. I have brought those items with me. The binoculars are quite good—they're German—perhaps you'll find them useful in your further work." He took a bag from his pocket and handed it to Hans.

"And now, my dear American, I will be on my way. I can help you no further. Let us forget this little encounter ever took place. I shall forget you, and you shall forget me. Good-bye!" He whistled to the dog, which came running up out of the creek. Then, with a little bow, he turned and faded into the dark.

Back in his room, Hans lay down on the bed. This mention of

Collins had reawakened the bad feelings he had had at the time. It was sad how much the man had trusted him—it was almost as though they'd had an instant bond. When he closed his eyes, he could see Collins's face and the look in his eyes as the driver shot him with the stun gun. The look had said, "You and I are in danger," when really it was only he who was in danger, and that his life was in fact over. What had it been like when he said good-bye to his wife for the last time? Did some little part of him know? As for Hans, how many more black deeds would he have to do before he finally could lie down, never to arise? How depressing to have turned out like this. He would have never imagined it as a child. It was all the fault of that wretched Heinz Kalmbach. The man had ruined his life. If only he'd stayed home where he belonged, none of this would have happened.

The night dragged on, and other dark thoughts plagued him. What chance did he have, in a place like America, with everyone against him? What was the point of all this, anyway? Wasn't it just a part of a meaningless struggle between two dead ideologies? Now, of course, it was far too late to get out. All he could do was succeed or die—it no longer mattered which. In the deadest part of the night, when he had turned the clock to the wall because he couldn't stand to look at it, some sense to life came trickling back. He thought of Mrs. Laibstain. It was for her he was doing this—not for the Director, not for socialism, not for the brotherhood of man. It was her image and her words that filled his mind. Tears came to his eyes. If only she were there to help him now! But she and her husband had long since joined their slaughtered kin. And now their voices joined the chorus of millions of others, calling out to be avenged. He felt driven on by legions of the dead.

The next morning Hans found himself on the parkway, heading toward the Nature Center. The sun had come out, and the parkway was beautiful. There were tall trees on both sides, an old graveyard that came down the slope right to the edge of the creek, and a hillside filled with daffodils. Passing under a high, arched bridge and then through a tunnel, he came to the zoo. Just beyond the parking lots, filled with school buses, he could see cages. Then the road forked, went up a hill, and soon led to the entrance to the Nature Center. Near it was a riding stable, and outside it, a woman on a horse.

The Nature Center was a long, low building with a deck in back looking out on the woods. In front of it, the American flag on a flagpole flapped in the breeze. Through the glass doors he could see displays with stuffed animals, and a man in a green uniform sitting behind the front desk. The nature trail began just beyond it. A few steps down it was a bench, and on it sat a woman in a dark coat. On her lap was a pair of binoculars and an open book with pictures of birds. She was thin with a pinched and wrinkled face, and her hands were those of an old woman.

"Good morning," he said. "Are you Ursula?"

"Good morning. I am." She closed the book and looked at him.

"A friend told me I might find you here. He also is a birdwatcher."

"I know. I spoke to him last night."

"He told you what I want?"

"He says there is someone you wish to find."

"That's correct. Mrs. Jahn. Can that be arranged?"

"I will try. But he did not tell me I would be dealing with an American."

"Do not be deceived by my accent. I am not an American."

"Then you speak German?"

"Yes."

She slipped into German easily. She had a slight Saxon accent.

"Come, let us walk a bit." She rose and started down the path. "You're younger than I expected. Over here we are all so old."

"You must have many memories of better days."

"Yes. The party gave meaning to life for many years. I find now that in my old age I have no substitute for it."

"Perhaps your work is not over. By helping me you are carrying it on. I'm told you knew Jahn."

"Yes. I was a courier. I had occasion to go to the East. My mother lived her last years in Dresden. She was very ill and I went to see her whenever I could. Many times I took things from Jahn to Berlin. And many times I brought things back. Half the items in his shop came right from the archives of the GDR. It was I who delivered the hundred thousand dollars in cash to him the day before he died. It was at this very spot that one of your colleagues gave me the money."

"What was Jahn like?"

"A frightened little man. For years he suffered from ulcers. He had a stutter. His business and his catalogue were all he seemed to care about. And his wife. They were very close. His death was terrible. They took him from his home and they hanged him in the basement of his shop. The rope was looped over a water pipe. They made him stand on a box of his own catalogues and then they kicked it out from under him. It took him a long time to die. Beforehand they'd made him open his safe. Everything in it—including the hundred thousand dollars—was gone."

"But you saw Mrs. Jahn after that."

"Oh, yes. We were friends, after a fashion. Over the years I went several times to the hospital. Your colleagues sent me there. I used to take her little treats and sit and talk to her. They would let us go out on the terrace. In all that time I was her only visitor."

"What did you learn from her?"

"Nothing. Every time I went, it was the same. She would talk to me about Jahn. She said he had gone back to the Republic and would return. But of course she knew he was dead. It was she who found him. It is what made her the way she is."

"Didn't they treat her at the hospital?"

"Oh, they gave her drugs. But that was all. No one could talk to her. No one there spoke German. And her English was gone—Jahn's death had driven it right out of her head. From the moment she found him, she never spoke nor understood a single word."

"Have you heard anything of her since she was discharged?"

"Yes. A few months ago she turned up rummaging around in the basement of her old house. It seems she'd hidden a key in the yard, and twenty-five years later it was still there. When she came out the door, she left it in the lock. It was right in the middle of the day. The present owner was at work, but an old couple who lived next door saw her leave and remembered her. They brought her into their house and called the police. She wrote my name on a piece of paper and the police called me down to interpret. When they asked her why she was there, she said she was looking for her husband. We waited while the owner went through the house, and when he decided nothing was missing, they let her go."

"What was she doing there?"

"I don't know. I think she must have been looking for something."

"Do you think she found it?"

"Perhaps."

"Have you seen her since?"

"Once, on the street. I bought her some food and some warm clothing. I tried to take her home, but she wouldn't come."

"Do you think you can find her tonight?"

"There's a chance. The street people know each other. They notice everyone and everything. They are the eyes and the ears of the city. There's one I sometimes give money to. I spoke to him this morning. He says he knows who she is. I've arranged for us to meet him at ten tonight."

"Where will you and I meet?"

"My car is parked on the south side of Albemarle Street, just west of Connecticut Avenue. That's only a few blocks from here. It's a blue Toyota, and the first three letters of the license are AJE. I will be there just before ten."

"Aren't you taking a risk by helping me?"

"What does it matter? The life I lead is no pleasure to me."

They had come to the end of the path. She raised her binoculars and pointed to a bird, high in a tree.

"Look," she said. "An Eastern Bluebird. A lovely creature. There's no bird that color in all of Germany." He focused on it, too—it seemed only inches away. Its breast was rosy, and its back a deep turquoise blue. As he watched it, it took wing and disappeared over the trees.

A few minutes before ten Hans turned down Albemarle Street and spotted Ursula's car. He drove two blocks beyond, parked, and walked back. As he approached, she was unlocking the door to get in. Once he was in as well, she took a pocket flashlight from the glove compartment and gave it to him.

"You may need this," she said. "We're picking the street person up in front of the metro station. He's very eager to help. I've promised him a hundred dollars."

They drove to the corner and turned down Connecticut Avenue. After a few blocks the apartment buildings gave way to a commercial section. Near a row of newspaper vending machines by the stairs leading down to the metro station stood a man in an army jacket and blue spandex pants. Curly gray hair stuck out from beneath his knit hat. Ursula pulled up and he came over to Hans's side of the car. Hans rolled down the window. The man bent down to talk. His face was florid and a double chin hung below his jaw.

"See that supermarket over there?" He pointed across the street. "We gotta go over there and get Freddy. He knows where the old lady's at. He's out in back, by the dumpster. I checked on him a while back. Let's go pick him up." He got in the back seat and slammed the door. A stale smell filled the car.

Ursula pulled across the street and into the alley behind the store. A refrigerator truck was backed up to a loading dock, and two men were unloading boxes onto a conveyor belt. Beyond, a dumpster loomed in the dark. A shadowy form ran along the top of it and disappeared inside. On the ground with his back braced against it sat a man gnawing on a crust of pizza. As they watched, he took a drink out of a bottle in a paper bag.

"That fucker, I told him to lay off the booze." The man in spandex got out and walked over to the man on the ground. "Get up, you drunken bastard," he said. "You're not going to fuck things up for me." The man didn't move. The man in spandex yanked him up, dragged him to the car and shoved him in the back seat. Ursula pulled back out onto the street.

"Where are we going?" said Ursula.

"Over by Georgetown Reservoir. Freddy says this old lady's got a spot right behind it. Been there since the fall—he knows right where it's at. Ain't that right, Freddy, you drunken fucker." He punched Freddy in the arm and Freddy groaned. Then the man leaned forward. "Hey mister," he said, "we didn't introduce ourselves. That ain't polite. My name's Tony. What's yours?"

"Tom."

"Tom, huh? Glad to meet you." He stuck a dirty hand up over the top of the seat. "This here's Freddy. A drunken bum, that's all he is. Now me, I'm different. I was in 'Nam. Got my service medal, right here." He fingered a piece of metal pinned to his shirt. Then he touched his sleeve. "See this patch? Hundred and First Airborne, Fort Campbell, Kentucky. The Screaming fucking Eagles. I jumped out of the fucking sky right on top of those fucking gooks. I blew away a whole shitload of them in my time."

"Really."

"Yeah, one of them shot me in the crotch, damn near blew my balls off. I was out there, all right. I was one brave bastard. They gimme a silver star. 'Galantry in action,' that's what it's for."

"Congratulations."

"Shit, what the fuck good did it do? Now the little yellow bastards are all over here."

"I guess they are. This old woman. So you know who she is."

"Yeah, we know her."

"What's she like?"

"Fuckin' crazy. She don't talk nothing but nonsense. Don't know what it is, but it ain't English. Can't understand a fuckin' word she says. What you want her for?"

"Just to talk."

"Yeah? Then you talk the same lingo she does?"

"Some."

The drunken one suddenly came alive. "What is she," he said, "your fuckin' mother?" They both laughed. The man in spandex kept looking at Hans. He had taken a piece of paper from his pocket and was squinting to read it in the poor light. The drunk looked at it and said, "Hey, I got one of them, too."

"Yeah?"

"Yeah. A guy outside the shelter gimme it. He was one of those, what do you call it?"

"Why don't you just shut the fuck up?" The man in spandex put the paper away. Then he leaned forward over back of the seat and peered at Hans from only a few centimeters away.

"Hey, mister, you look like you're Swedish or something. Where you from, anyway?"

"Baltimore."

"Baltimore, huh? I know Baltimore. What part?"

"The nice part."

"There ain't no fuckin' nice part in Baltimore. Hey, what did you do to your cheek? Looks like your girlfriend got pissed at you. What for? You fucking somebody on the side?" They both laughed again.

"Something like that."

They drove on through the dark. They passed a hospital and then two embassies, one behind heavy gates in a woods, the other on a hill, bathed in light from spotlights set into the lawn. On a street near a fire station they turned sharply to the left, and the reservoir appeared on the right. It was the size of a city block; around it ran a cyclone fence, topped with barbed wire. All along were signs that read "No Entry." In the light from the moon, Hans could see ripples on the water and a cement pier that ran down the middle of it. On the block beyond, amid houses and apartment buildings, were the lights of a little store.

"See that deli?" said the man in spandex. "We gotta stop there and get Freddy some coffee, otherwise he ain't gonna make it. Just pull up in front. I'll go get it. Mister, you got a buck?"

He went into the store and disappeared down one of the aisles. In two minutes he was back, getting into the car and handing the coffee to Freddy. They turned down the first street to the right and drove to the end. Now they were in a residential neighborhood that faced a park overlooking the river and the bluffs on the other side. The man in spandex had to help Freddy out of the car. Half the coffee was down the front of his coat. They walked past a picnic table and between some large pines. The drunk stopped, braced himself against one of them, and urinated on the trunk. Then he lurched down a little incline to a path. It was broad, and in the middle were the overgrown tracks of an abandoned railroad. The two set off ahead. The man in spandex kept turning around and looking back down the path. Hans found this very unsettling. He began to note the lay of the land. To one side, behind a tangle of vegetation, was a fence enclosing the back side of the reservoir, and to the other, a steep, wooded slope that ended after perhaps fifty meters in a drop-off to a road. Below them cars sped by, and in their lights, he could see the yellow double-line in the middle. Beyond that, behind a low stone wall, was a canal, more woods, and the river.

All along the path were telephone poles. Hans counted them as they passed. At the fourth, the drunk stopped. He swayed unsteadily for a moment. Then he lifted his arm and pointed to a trail, barely visible, that led down the slope.

"She's down there."

Ursula shined her light at a thicket a few meters away. In the middle was a figure lying on the ground, covered with blankets. Above it was a black plastic sheet, suspended on four sticks, stuck in the ground. All around were empty cans and bottles. In the light the figure stirred, and a face peered up at them. It was the face of an old woman.

He turned to Ursula. "Is that her?"

"Yes, that's her."

"What did I tell you?" said the man in spandex. "Hey, you got our money?" He held out his hand. Hans counted out a hundred and gave it to him.

"What about Freddy?" said the man. "He's the guy who brought us here. Shit, don't he get nothing?" Hans counted out a hundred more and handed it to the drunk, who peered at it and stuck it in the pocket of his shirt.

"Pleasure doing business with you, Mister. Well, that's it for us. We won't be sticking around. Whatever you gotta do, you go do it." The man in spandex seemed in a hurry to leave. He had a grip on the drunk and was practically dragging him back down the path.

With Ursula ahead, they started down the slope to the old woman. It was muddy and treacherous, and they held onto trunks and roots. The old woman watched them, silently. When they got close, Ursula stopped.

"Frieda," she said. "Frieda Jahn."

The old woman rose on her elbow. "Who speaks?" Her words were German. Her voice was gravelly and weak.

"It is I, Ursula."

"Ursula. Why have you come here?"

"I have brought someone to see you."

Hans stepped forward and knelt beside her. She looked up at him. "Unknown man, who are you?"

"I have come from Comrade Wiehle. He sends you his greetings."

"Comrade Wiehle. It is Comrade Wiehle who sent Jahn here. Then you are from home."

"Yes."

"Who would come all the way from home to see me? No one! Only Jahn! Everyone else has forgotten me. Are you Jahn? You do not look like Jahn."

"No, I am not Jahn. But I will be Jahn if you wish me to be."

"Yes. Jahn. That is what I shall call you. And you shall call me 'darling.' That is what Jahn called me. No one has called me that since the day I last saw him."

"Yes, darling."

The old woman pulled herself up and sat, her arms hugging her knees. "Dearest Jahn," she said, "tell me about home. What is it like there? I've heard many things! Are they true? Has it changed?"

"No, it is still the same."

"Then the Wall is still there? And the Palace of the Republic?"

"Yes, they are both still there."

"And the May Day Parade. Do they still have the May Day Parade?"

"Yes, they still do."

"Berlin was always so happy on that day! The flags, the banners! The party leaders on the review stand! The workers marching past! It was my favorite day of the year! You and I used to march in it, too, holding hands. Do you remember?"

"Of course I remember."

"Our garden in the garden colony at Köpenick. How lovely it was! How filled with flowers! Do you still have it?"

"Yes, I still do."

"Oh, how I miss it! Have you kept it up?"

"Yes. It is as beautiful as ever."

"You always said you were going to buy a new garden dwarf for it. The old one was so cracked and discolored. Did you?"

"Yes, I did. He stands where the old one stood. He has a peaked hat and he is holding a spade."

"How I wish I could see him! And the fountain. Is the fountain still there? And does the blackbird still nest in the hedge by the path?"

"Yes, the fountain is there. And the blackbird is there as well. He sings for me every evening."

"Dearest Jahn, I've waited for you so long. I never gave up hope. I knew you would come. I told them nothing! I told the Americans nothing! This is a hateful place. They have treated me badly. I am not the same as when you left."

"Darling, in my heart you have not changed." He sat by her and stroked her hair. She was ancient and wizened, and her clothing was in rags. On her chin was an open sore.

"Kiss me, dearest." Hans leaned forward and kissed her. Her lips were trembling. She parted them. A horrible taste filled his mouth and reached down into his throat. But as her rough hand caressed his cheek, it melted away.

"My dearest Jahn, I have what you gave me to keep for you. For many years it lay hidden, but I have it now."

"What is it, darling?"

"This!"

She reached down the front of her shirt and pulled something out. In the dark he could see that around her neck was a ribbon, from which something hung. He fixed it in the beam of his light. It was a Maltese Cross; the outer end of each arm was flared into two points. He reached down and turned it over. On the back was engraved "H. Goering, 1917." It was the Reichsmarschall's *Pour le Merite*, missing since 1945.

"Where did you get this?"

"Dearest, don't you remember? A dying man brought it. You gave him money for it. Twenty thousand dollars!"

"A dying man?"

"Yes. A man from the country. He was gray and sick. He could hardly stand. You made me get him a chair. He said he was an American soldier. He said he guarded Goering at Nuremberg. Goering gave it to him for a favor."

"What kind of favor?"

"He never said."

"Do you know his name?"

"No. He never told us."

"Darling, tell me. I know it was a long time ago. But was there ever anyone else? Was there ever a man on a motorcycle?"

"Yes! Not a man, but a boy! He was no more than sixteen! He came to the shop a few days later. He was coarse and brutal-looking. He spoke German. He had a Berlin accent. He said he knew you'd given money to the dying man. He wanted money, too. And he had something to sell. A party badge! It was Goering's, too!"

"I remember that badge. And didn't he have a photo, too?"

"Yes! Of a little girl, holding a figure of a man with a sword. He was killing a snake! The boy said the girl was his cousin. He said he could get what she held, but that it would cost thousands! You told him you'd get the money, and he said he'd come back in a week. Then he left. How excited you were. Don't you remember? You said, 'This is what we've been looking for! It means we can go home! We can leave this wretched place forever!' We were both so happy!"

"But what happened?"

"The next day he was supposed to come. But instead the SS came, in the middle of the night! They had pistols and whips and a dog! There were two of them, dressed in black! They had the Death's Head on their caps. I saw them from the staircase! I ran in the closet and hid! I heard the door close, and when I came out you were gone!"

Suddenly, above them on the path, there were voices. The man in the spandex pants was back. With him were two others. As they got closer, he could see they were broad at the shoulders and carried sawed-off baseball bats. The man in spandex was standing at the top of the trail, looking down and pointing.

"That's where they are," he said. "Right down there."

"The guy, too?"

"Yeah, him, too."

"You sure he's the right one?"

"Yeah. He's got the eyes. He's got a scratch on his face. He can talk German. That fucking old lady, she's another fucking kraut. There's some other old bitch down there, too."

"We don't care about them. Just the guy. You gonna help us?"

"Me? Shit no, I ain't goin' down there."

"Hey, I thought you said you were in Vietnam. Just pretend you're back in the jungle."

"Fuck that. I don't like that dude. He's a spooky fucker. His eyes are cold, it's like they're looking right through you."

"A real hero, aren't you? You dumb piece of shit. You're a disgrace to the white race. No wonder the gooks won."

Suddenly a bush near Hans lit up. Then a beam shone in his eyes. Shading them, he could see two men only a few meters away.

"Mr. Hunter," said one of them. His voice was forced and jovial. "Hello! Come on up. Nothing to worry about. We just want to talk to you."

"Jahn! Run! It's the SS! It's them!" Mrs. Jahn skittered backwards over the ground, like a crab. Ursula scrambled after her. Bottles and cans rolled down the hill. In a moment they were out of sight. The beam stayed fixed on him. The men started forward, moving carefully, their bats raised. Hans took a deep breath. Then he launched himself down the slope, crashing through the brush, through vines with barbs that caught on his clothing and dug into his flesh. At the bottom he came abruptly to the top of a retaining wall built into the hillside. The light followed him, but the men stayed behind. The drop-off to the road was at least four meters. Below him, cars raced by. It was dizzying, and for the first time, he felt afraid. The top of the wall was crumbling, and it was hard not to go over the edge. He moved along the top, pushing branches aside. Soon the woods on the slope grew thicker, and the path above was nearly out of sight. Everywhere were tall trees with ghostly pale trunks.

He thought back to his training days in the border troops. They often held exercises in the forest, some playing traitors trying to flee across the frontier, and others a patrol sent to hunt them down. He remembered the sergeant—a decorated veteran who had himself shot two men trying to cross. To the patrol, the sergeant had said, "Men, by your honor, by your oath to defend the German Democratic Republic from its enemies, foreign and domestic, do your duty! When you are at your posts, show no mercy! If anyone tries to cross to the other side, shoot him down like a dog! These people are vermin. They are out to destroy the state and plunge Germany back into fascism!" And to those playing the traitors, he said, "Men! Do not make it easy for them. You must think like crafty fascists yourselves. For now, you are an enemy of the state! Use the terrain. Find a hollow, fit your body into it, and hide your shape with leaves and sticks. A week's leave for those of you who make it!" Hans looked around. He walked a few meters up the slope, picking his way carefully. Passing cars masked the sounds. Near a fallen tree there was a slight depression. He got to his knees and lay down in it, facing the road. Beneath him the leaves were wet—he could feel water soaking through to his skin. He rubbed dirt on his face and pushed his hands and feet beneath the leaves. Then he lay perfectly still. The two men had run ahead on the path, and one had gone down the slope to the wall. Now they were working their way back toward him, one shining his light up the slope, the other down.

He heard them talking as they approached. Some of the words were meant for him. "Mr. Hunter, come out! We mean you no harm. You might as well make it easy on yourself. Don't make us angry. You can't get away. Every bum in the city has your description in his pocket."

They came ever closer. Now the man at the foot of the slope was only a few meters away; Hans could almost hear him breathing. Slowly he lifted his head and looked, his eyes slits. The man was moving along the top of the retaining wall, coming his direction, stopping every few paces to shine his light up the hill. The light played along the ground nearby. The man stood silhouetted against the lights of the road. What had the sergeant said? If you see your enemy and he does not see you, you must use that moment well. You must be patient. You must wait for him to make a mistake. And then you must strike! Hans watched. Now the man was holding his light in one hand and the baseball bat in the other. At a spot on top of the wall blocked by a branch, he put the baseball bat and the light on the ground, pushed the branch aside, and started to step around it. For a moment he was half-poised over the abyss, and no more than three meters away. Hans dug his shoe into the ground and rose silently to one knee. As the man let go of the branch, Hans burst from his lair, striking him in the chest with the flats of both hands. The man threw his arms out and fell backwards off the wall, into the path of a car. His body flew forward through the air and the car hit it again, tires squealing. Then the car spun around, flipped over and crashed into the wall on the other side. There was a hissing sound and the screech of grating metal as someone inside tried to open the door.

Above on the path the other man was shouting "Jack, Jack, what the fuck's going on? Where are you? You all right?"

Hans picked up the bat and stood, legs apart, facing up the slope. As the man's light shined on him, he held the bat aloft. "You fucker," said the man, "where's Jack?"

"Jack's dead. Now it's your turn." He took a step forward. The man turned and the light went off. Then came the thud of footfalls receding into the distance.

Hans made his way up to the path. At the trail to Mrs. Jahn's camp he stopped. The camp was abandoned. Already one siren was blaring, followed by another. Down on the road there were flashing red lights.

He came up from the path into the park. On the street, he could see that Ursula's car was gone. Behind where it had been was a motorcycle. By a picnic table, the drunken derelict lay in a heap. Hans shined his light on him. There was vomit down the front of his coat, and blood oozed from his nose. Hans could see that the pocket of his shirt had been ripped open and the money was gone. He looked up at Hans with stupid eyes. Hans reached into the man's coat and pulled out a paper. He turned his light on it.

"Wanted!" it read. "A dangerous traitor to the Aryan race! In Washington, DC a man claiming to be John Hunter of Columbus, Ohio, attacked and viciously beat a racial comrade. There is a reward of one thousand dollars to anyone who can report his whereabouts. He is of Aryan appearance with high cheekbones, thin lips, pale blue eyes, and light blond hair. He may have a scratch on the right side of his face. He speaks both perfect English and German. If you see him, call the Alert Network of the Aryan Youth at once. We are on the streets right now. Call us and we will come to you." And then there was a telephone number.

Hans started back to his car. It was a long way, and it took more than an hour. He stayed on the side streets and stepped into the shadows whenever a vehicle went by. Once a motorcycle cruised down the street while someone on the back shined a light between the parked cars and onto the sidewalk a block away. Whenever he passed beneath a streetlight, his shadow seemed like that of someone coming up behind him. Back in the motel, he washed his face and hands and changed clothes. Then he went into an all-night drugstore and bought some skin-colored cream in a little tube. In front of the mirror in his room he dabbed some on the angry red line on his cheek until it was almost gone.

He lay down on his bed and closed his eyes. He thought about the man from the country who had guarded Goering at Nuremberg. What favor could he possibly have done for Goering to earn him a gift like that? There was one, of course. Of the condemned at Nuremberg, only Goering had escaped the rope. The night of the hanging, as he lay alone in his cell, he'd bitten into a cyanide capsule and died in an instant. Where did he get it? Someone must have slipped it to him. Who had been around Goering during his last hours? Wasn't this documented anywhere? He remembered the book he'd seen in the Georgetown University Library, *The Mysterious Death of Hermann Goering*. Maybe the answer lay there.

As he lay there, vainly seeking sleep, the sound of the "Ride of the Valkyries" came from the bed stand. It was Foerster's phone. He put it to his ear. On the line was the same hard, suspicious voice.

"Leutnant Klug!" it said. "Oh, yes, now I know for a fact who you are, you son of a red whore! Small wonder you showed such interest in the archives of the Border Troops. And now I have found someone who saw you in Berlin. In fact he is with me right now. His description of the man who murdered Ingeborg Mohr matches exactly how Foerster describes you! Of course you had every reason to kill her, didn't you? She was about to expose you! And now you go from that crime to another. Thanks to you, a young man has fallen in the service of his race. You have given us a martyr. His comrades will bear him, a hero, to his grave. And we will seek revenge! And don't think we will leave matters to the police. They are too easy on swine like you. You and I will soon meet face to face. And then I and my comrades will deal with you in the time-honored way that National Socialists deal with their enemies!" The man's voice had taken on a triumphant tone. "But I have no time now for you and your petty crimes. I'm about to acquire something we will use to change history. It may be that you know what it is. You were looking for it, weren't you, you fool! But forget it! You'll never see it! Just at sunset I will meet the man who has guarded it for many years. By tomorrow night it will be in my hands." There was a click, and the man was gone.

---CHAPTER 10---

𝕿𝖍𝖊 𝕸𝖆𝖓 𝖋𝖗𝖔𝖒 𝖙𝖍𝖊 𝕮𝖔𝖚𝖓𝖙𝖗𝖞

The next morning Hans drove across the bridge and headed toward the library. A block away he found a space with a meter and pumped quarters into it until he had no more. Down the block he could see a street person sitting on the curb, across from the main gate. He doubled back, went two blocks out of his way, and entered the campus through a lower gate.

At the library, he headed back to the fourth floor. During the week, the library was a much different place than on Sunday. Now it was noisy, and there were lots of people. A young woman, wearing headphones and bobbing to rhythms only she could hear, was pushing a metal cart down the rows between the stacks and putting books back on the shelves. A workman on a stepladder was changing a light in the ceiling. Two Hispanics were sweeping the floor and emptying the trash. A few students were in the carrels, hunched over laptops. On chairs in front of the window looking out on the campus sat two others, dozing, their feet propped rudely on the heating register. On one side, the windows facing the river looked out over a parking lot, and from below came the whine of the compactor of a garbage truck, followed by a beeping as the truck backed up. Soon he was at the same spot in the stacks he'd been three days before. The book he'd remembered was still there. It was called *Cheating the Hangman: The Mysterious Death of Hermann Goering*, by someone named Patrick Callahan.

He took it to a carrel and opened it. Bound in the center were several plates with photographs of Goering: Goering standing by his plane as a young pilot in von Richthofen's Flying Circus; Goering in dramatic half-profile, wearing a party uniform, the *Pour le Merite* around his neck; Goering resplendent in the uniform of a Luftwaffe general, posing with his new bride; Goering at the moment of his arrest, eyes cast down, unpinning a medal from his shirt; Goering in the docket; Goering in his prison tunic; and Goering dead, laid out on the cot in his cell.

Hans turned to the introduction. "Hermann Goering," it read, "the number two man in the Reich, head of the Luftwaffe, and close confidant of Adolf Hitler, was tried for war crimes at Nuremberg and condemned to death by hanging. But in the very hours before the hanging was to be carried out, on October 16, 1946, he committed suicide by biting into a glass capsule filled with cyanide. He died with a twisted grin on his face, mocking his captors. And all over Nuremberg, all over Germany, people were saying, 'Did you hear? Our Hermann cheated them. He got the last laugh.' Goering's suicide was a major public relations disaster for the Allies, and they vowed that someone would pay. They asked then the question that everyone has asked since: how could Goering get a cyanide capsule when his entire cell and his person were subject to daily search? Who could have been in a position to give it to him? Goering died clasping a note, saying he had had it with him since before his arrest nearly a year and a half before, but this hardly seems likely. It is much more probable that one of his last visitors somehow managed to slip it to him—his doctor or his attorney—or that it was even planted by an American guard during the final search of Goering's cell."

Hans turned to the chapter called "Goering's Last Days."

"In the days between hearing the sentence and the day of his death," it read, "Goering paid an emotional farewell not only to those few visitors he was allowed, but to the Americans who had guarded him. In that time he gave away many of his personal possessions. He also left behind a tantalizing riddle. Only two days before he died, he boasted to the prison psychologist, an American major, that Hitler had outwitted the allies, and that a secret organization existed to keep his ideas alive and to assure they would someday return to rule the world. He claimed this group had buried treasure and sacred relics of the movement in a secret place beneath the streets of Berlin, and that no one would find them, though thousands passed by the spot each day. But when pressed, he became sullen and morose and refused to say more. Is there any truth in what he said? Scholars have debated this for years, but not a shred of evidence to substantiate his claims has ever come to light."

The rest of the book consisted of chapters on each of the suspects, and the conclusion. One chapter was called, "The German Lawyer," another, "The Personal Physician," and another called, "The American Lieutenant." Skipping the others, Hans turned to the latter and began to read.

"Among the American guards there was a young lieutenant, Ted McCracken, of Elkins, West Virginia, who became a particular favorite of the Reichsmarschall. They shared a passion for hunting, and Goering gave the young man several gifts. Strangely, no one questioned the propriety of this relationship. McCracken was in charge of the detail the night Goering committed suicide. It was he who discovered Goering's lifeless body in his cell."

Hans paged through the chapter to the end. The last paragraph read, "McCracken, who died in 1975, was cleared of any wrongdoing in the case, but lived much of his life under a cloud of suspicion. Did McCracken do it? My own feeling is, no. A simple country lad, he was a classic American type in the best sense, a man incapable of guile. Far more likely is that it was a plot hatched between Goering's lawyer and his personal physician."

Hans closed the book. Who had actually given the cyanide capsule to Goering was of little interest to him. But incapable of guile or not, McCracken was quite apparently the one who had sold the *Pour le Merite* to Jahn. Even the date fit. The year McCracken had died was the year the man from the country had turned up at Jahn's shop. Putting the book back on the shelf, he went down the stairs to a phone near the exit and used one of his cards to call West Virginia information.

A man's voice came on the line. "What city, please?" it said.

"Elkins."

"Yes?"

"Do you have a listing for Ted McCracken?"

"Just a moment. There's a Rodney McCracken, but no Ted. Do you want that number?"

"Yes, please." In an instant the operator was gone and on came a computerized voice, saying the number and then repeating it. Hans copied it down, dialed it, and in a moment, he was talking to a man at the other end of the line.

"Mr. McCracken?"

"Yes?"

"I'm looking for someone who might be a relative of yours, Ted McCracken. My dad was in the service with him, over in Nuremberg, right after the war. Dad's hearing is pretty well shot, so I'm making some calls for him. He's getting kind of sentimental about the old days and he's trying to find some of his old buddies. He's got some pictures to share with them."

"Well, in Uncle Ted's case, I'm afraid your dad is a little late. He died over twenty-five years ago."

"Really. I'm sorry. How about his wife? Maybe she'd like the pictures. Is she still alive?"

"No. That's a sad story."

"Oh?"

"Last Labor Day someone murdered her, right in her house. Hanged her in her basement. Poor old lady. She had to be at least seventy-five."

"That's horrible! Is there anyone else? Did they have any children?"

"Yes, one. Bernice Green. She still lives around here, out on Cheat Mountain Road."

"Thank you. Maybe I'll give her a try."

He hung up. Another hanging. That certainly tied the McCrackens to the case. But why? What did the old lady have that anyone wanted?

Back at the motel, Hans packed his few things into the car, checked out, and headed for West Virginia. It felt good to leave Washington behind. With every kilometer he felt more at ease. For a while, the landscape and the road through it were no more than gently rolling, but in an hour or so, he came to mountains, and the road began to climb. At the crest of a ridge he came to a sign reading "Welcome to Wild, Wonderful West Virginia—We're the Place To Be in the Twenty-

First Century: We're Proud—We're Growing—And Our Time Has Come At Last!" Further on was a billboard, showing a great, dripping sandwich, held forth by a clown. "McDonald's, Way Ahead of the Rest," it read. "Try the Millenium Burger—The Sandwich for the Next Thousand Years!"

These were really the first mountains he had driven through since his days in the Harz Mountains near the border with the West—but this was hardly the same. Here there were a dozen twists and turns in every kilometer—it made him queasy. At one point, feeling sick, he pulled over, got out of the car, and walked over to the edge of the road. Below him was a ravine, and all down it were black plastic bags of trash, most of which had burst open. At the very bottom was an old washing machine and a rusted car body, half-covered with brush.

In a few more minutes he came to a little town in the middle of a forest. At a crossroads was a café with a few pickups parked outside. Thinking food might settle his stomach, he went in and sat at the counter. To save time, he ordered the special from the chalkboard. Within five minutes, the waitress had set it down in front of him. It was a slab of meatloaf under a thick gravy, with pickled beets and potatoes whipped into a sort of pudding, on top of which a crust had formed. With it came two spongy rolls and two little tubs of spread. The coffee was very black and had a burnt, bitter taste. He ate what he could of it, left a few dollars on the counter, and left.

This day was quite different from the days before. It was chilly. A front had moved in, and a cold fog had settled in some of the hollows. Up here there were few signs of spring—the trees were as bare as in the dead of winter. Toward the tops of the mountains there was even a patch or two of snow left in the woods, and some of the farm ponds had a skim of ice around the edges. For a few kilometers he got stuck behind a school bus that stopped every two or three minutes, flashing its lights and projecting stop signs from the sides. Children in jackets with hoods went running down the lanes to their homes. Every so often came another little town with a grocery, a filling station and a few rundown clapboard buildings. After another hour or so of this, he came to a great rock formation of bare towers sticking up out of the forest. Right beyond that, the road toward Elkins left the valley and headed up another ridge. Ahead of him, an old car spewed out clouds of black exhaust. Finally it turned and disappeared down a rutted dirt road.

At a filling station on the outskirts of Elkins, he looked up Bernice Green in the phone book and got directions to Cheat Mountain Road. It turned out to be a winding road on the side of a hill. There were houses all along with names on the mailboxes. At last he came to one that read B. Green. The house was small and neat and painted a light gray. In the back was a garage with an old basketball hoop nailed above the door. Across the street was a graveyard.

Leading to the house was a steep stairway with a heavy railing bolted into the cement. Next to the porch, a crocus peeked through a patch of snow. Hans walked to the top. He rang the bell and waited. In a minute a heavy woman in a print dress came to the door. She had short, curled gray hair and looked in her late forties. She looked Hans up and down, holding the door open no more than a crack.

"Mrs. Green?"

"Yes?"

"Can I talk to you for a moment?"

"You're not a Jehovah's Witness, are you?" she said. "Or a Mormon? You kind of look like one. Because if that's what you've come for, save your breath—I'm a churchgoing Baptist, and I'm not about to change for somebody who just turns up at my door, and that's a fact."

"No, no, it's nothing like that. My name is Tom Bradford, and I'm an attorney from Trenton, New Jersey. Are you the daughter of Mrs. McCracken? I was looking for your mother, but I'm sorry to learn she's recently deceased."

"Yes, God rest her soul. Since last September. What did you want to see her about?"

"It might seem kind of strange to you, to hear about this so many years after the war, but I represent the family of Hermann Goering— they're looking to recover mementoes that might have sentimental value to them. I can offer some compensation on behalf of the family and a foundation established by the children of veterans of the German Luftwaffe. And both also want to express their thanks to people who were kind to the Reichsmarschall during the last difficult days of his life. I understand that your late father was one of them."

"Well, I don't know how much I can help you, but if you want, you can come in. But I want to see your driver's license first. Just hold it up and show it to me through the door. After what happened to Mom, I'm pretty wary of strangers."

"I understand." He took it from his wallet and held it up. After peering at it and looking back at him, she held the door open and led the way into the room. Her legs were white and puffy and laced with varicose veins; she wore slippers that flapped against the linoleum floor. On the television at the far end of the room, there was a preacher pacing back and forth on a stage, holding up a bible and shaking it, while an 800-number rolled across the bottom of the screen. She stepped over and turned it off.

In the room there was a rocking chair and a recliner with a lever on the side. On the floor lay several braided scatter-rugs, and in the corner stood a grandfather clock. On the coffee table in front of the sofa were a copy of *Soap Opera Digest* and *TV Guide.* On the mantle over the fireplace were several photographs. One showed two boys, holding fishing rods, posed next to a pickup truck. Hans nodded toward it.

"Nice looking boys," he said. "Are they your sons?"

"Yes," she said, "Jarrel and Tom. That's Jarrel there on the right. They both moved up to Detroit, where their daddy lives, as soon as they got out of high school. Can't keep young folks around here anymore. Got jobs in the auto plant. They keep asking me to move up there with them, and I'm just about ready to go. Now that Mom's gone, there's no reason in the world to stay around this old town. Never did like it much anyway. And nowadays it's mighty lonesome up here. Have a seat, Mr. Bradford. Would you like some coffee? I got a pot on the stove."

"That would be nice."

"Sugar and cream? I always like lots of sugar and cream in mine."

"Just black, thank you."

She shuffled into the kitchen, and a few minutes later came back with a cup and some cookies on a plate. Each cookie was two dark wafers with a sort of white paste in between. The plate had a pavilion in the center of it, under the cookies, and near the rim were the words "World's Fair, Flushing Meadows, New York, 1964."

"Sorry, these cookies are just store-bought—I don't do much baking anymore."

"Oh, they're fine. That's a pretty plate. Did you go to the World's Fair?"

"Yes. Mom and Dad took me up there. I was real little, just about to go in the third grade. It's the longest trip we ever went on together! I remember that Dad was already coughing a lot then. Cigarettes, three packs a day! He liked the no-filter kind. That's what did him in, in the end. He picked up the habit in the service. Mom was always trying to make him give it up, but he was hooked, that's for sure. From the time I remember, he always had a damn cigarette in his hand. He died when he was only fifty-five years old. Makes me sick to think it, but both my boys smoke, too."

"I heard a little bit about your dad. He sounded like a very nice man. It's not hard to figure out he was a hunter." Over the mantle was a deer's head, and on the floor in front of the fireplace was a bearskin rug.

"Oh, yes, he lived for the hunting season. I swear, come the fall, he spent more time in the woods than he did in the store. Maybe that's why the business started to fall apart. Plus he was always giving people credit. That's a bad idea around these parts."

"He had a store?"

"Yes. He came back from the war with a little money saved up and set up a furniture store here in town, right on the main street. That was back before everybody shopped at the malls. But he never did do real good at it. He liked nice pieces, the kind that come from North Carolina, but around here people only want junk. Guess that's all they got the money for. By the time he died, he owed practically as much on it as it was worth. We couldn't keep it going, Mom and me, we had to sell out. But still, somehow he managed to leave us with enough money to keep us going for a while. Don't know how he did it, but he always thought of his family first. He was a good, good man. I still miss him."

"That's him right there, isn't it?" Next to Hans was a bookcase, filled with popular novels and a collection of Reader's Digest condensed books. On it was the photo of a young man, in football gear, kneeling on one knee, his helmet under his arm. Flanking it were a couple of trophies.

"Oh, yes, that's him all right. He was a real good athlete. Football, basketball, track—he was good at all of it. He was the star quarterback at the high school. They were state champions two years in a row. Skinny but fast, that's what he was. And so handsome. Mom said every girl in the school was crazy about him—her included—but he never gave her a look until he came back from the service. They gave him an athletic scholarship to the little college here in town, and that's why when he went in the army they made him an officer. He was real proud of that. He was in the war just at the end and then they kept him on in Germany and stationed him at Nuremberg, where they had the trials. That's where he met Mr. Goering."

"Did he ever talk about Mr. Goering?"

"Oh, yes."

"What did he say?"

"Oh, he liked him. He said Mr. Goering was a very nice man. He wasn't like those other Nazis, Hitler and the rest of them. All those bad things that happened to the Jews, my dad said Mr. Goering didn't know about any of them."

"So you already know quite a bit about Mr. Goering."

"Just what Dad told me. I know Mr. Goering was a hero in the First World War. That he won the highest medal of the time and that he shot down a bunch of enemy planes. I know that Mr. Goering's first wife was a Swedish countess, and he loved her more than anything in the world, and that when she died he built a big house and named it after her. I know he collected paintings, and the whole house was full of them. I know that when he got married again, his second wife was an actress who had lots of Jewish friends, and that she and Mr. Goering helped a lot of them to get out of the country."

"That's what I've heard, too," said Hans, who had heard nothing of the sort. For Hermann Goering to portray himself as a friend to Jews in a time of trouble was obscene—the man was as bad as the worst of them. He looked down a moment and went on.

"Did your dad get to know Mr. Goering pretty well?"

"Oh, yes, when Dad was guarding him, he and Mr. Goering used to talk about all kinds of stuff. Hunting, especially. They spent hours swapping stories. Before he died, Mr. Goering even gave my dad a beautiful shotgun, all engraved with German hunting scenes. I remember there was a wild boar on it, running through the woods, being chased by a pack of dogs. Dad used to have it over the mantle in the den."

"The family has told me about that shotgun. Didn't it have an inscription on it?"

"Yes, I think it did."

"Where is it now?"

"I wish I knew. It's one of the things that got stolen from Mom's house."

"I'm sorry. But how could Mr. Goering give it to your dad? He couldn't have just had it there in his cell."

"Oh, no. He got word through to his wife. Dad used to smuggle out letters that Mr. Goering wrote to her. She had a lot of her husband's things hidden out in the woods. Otherwise everything would have been stolen! She lost a lot as it was! After the war it was really tough over there. Mrs. Goering was strapped for cash. She and her daughter were practically starving! Dad felt sorry for them. He helped her sell some of this stuff to friends of his in the army. He always got a good price for her, and he never kept any of the money for himself! That was one reason Mr. Goering gave Dad the shotgun. They were both really grateful to him."

"Did your dad have anything else from Mr. Goering?"

"Just little things, like a watch, and a cigarette lighter."

"How about military items? Like a ceremonial dagger, or a baton, or any medals or decorations? Those have great sentimental value. The family would particularly like to recover them."

"There might have been. I'm not sure. I remember some kind of cross on a ribbon Dad showed me once or twice. I don't know if it came from Mr. Goering or not—Dad had a lot of other souvenirs from the war. Swords, flags, all kinds of stuff. It hasn't turned up, so maybe it got stolen, too."

"I know this must be painful for you, but what exactly happened to your mother?"

"Yes, it is hard." She took a tissue from her pocket and dabbed her eyes. "I'd seen her earlier in the day. Poor old lady. Whoever did it, was real mean to her first. They tied her to a chair and set her clothes on fire, and then they hanged her. It makes me sick to think about it."

"That's horrible! Why would anyone do that?"

"There were stories that Mom kept money around the house."

"Do you think she told them where anything was?"

"I don't know. Maybe she did. They like to tore the whole place apart—there were even some floorboards ripped up in the bedroom."

"Were there any suspects?"

"Nope. Not a single one. There's some bad boys out here in these hills, but none of them that bad. But it was Labor Day Weekend, so there were a lot of people on motorcycles around, from out of town. The police always figured one of them did it."

"Did you give the police a list of missing items?"

"Well, no. I told them about the shotgun, but that was all. And I didn't say where it came from. As for that cross, I hadn't seen it in years, anyway, not since before Dad died. Dad was sensitive about those gifts. He thought if he told anybody, the government would come and take them away from him. Mom and I weren't supposed to mention them. And he never let anybody but us into the den. But now I suppose it doesn't really matter."

"Did your father ever do anything else for Mr. Goering?"

"Oh, little things. He used to bring Mr. Goering chocolate from the PX. Mr. Goering loved Hershey bars, that's what Dad said. And M&Ms—Dad said he used to eat them by the handful! And Dad took canned food to Mrs. Goering and Mr. Goering's sisters a few times. And cigarettes. Those were as good as money in those days! Once he bought a little teddy bear for Mr. Goering's daughter, Edda. Mostly, I think, Dad was just nice to him. All Mr. Goering's old American friends, like Charles Lindbergh, turned their backs on him, once he got in trouble. But Dad wasn't like that. He never turned his back on anybody. He accepted people the way they were. I think you have to forgive people for the bad things they've done, especially if they're really sorry. Mr. Goering said that knowing my dad convinced him that Americans were still good."

"Do you have any photos from those days? I'd love to see them."

"Well, I've got an album in the back room somewhere. Won't take me a second to get it. It's all the pictures Dad took over there."

She went into the back room, slippers flapping against the floor, and in a minute emerged with a worn photo album in one hand and a silver framed picture in the other. Then she sat down on the sofa and motioned for him to sit next to her.

She held out the picture for him to see. It showed the Reichsmarschall at the height of his powers, in full dress uniform, holding his baton. It was signed, "To Ted McCracken, with many thanks for all your kindnesses, your friend, Hermann Goering."

"Dad used to have this on the top of his dresser," she said, "right next to a picture of his parents."

"It's very nice."

"Yes. There are more pictures of Mr. Goering in this album. My dad used to show it to me when I was a little girl. We'd sit together on this very sofa. I haven't looked at it in years—not since right after he died, in fact. It was too painful." She began to page through it.

"Here's Dad in his uniform. And here's the Palace of Justice—that's where they had the trial. And here's downtown Nuremberg—not much left of it, is there? They say it's all built up again, just the way it was before." It was a photograph of utter ruin and desolation. There were a few walls of buildings standing, surrounded by rubble. It was hard to tell if there had even been a street there at all.

She paged through farther. There were lots of other photos in the album, of life in the military, in Germany. There were thin people, some of them in old German army coats, picking their way through the ruins. One was of an old woman, begging, holding out her hand. On the next page was the photo of people inside a tavern, with a bunch of GIs and several young women.

"See this whole group of people, having a good time? That blonde woman is somebody Dad knew over there. Pretty, isn't she? She was only twenty or twenty-one. Helga. Her husband had been killed in the war, and she had a little boy named Joachim. Isn't that a funny name for a little boy? See these blank spaces here? There were some other pictures of Helga there, but after Dad died, Mom went through the album and took them out. I don't know why, really. He didn't even really know Mom until after he came home."

She turned the page and stopped at a photo showing Ted McCracken, in civilian clothes, next to an attractive, well-dressed woman and a little girl.

"Here's a photo of Dad with Mr. Goering's family. That's Mrs.

Goering right there. That poor woman went through a lot! And there's Edda. She was just a little girl when her father died, only eight or nine. That's sad, isn't it? The last time she and her father saw each other, they cried and cried. At that point, they already knew he was going to die. Dad was there, too, and when he told me about it he got all choked up."

"How did your dad and Mr. Goering talk to each other? Did your father speak German?"

"Oh, no, not a word. But Mr. Goering knew some English. And there was someone else, Hanno, who translated for them."

"Hanno? Who was that? A German?"

"Well, not really. Sort of a German. His parents came from Germany, but he was an American. A soldier. He was one of the guards."

"Are there any pictures of him?"

"Oh, yes. Here. That's him. Next to his motorcycle. My dad said he was a great mechanic—he used to repair jeeps and motorcycles that everybody else had given up on. This is the German cycle he had—it was a BMW, made for the German army—God knows how he kept it going, that's what my dad said. He bought it for ten cartons of cigarettes! He used to ride it all over Nuremberg. People thought he was a German because he could talk it so good. For a joke, sometimes he told people he'd been in the SS, and they believed him. In fact he had an uncle or a cousin who came to visit him—that person really *had* been in the SS. Dad and Hanno got some of their souvenirs from that guy, I think."

"What was Hanno's last name?"

"Oh, Lord, I don't remember. Dad never called him anything but Hanno. But Dad usually identified people on the back of the photos. Let's take a look." The picture was held into the album by four little mounts at the corners, glued to the page. Bending it slightly, she slipped it out of the mounts and turned it over. On the back, in fading pencil, were the words "Cpl. Hanno Schmidt, Nuremberg, Germany, June, 1946."

"Do you think Mr. Goering might have given things to Hanno, too?"

"He might have. Hanno used to spend a lot of time with Mr. Goering, talking German. My Dad said he never knew what they were saying. When Hanno was on duty they'd talk through that slot in the door. The rules were, that a guard had to be watching every prisoner all the time, ever since one of them killed himself in his cell. See? Here, here's where Mr. Goering lived." There was a photo of her father at the door to Goering's cell, with the name "H. Goering" on a sign at the center, and a panel that slid back so the guard could look inside.

"Schmidt. That's a pretty common name. Do you know where he was from?"

"Oh, I've forgotten. Somewhere in the Midwest."

"Do you know what became of him?"

"Yes, I know, at least up to a point. After Mr. Goering's death, Dad stayed in Nuremburg for a while, but Hanno got himself transferred to Berlin. He was military policeman there during the blockade, chasing down black marketers. He always wanted a nice German girl—American girls weren't good enough for him—and he found one over there and married her. He brought her back home in 1948 and went to work in a motorcycle factory. Just the right place for him, that's what my dad said. As far as I know, he stayed there the rest of his life. He may still be alive, for all I know. But I haven't heard anything about him since Dad died—he never even wrote to say he was sorry! And Dad had done him a favor, too."

"What kind of favor?"

"Hanno sponsored some people to come to the States. Some relatives of his wife's—his wife's sister and her husband. This man hadn't even been in the war—he'd been injured in a factory accident. But one sponsor wasn't enough in those days—they needed two—so Dad agreed to be the other one. I don't think he ever even met the man. But he and Hanno used to stay in touch, a little. My dad sent a picture of me as a baby to Hanno and Hanno sent a picture of his little boy, who was born a couple of years before.

"So that was in the mid 1960s some time."

"Don't I wish! It was 1956."

"Did you ever meet this Hanno?"

"Yes, once. Hanno and his family came by here, a few years before Dad died, on their way to Florida. They had a nice car, like they had some money. I must have been nine or ten. I remember that Hanno's wife could hardly speak English—she just sat on the sofa and nodded her head. Can you imagine that? She'd been in this country for twenty years, and she could hardly ask how to get to the bathroom! Mom got so sick of trying to talk to her that she gave up and went in the kitchen. Hanno's son was there, too. He must have been twelve or so. I remember we sat in the den. That was unusual! Dad never let visitors in there! I remember that Hanno's son wanted to see the shotgun, so Dad took it down and let him hold it. I remember, he got real excited. But he kept pointing it at people, so Dad had to take it away from him. That may have been one of the times I saw the cross with the ribbon on it, because I think Dad took that out, too. After a while Dad and Hanno wanted to talk, so they sent me and Hanno's son outside. What a rotten kid he was! He got me behind the bushes and tried to do something dirty to me. When I stopped him, he pushed me down and made me cry. I came in and told Mom and she went out and slapped him right in the face! After they'd gone, Mom told Dad she'd never let any of those people set foot in her house again."

"This son. What was his name?"

"Oh, I don't remember."

"Did your dad ever hear from Hanno again?"

"Well, once that I know of. We went through some hard times. When my dad got sick there were a lot of bills, and Dad started to think that maybe some of that stuff he'd gotten from Mr. Goering might be worth some money. In fact when he was thinking of selling something, he called Hanno up. I heard Dad talking to him. But I guess Hanno didn't want dad contacting him, or he got mad for some reason, and they had a big fight over the phone."

"Did your dad ever sell any of the items?"

"I think he might have. He took a trip to Washington. He wouldn't tell us why he was going. It took all the strength he had. A month later he was dead."

Meanwhile, she had turned to the last page. There was a photo of Goering in his cell, looking up from his chair. His face was deeply lined, and his clothes hung slack on his frame. "This is the last picture my dad took of Mr. Goering. Doesn't he look sad, the poor man? Two days later he was dead. My dad felt really bad they were going to hang him. He said it was a good thing he died the way he did."

"Yes. And the family is very grateful for it. Did your dad ever say how he thought Mr. Goering got his hands on a cyanide capsule?"

"No, he never did. A few people tried to say that Dad gave it to him. But that's ridiculous—Mr. Goering had it hidden in his cell the whole time. He even left a letter saying that. Besides, it was official German issue—where would Dad get something like that? And if anybody gave him the capsule, it was his German doctor, not Dad. The army investigated Dad thoroughly. They pulled him off duty for a couple of weeks and made his life miserable. Even after the war, a couple of people from the government came up here, snooping around, asking where Dad got the money to open his store. Once or twice reporters came, too. And sometimes, you know, somebody who wanted to ask him about Mr. Goering would call up, but he would never talk to them. But after a while, people kind of forgot about Dad."

She sighed. Then she closed the album and put it on the table.

"Mom and Dad are buried right across the street. I go see them most every day. Would you like to come with me to pay them a visit?"

"Yes, I would."

From beneath the sofa she took some worn tennis shoes and pulled them on. "My feet get swelled up so bad," she said, "these are the only shoes I can wear."

Going down the stairs she held onto the railing with both hands, letting herself down one step at a time. Crossing the road, she leaned on Hans's arm. On the pillar next to the iron gate were the words "Mount Calvary" and the date, "1871." Many of the graves had plastic flowers, and some had little American flags stuck into the ground. Right inside the gate was a column with a shrouded figure on top. It cast a long shadow in the late afternoon sun. She stopped in front of it.

"See this? Sometimes people come and take pictures of it. It's famous around here, it's even in a local guide book. See what it says?"

On the column were the words, "This monument is erected by John and Agnes Belmont in memory of all those from Elkins who died in the Spanish Influenza of 1919, including four beloved members of their own family: James Belmont age 62, Martha Harper age 59, Henry Belmont age 3, William Belmont age 1. You took our parents and our children, leaving us to mourn."

"That's sad."

"Yes, isn't it? During the influenza my grandma told me there were funerals here day and night. She lived right here in this house and watched them. My own grandpa got it, but he pulled through okay. She was scared she was going to get it, too! She was pregnant with Dad then."

A few meters down a gravel path was the McCracken family plot. It was enclosed by low pillars, between which hung a heavy chain. On the largest stone, under a cross, was the inscription, "Theodore John McCracken, First Lieutenant, U.S.A. 1920–1975. Our Beloved Husband and Father, Asleep in The Lord." Next to it was a smaller marker that read "Theodore John McCracken Jr. 1959." Beneath the name was a little lamb, in repose, and the words, "You were with us just a week, but you stole our hearts away."

"Here's where Mom and Dad are. See the way the ground has settled over Dad? That happens after a few years. They say it's because the coffin collapses. And Dad's been down there a long while. Right next to him, where the ground still looks all dug up, that's where Mom is. I don't have the stone up for her yet. Once I do, I'm going to plant some grass and put in a few flowers around the edge, even though it's real hard for me to do that kind of work nowadays. Those right there are my grandparents. My grandma lived to be an old lady. She outlived Dad by ten years! And that little stone is for my little brother. He came along three years after I did. After that, Mom couldn't have any more children."

"That's too bad."

"It is. Life is a long, sorry business, that's for sure. Sometimes I come in this graveyard, and I wonder what it's all about. Do you know something? Dad and Hanno were there at the hangings. The gallows were put up right in the gymnasium where the boys played basketball. Can you imagine that? They took the condemned men out of their cells one at a time and hanged them in the middle of the night. Dad watched while each one walked up the stairs to the platform and then while the hangman put the nooses around their necks. Then he'd pull the lever and they'd fall right through the floor. Every time, there was a horrible thud and a cracking sound. It made Dad sick, but the hangman seemed to enjoy his job! Afterward he wanted to buy everyone a drink, but nobody wanted anything to do with him. Dad was in charge of the detail cutting the bodies down and loading them onto a truck. They put Mr. Goering's in with the rest of them. Hanno was the one who drove it, and Dad sat up in the front with him. There was a whole convoy, six trucks in front of them and six in back. They took them to a crematorium in Munich and then threw the ashes in a canal. Dad told me that he said a little prayer for Mr. Goering at the time."

They walked back across the street. Holding the railing, she struggled up the stairs and stopped in front of her door.

"Sorry I couldn't have helped you more," she said.

"Oh, no. You've been very helpful. And it was nice to meet someone whose father was so kind. You know, I've never told anyone this, but I have a theory about that poison capsule. Hanno was one of the guards who searched Mr. Goering for the last time. Hanno could have hidden the capsule for him."

"That's true."

"And here's something else. I'm only telling you because you're a friend of the Goering family. My father left an envelope, to be opened only after his death; Mom read it and then she burned it. I remember, it made her real upset. She wouldn't tell me what was in it, but she said Dad had done something he shouldn't have done. You know what I think? I think he created a diversion while Hanno hid that capsule. Maybe he dropped something. I don't know."

Hans shook her hand and gave her a sympathetic smile. Her story sounded all too probable. How had it happened? It wasn't hard to imagine. A fresh-faced boy from the country would have been no match for a wily old frog like Hermann Goering. A few gifts and kind words, and Goering had an admirer for life.

He drove down the main street of Elkins. There were a few restaurants and shops, none of them very big. Probably there was a mall somewhere that had sucked all the business away. He wondered where the furniture store had been. On the way out of town he passed a motorcycle dealership. At a phone right beyond it, he stopped and called them up.

"I'm thinking of getting a motorcycle as a graduation present for my son," he said, "but I don't know whether to buy him an American one or a foreign one. I hear the Japanese ones are pretty good. What do you think?"

"Oh, no, get an American cycle, they're much better made, and they've got a much better resale value."

"Where do they make them, anyway?"

"Up in Milwaukee—that's the motorcycle capital of the world. Both the U.S. companies are there, Harley-Davidson—they're the top of the line, the Cadillacs of motorcycles—and Wisconsin Motors. We don't carry any of the Wisconsin bikes, but we get a used one every once and a while. They're favorites with the motorcycle gangs. They're big, heavy bikes with lots of chrome on them and souped-up engines and a rotten safety record. You practically have to wear a suit of armor to ride one. They make as much noise as a 747, and they can hit 150 mph! The top model they call the Satan Cycle—it goes for over fifty thousand bucks. They get used a lot at monster truck rallies and in movie stunts. They're evil, beautiful machines. You could ride one of those damned things into hell itself and right out the other side. Some they ship over to Russia and Eastern Europe—the gangsters over there like them. Some of them have bulletproof glass on the front. Secretly, I think they're kind of neat. But they're definitely not for your average rider. If you're looking for a good bike that'll never let you down, get a Harley."

"Thanks. You've been very helpful."

Hans pulled out his map and looked for Milwaukee. He had only a vague idea where it was, but soon he found it: a yellow blotch by one of the Great Lakes, north of Chicago. It would surely take many hours to get there—it was hundreds of kilometers away. One could drive back and forth across Germany and still not have gone as far. With a cup of coffee he bought at a drive-thru, he took the road out of town toward the north. The mountains gave way to hills, and the day faded away and turned to night. Just as the sun dipped below the horizon, he pulled over to the side of the road and took out Foerster's phone. He found Prober's number in the list of names and pressed *connect*. The phone rang perhaps a dozen times, and then the line went dead.

In a few hours he came to the Interstate going west. Soon again he was surrounded by speeding trucks, some with two and even three trailers attached. There were moving trucks, there were tanker trucks with ladders up the back, and there were buses with a running dog painted on the side. It struck him then that the most alienating part about America was the shape of the cars, the trucks, and the buses.

As he drove, he thought of what this woman had told him and how it fit with what he already knew. It was clear the brother-in-law of Hanno whom McCracken had sponsored to come to America was the German hero picked by Himmler. Hadn't the Director said that the hero's records were being falsified to show he'd been injured in an industrial accident, just like this brother-in-law? And what about Hanno himself? The Director had said that a German-speaking American soldier had arrested the artisan who'd made the icon. Wasn't that just when Hanno was stationed in Berlin? The tumblers were clicking into place, and the lock was opening. Then there was the matter of Hanno's son and the shotgun. That was the shotgun the man on the motorcycle planned to sell to Prober in Berlin. The young man who had sold Goering's badge to Jahn and given him the photo of the icon was the same man who had hanged both Mrs. McCracken and Ingeborg Mohr. There was little doubt that he was Hanno's son and the nephew of the German hero. But why had it taken him twenty-five years to reappear?

He stopped to eat at a chain restaurant right off the highway. He sat at the counter. The grills were behind a partition with an opening in it, to pass out the food. From behind it came the diabolical sound of a hundred items frying at once. Foerster's phone was still in his pocket. It was giving out weak little beeps, as though it were dying. At the end of the meal, he took it out and tried to turn it on, but it was dead.

He drove again until late. Just outside Columbus, he took a road paralleling the interstate until he found a motel. It was a shabby place, with peeling paint and a flickering neon vacancy sign. Behind the counter sat an East Indian man, reading a newspaper and having a cup of tea. He wore a turban and was very dark. The lower part of his face was shrouded in a beard. In the dim light, it was hard to tell what he looked like at all. Paying in cash and taking a key, Hans went to his room. Inside it was hot, and the toilet was running. Such things no longer mattered to him. He took off his shoes and lay down on the bed. It was ten-thirty when he closed his eyes and three when he opened them, and he knew it was time to go on.

CHAPTER 11

The Perfect Aryan

By dawn he was in Indiana, first approaching the ring-road around the capital city and then leaving it behind. The mountains of the previous day had given way to monotonous country that stretched on and on, like the steppes of Russia. There were farm buildings in a flat landscape. There were filling stations with convenience stores on the off-ramps. There were desolate motels, set in the middle of nowhere. The sky had grown leaden and ominous. It was a place where gigantic weather systems came whirling out of nowhere and flattened whole towns. To dispel heavy thoughts, Hans turned on the radio, but it offered no relief—all he could find was country music or incomprehensible street-chanting. At last the sights began to change. First came an area of abandoned, rusting factories, looking much like the parts of eastern Germany that had fallen into ruin after it had been swallowed by the West. Then came neighborhoods with shabby, unpainted houses and junked cars, giving way gradually to a vast city where a huge building rose up out of the mist—it was hard to believe it was real. Then as the city faded into his rearview mirror he found himself on a road many lanes wide, choked with traffic, with periodic lines at toll stations, where drivers threw money out their windows into metal baskets and then sped off. Toward eleven he pulled into a rest stop to buy gas and to revive himself with a cup of coffee. It had a restaurant built right out over the roadway where one could sit, sip a drink, and look down at the tops of speeding trucks only two or three meters below. A few kilometers on came the state line of Wisconsin with a welcome station, where he stopped to pick up a map of Milwaukee. Back in the car, at last he found a station playing classical music—a Bach concerto for four harpsichords. He listened for a while, but gradually it began to get on his nerves, like everything else. There was something inexorable and relentless about it, like a freight train moving down the tracks.

Soon he came to the outskirts of Milwaukee. First came an enormous landfill with trucks dumping loads of trash while thousands of gulls wheeled about in the air. Then came an airport, followed by a long, elevated road over an industrial district near the lake. Taking a turn to stay near the water, he found himself at a park by the lakefront, where he got out of the car near a breakwater that stretched far out into the lake. Near it was a narrow, sandy beach where tiny waves washed against the shore. He looked out at the water. The lake was so huge that it seemed like the sea, and far out on it was a ship. Walking a few hundred meters along a paved walk above the beach, he passed an old couple with a dog. All three of them were fat and slow. They looked like they'd been dropped there from the streets of Berlin. Hans got back in the car and drove farther up the lake. It was pleasant there—not a bad place for a Nazi to hide. Up a hill was an ancient water tower, and farther along came an area of vast houses set back from the road, some barely visible through the trees. A few minutes beyond that, he stopped the car at a point that gave a fine view up the shoreline. Far away the land jutted out into the water, forming a large bay. He got out and walked over to the edge of the bluff. The lake was eating it away, and several trees had tumbled down onto the beach. Some day the spot where he stood and the entire hillside as well would crumble into the lake.

By then it was well past one. Stopping at a motel, he went to the phones and looked up Schmidt in the residential directory. The Schmidts took up half a page, but there was no Hanno. Then in the commercial directory he looked up Harley-Davidson and Wisconsin Motors. First he tried Harley-Davidson, asked for personnel, and was promptly put on hold. Against a background of more country music came a bright female voice saying, "This year is our hundredth anniversary! Come to Milwaukee and join the celebration! And remember, think Harley and always wear your helmet!" In a few seconds, someone came on the line.

"Personnel," said a woman's voice, "this is Gretchen Stahl. How may I help you?" She had a flat, nasal way of speaking that was new to him.

"I'm an attorney looking for the heirs to a parcel of land in Germany. I'm calling because I was told that one of them might possibly have worked for your company, but that he probably retired fifteen or twenty years ago. Is there any way you could help me get in touch with him or his heirs?"

"A long-lost uncle died, huh? Wish that'd happen to me! Okay, let me look him up in our employee database. It goes all the way back to 1952. It'll only take a second. What's his name?"

"Schmidt. Hanno Schmidt."

"Schmidt. Schmidt. Let me see. Probably a dozen Schmidts in here. Schmidt, Arnold. Schmidt, Ben. Schmidt, Dale. Schmidt, Frank. Schmidt, Gustav. Schmidt, James. Schmidt, Larry. What was his first name again?"

"Hanno. H-a-n-n-o."

"Hanno. Huh. That's a new one. No, sorry, lots of Schmidts have worked here, but no Hanno. You sure that was it?"

"Pretty sure. Isn't there another motorcycle company here in town? Maybe that's where he worked."

"Wisconsin Motors? Well, good luck getting anything out of them! They wouldn't know a database from a nuclear reactor! Besides, half the people who work there probably don't give their right names—they're in the witness protection program." She laughed, and a moment later he was dialing the second number.

The phone rang and rang. At last someone answered. This time it was a man.

"Wisconsin Motors," he said. His voice was deep and wheezing, as though he had to force out every breath.

"Could I speak to someone in the personnel division?"

"I'm the personnel division," said the man.

"I'm looking for someone I think used to work there. His name was Hanno Schmidt. Any chance you can help me?"

"We don't give out information like that over the phone."

"You don't? Is there any way I could get it?"

"If I took a look at you, maybe I'd give it to you, maybe not. I gotta tell you something in advance. You better not be working for no collection agency. My boys don't like to be bothered on the job by people like that. They can get real nasty."

"No, no, it's nothing like that."

"Look, I'm real busy today. If you come right now, I can see you. Otherwise, forget it."

Wisconsin Motors was down in the industrial valley, near where a narrow river spilled dirty water into the lake. Overhead was the road, clogged with traffic, and in the valley was a railroad yard, with switch engines and strings of boxcars. The buildings were shabby and old. Most were of cream-colored brick, darkened with grime. Interspersed with a few rundown houses were foundries, warehouses, trucking companies, and taverns. Wisconsin Motors lay at the end of a dead-end street. Next to it, behind a chain-link fence topped with barbed wire, was a parking lot full of motorcycles and a few old cars, most with frames rusted out along the bottom. In the windowless wall facing the sidewalk was a door marked "deliveries." Inside it sat a man on a stool, behind a wire mesh window. He was chewing on a toothpick and reading a comic book. On his desk was a phone with a rotary dial. The man looked up.

"You got business?"

"Yes. I'm here to see the personnel manager."

"He expecting you?"

"Yes."

"Sign in." The man pushed a sheet of lined paper toward him, on a clipboard. Hans wrote down the name "Tom Bradley" and the time. The man took back the clipboard without looking at it. "Up the stairs," he said.

At the top of the stairway a door opened onto a metal catwalk that went out over the factory floor. Below, motorcycles in various stages of assembly moved down the line, past workers at their stations. Some were welding fenders onto the frames, others were putting seats and headlights into place, and at the far end of the line, a man was riding a cycle out the back door and up a ramp into a truck. Overhead the ducts of a huge ventilation system sucked the fumes out through the roof. An immense American flag covered the front wall.

At the end of the catwalk was an office, glassed in, looking out over the floor on all four sides. A stairway led down to the work area. Inside sat a man at an old metal desk. Hans knocked. The man looked up and nodded at him to enter. On his desk was an overflowing ashtray and a Styrofoam cup half full of coffee. The man was middle-aged and fat. The buttons were practically popping off his shirt.

"You the one that called?"

"Yes."

"What's your name?"

"Tom Bradley. I'm a lawyer from Trenton, New Jersey."

"You got a license or a certificate or something like that?"

"Sorry. Only back in my office."

"What do you want with this guy?"

"His wife was from Germany. Her brother died and left some property to her or her heirs. If nobody over here claims it, it goes to the government."

"The government, huh? Fucking governments are the same everywhere. What was his name again?" he said.

"Hanno Schmidt."

"The name sounds familiar. Can't say I remember him."

"Is there anybody else here who might?"

"Old Bronkowski, maybe. The toothless old fucker's been here since 1962. Let me call him up off the floor."

Through the glass in the office, Hans looked down at the assembly line. The man dialed a number and spoke into the phone. His voice blared out throughout the floor, and everyone looked up.

"Bronkowski, Bronkowski," he said. "Get your ass up here."

An old man, perhaps sixty, left one of the benches and came up the stairs, holding onto the handrail. The top of his skull was bald and shiny, but down his back hung a long, gray ponytail. His lips were collapsed over his gums, and his cheeks were deeply creased. Once inside, he looked at Hans suspiciously and wiped some grease off his hands on a rag in his back pocket. He wore a T-shirt with the words, "Wisconsin Motors—We Build the Best," across the chest, and beneath them, a skull and crossbones.

"Tell old Bronkowski who you're looking for. Only speak up. He don't hear so good."

"Mr. Bronkowski," Hans said, "I'm looking for a man named Hanno Schmidt. He or his heirs may have come into some property. He must have worked here last fifteen or twenty years ago."

"Hear that, Bronkowski? Hanno Schmidt. You know the guy?" The man was talking as loud as he could. It sounded as though his voice-box were about to rupture.

"Yeah, I know him. Worked next to him the first twelve years I was here."

"Have you seen him since?" said Hans.

"When people leave this place, they don't come back to visit."

"Do you know where he lives?"

"Used to live right off Capitol Drive. Don't know about now. Nothing but niggers up there now."

Meanwhile the man behind the desk had lit a cigarette. He was sucking on it and blowing the smoke out his nose. It was apparent he was starting to lose interest. "Think I should give this guy his address?" he said.

"What the fuck do I care?" The old man was already turning around, ready to go. On the back of the T-shirt was a demon riding a motorcycle and grabbing a bare-breasted blonde around the waist. Her face was distorted into a scream. Meanwhile, the man behind the desk was shuffling through a card file until he pulled one out.

"Here you go," he said. "Schmidt, Hanno. Hired 6/17/49. Retired 4/26/87. That's where he lives, at least when he left here." The man held out the card briefly, one dirty finger under the address, and put it back in the file. Then he turned back to his desk.

Schmidt's house was on a numbered street and easy to find. It was a bungalow, painted a dingy gray, with a hand-lettered "for sale" sign in the yard. The shades were pulled, and the driveway was empty. Last year's un-mowed grass and un-raked leaves littered the lawn, and stalks of weeds grew out of the cracks in the front walk. In the yard next door, an old black man was down on his knees on a piece of cardboard, digging with a trowel in his front garden. He wore rubber boots, work gloves, a knit cap, and a thick jacket. Hans went up to the door and began to rap on the glass. The old man looked up and shook his head.

"You can knock to Judgment Day, ain't nobody comin' to the door in *that* place."

"Isn't this the residence of Hanno Schmidt?"

"Used to be. He still owns it, but he don't live there no more."

"I see. Do you know where I could find him?"

The old man put down his trowel, rose uncertainly to his feet, and walked over to the edge of his property. He took off one of his work gloves, flexed his fingers, and winced.

"He's in one of them rest homes, up along the lake," he said. "That's where white folks go when they gets soft in the head. Black folks, they just stays home."

"That's what happened to him? He got soft in the head?"

"Yes, I reckon. He sure was actin' strange. Didn't seem to know where he was half the time. Used to wander right out in the street. Damn near got hit by a truck one time." The old man shook his head again and chuckled.

"Did you know him very well?

"Didn't know him at all. I lived next door to him for fifteen years and didn't talk to him once. He don't talk to no colored folk. We not good enough for him."

"Really? In fifteen years he never even said hello?"

"Not to me, he didn't. Every time he come out the house he just look straight ahead and go right to his car."

"How about his wife?"

"Never did see her. She died years ago, 'bout the time their boy went off to jail. They say that broke her heart. After that, she done just give up. She knew when he come out, she wouldn't be around no more. Thirty years, that's what they give him. They said he was a juvenile. He weren't no juvenile. His soul's as old as Satan's."

"Thirty years? He must have done something pretty bad."

"Yep, pretty bad, pretty bad. You don't go to jail for no thirty years for farting in church. Far as I'm concerned, jail was too good for him! They should have put him down like a dog! Down in Chicago, when I was a young'un, you did something like what he did, they strap you in the chair and make a light bulb out of your ass!"

"Really? What did he do?"

"He went and raped and murdered a sixteen-year-old girl. He was all drugged up, that's what they say. Cocaine, heroin, booze, pills, ain't nothin' he didn't try. But that ain't no excuse! You got to have something rotten down inside you to do what *he* did. Crazy, that's what he was! Dressed up like one of them Nazi soldiers and went after her with a knife. Cut her up so bad her own momma didn't know her. Left her hanging in her garage. Folks say she was a real pretty little thing. Lived in that house over there, right down the block." He pointed at a house across the street, much like all the others. "Colored family lives there now. They were the first colored to move into this neighborhood. After their little girl died the way she did, her parents, they didn't want no more to do with that place. They didn't care who they sold their house to. Schmidt, he'd have moved out, too, I reckon, but that boy's legal bills cost him all his money."

Hans remembered the story McCracken's daughter had told about him. "Was the son always so bad?" he said.

"Oh, he was trouble, all along. They threw his ass out of school when he was fifteen."

"Is he still in jail?"

"Nope. He done serve his sentence. Every day of it. When his time was up, they had to let him go."

"How long ago was that?"

"Must be eight, nine months. It was back in the summer. Turned up here one day on a motorcycle. Roared up and down the block just to let folks know he was back. He hadn't been here in thirty years. Back then there was nothing but white folks here. Must have been a shock for him to come back and find people like me around." He gave another low chuckle.

"He can't be so young anymore."

"That's right. He's forty-seven, forty-eight. Strong, though. He didn't have nothin' to do in prison but lift weights. That's what them boys do in there. And they all come out worse than when they went in."

"How about now? Does he ever come around?"

"Oh, he comes around all right. Rides his motorcycle by here every so often. Him and his friends. They in a gang—the White Aryan Knights Motorcycle Club; that's what it say on their jackets. A big old swastika on top of an American flag, that's their symbol. They like to come through here and scare the colored folk. One of them, he drove his motorcycle right over my lawn, really tore up the grass! They always wear them, you know, German helmets. Hadn't seen him in a while, but four, five days ago he come around by himself, on a brand new bike, a huge damn thing. Had the devil painted right on the gas tank. Want to show off to people, you know? Seems like all of a sudden he got some money. He's up to dirty business, that's for sure. Course after he took his daddy off to the rest home, he sold off every livin' stick of furniture in that house."

"Really?"

"Yes, sir! He sure was mean to that old man. Treated him worse than a dog! Old man used to whimper like a baby. I almost felt sorry for him. One day, though, the boy dragged him out the house and shoved him in a car—old man was kicking and screaming—and that was the last we saw of him. And that boy, he's crazy as ever! He's still up to his old tricks! You know what I seen a few weeks back? Him, through the window, dressed up in one of them Nazi uniforms, like the Hitler people wear in the movies, just like when he killed that girl. He gonna kill somebody else one of these days."

"I don't doubt it. This old Schmidt, did he have any friends?"

"Friends? He weren't too social. There was one old man, used to come by sometimes. They say, he was Schmidt's brother-in-law. Haven't seen him in a long while, though. He was just as bad as Schmidt! One time, he called my grandson a little nigger-boy, made him cry. Both of them, mean as snakes."

"What was his name?"

"Never did know that. But he was another one of them Germans. That's all they ever talked to each other. German, German! The whole damn family! Decent folk never knowed what they was talking about!"

"Old Schmidt, which rest home is he in?"

"Place called Lakeside Manor. Out on Port Washington Road. My sister's girl, she a nurse up there. He won't have nothin' to do with her. Won't hardly let her in his room. Still hates the colored. Everything gone in his brain 'cept that."

〜

Following the old man's directions, Hans drove down Capital Drive to the entrance to the Interstate and headed north. In a few kilometers he got off onto an access road. The rest home wasn't hard to find. It sat in the middle of a field, not far from the highway. There were piles of snow in the parking lot and a glaze of ice on the front walk, sprinkled with sand. The landscape all around was flat and dismal. Just inside the first of the double doors he was hit by a blast of heat. He wiped his feet on the corrugated rubber mat and went up to the desk. The woman at the desk was on the phone. Her tone was annoyed.

"I'm sorry, he died Tuesday and it's already Friday. After two days we charge storage of a hundred dollars a day. If you'd just give me the name of a local funeral home, I could have them pick him up. Yes, yes. I understand. I know it's a long way away. I know. I know. But he is your father, after all. Just a minute." At that she put her hand over the receiver, looked up at Hans and said abruptly, "Yes?"

"I'm here to see Mr. Hanno Schmidt."

"D-wing. End of the corridor and turn left. Just ask at the station there." Then she waved her hand dismissively and went back to her call.

Hans walked down the corridor. There were rooms to either side. Old people sat in the hall, in front of them, in wheelchairs. Some wore neck-braces, while others sat with their chins on their chests, drooling onto their shirts. A couple of them rolled their eyes up at him and smiled vacantly. In a large room halfway down the hall, a few people sat propped up on sofas in front of a television, watching a game show.

At the station in D-wing, a pretty young black woman was preparing medication and laying it out on a cart. There were syringes, pills, and liquids in little paper cups. Next to them was a logbook with names and room numbers.

"Excuse me," he said to her, I'm here to see Mr. Hanno Schmidt." She gave him an unfriendly look.

"What you want to see him for?"

"It's a legal matter."

"You're not a family member, then." She relaxed a bit.

"No. I'm an attorney."

"Just a moment." She rang a bell and in a minute a young black man walked up. He wore a light blue cotton shirt and pants and a hairnet.

"Cameron, can you take this gentleman to Mr. Schmidt? He's not a family member. He's an attorney."

"Sure thing." The man smiled and nodded his head.

As they walked down the hall, the man said, "Mr. Schmidt—you ever see him before?"

"Never in my life. What's he like?"

"Well, let me tell you," said the young man, "most of these old folks, they're sweet, they're no trouble, they're just off in their own little world. Not Mr. Schmidt, though. Old Hitler, that's what we call him. Anybody come near him, especially somebody like me, he try to scratch 'em and bite 'em. Finally we had to take his teeth away."

"Do you ever talk to him? Does he make sense?"

"Not to me he don't. He don't talk English no more."

"Think he'll recover?"

"Recover? There's only one way to recover from this place, brother."

He stopped and pointed into one of the rooms. "There he is," he said. "Mr. Schmidt. That big bruise on his head, that don't look good, I know it. But he threw hisself out of bed last week, and that's the God's truth. That's why we got to tie him down. And don't worry. We change his diaper, just ten minutes ago. He's clean as a baby." The man chuckled, turned around, and walked away.

The curtains in the room were drawn, but the fluorescent lights in the ceiling were as bright as the sun. It was very spare. There were no books, no newspapers, and no television. There was nothing but a chair, the bed, and next to it, a stand. Hans walked over to the bed and looked down. In it was an old man on his back. His wrists and ankles were loosely bound with leather straps to the frame. He was very thin. There was a gray stubble on his chin, and over his collapsed chest was a stained nightshirt. The bruise on his head was still dark, but had started to fade around the edges. Hans pulled up the chair and sat next to him. As he watched, words began to form on the old man's lips.

"Water, water," he said, in a whisper. The word he used was German, and he gave it a prolonged hiss in the middle.

"Herr Schmidt, I will give you water," said Hans. At the sounds of the German words, the old man opened his eyes and looked into his face. Hans filled a glass from a pitcher on the stand, cradled the old man's head, and helped him take a drink. Some of it dribbled from the corner of his mouth onto his neck. When the glass was drained, Hans dried his face with a tissue and gently lay his head back on the pillow.

"Who are you?" said the old man.

Hans leaned down close to his ear and said, "I am a messenger from Germany."

"Who has sent you?"

"Who do you think?"

"The Reichsmarschall!" His voice was weak but clear. His eyes grew bright. It was like a part of his brain had suddenly come alive.

"Yes. The Reichsmarschall. It is through him that I found you."

"Why are you here?"

"I have come seeking the hero."

"The hero who guards the secrets of the Aryan race!"

"Yes, that is the one!"

"Are you the new Siegfried, Prince of the North?"

"I am."

"Do you know the hero's real name?"

"Yes. Gottfried Lenz. That is his real name."

"Yes! And do you know the answers to the three questions?"

"I do. Do you know them yourself?"

"Yes, I do!"

"Then you must prove it to me, Schmidt. I must be careful. I must know if you are telling the truth."

At this the man lifted his head. "I know that the Jew is the enemy of man, that the Aryan fights the Jew, that the Siegfried League guards the holiest place in all the world."

"You speak truly, Schmidt. Now I want you to recount to me your deeds so that I can record them for all time. You yourself are a hero. There is a place for you in the sacred chronicles of our race. You helped the Reichsmarschall, didn't you?"

"Yes."

"What did he say to you?"

"He said, 'The time is coming, Schmidt. They will hang me! That is no way for a German hero to die! Schmidt, you must help me!'"

"And what did you do?"

"I did as he asked. I went into the town, to a man he sent me to. I wore my civilian clothes. Everyone thought I was a German! The man knew I was coming. He gave me a capsule for the Reichsmarschall."

"Why did you help him, Schmidt?"

"My father raised me to be true to the Fatherland. He was in the Kaiser's army in the Great War. He was wounded at Verdun. He only came to America because the Jews were ruining Germany, and he and his family were starving. But he never forgot his country. He worshipped the Führer. He told me that when I went to Germany, I should do what I could to help the German people."

"But what of the capsule? Did anyone help you?"

"Yes. An American. A soldier. A lieutenant."

"What was his name?"

"His name was McCracken."

"Why did he do it?"

"He did it for money. He agreed to help us. I gave him three diamonds from the Reichsmarschall. They were taken from Jews. He did what we asked."

"What was the plan? It is important that you tell me!"

The old man had lifted his head. Spittle drooled out the corner of his mouth. His words were clear but slow. "It was during the last inspection of the Reichsmarschall's cell, the night of the hanging. I put the capsule in the rim of the toilet just as the lieutenant stepped in front of me and blocked the view from the door."

"And after the Reichsmarschall died. What then? Had he asked anything else of you?"

"Yes. He asked me to seek out the hero. The bravest living member of the German race. This man had been charged by the Führer with a sacred task. The Reichsmarschall asked me to protect him, to give him aid. He asked me to bring him to America."

"Where was he?"

"Underground, in Berlin."

"Beneath the Rheinsberger Strasse."

"Yes!"

"It was noble of you to help him. How did this man know that the Reichsmarschall had sent you?"

"I had the Reichsmarschall's Golden Party Badge. That was the proof."

"I must see it also. Where is it now?"

"It is gone. My son stole it. My son is the great shame of my life. I should have killed him in the crib!"

"What did your son do with it?"

"He sold it to a man who had a shop near Washington. A man who bought and sold things which should never be bought and sold! Because of my son, he could have found out who we were! He would have exposed us. He was a traitor to Germany! He was a tool of the Bolsheviks!"

"So you and the hero went to get the Golden Party Badge back."

"Yes! We beat my son until he told us what he'd done with it."

"Then you went to see this man and you killed him."

"He deserved it! He had other things as well—the sacred patrimony of our race. We held a summary court martial, according to SS regulations. We sentenced him to death, and we carried out that sentence! Like the traitor he was, he died by the rope!"

"And you recovered the Golden Badge."

"Yes! But when my son got out of prison, he stole it again. He tortured me until I told him where it was! Now it is gone forever."

"Still, Schmidt, you have done your duty. And so has the hero. Now I must seek him out. It is I who will take up his mission. That is why I am here. You must tell me how to find him. The last I know of him, he was beneath the streets of Berlin! Let me show you something of great value. I am here to award it to you in the name of the Führer. Once I have found the hero, I will return and present you with it."

From his briefcase Hans pulled the box with his grandfather's Knight's Cross, opened it, and held it up for the old man to see. The old man's fingers caressed it. Tears came to his eyes and rolled down his cheeks.

"Schmidt, Schmidt, but to give it to you I must first find the hero. Where is he?"

The old man's voice had dropped to a whisper. Out in the hall a cart clattered by. An old woman on the arm of a nurse shuffled by the door. Hans leaned forward and put his ear to the old man's mouth. "He lives in a house on Maryland Avenue in the suburb of Shorewood. It is on the corner, on the side toward the lake. When you see the backyard you will know you have come to the right place. It is a bit of the Fatherland. He and I created it together. You must go to him at sundown. He is ill. He has little strength left. Only enough to fulfill his final task! His daughter speaks for him. When she takes you to see him, you must tell him that I have done my duty!"

"I will, Schmidt!"

"He will give you that which you seek. I have seen it just once! It is the badge of your office! When you hold it in your hand, you must pull the sword from the dragon's heart. Only you are allowed to do that! Now leave me and go!"

CHAPTER 12

Siegfried

Maryland Avenue was a tree-lined street through a residential neighborhood a few blocks from the lake. Along it were middle-class houses with small yards. Already it was late afternoon, and just a sliver of the sun peaked above the horizon. Hans slowed down at every corner, looking into the backyards. Most were no more than well-trimmed lawns, still brown from the winter. In others were children's toys—swing sets, sandboxes, tricycles, and little wagons. At last he came to a house with a backyard unlike the rest. Behind a low, picket fence he could see a raked gravel path, carefully laid-out beds of daffodils, a fountain, and a garden dwarf. In the middle of it was a small garden house with bright red shutters. It looked exactly like a plot in a garden colony in Berlin. The house itself was a well-kept bungalow with a porch and trimmed bushes in the front yard. The curtains were drawn.

Hans walked up the walk and onto the porch. Just as the sun dipped below the horizon, he rang the bell. From inside came the barking and growling of dogs. One of the curtains drew aside for a second, and then he could hear bolts being drawn back, and at last the door opened. Facing him stood a trim woman in her late thirties, her blonde hair in two braids that fell to her shoulders. Her cheekbones were high, and her chin was sharp. Her eyes were piercing and blue. Behind her, propped in the corner, was an automatic machine-pistol. Behind her was the control panel for an alarm system with a flashing yellow light.

At her side were two German shepherds, their teeth bared and their ears back. Hans addressed her in German.

"I have come to see Gottfried Lenz."

"Who are you?"

"Do you not know?"

"Yes! You are the new Siegfried! The anointed one of the snow-blond hair and icy eyes. The Keeper of the Flame of the Aryan Race. You have come for the sword, Notung."

"Yes."

"Welcome, hero. It is as my father said. Enter!" As she stepped aside, she spoke to the dogs. "Reinhardt! Heinrich! Stay!" They crouched in the front hall and glowered at him, their lips curled.

He stepped into the room. It was a living room in an orderly working-class household. It was spotless. The surface of the mahogany coffee table had been polished to a high gloss. Lace doilies covered the arms of the green plush chairs. A knit afghan lay folded on the sofa, and there were Persian rugs on the floor. On one wall was a cuckoo clock, and next to it, a plaque from Wisconsin Motors naming Gottfried Hartmann as worker of the year, 1972. On another wall was a painting of a lake in the Bavarian Alps, with a church on the distant shore. On a side-table by the sofa was a photograph of two couples standing in front of the Brandenburg Gate with the Wall just behind them. The men stood tall and straight, with the women between them, smiling and holding hands. They were dumpy and middle-aged and looked alike. On the mantle was a figure of Meissen porcelain, an eighteenth-century woman in a hoop skirt and tall, white wig, holding a parasol, while at the edge of her skirt stood a little terrier on its hind legs. Over the figure hung a picture frame covered by a black curtain, on which was embroidered a gold Maltese Cross. This was the room where the photograph he had seen in the bunker had been taken. The woman before him was the little girl who had held out in one hand the icon of the Siegfried League, and in the other, the necklace with the Star of David.

"Are you the daughter of Gottfried Lenz?"

"I am."

"Where is your father?"

"My father is here. But he is not well. I speak for him. He sees no visitors except those I take to him. Once you and I have talked, we will go to him." She pointed to the sofa. "Sit there," she said, "but make no sudden moves. If the dogs think you are a danger to me, they will tear you apart!"

"What do you fear?"

"There is someone who would come here to rob me. But he is afraid. He knows the dogs would kill him. I have trained them with his scent! Whenever I leave the house, I take one with me and leave the other here, on guard."

She sat on the other end of the sofa and looked at him intently.

"Where are you from?"

"I am from Berlin."

"The capital of the Reich! I know it well. As a child I went there every summer. My grandparents lived there, in Neukölln."

"You grew up speaking the mother tongue?"

"Yes. I was kept separate from other children. I was raised in the sacred mysteries of our race."

"As was I. It is proper that a German child be so raised. But tell me about the one who threatens you."

"He is my cousin. He is five years older than I. His mother and my mother were sisters. As children we were close. He was raised like I was. Our storybooks were about traveling Jews who kidnapped children and cut out their hearts. We played games our fathers taught us—games other children did not play. Pin the nose on the Jew. Hunt down the partisans in the forest. Hang the traitors who betray the Fatherland. Defend the sacred borders of the Reich. But my cousin was not like me. He changed! He forgot our ideals! He was corrupted by America! He is a thief and a murderer. He polluted his blood with drugs. But you! Tell me about you! You're a good German boy, aren't you? No Jews in your family?"

"No. There are no Jews in my family. I come from peasant stock in the Mark Brandenburg, where my family has dwelt on the land as long as records stretch back. We were farmers, blacksmiths, and harness-makers."

"Then look at me!" She leaned forward and examined him closely; she touched his face. "You haven't got that crafty look. A Jew can't look a German in the eye! But show me proof of your racial purity!"

Slowly opening his briefcase while looking toward the dogs, Hans took out the SS Suitability Certificate his aunt had given him, along with the family tree. On both were the seal of the Third Reich and the word "Approved." She looked at them, held them to the light, and handed them back.

"Many German families have such documents. Even some who live here. But can you show me proof that you are from a line of heroes?"

"Yes," said Hans, taking out the cedar box and the photograph. "This is my grandfather's Knight's Cross. Here is a picture of my father, as a boy, with the Führer. It was a proud moment. My father taught me what it means to be a German."

"The prophesy taught me by my father says that the hero must have shed blood for Germany. Have you shed blood for Germany?"

"I have."

"Then show me your wound!" Just as he had for Breitbach, Hans lifted his shirt and showed her his scar. She leaned forward and touched it, gently pressing down on the center.

"It is exactly like the scar of my father! But still, I must be careful! You must prove yourself to me! You must answer three questions! They are the questions taught me by my father, who learned the answers directly from our Führer."

"I do so willingly."

"First, what is the Jew?"

"The Jew is the enemy of mankind."

"Correct! Now, who fights the Jew?"

"The Aryan fights the Jew."

"You answer true, hero. Now, the last question. Who guards the room where the sacred relics of our struggle lie hidden?"

"The Siegfried League guards that room."

"Yes! That room is a sacred and holy place, deep beneath the capital of the Reich. If the Jews were to find it, they would profane and destroy it—the ultimate triumph of the world poisoners over the Aryan race! But the new hero will guard it until Germany shall rise again! Now you must pass the tests to determine if you are the one! Follow me!"

She arose and led Hans down a hall past two closed doors to a third, which she opened and then closed behind them. The shades in this room were pulled, too. She turned on a switch, and bright lights shown from the ceiling. It looked like a physician's examining room. Against the wall was a metal cabinet with a glass-fronted door. Laid out on white cloths on its shelves were medical instruments, and in a bookcase next to it were several anatomical texts. On one wall was a color chart, in German, labeled "The Noses of Man," with sets of noses labeled "Aryan," "Mediterranean," "Slav," "Mongol," "Negro," and "Jew." In the center of the room were two metal stools with revolving seats, and beneath one was an irregular, faint stain. Outside the door he could hear the dogs sniffing about and growling. She took a white smock from a hook on the door and put it on.

"Sit here!" she said, moving one of the stools in front of him. "Let your arms hang at your side!" A metal rod rose from the back of the seat, and at the top were padded clamps. As he sat, she placed the clamps against his temples and tightened them.

"Look straight ahead," she said. "You must hold very still!" She leaned forward and looked into his eyes with a little light, while holding up next to them a series of cards and looking from his eyes to the cards before laying one aside. Next from the cabinet, she took a pair of calipers and a book, which she opened on a counter beside her.

"These are from the Racial Institute in Berlin," she said, "as is this book of measurements, diagrams, and instructions." With the calipers she measured his skull, his nose, his lips, the distance between his eyes, and his ears, each time pausing to write the results on a form on a clipboard. When she had finished, she said, "Now, show me the skin on the underside of your arm." Again, she held a series of cards, placing them against his skin and then laying one aside. Last, with a silver scissors, she cut a lock of his hair and compared that against another set of cards as well. Then, with the clipboard and the cards in front of her, she did a series of calculations and compared them to a chart in the book. At the end, she closed the book and put the clipboard and the cards away.

"You have passed the test!" she said. "All of your measurements fall at the exact mean for a true Aryan. It is as though the Institute used you for their model!"

"Why have you done this?"

"You understand that I must take great care. A false pretender came here before you, just two days hence. He was sent by my cousin. He was an agent of the world poisoners, the enemies of mankind. He wanted the sacred symbol. He understood nothing! He offered me money for it, the swine! He offered me even more if I would tell him the location of the sacred room! I told him I would do as he asked, but that I wanted to take his measurements first. That is how I knew who had sent him. He sat where you sat. I compared his eyes and skin against my cards. I took a lock of his hair. I measured his skull. I measured the width of his nose and the thickness of his lips. I did the calculations and compared the results with the tables in the book. He failed! His nose was not the nose of an Aryan! Nor were his eyes! They were a strange color I could not match to my cards! Nor was his hair! It was dyed! I saw that it was dark at the roots! And it was the curly hair, not of an Aryan, but of a Semite! The blood in his veins was tainted! His German was tainted, just like his blood! He spoke with an accent that reeked of the language of the world poisoners."

"Where is this man now?"

"He is here!"

With this she spun his seat around and threw open the door to a closet. Slumped in the corner sat a man, about forty-five, with short, wavy, dark blond hair. The bridge of his nose was concave, no doubt the result of an accident. One of his eyes was partly open, and his lips had curled back from his teeth. His chin rested on his chest, and his shirt was caked with blood. It was clear what had happened to him. His dyed hair and his broken nose had cost him his life. At the end of the test, as he had sat on the very stool Hans sat on now, she had slit his throat.

"I expected him to come. My father told me that the true hero would be preceded by a false pretender. He learned that from our Führer. The Führer knew all this from a man who could read the stars. The Führer told my father that the true Siegfried would come at sundown before two days had passed. It has happened just as the Führer said! Now, arise!"

Hans stood, and she stood also and looked him in the eyes.

"Hero, there is a task that I shall set you. You must perform it before my father will see you. If you fail, it will cost you your life."

"Very well. What is it?"

"You must take my revenge for me. It is your duty! My cousin. It is he who sent the false pretender. His crimes are many! When I was a child, he defiled me! You must go to him. You will find him under the viaduct near the lake. He works for a wrecking company there. It is just beyond the Coast Guard station. He is there every night. You must kill him and bring me his head! Only then will my father receive you. Only then will he give you the key to the secret chamber."

"Your cousin. How will I know him?"

"He is strong. His chest is wide, and his arms are thick. His hair is the color of mine. In his ear he wears an earring shaped like a coiled snake. He walks with a limp. His knee is not bone, but steel!"

From the drawer in the cabinet she took a dagger. The dagger had an ivory handle with a silver swastika set into it.

"To kill him, you must use this! I have cleaned and sharpened it. Yesterday it was wet with the blood of the false pretender, and tonight it will be wet with the blood of the traitor! You must show it to him. He will know what it is for! And then you must stab him in the heart! But this dagger won't be enough for you to bring me what I ask."

Taking a hacksaw from one of the shelves, she handed it to him and said, "Just as his arms are thick, his neck is thicker! Take this. It is a surgical saw, used in dissections at the Racial Institute. You will need it! Now go, and may the spirit of our Führer go with you!"

In silence she led him to the front door. As he left, he could hear the bolts snap into place behind him. He walked to the car, the dagger in his belt and the saw beneath his coat. The sun had set long ago. Clouds had come in from the west and a wind was blowing. A few cars went by. Through a lighted window next door, he saw a family seated around a table, eating a meal. Up the street a man wheeled a trash can out to the curb. A jogger in a sweatshirt ran by, the hood pulled up against the cold. All around him, ordinary life was going on. Driving to the lake, he turned right and headed toward the viaduct. He was hardly aware of time passing or of the direction he took. In a few blocks, he bore to the left and entered the drive that went along the shore. To his right, the city was ablaze with lights, but to his left the lake was a black void. He drove out onto the viaduct, over the industrial area where Schmidt and Lenz had once worked. At the end he drove down the exit and turned beneath it. Before him was the lake and the Coast Guard station. The viaduct loomed above. A few hundred meters away, he could see the lights of the wrecking company. In the other direction were the lights of a distant neighborhood. With his headlights off, he drove behind one of the pillars that held up the structure and parked.

He sat for a moment, looking out at the water. He felt quite calm. Getting out of the car, he lay out the tools he would need for the night and put them in a bag. He took off his street shoes and put on his running shoes. Then he took his grandfather's Knight's Cross out of its box and put the ribbon around his neck. A cold rain was falling, mixed with a few flakes of wet snow. A mist hung over the lake. He walked down the road toward the wrecking company, passing more pillars on the way. The road was muddy with deep ruts. There were puddles everywhere, with a skim of ice at the edge.

The wrecking company was surrounded by a high, chain-link fence topped with coils of concertina wire. Its perimeter was lit with powerful lights mounted on steel poles. Spaced along the fence were signs with, "No Entry!" in large, black letters. The gate was chained and locked with a large padlock. Behind it were row after row of wrecked trucks and buses—they stretched to the other side of the viaduct and beyond. Beyond that he could see railway coal cars, piles of coal partly covered with snow, and the stacks of a power plant. A few meters inside the gate was a tarpaper shack, and parked before it was a motorcycle—an immense white machine with chrome trim. The lights were on in the shack. He took the binoculars from his pocket and lifted them to his eyes. The image they gave him was crisp and clear. Through the window he could see a man with a beard and brown hair down to his shoulders. He wore jeans, a leather jacket, and heavy black boots. He sat with his chair tipped against the wall, a beer in his hand. On the floor beneath him was a row of empty bottles. Behind him on the wall was a Nazi battle flag and a banner with a swastika over an American flag. On it were the words, "White Aryan Motorcycle Club, Milwaukee, Wisconsin." Hans walked the length of the fence, looking for a weak spot—there was none.

He stood beneath the viaduct, his back to one of the pillars, waiting. The minutes went by, and the wind picked up even more. Paper and plastic bags blew about. Gusts carried them high in the air and out over the lake. In the shack the man had barely moved. In a few minutes—it was hard to say how long he had been there—he heard a low rumbling. In the distance were four bright, moving lights with a row of flashing yellow lights above them. He stepped behind the pillar and watched from the shadows. A huge tow truck came into view, splashing through the puddles and churning up the mud. As it went by, he saw it had another truck in tow—a delivery truck from a laundry, its front smashed in and the door on the driver's side hanging open. It pulled up to the gate and stopped. The driver got out, limped to the gate, unlocked it, and swung it open. As the man climbed back into the truck, Hans ran forward, crouched low, jumped through the door of the towed truck, and threw himself on the floor. The seat had been knocked off its bolts, and glass from the shattered windshield lay all around. Jammed beneath the brake pedal was a shoe. The truck jerked forward and stopped again, and then came a blast on the horn. The man ran out of the shack, pulled the gate shut, and re-locked it. He passed no more than three meters from Hans's head.

He shouted up at the driver, "Kurt, whatcha got?"

The driver leaned out the window and shouted back. "Dumb fuckin' nigger hit the wall on the expressway. Motherfucker's fat black ass shot right through the windshield. Eight-wheeler squashed him like a bug. Cops said the fucker's guts came shooting right out his mouth. Shit, I wished I'd of seen that." They both laughed. The other man jumped in the cab. The engine roared, and the truck jerked forward again. At the back fence it stopped. Hans jumped out and slipped between two rows of wrecked vehicles. He stopped by a yellow and black bus marked "Milwaukee County School System." It was smashed in on the side, nearly folded in two, as though it had been hit by a train and dragged it along the tracks. On the ground nearby was a heavy tire iron, nearly a meter long. Hans picked it up and looped the bag with the saw under his belt. He could hear the whir of a motor as the driver lowered the delivery truck, and the clank of a chain as the other man unhooked it. Then they got back in the cab and drove to the front. Hans watched through the binoculars. They got out and slammed the doors. The driver walked over to the cycle and lingered near it. He patted its seat and ran his fingers gently over its gas tank, as though it were alive. They went into the shack. Then all was silent.

Gripping the tire iron, Hans walked around to a window on the side. The man with the long hair was in his chair, his back to the wall.

The driver sat at the desk, facing the door. Hans looked at him through the binoculars. He had a broad chest and coarse, brutish features. His face was pockmarked, and his eyes were pig-like slits. His arms were thick and blue and red with tattoos. He wore an SS helmet and was cleaning a shotgun, which he had open, looking down the barrel. Over him on the wall was the poster for a neo-Nazi rock group. It showed three men in SS uniforms playing guitars, while in the background were guard towers and shadowy figures behind a barbed wire fence. Beneath them were the words, "The Buchenwald Boys, In Concert, Skokie, Illinois, June 4." A boom box, perched on a shelf above the desk, was blaring mechanical sounds and raw, insistent screams. Nearby was a space heater, and on the floor were weights and barbells.

Hans watched them through the window. By standing in the shadows a couple of meters back, he was out of sight. Fifteen minutes went by, then ten more. The man with the long hair had finished one beer and opened another. Hans waited for something to happen. Finally the man with the long hair stood up and lurched to the door. He walked out into the yard, then turned and went between two rows of wrecked vehicles, piled one on top of another, their roofs crushed. Hans followed silently a few paces behind. Halfway down, the man stopped and fumbled with his pants. A few seconds later, a stream of urine was splashing into a puddle. Hans waited. As the man bent forward to zip his fly, Hans stepped forward. He raised the tire iron with both hands and brought it down with all his strength on the man's skull. The man fell face down into the puddle. His fingers clutched the ground, making furrows in the mud. Hans put his foot on the man's neck and pushed his head down into the water. A few bubbles came up and then stopped.

Hans stood a moment, listening. A slick of oil glistened on the puddle where the man lay. It was quiet, save for the wind and the faint sounds of traffic on the viaduct above. In the distance came the whistle of a train. He walked down the row toward the end. Beyond the rows of wrecked vehicles lay a field of cement blocks and slabs, stretching at least thirty meters to the fence. They were piled one on top of the other. Some had steel rods sticking out of them. They were all kinds of shapes and sizes. One was like a pillar, another like an arch. They looked like the remains of the structure the viaduct had replaced.

There were narrow passages between them and hundreds of nooks and crannies. They were like the ruins of a bombed city. The only light came from one of the spotlights fixed to a pole near the fence. On the other side was a cinder road. A lone dump truck came down it, rattling and splashing through the potholes. It weaved back and forth, and he could hear the grinding of the gears. It was like it was being driven by a child. As it went by, he could see through its window a shadowy form and the glow of a cigarette. Hans watched until its taillights were out of sight.

Keeping to the shadows, he made his way through the rubble to the fence and moved along it toward the front gate. The ground was wet. He could feel the water seeping into his shoes. The lights at the front gate made it nearly bright as day. The gate was lower than the rest of the fence, but still close to three meters high. Instead of concertina wire, it was topped only by a few strands of barbed wire. It occurred to him that keeping the man inside was more important than getting out. They would fight to the death like two scorpions in a bottle. Stepping up to the padlock, he took some dirt between his thumb and forefinger and pushed it into the key slot; with a sliver of wood he jammed it in further. Then he pushed the sliver into the lock as far as it would go and broke it off.

Silently he walked back toward the shack. Several wrecked police cars were parked in a row facing the side, their trunks to the fence. Some had the doors smashed in, and others had the hoods up and the engines missing. He found a spot between two where he could see both the window and the porch. He crouched down and waited. The cycle was parked right outside the front door where the man could look out and see it. It was a beautiful machine. Its chrome glinted in the light from the shack. Its seat was black leather, its side compartments snowy white. The head of Satan on the gas tank was as black as tar, with red eyes and fiery nostrils. How often the man must have lain in his cell, dreaming of it. It was like a lover—better than any woman.

He again looked through the window. The man in the helmet was still working on the shotgun. He was polishing the barrel. He had a rag and a little jar into which he kept dipping it. From time to time, he held the gun to the light to admire his work. Hans could see there was carving on the stock and engraving on the barrel. As time went on, the man worked more and more slowly. Finally he pushed the rag and the jar aside and just stared ahead, the shotgun on his knees. Minute after minute passed, and the man barely moved. Finally Hans stood up and threw a rock so that it bounced on the porch and through the door. The man jumped up. From the drawer of the desk he took a handful of shotgun shells. He put two in the chambers and the rest in his pocket. Then he limped to the door, gripping the gun and pointing it ahead. He stood on the porch and looked around. Hans crouched back between the cars.

"Jerry, you stupid fuck," he called out into the yard, "what the fuck you doin'?"

There was silence. The man moved a few steps out into the yard. Hans could hear his footfalls in the mud. The man took off his helmet and listened. Crouching down, Hans looked at him through the binoculars. When he turned his head Hans could see the glint of an earring—he could almost make out the shape of a snake. "Jerry," the man called out again, this time louder, "where the fuck you at?"

Hans stared at the man's head. What did something like that weigh? Five kilos? Ten? Could he really get it off that body and put it in a bag? He'd already killed one man that night, but this was worse. If he could cut off a man's head, couldn't he do anything? Couldn't he rip a child from its mother's arms and dash its brains out on a rock? Couldn't he club an old woman and shove her into the gas chamber?

The man put the helmet back on and adjusted the chin strap. He peered out into the dark. He walked back and forth, stopping to listen. At last he spoke. His voice was tense and low.

"Whoever's out there, don't fuck with me," he said. "I'll fuckin' kill you. Who the fuck is it?"

Hans lay down and cast his voice beneath the car. "It is I," he said. His words were German.

For a moment the man froze. Then he turned slowly toward where Hans lay hidden. Hans could see the man's boots pointing in his direction. The man spoke again. His voice was lower.

"What do you want?"

"You know what I want. Did you not expect me? Did you not know I would come some day? You are a traitor to the Fatherland. You are a murderer and a thief. Sentence has been passed on you. I am here to carry it out."

"Sentence? Who has passed sentence on me?"

"All those you have betrayed. Your father. Your uncle. Your cousin. They have sent me. They have given me a dagger. They say you will know what it is for."

"Fuck you! Fuck you all!"

The man crouched down and peered toward him under the car. He lay forward on his stomach and put the shotgun to his shoulder. Hans could see it pointing right at him. He rolled out of the way just as there were two blasts. The car rocked; a tire exploded; part of the frame was blown away. He heard the click as the man cracked the gun open and put two more shells into the breach.

Hans rose to his feet. Bent low, he ran around the back of the shack. There were two orange bursts of flame as the man fired again. The pellets, like metal rain, hit the cars. Behind him the motorcycle roared to life. Hans ran toward the far end of the yard, past row after row of wrecked buses and trucks rising high over his head. He ran down between the last two rows and stopped. Just a few paces away were the ruins. He stood and waited.

The roar of the engine grew louder. The cycle was going up one row and down another, looking for him, working its way closer. Soon it was only one row away. In the gaps between the vehicles, Hans could see its light moving slowly by. At the far end it turned into the row where he stood. It stopped. Hans stepped into the light and faced it. His legs were apart, and his hands were on his hips. Out of the mist, the light moved slowly toward him. He could see the man, one hand on the handlebars, the other with the shotgun. Hans took a deep breath of the cold, damp air. He fully expected to die. What did it mean to be a hero, anyway? Was it no more than a delusion and a mental trick? Was it just seeing one's place in the universe and knowing that whether one lives or dies, it's all the same?

The rest of the world dropped away. He felt apart from the events of his life. His childhood, his years on the border, his work for State Security—none of it meant anything. He had entered a place where nothing could touch him. Perhaps it was the place Gottfried Lenz had been. Perhaps his grandfather had been there, too.

The motorcycle got closer. Its light shined in his eyes. He felt the vibrations of its engine in his chest. Now it was only a few meters away. The man stopped. Now he gripped the shotgun in both hands. He leveled it and sighted along the barrel. Hans stepped back, turned, and melted into the ruins.

He entered a passage between the blocks. He moved down it quickly. It was random, formed only by how the blocks had fallen. Sometimes it twisted to the right, sometimes to the left. In some places it was blocked by crumbling cement that he had to climb over. In others, it was so narrow he had to turn sideways to get through. On either side were other passages. He tried a few. Some went on and on, and others ended in a wall. It was like a maze. In places the piled-up blocks rose four or five meters high. The wind had come up. It whistled through the arches in the viaduct above. The tones were deep and hollow. It was almost like a choir. The pole with the light swayed. There were moving shadows everywhere. They seemed to creep through the ruins and peer around the corners. They were like gaunt, starving people with sunken cheeks and sunken eyes. They seemed to reach out to him in their misery.

He kept moving, twisting and turning, following one passage, then another. Deep inside he came to an open area, no more than a few meters square. The ground was bare; it looked smoothed away. On one side grew a tree, hugging the blocks, its trunk no bigger around than his wrist. He stopped and listened.

In the distance he could hear the engine of the motorcycle idling. Over it came a voice, drifting toward him on the wind. Its words were English. "I know who you are," it said. "You're that fucking border guard. You killed Jerry, you fucking red bastard. I'm coming in after you. I'm gonna blow your fucking balls off!"

Hans cupped his hands to his mouth. He turned in the direction of the sound. "Speak German, if you still can," he said. "Do you want to die with American words on your lips?"

A few minutes passed. He left the open area and moved down another passage, slowly. At any corner he might be blown away. Now the wind had died down. Nothing moved. The shadows were frozen in place. It was silent, save for the distant rumbling of the cycle. His mind was cleansed. He saw only what was around him. He thought only of the task ahead.

He turned into a narrow passageway. It ended in a few paces. Ahead, the piled-up blocks formed a staircase. Each step was no more than a few centimeters wide. He started up it, pressing himself against the blocks and turning his feet sideways to get a better hold. His ankles ached; every step up was agony. A railing was set into a block on the top. He grabbed hold and pulled himself up. At the highest point, he was on his feet. He was at least four meters off the ground. He could see out in every direction over the yard. It was like being back in his watchtower on the frontier. He was alert, just as he had been then. He scanned the ruins. He looked for the slightest contrast; the slightest change.

The man must be down there, creeping around. There was no sign of him. The motorcycle was at the end of the row, its lights on, its engine running. For several minutes, there was nothing. Then he saw the hint of a shadow moving forward. It fell on one block, disappeared, then reappeared on another. Then it was gone again. A few minutes passed. At last, there it was, again. Now he could see the top of the helmet and the glint of the shotgun. The man was working his way forward. In a few more steps, he would reach the open area.

Hans moved over the blocks. There were gaps between them, sometimes more than a meter wide. Each time he came to one, he sprang silently across. The blocks had rough surfaces, so the footing was good. The light on the pole was ahead of him, and his shadow was behind. He saw the helmet again, a few meters on. Then it stopped. He could see it turning. He stepped down and hid behind a block. When he rose, the helmet had moved on, and now he could see the man, the shotgun pointed ahead, his head bobbing up and down as he limped down the passage. Hans crept closer, his prey in constant sight. Soon he had closed to within five meters. Now the man was just entering the open area. In the faint light, Hans could see the vapor of the man's breath. The prize was nearly in his grasp. He tensed, he looked ahead, and he judged each place his foot would fall. He touched the Knight's Cross and called on his grandfather for strength, not for his evil deeds, but for his mad ferocity. He crouched down, his left foot forward and his right foot back, like the runner he had been in his youth. In his mind he saw the field judge raising his pistol. The sinews in his leg tightened. He heard the crack of the shot. He sprang from one block to the next. At the fourth step, he leapt out into the open space and landed on the man's back. The man fell forward, dropping the gun. Hans grabbed the helmet and yanked it back. The chin strap was around the man's throat. He began to twist the helmet, tightening the noose. The man lifted his hands weakly to the strap. His breath had stopped. Why not keep twisting and give to him the death he had given others? But that was not the way he was to die. Abruptly Hans let go and jumped back. He picked up the shotgun and pointed it at the man. The man rose to his knees. He was shaking his head and breathing again in great gasps. He pulled off the helmet and dropped it to the ground. He struggled to his feet and faced Hans. Then he turned and staggered into a passageway. Hans heard his gasps receding into the distance.

Hans braced himself on the tree and climbed up the blocks until he could just see over the top. The man was just coming out of the ruins. He got on the motorcycle. It roared to life. A black cloud of exhaust hung in the air. Hans watched its taillights as it raced toward the front gate. He pulled out the binoculars and lifted them to his eyes. He saw the man stop at the gate and get off the motorcycle. He watched as the man found a key and began to struggle with the lock. He pushed it and pulled it, but it held fast.

Hans left the ruins and walked toward the gate, holding the shotgun. There was no hurry. He felt like someone else was taking the steps. Soon he was just a few paces away. The man saw him and dropped the lock. He gripped a bar of the fence and started to climb. Hans moved closer. He lifted the shotgun and pointed it at the man's waist. The slightest pressure would blow him in two. The man looked back. "Herr Leutnant," he said. "Don't do it. Don't shoot." His words were German. Hans lowered the gun. He turned it toward the motorcycle and emptied both barrels into the engine. The motor's roar turned to a whine. The headlight flickered and went out. Then all was silent. Hans let the gun fall to his feet. He felt the dagger in its sheath at his belt and gripped its hilt. He pulled it out and held it high.

The man was breathing hard. His breaths were almost sobs. He put his foot on the chain with the padlock. Now his head was level with the barbed wire. He gripped it and pulled himself up. Hans could see the barbs going into his flesh. He could see the blood running down his wrists. The man's foot found a crossbar. He struggled higher. He had one leg nearly over the top. As he pulled himself up, Hans jumped up, grabbed him by the belt and wrenched him free. He fell off the fence and hit the ground on his back. Air exploded from his lungs. Blood dripped from his fingers, and two lines of flesh were gone from his hands. One leg lay twisted beneath him. He lay there, blinking stupidly. Hans loomed over him, the dagger raised. "You hanged Ingeborg Mohn! You stole money from the state! In the name of the German Democratic Republic, I execute on you the sentence of death!" With all his strength, he plunged the blade into the man's chest.

Everything slowed down. The man looked exhausted; his eyes were dull, and his face chalky white. Through his parted lips Hans could see his broken, rotting teeth. Blood began to trickle out of the corner of his mouth. His breath came slower and slower. Then a wave of blood poured over his lips. As Hans watched, his face turned blue, his eyelids fluttered, and he died.

He walked back between the cars to where he had left the bag with the saw. What came next seemed simple enough. He pulled the dagger from the man's chest and lay it on the ground. Then he rolled the man onto his stomach. He placed the teeth of the saw on the back of the man's neck. His neck muscles were massive. In death they bulged out like knots. The saw ripped through the tendons and the blood vessels and into the bone. The handle was sticky, and his hands were covered with blood. Just beyond the bone the saw got stuck. To free it, he used the dagger to cut away some of the flesh. At last the head fell forward from the trunk into the mud. He grabbed it by the hair and put it in the bag; then he dropped in the saw and dagger and tied it shut.

He picked up the shotgun. In the light from the spotlight he looked at it. It was beautiful. The stock was polished mahogany, and the barrel was inlaid with silver and gold. On it was the scene of a pack of dogs cornering a wild boar. The inscription read, "To Reichsmarschall Hermann Goering, the Reich's Greatest Sportsman, from the Reich Hunting Association, on the occasion of his forty-fifth birthday, January 12, 1938." He carried it over to a row of crushed vehicles piled on one another. He found a gap between them. Barrel first, he pushed the shotgun into it until it dropped down and disappeared.

At the gate the key was still in the lock, halfway in. He tried to push it in or pull it out but it was hopelessly stuck. He went back to the cycle and pulled the key from the ignition. There were other keys with it. He carried the bag over to the tow-truck and climbed into the cab. He tried the keys until he found the one that fit and started it up. Slowly he drove the huge vehicle until it faced the gate, then he backed up as far as he could. In low gear, he let out the clutch and pressed the accelerator to the floor. The truck roared forward, crushing the cycle and grinding the body into mud. It hit the gate, ripping out the metal fence posts, shorting out the lights, and wrapping the fence around its front. Then it rolled over the top and broke free.

He went back to the car and drove up along the lake. In a few kilometers, he came to a parking lot next to the water. As he turned into it, he could hear the head rolling around in the trunk. He stopped and walked over to the rocks by the shore. Dark water lapped against them. He took the Knight's Cross from his neck and threw it far out into the lake.

As the clock in the car showed eleven-thirty, he pulled in front of the house. The neighborhood was dark. Carrying the bag, he climbed the steps to the porch and knocked on the door. He heard the bolts slide back. This time the dogs were silent. The woman stood aside for him to enter. In the living room, the curtain over the portrait had been drawn back. It was a photograph, enlarged in a silver frame. There, with one hand on the shoulder of the young Gottfried Lenz, stood the Führer. He looked weak and senile, a slack smile on his face.

"Welcome, hero!" She addressed him familiarly. "Have you brought what I asked?"

"I have."

"Show me!" He held out the bag to her. She carried it into the kitchen, opened it, and dropped the head into the sink. Its mouth and eyes were open; its hair was matted with blood. Shreds of flesh hung from the severed neck. She turned on the water and held it under the tap. Clots of blood and tissue clogged the drain; the liquid filling the sink turned red. Then she set it in the dish rack and dried her hands. She smoothed the hair away from its forehead. "See this earring? I gave it to him when I was twelve years old. We were so close. He was like a brother to me." She picked up the head and kissed it on the lips.

"Now, both of you shall come with me!"

Carrying the head before her, her arms stretched out, she led him into her bedroom. She pointed at the bed.

"Sit there!" she said.

She put the head on a dish on her dresser, its face toward the bed. On either side were candles, which she lit. Then she closed the door and looked at him in the flickering light.

"Hero, there is one last test. I must examine your penis. It must be strong and true, a German penis, not a Jew's penis with the tip cut off and thrown to the dogs." She knelt before him and removed his shoes and socks. Then she unbuckled his belt, pulled down his trousers and underwear and spread his knees apart. He could feel her fingers touching him, pulling back his foreskin.

"It was my destiny to give myself only to the hero. But my cousin profaned me! Only you can make me clean again! "

She unbuttoned his shirt, removed it, and slipped off his undershirt. Then she stood and undressed quickly. She gently pushed him so that he lay down and then she lay close to him. She went over his body from head to foot. There was a cut on his hand he hadn't seen. She held his hand gently and licked off the congealed blood. His knees were stained with blood that had soaked through his trousers. Rising and going into the bathroom, she came back with a warm cloth and washed him off. Then she began to fondle him and kiss him. She put her lips close to his ear.

"The traitor's seed polluted me," she whispered. "But your seed will cleanse and purify me and prepare me for death."

She gripped his wrist and pulled his hand down between her legs. "See, hero? We are racial comrades, you and I. I am doing just as my father instructed. I am ready for you. Do you not feel it? I have been ready for you since the instant you walked through the door!"

She lay back, her legs spread, and guided him on top of her. How could he do this? By thinking of Sonja Davidovna? No, it was obscene to think of her while grappling with this beast. So he thought of duty, and his body responded. He slipped inside her and pushed forward.

The whole room spun around. It was like being drawn into a vortex. At its edges was everything horrible he had seen: the head he had cut from the man on the motorcycle; the man whose skull he had fractured and then drowned; the body of the Aryan Youth flying through the air and the car flipping over; Ingeborg Mohr swinging by a rope from the ceiling; Prober in the closet, soaked with blood; even Heinz Kalmbach, cut to pieces by gunfire. He had to hold tight to keep from joining them. And as he held her, barely moving, she thrust herself against him again and again, nearly lifting him off the bed, until at last, as she dug her nails into his back and her teeth into his neck, he came.

Then they lay quiet. In a few minutes he could feel himself disengaging from her.

"You are leaving me, hero. There, you are gone! Wait here a moment! "She rose and in a few minutes she came back with underwear, socks, trousers and a shirt.

"Put these on! They belonged to my father! It is time! Now we will go to him!"

Picking his keys and his wallet out of the bloody clothes, he dressed in those she had brought him. They fit well. Then, picking up the head, she led him into the hall and opened the door opposite. The room was dark and cold. She turned on the light. It was an ordinary bedroom. Flower-patterned wallpaper covered the walls. There was a bureau with family photos on it, and above it, a dressing mirror. There were white lace curtains on the curtain rods, but behind them, black shades were pulled and taped to the window frame. There was a bedside table and a bed. In the bed lay a man, dressed in the black uniform of the SS, a cap with the skull of the Death's Head division on it, and the Knight's Cross with Golden Oak Leaves around his neck. On the bedside table was a book, face down, an empty glass and a stained plate. His eyeballs had shriveled and dried up, leaving crusted eye sockets. His teeth were exposed, and the bone showed through at the cheeks. With pillows, his arm had been propped up in the Nazi salute and in his outstretched, bony hand, he held forth an object: the icon of the Siegfried League. He had been dead a very long time.

"Father," she said, "I have brought you the hero! I have done as you asked! I told everyone you had gone back to Germany. I have not disturbed your sleep until the day the hero arrived! He has brought you a great gift! Behold, Father, the head of the traitor!" With that she held up the head by the hair and set it on the bureau, facing the corpse. She turned toward the bed and continued to speak.

"This is the new Siegfried! Father! Give him the icon!"

Then she turned toward Hans.

"Take it from him! It is an unbroken chain! My father received this icon from the Führer's hand, and now he passes it on to you."

The corpse's bony fingers were wrapped tight around the icon. He gripped the bones of the wrist. He broke the fingers' grip with a dry, cracking sound. Bits of bone and dried flesh flaked onto the bedspread. The icon came free. He held it toward her and withdrew the sword from the dragon's heart.

"Hero," she said, "my father told me that only the hero would know to do that! Now you must take a sacred oath. It is the oath that the Führer made my father swear. My father taught it to me as a child." From the bedside table she picked up the book and turned it over. It was *Mein Kampf*.

"Put your left hand on this and raise your right in the German salute!"

Hans clicked his heels and held his arm out, as his grandfather and father had done before him.

"Repeat after me! 'By all that is sacred to me, by my faith in the German Reich, by my allegiance to my Führer, Adolf Hitler, I swear to guard the holy place. If I fail in my duty, may I be struck down at the moment of my greatest triumph!'"

Hans spoke the words after her. As he said them, he thought of Mrs. Laibstein and her wonderful face, which time had made beautiful to him. He thought of the oath he had taken to her at her deathbed and repeated in the cemetery, and he thought of the oath he had sworn under the Rheinsberger Strasse, and it seemed to him that those were the words he was saying.

"Now you must go there! You must see it for yourself!"

"Where does it lie?"

"It is in Berlin-Tempelhof, right across the boundary of Kreuzberg. It is where the General-Pape-Strasse meets the Loewenhardt Damm. There is a great cement pillar there. It is round. It is cracked with age. It is in an empty lot in a forgotten corner of the city. It was placed there at the Führer's command, near the site where the Great Arch was to arise. Nearby are apartment buildings and a garden colony. The sacred room lies beneath it. There is an iron stairway, which leads to steel plates at the base of the pillar. There is a secret door there. It cannot be seen from the outside! You must take a wrench. Set in the steel is a row of ten bolts, which protrude enough to be gripped. Twist the fourth bolt from the right and push it, with all your strength, to the left. That will reveal the panel, which also cannot be seen until it is moved. Behind it is a keyhole. Insert the key and turn it all the way around, then push with all your might, and the door will open! You must leave the key in the door while you are in the sacred room and remove it only right before you shut the panel again! Go at night when no one will see you."

"You have been there?"

"Once. As a child. But I did something foolish! You must make it right for me! I will tell you of it." She sat on the bed next to the corpse and took its hand.

"My father and I were very close. We were in Berlin visiting my mother's parents. I was only eleven. Late one night, my father woke me and told me to get dressed. He told me to be very quiet. We crept down the stairs. Everyone else was asleep. He said it was a special night and one I should always remember. We got into the car and drove to a place by the Wall. He said that right on the other side was a graveyard, and that a great hero lay buried there—a winner of the Knight's Cross. My father had a bag with him. In it were two wreaths. He took out one with a ribbon on it. He showed it to me. On the ribbon was the figure of Siegfried slaying the serpent, with a motto below it, and the words, 'German Hero, Rest in Peace!' We both placed our hands on it, and then my father threw it over to the other side. Then we drove to a place near the S-bahn tracks. That is where the pillar is! My father took torches out of the trunk of the car. We went through the gate into the garden colony and then through the fence. He took the bag with him, too. We walked around the pillar and down the stairs. We slid aside the panel, just as I have told you, and with the key my father opened the door. There were more stairs, going down and down—it seemed like forever! At the bottom was a passageway with doors to the side. The first was closed, but the second was open. My father shined the light in. On the floor was a wooden chest, open, filled with jewelry. It was beautiful! How it sparkled in the light! There were necklaces, rings, bracelets. I had never had a single piece of jewelry in my whole life!

I so wanted to pick them up, but my father took me by the arm and pulled me away. Down the hall we went, past another door. At last we came to a chamber. My father gave me the light and lit the torches. He put them in brackets on the wall. The flames lit the room. It was like a church! All around were beautiful mosaics depicting great events in German history. There were figures, glowing, like saints, and other figures, demons all in black, with fiery eyes. My father told me that it showed the struggle between good and evil. It was the most beautiful place I have ever seen! I held Angelika up so she could see, too."

"Angelika?"

"Angelika. My doll. She went with me everywhere. I had no friends. I have lived my whole life without friends. But Angelika was my friend. Her hair was blonde, and her face was white as snow. I loved her more than anything! She was with me, but my father left me. He told me to wait there while he went into another room that only he could enter. He disappeared down a passageway on the other side and was gone. The minutes went by, but he did not return. I grew tired of waiting for him. I was just a child! I thought of the room with the jewelry. I took my light, and Angelika and I went back. I just wanted to see it. I hadn't planned to take anything! I went in the room and opened the chest. I picked up the thing I liked the most—it was a long gold chain with the star of the Jew on it—but I didn't care. It was beautiful! I put it around my neck. It made me feel so pretty! I sat Angelika on the floor, and I walked back and forth, modeling it for her. I wanted it so much! Why should I not take it? The Jews had so much, and I had so little! Then in the distance, I heard a door close. It was my father, coming back. I was afraid! I slipped the necklace into my pocket and ran back to the room with the figures. I didn't have time to take Angelika. I left her right where she was sitting, and she is sitting there still! When I came home, I hid the necklace! Whenever I was sad I took it out and put it on. It was like magic! It made me feel so much happier! One day I was wearing my mother's gown. My cousin and I were playing my favorite game. I was the Princess of the Reich, and my cousin was the handsome young SS officer the Führer had assigned to guard me. Like a fool, I took out the necklace, and then while my cousin waited downstairs I took the icon from its hiding place—only my father and I knew where it was—and I let him take a picture of me holding both of them! And when I grew to be fourteen, he told me that unless I gave myself to him, he would show the picture to my father! So I did what he asked. Now he has paid for his crime, and soon I shall pay for mine."

She reached into her pocket. "Here is the necklace. You must find the chest and return it!" With that, she dropped it into his hand. Then she arose.

"My mission is over," she said. "There is but one thing left to do. Reinhardt, Heinrich, come!" The dogs came into the room. She grabbed the muzzle of one, forced open its mouth and threw in a capsule she had taken from the dresser. Then she held the muzzle shut and blew into its nostrils. As she did the same to the other one, the first was already lying on its side, specks of foam at its lips, wracked with spasms. A few seconds later, both lay still.

She opened the closet door. On the floor were four five-liter metal cans. She opened one and poured the contents on the corpse and around the bed. The smell of gasoline filled the room.

"This is my father's wish! I shall empty them all right here and then I, too, shall lie down on the bed! Flee, hero! Flee the flames! When I close the door, you shall have one minute to escape!"

Shoving the icon into his pocket, Hans ran out of the house and jumped in the car. At the corner, he made a U-turn and came back by. In the middle of the next block, he looked in his rearview mirror. A sheet of flame shot from the front of the house. The whole street was lit with an orange glow. Already a light had come on upstairs in a window of a house opposite. In a few more blocks he pulled over and turned off the lights. Police cars and fire engines sped by.

He drove to the west, avoiding the viaduct, and then to the south, toward Chicago. First he took the Interstate, but then left it for a road that wound through town after town, with dozens of stoplights in each. Seeing an all-night drugstore, he stopped to buy some cotton and some alcohol. A few kilometers on, he found a motel. The clerk was in a secured office with heavy glass and a bolted door. Hans put his money into a metal tray and pushed it through to him. The clerk put in the key and pushed it back. Once in the room, he first took a shower and then stood in front of the mirror. There were tooth marks in his shoulder and scratches on his back. As best he could, he swabbed them with alcohol and lay down on the bed.

The night was disturbed. It seemed like sleep would never come. There was a new sound, one he had never heard before. Voices came from beneath the floor. Finally he got out of bed and lay on the rug and listened. It was hard to say if he were awake or asleep. Far below him there was a moan that rose and fell. Sometimes it sounded like one voice, sometimes like many. The room was dark as death. Even with his eyes wide open, he could see no speck of light. The night light he had left on in the bathroom was out. The light of the clock was gone. Suddenly he heard a dull thud in the distance, then another. They came a few seconds apart. Each one seemed closer than the last. The windows began to rattle. Then came the drone of the engines far above him. He imagined there were black dots covering the sky. It seemed like the end of everything. But as he awoke, the dots slowly faded and the drone of engines turned into the drone of the fan. Sunlight streamed through a crack in the curtains. He looked at the clock. It was nearly ten, and the cleaning crew was moving down the hall.

He drove to the airport and parked in the garage. Noting the row and the space, he called the 800-number to report where it was. In a stall in the men's room, he took the second passport from the lining of his bag, and by evening, he was on a plane to Berlin.

CHAPTER 13

Germania

The flights back had been long and delayed. First there were three extra hours in New York, with nothing to do but stare at the walls. Then, due to the missed connection, there were two more in Frankfurt. When he rose at last from the last seat on the last flight, every limb was numb. He felt like an emissary from the dead to the living. It was early afternoon, and a light rain was falling. In front of the terminal, not a cab was in sight.

It was best, at any rate, just to melt into the crowd. Joining a group of Turks waiting at the bus stop, he rode first to the U-bahn at Jacob-Kaiser-Platz, then changed to the S-bahn at Charlottenburg, and finally back to the U-bahn at the Alexanderplatz. After nearly an hour underway he arrived at the Bernauer Strasse station, and from there walked to Breitbach's, carrying his things. What a relief it would be to give this cursed icon to the Director and walk away from it all. As for that necklace, he felt like dropping it down a sewer. But how could he possibly forget the past few days? It was only as he sat on the plane that it had begun to strike him: now he'd killed four people in his life. How had that made the world better for anyone? As for those relics, it was better to let the dust of history settle on such things. With any luck, he could go home and never hear about any of it again.

On the Rheinsberger Strasse, Breitbach's cab was parked in the courtyard of his building. Hans put his hand on the hood—it was cold. He rang the bell, and when nothing happened, he rang again. Finally, he heard the bolt being drawn back and the door opened just a crack. Then it creaked open all the way, and there stood Breitbach in his nightshirt, shading his eyes and staring weakly out into the light.

"Herr Doktor," he said, "so you're back from America! What a pleasant surprise! The Director will be so pleased to see you. He's talked of little else since you left!"

"I'm here to make a report to him, Herr Breitbach." To himself, his voice sounded like it belonged to someone else, but Breitbach appeared not to notice.

"Of course! But tell me. Your trip. Was it successful?"

"After a fashion."

"After a fashion? That sounds ominous. Did you recover the money?"

"No."

"Then the Director will be disappointed!"

"I don't think he will be, Herr Breitbach."

"Perhaps you're right, Herr Doktor. We'll see soon enough!"

Breitbach, meanwhile, had locked up the front door behind them and was now going through the ritual of unlocking the door to his flat—he'd apparently locked it only to take those few steps from his threshold to the courtyard. Soon, after discretely stepping behind a screen to put on his clothes, he straightened up his rumpled bed and pulled it away from the wall. Then he opened the panel and led the way down the stairs to the bunker.

"The Director has been quite busy since you left, Herr Doktor," he said as they reached last step and set out down the corridor. "I've never seen him like this. He hardly eats or sleeps—he just works on his model, eighteen or twenty hours at a time! It makes me weary just to look at him! And he's always sending me out for some little thing— paint, varnish, sandpaper, a new tool. If I'm not back inside an hour, he throws a fit! And he's made me lay in enough food to last a year!"

Having walked past the room where Gottfried Lenz had once lay hidden and where Schmidt, the American soldier, had sought him out, they entered the large room where the Director had sat when Hans first set eyes him. This time, however, there was no sign of him, though the plants, the fish, and everything else were in their accustomed places.

Breitbach led the way past the workshop, and after knocking softly, opened the door to the room at the back, where the Director stood, wearing a white smock, working on Germania. The spotlights on the ceiling were on, and it was blindingly bright. The Director looked up and nodded.

"Ah, Herr Doktor! So you have resisted temptation and returned from America!" He then looked down and went on with his work.

"Yes, Comrade Director."

"See here!" he said, holding up the model of a building, "The Hall of Heroes! I'm just putting on the finishing touches! And look at this! The Great Hall and the North-South Axis, finished just yesterday! My masterpiece! The Great Hall is like a medieval cathedral, but even more magnificent! It follows the Führer's plans to the last detail! I've even built it to scale! What do you think of it?" He stood aside so Hans could see. Consisting of a square base some twenty-five centimeters on a side, it was crowned with a massive dome, fully thirty centimeters high, which towered above the rest of the city. Each column around the base, each window, and each square in the pattern that adorned the dome itself had been laboriously carved into the wood, sanded smooth, and painted a glistening white. At the very top, perched on a golden orb, was a silver eagle with the swastika of the Third Reich, and on each of the hundred flagpoles that ringed the square where the Great Hall sat was a tiny Nazi flag. Before it and behind it stretched a wide boulevard, lined with buildings of a similar, but less grand, neoclassical style. Along the boulevard there were little trees made of wood and thin wire and tiny metal streetlamps. It was remarkable.

"It's beautiful, Comrade Director."

"Yes, isn't it! But tell me. It's so hard for me to track the days from this tomb. It seems but an instant since we saw you last. How long have you been gone? "

"Eight days, Comrade Director."

"Eight days! Eight days in America! Did you like it there?"

"Not very much, Comrade Director."

"No? And what was it like?"

"Rather like the new Germany, only dirtier and noisier."

"Ha! So you have returned with your ideals intact!"

"Yes, Comrade Director."

"I knew that you would. Didn't I tell you, Breitbach?" The Director had turned to Breitbach and was giving him a look both amused and severe.

"You did, Comrade Director." Breitbach's voice was slightly peevish. "He may have returned with his ideals intact," he went on, "but unfortunately he has not returned with the money."

"The money doesn't matter, Breitbach. Money can be replaced! But Herr Doktor, have you brought with you anything else?"

"Yes, Comrade Director. I have found what you sent me for."

"The icon. The icon of the Siegfried League."

"Yes."

"Then you have succeeded where Jahn had failed! You found in eight days what he could not in fifteen years! I knew you would! After all, dear boy, you are the historical imperative made flesh and blood! You were destined to find it! I knew it the first time I set eyes on you! Let me just put this in place, and I'll come over and take a look at it." Taking a tube from the pocket of his smock, he squeezed a thin line of glue onto the bottom of the Hall of Heroes and pressed it into place. Then he stood back, wiped his hands on the smock, and gave a little sigh of satisfaction.

From his briefcase Hans took the icon and gave it to him. The old man turned it over and over in his hands. Then he took the sword, pulled it from the dragon's heart, and held the key aloft.

"See this, Breitbach? Genuine! This is the culmination of my life's work! We are fortunate, you and I, to have lived to see this moment. Think of all who have touched this icon! Think of who created it and why! It is like a glowing coal snatched from the pit of hell! The fascists would give their lives to have it, yet it is we who have it, not they! Tell me, Herr Doktor, where did you find it?"

"I got it from the daughter of a man named Hartmann."

"Hartmann? Who was that?"

"He was the hero chosen by Himmler. The one who accompanied the relics to the Black Vault and locked it up."

"Gottfried Lenz."

"Yes."

"Wonderful! Where was he?"

"In Milwaukee. It's a town in the Middle West where many

Germans have settled. It was the perfect place for such a person to hide. An American soldier, sent by Goering, found him here in this bunker and brought him to America."

"And why did he do that?"

"He was a fascist sympathizer, Comrade Director, the child of German immigrants. He was brought up to worship Hitler. Somehow he ended up as part of the guard at Nuremberg. It was he who gave Goering the cyanide capsule."

"And this Gottfried Lenz, what did he do all those years in Milwaukee?"

"He built motorcycles, Comrade Director."

"How about Prober? Did you find him as well?"

"I did, Comrade Minister. He is dead."

"Really? And did you kill him?"

"No, Comrade Director. He was killed by Lenz's daughter. She was the little girl in the picture that Jahn sent you. Prober came to see her and tried to buy the icon. She had racial charts and measurements. She told him she'd sell it to him only after she measured his head. When he didn't fit the charts, she cut his throat."

The Director gave a little laugh. "So he didn't measure up? Amusing! A victim of his own philosophy!"

"Yes, Comrade."

"What of Lenz himself?"

"He is dead, too, Comrade Director. He died at home in his bed, an old man. His daughter dressed him in an SS uniform and left him there. She hid his death from the authorities and continued, I'm sure, to collect his pension."

"So the directions to the Black Vault. That knowledge died with him?"

"No, Comrade Director. His daughter had been there. He had taken her there once as a child. She told me where to find it."

"Excellent! And where is that?"

"It lies near what was to have been the North-South Axis of Germania, beneath a test pillar for the Great Arch. The pillar is still there. She remembered the S-bahn tracks nearby, and a garden colony. She said it's a spot filled with weeds and trash, behind a fence, where no one goes. At the base of the pillar is a sunken passageway all around it. On one side there are some iron stairs, leading down. At the foot of those stairs there are ten bolts set into the wall. If one uses a wrench to twist the fourth bolt from the right, one can then push it to the left and slide back a hidden panel, beneath which is a keyhole. The key of the icon fits into it. Once the key has been turned, one can push open the hidden door."

"I know of the spot! It's just here!" With a pointer the Director touched a spot a short way from the Great Arch. "I thought to look there myself, but I could not, since it was in the West. But I've read of it. Yes, it's true, the Führer had this pillar built there, supposedly to test the substrate to see if it would bear the massive weight of the Great Arch. The Great Arch was one of his favorite projects! It was to have carved on it the names of the 1.8 million German soldiers who fell in the Great War. The test pillar and the plans for this model are all that exists of Germania! How fortunate the Black Vault is in such an out-of-the-way spot. How brilliant to place it there! No one would have ascribed any significance to it unless the Great Arch had actually been built! Had it been under the Friedrichstrasse, or the Potsdamer Platz, it would have long since been discovered."

"Yes, Comrade Director."

"This daughter of Lenz. Where is she?"

"She is dead, also, Comrade Director."

"Your work?"

"No, her own. After she gave me the icon, she set her house on fire and burned up with it."

"Amazing. So you killed no one at all?" The Director sounded disappointed.

"I killed a hooligan in Washington. And I killed the son of this American fascist, and another hooligan who was with him. The son had stolen Goering's Golden Party Badge from his father and sold it to Prober. He was a murderer and a drug addict. He had been in prison for many years. It was he who hanged Ingeborg Mohr."

"So this Lenz, the greatest living hero of the Third Reich, lived for fifty years in America, working first as a mechanic in a motorcycle factory and then sitting around, no doubt, drawing his pension from the state?"

"Apparently so, Comrade Director."

"What of this American fascist, the one who protected him?"

"He built motorcycles, too."

"And he is still alive?"

"Just barely, Comrade Director. He is an old man in a nursing home, confined to his bed."

"So all this time these evil men lived in America, growing old and weak, leading their meaningless little *lumpen* proletariat lives, building motorcycles! And by the time the Wall fell and fascism began to reemerge, they were too feeble to seek out that place again! You see, Herr Doktor, this is the historical imperative at work! How can anyone doubt its truth? And now we, instead of they, will go there! This very night we will stand where they sought to stand but could not! It is we who shall find the relics! It is we who shall interpret them to mankind! It is time at last for me to leave this place and go up into the world! Dear boy, you have set me free! You are the hero who redeems Germany! You are the Red Knight! Comrade Breitbach, you are to be commended for extracting a diamond from the wreckage of the state! I will see that you, too, are honored for your work!"

"Thank you, Comrade Director."

"What time is it, Breitbach?"

"It is afternoon, Comrade, shortly past fifteen hundred hours."

"What month is it?"

"It is April, Comrade Director."

"Good! That gives you plenty of time to seek this area out during the day and tell us what we can expect there. Then tonight, around one, the three of us will go there and make our way down beneath it and into the chamber. Breitbach, there are other preparations to make. Besides the wrench, you must bring torches and a crowbar. And I have several things that I must do. Herr Doktor, you must go home and rest. Breitbach will come for you at midnight."

Back at his flat, Hans knocked on Professor Eisenstein's door. In a moment it opened, and there stood Sonja Davidovna. She looked even more beautiful than he had remembered. Her skin was very pale, her hair was jet black, and there were golden flecks in her gray eyes. She gave a little cry of surprise and embraced him, but then stepped back.

"Herr Doktor, you look different! What has happened to your hair?"

"I had it cut in a new style. Do you like it?"

"No! It looks terrible! Whoever did that to you, you must promise me you will never go to that person again!"

"Very well, Sonja Davidovna, I promise."

"And you don't look at all well! You look as though you hadn't slept or eaten for days! You look, too, as though you'd been in a fight! I am very concerned about you!" And the expression on her face told him she was telling the truth.

"I'll soon be all right, Sonja Davidovna."

"I have thought of you many times since you left, Herr Doktor." She had taken hold of his hand in both of hers and continued to hold it tight.

"And I have thought of you."

"Then why did you not write to me, or give me a call?"

"That would have been impossible, Sonja Davidovna."

"Impossible? What have you been doing? And where exactly have you been?"

"Some day perhaps I will tell you, but not now. But there is one thing I need to know. Has anyone been to my apartment?"

"Only I. When you left, I went in and straightened it up a bit. I hope you don't mind."

"Not at all, dearest Sonja Davidovna."

"Do you want your box back?"

"Not just yet, Sonja Davidovna. If you would keep a few hours longer, I would be grateful to you. I must go out this evening. I have a little errand to run."

"A little errand? What sort of little errand?" She eyed him suspiciously.

"Oh, nothing, really. It won't take long."

"Nothing, is it? Then you will not mind if I come along. I feel the need of an evening stroll."

"No, dearest Sonja Davidovna, I'm afraid I must go alone." She set her lip and looked at him like an angry child.

"It disturbs me, Herr Doktor, that you do not trust me." At that point, she released his hand and stepped back over her threshold.

"I trust you more than anyone."

"You certainly do not show it! When are you leaving?"

"In a few hours. I need to rest a bit. Then a colleague is picking me up at midnight. I should be home well before dawn, and I shall see you in the morning. Perhaps we can have coffee together. But now, dearest Sonja Davidovna, I shall need my key."

"Very well," she said, reaching into her pocket and holding it out to him. As he took it, she gave him another angry look and shut the door.

Inside his flat, everything was changed. It was spotless. The stains in the kitchen sink were gone, and the leaking faucet had been fixed. The refrigerator had been scrubbed out, and a broken cabinet door had been set right. The windows were clean. The cracks in the ceiling had been plastered over. A spot near the radiator where the paint had peeled off had been touched up. His books had been shelved and ordered by subject, and his papers put neatly in a stack on his writing-table. In the bedroom there were clean, white curtains at the windows and a new cover to the featherbed. His laundry had been done, his shirts and trousers pressed and hung in the wardrobe, and the whole place smelled clean and fresh. It was like coming home to a different place, and for the first time in many years, he felt happy to be there. Of course it was a pity he had had to offend even for a moment someone who meant so much to him, but he would soon make it up to her. For the time being, he could think of nothing but rest. Setting his alarm, he lay down and sank slowly into sleep. He found himself at last in a place of peace. All was silent. He lay on his back, his arms at his side. Gentle hands undressed him. They anointed him with oils. A sweet smell filled the air. They rubbed his temples, they rubbed his chest. His scar had disappeared. The hands placed his feet together and crossed his arms on his chest. He lay very still. The candles at his head and feet cast a soft glow. The shadow of the flame flickered on the wall. Then it faded away and was gone.

CHAPTER 14

The Black Vault

Shortly before midnight he left the flat. He knocked lightly on Sonja's door, but there was no answer. No doubt she was asleep.

Breitbach was already at the curb, waiting by his cab, and soon they were heading down the Greifswalder Strasse. At that hour, the streets of Prenzlauer Berg were nearly deserted.

"I've gone down to take a look at that pillar, Herr Doktor," said Breitbach as he turned toward the Eberswalder Strasse. "I've been by it hundreds of times. I've often wondered what it was."

"What does it look like?"

"It's nothing but a big, round ugly hunk of cement. There are cracks on the side, with trees growing out of them. It's in the middle of an empty lot at a corner where two diagonal streets intersect. I can see why it's still there. It would take more effort than it's worth to knock it down and cart it away."

"Did you find the bolts in the metal at the foot of the iron stairs?"

"Yes, I found them all right. It's just as you said."

"And the panel?"

"That, too. With a little work I was able to loosen the fourth bolt and push it aside. Behind it is the keyhole. I've put a bit of oil in it. The key should work just fine."

"Are there people around there?"

"Not many. On one side there's a parking garage for an apartment building and on the other a garden colony. The whole area around the pillar is fenced off, but it's easy enough to climb over in a spot out of sight of the building. As for tonight, the gardeners won't be around. And once you get beyond the fence, the brush conceals you."

Meanwhile they had arrived at the Rheinsberger Strasse, and ten minutes later they found the Director in the back room, still working on Germania. The model had changed even in the few hours since Hans had last seen it. Now the North-South Axis that led from either side of the Great Hall was lined with miniature troops, and in the center of the boulevard was a black car with the top down. At the back of it stood a tiny figure, its arm stretched out in the Nazi salute.

"Herr Doktor, come and see what I've put in as the final touch! The Führer in his open car! It represents him on the day of the massive celebration to mark the declaration of Germania as the capital of the world!" He gently touched the little figure on the top of the head. "Good-bye, my little Führer!" he said. "Perhaps I shall bring you a gift when I return!"

They went into the other room. "I have put out some clothes for you, Comrade Director," said Breitbach. A sweater and a coat were laid neatly on the chair.

"Very thoughtful of you, Comrade." The Director put on the sweater but left the coat where it was.

"Are you dressed warmly enough, Comrade? There's a chill in the air."

"I shall be warm enough, Comrade Breitbach."

With him the Director had a canvas valise. Breitbach slid back the door, and they started up the stairs. The valise seemed heavy, for once or twice he stopped and put it down. But when Breitbach offered to give him a hand, he pulled it away and said sharply, "No, I'll bring it myself!"

Once they had stepped into Breitbach's bedroom, the Director watched with interest as Breitbach closed the secret door. "Very clever, Comrade Inspector. So the button to open the door is set under the panel behind Comrade Mielke. A nice touch! One Comrade Mielke would have liked. Look at it! Even with the portrait removed, no one would find it in a thousand years!"

As they passed into the living room, the Director stopped and looked around.

"So here I am back in your flat, Breitbach! It looks little different from when I saw it last. Everything in its place! Not a speck of dust to be seen! You're a good socialist, Comrade Breitbach. Perhaps the best I have ever known!"

"Thank you, Comrade Director."

At the door he watched carefully as Breitbach went through the ritual of unlocking and relocking it. At last they stepped into the courtyard. The Director stood and breathed the night air.

"This is my first time above the ground since November 12, 1989! You recall when you brought me here! Even then they were on my trail!"

"Yes, Comrade Director."

"Where are the torches, Comrade Breitbach? And the tools?"

"In the trunk, Comrade Director. Everything is there. Shall we put your valise in there as well?"

"No! I shall keep it by me!"

As Breitbach closed the car door after seeing the Director into the back seat, he said to Hans in a low voice, "Herr Doktor, tonight, when we reach our destination, the Comrade Director intends to present you formally with a high decoration. He's very excited about the prospect. He's already showed it to me. You might be so kind as to indulge his little fancy."

"Of course, Inspector Breitbach."

They pulled out of the courtyard onto the Rheinsberger Strasse. Only a car or two was in sight. After a block, they turned left and proceeded down the Brunnenstrasse. Nearly every shop had a neon sign, and advertising placards covered the sides of the buildings.

"Is the whole city like this?" said the Director.

"Yes, Comrade Director."

"It's monstrous! Worse than I had imagined! I recognize almost nothing!"

They turned right on the Invalidenstrasse and were soon crossing the canal that had once marked the frontier. Everywhere near where the Wall had once stood, there were new glass and steel buildings with lights in nearly every window. Like an excited child, the Director pressed his face against the glass.

"Are we in the West, Herr Breitbach?"

"Yes, Comrade Director."

"What is this place?"

"It's the site of the new government. Those buildings are the ministries."

"And many people work there?"

"Thousands, Comrade Director."

Turning south, they passed the Reichstag and the Brandenburg Gate to their left. A block or two farther was a great hole in the ground from which rose the structure of yet another new building. There were lights on the cranes, and they could see workers on the girders. Sparks from a welder's torch fell several stories toward the ground. Heavy trucks filled with earth rumbled up out of the pit. There came the faint sounds of drilling and pounding—the sounds of the new Berlin taking shape.

"Does it never stop?"

"No, Comrade. It goes on day and night. It's the greatest construction project of all time."

"And where was the Führer's bunker?"

"Just across there, Comrade, on the other side of that hole."

"What is in that hole?"

"It's a sort of monument, Herr Director. To the murdered Jews of Europe."

"They died by the millions and that is what they get? A hole? But Breitbach. Over there. Is that the zoo?"

"Yes, Herr Director. The park, and beyond it, the zoo."

"My mother often took me there as a child. We lived only a few blocks away. After the surrender I wandered through it. There were dead animals in their cages. Starving Berliners were cutting them into pieces and carrying them away."

Soon they came to another massive group of new buildings. Several streets came together there, and there were underground stations for both the U-bahn and the S-bahn. The place was lit up as light as day.

"Where are we now, Comrade Breitbach?"

"This is the Potsdamer Platz, Comrade Director. It's the new main square of Germany and all Europe."

"Yes! I know this place as well! I stood here as a boy! It was March 1945. I was in the Hitler Youth. I was an artillery helper. It was I who handed the shells to the gunner who put them into the breach. Our gun emplacement was right here! The American planes came from just beyond those trees! Hundreds of them! We fired round after round at them! Finally we hit one! Flames shot out of the wing. It began to spiral. Pieces were falling off it! It hit the ground and blew up. How happy we were! We embraced and shouted for joy! But what difference did it make? The war was lost. Germany was an ash heap. Yet they kept coming! They destroyed this city, they killed my mother, my little brother burned up her arms. I am the only one left! The brutes! How I hate them!"

Breitbach drove on, slowly. The streets were clogged with traffic. A line of taxis stood in front of one of the buildings. A crowd of unruly youths was pushing toward the entrance. They were shouting and laughing and spilling out onto the street.

"Why are all those people trying to get into that building?"

"It's a theatre, Comrade."

"And it's opening its doors at this hour of night?"

"Yes."

"What's playing there?"

"A concert, Comrade. An American rock group. There are concerts like this nearly every night."

A drunken youth with spiked hair and a ring through his lip came up and pounded on the window of the car. The Director shrank back. Breitbach kept moving ahead. Slowly the crowd parted, and they drove on.

Proceeding down the Potsdamer Strasse, they passed the Kleist-Park, where Ingeborg Mohr once plied her trade. They turned onto the Kolonnenstrasse and soon crossed the bridge over the S-bahn tracks. Ahead they could see the pillar looming in the faint light, along with a parking garage, and behind that, an apartment building. Breitback pulled down the darkened General-Pape-Strasse and parked the car. Another car went by and disappeared into an alley down the block. Then all was quiet.

Breitbach opened the door for the Director. They stood a moment, looking back at the city. They could see the glow of its lights against the clouds. "Look!" said the Director. "The Führer's dream! Germania!"

Breitbach opened the trunk and took out the torches. They were thick and tapered and smelled of tar. There were three of them. Breitbach gave them to Hans while he brought a flashlight and a crowbar. They set off toward the pillar with the Director between them, carrying his valise. The little procession moved toward the gate into the garden colony. By the streetlight, Hans could see on it a sign that read, "Jasmine Way." To the right the huts of the garden colony were scattered among the little plots of land, and to the left, the test pillar rose above them. Hans could see little trees growing from the cracks. Toward the top, metal rods stuck out all around. The wire fence separating it from the path was low and half falling down. They stepped over it and pushed through the brush. On the ground all around was trash—bottles, cans, a car battery, chunks of cement. Breitbach led the way. On the side facing General-Pape-Strasse and the S-bahn tracks, right at the base, was a set of metal stairs leading down. At the top of the stairs, Breitbach stopped.

"Wait a moment, Comrades," he said, "I have left the wrench in the car." He lay the flashlight and the crowbar down and disappeared.

The Director put his valise down for a moment and looked up at the pillar.

"See, Herr Doktor?" he said. "This is all that remains of the Führer's dream. The fascists would make it a holy place. In 1943 a firm was engaged, supposedly to test the capacity of the substrate to support the weight of the Great Arch, which was to be close by. The site was guarded by the SS, and this pillar was put up in the spring of 1944. It was built by inmates, most of them Jews, from the Sachsenhausen Concentration Camp. They were kept in a barracks apart from everyone else. Once it was finished, they all disappeared, as did the owners of the firm, murdered, no doubt, by the SS. It's like the tombs of the Pharoahs—built by slave workers who were then put to the sword!"

Breitbach returned, picking his way through the brush. He went down the stairs in front of them. With the flashlight, he shined a circle of light on the line of bolts. While Hans held the light, Breitbach took the wrench and loosened the fourth from the right and pushed the panel back. Behind it was a recessed keyhole and a knob.

"Herr Doktor," said the Director, "you have earned this honor. You must insert the key."

Hans pulled the key from its sheath, put it in the keyhole, and turned it slowly until he heard a click. Then all three pushed against the door. Slowly it creaked open. Before them was a short passage and a set of stairs leading down. It was black as pitch. The Director paused. "Comrades," he said, "bid farewell to the world above. You enter a world where time has stopped. Few who entered this place have ever returned!"

Breitbach shined the light ahead and they started down. The Director moved slowly. He began to speak. "On the night of 30 April 1945, a ragged little band left the bunker and came, first in an armored vehicle preceded by two motorcycles, and then on foot, down the S-bahn tracks. Among them were Dr. Goebbels and our hero, Gottfried Lenz. Think of it! The twisted little doctor himself limped down these stairs."

The stairway was long, as long as that to the bunker on the Rheinsberger Strasse. Down and down it went, into the earth. The air was moist and dank. It was quiet, save for the faint rumble in the distance of a train of the S-bahn. Set into the wall was a handrail, which the Director held with one hand, gripping his valise with the other. Slowly he made his way down the stairs. At the bottom was a corridor, its walls lined with tile, with metal doors set into the walls to the side. At the first one he stopped.

"Breitbach!" he said. "Let us look inside!"

Breitbach lifted the latch and put his shoulder to the door. Slowly it swung open. He shined in his light. It fell on row after row of metal shelves with hundreds of file boxes. Breitbach stepped closer and played his light back and forth on them. Each box was neatly labeled with a name: Auschwitz, Treblenka, Sobibor.

"What are these, Comrade Director?"

"The archives of the destruction of the Jews!" The Director took a box from the shelf and opened it. It was filled with documents.

"See?" he said. "The weekly reports from the death camps. The SS insisted on an exact accounting. Every death, every incinerated corpse, was carefully noted and entered into the records. A great treasure trove for scholars! At last it will be possible to determine, down to the last child, exactly how many Jews perished in the Holocaust! Comrades, what you see before you is a vast ledger of death!"

Set into the wall near the door was a marble tablet. At the top were the words "This memorial is dedicated to those who gave their lives that Europe might be free of the scourge of Jewry. Each of these sons of the Reich answered the call of his Führer. Each took up the sword of righteousness and smote every Jew that came in his path. Though first among the Jew-killers, each fell victim to the cunning and treachery of a Jew and died the martyr's death. All Germany honors them and we, their brothers in the SS, erect this monument to their memory. We will remember forever their sacrifice to purify our race." Below, in two columns, was a list of names.

"Look, Comrades," said the Director. "Those who appear here were the worst and most depraved of the lot. Heads of special units that shot women and children in the woods! Death camp guards who sealed the gas chambers filled with humanity and dropped the pellets into the acid! Swine, all of them! More than bringing shame on Germany alone, they have brought shame on the whole human race!" He leaned forward and spat on the tablet. Breitbach played his light down the list. As Hans watched, the light fell on the name of his grandfather.

They returned to the corridor. Some of the tiles had fallen off the walls, revealing cement laced with cracks. Ahead was the second door. It was ajar. They pushed it open and stepped inside. On the floor was a wooden chest, its lid thrown back. On the bottom of it were necklaces, bracelets, and rings. The Director picked up a few and let them run through his fingers.

"Look at this," he said. "A handful of trinkets and keepsakes of women and children long since dead. Worth no more than a few thousand euros! By early 1945, it's all that Bormann was able to scrape together from the camps! Everything else the SS had stolen years before! The filthy beasts! They went to South America, their pockets stuffed with the gold of their victims. Comrades, it's just another fascist lie. There is no Treasure of the Jews." Hans looked into the shadows at the limits of the light. Propped against the wall sat a doll. Her hair was blonde, and her face was chalky white. She sat motionless, staring straight ahead, just as she had for thirty years. As the Director and Breitbach turned to the door, Hans hung back. He took the necklace from his pocket, bent down, and dropped it in the box.

They went back into the corridor. A few paces on was yet another door. Three bolts held it shut. Breitbach oiled them and slid them back in turn. He pushed, but the door held firm.

"Comrade," he said, "something is holding it shut."

"It is the dead, pushing back. Herr Doktor, you must give him a hand."

Hans put the torches on the floor. The Director held the light. Hans and Breitbach braced themselves against the door and pushed. The door held fast. A full minute passed, and nothing happened. It seemed hopeless.

"Harder, Herr Doktor, harder, Breitbach!"

Hans pushed until every sinew in his body felt ready to snap. He breathed as deeply as he could, but nothing seemed enough. Pain shot up and down his arms and legs and into his chest. In the faint light, he could see Breitbach next to him, the tendons in his neck standing out like cords. At last he felt the tiniest tick, and the door began to move, a millimeter at a time. There was a scraping noise, as though the bottom of it were grinding something into the floor. Farther and farther it went, until at last they could step inside. They were in a room, bigger than any they had been in yet. Breitbach shined his light around. There were wooden chairs and a table, with pools of wax on it that had once been candles. In the corner were two buckets. Scattered across the floor were dark little piles. As he recovered his senses he could see they had once been human beings. Mixed with the bones were the remains of striped uniforms, and on them the six-pointed yellow star. Death had caught some on their knees, their hands clasped. Others lay stretched out on the floor, their fleshless heads toward the door. Along the walls were three-tiered wooden bunks. In one lay a skeleton, a bony arm draped over the side, a pair of glasses over its empty eye sockets. Its dead fingers clutched an open locket with the picture of a child. Hans felt weak. No photos of piles of the dead or of bones in the ovens of the crematoria had prepared him for this. He felt the urge to lie down on the floor and join them.

"Comrades," said the Director, "these are the slaves who built this place. Craftsmen and artists, locked up here and let out only to work. The most talented of their race, picked from concentration camps all over Europe, kept here for months! Once they came down the stairs, there was no return. Above on the streets the world had forgotten them! When their labors were finally done, the SS shut them in here for good! While the Red Army chased the last fascist rats through the sewers of Berlin, they died here in utter darkness! Look at them, the poor devils, trying to suck the last bit of air from under the door. Did the God of Abraham and Isaac comfort them in their last hours? Did they think he would free them from this place? Come! Let us go on! It is obscene to disturb them in their sleep."

They turned their backs and continued down the hall. There were no sounds but their footfalls. Hans felt he wore boots of lead. Each step onward took all the strength he had. A few steps ahead the Director stopped.

"We are approaching the Black Vault," he said. "We have but one more stop along the way. Breitbach, leave your flashlight here! It is time to light the torches!"

Breitbach took a torch from Hans and lit it. He handed it to the Director and then lit two more. Soon they were moving down the passage again, the torches held high. The flames flickered on the walls. At the end, the corridor opened into a circular chamber with a passage opposite. The Director stepped in and walked to the center.

"Those brackets on the wall! Let us put the torches there!"

The flames lit the room. The ceiling was high, like the vault of a chapel. On the wall were mosaics in many colors, with figures larger than men. Bathed in a cloud of light and clad in shining armor stood Hitler, the visor of his helmet raised to reveal his face. On his breastplate was a golden swastika. His sword was drawn, and he held it aloft. To either side of him stood other figures in armor.

The Director began to speak. "Comrades, behold before you the allegory of the destruction of the Jews. Is it not magnificent? The Führer casting the Elders of Zion into the pit of hell! The artists who created it were as great as any who build the great cathedrals. While their wives and children died in the camps, they were kept alive to do this work! Every figure is perfect! See who stands at the Führer's side? The heroes in the war against Jewry! The worst and most depraved anti-Semites the earth has ever vomited forth! Richard Wagner, Houston Stewart Chamberlain, Karl Lueger—together they planted the seeds of Jew-hatred in the Führer's mind that reaped a harvest of death! And see who is clustered behind them—the worst of the Nazi hyenas—Himmler, Heydrich, and Goebbels!"

Hans looked at the Führer. His face seemed illuminated by an inner light. There was no shadow of anger on it. His gaze was pure and steady, the look of a prophet, the look of a saint. Moving forward around him were the Aryan knights, with the double lightning bolt of the SS on their shields and the Death's Head on their helmets. Shrinking before the knights were dark and bearded figures with glowing eyes, clutching their scrolls. In their midst stood the Chief Rabbi, with billowing prayer shawls, holding up a bony hand. Around him were piles of gold and silver, while a mob of dark-skinned, ape-like rabble clung to the robes around his legs. Behind them, like a vast furnace, were the flames of damnation. The Aryan Knights were driving them back; some teetered on the brink, others, their robes already aflame, fell into the fire. Over the Führer shone the sun, a bright orb, high in the sky, but over the Jews, the sky was as black as night. Behind the Aryan Knights were blonde women and their blond children, some still at the breast, and in the distance, bathed in light, were the domes and spires of a magnificent city—Germania. The Director stretched out an arm toward it.

"See there?" he said. "The Great Arch! And there is the Great Hall! This is my triumph! Mine is like it in every way! But let us move on! Bring your torches! We are approaching the end of our long journey!"

They walked into the passageway before them. It stretched on into the darkness. On its walls stood rows of knights of the SS, the shoulder of one touching that of the next, their shields held before them. Their eyes were an icy blue, their faces blank and the same; they seemed to be closing in on him, reaching out and taking hold of him, dragging him away to be one of their own.

At the end was a stone arch, and set into it was yet another door. On it, in raised relief, was Siegfried, plunging his sword into the serpent's heart. On the arch above was a swastika over the globe of the earth, and an inscription. Breitbach held up a torch, and the Director read out the words. "'We shall turn the black night of death into the shining dawn of final victory!' Those are the words of Joseph Goebbels! The Nazi mythmaker! This is his last transcendent effort. He understood how symbols change history! Comrades! Behind this door lies the heart of Germania. The Black Vault! Let us enter!"

All three put their shoulders to the door. There was a creaking and screeching, almost like a human voice, as it slowly swung open. They entered. They were in a chamber, smaller than the last, no more than a few paces on a side. Its walls were of the blackest marble. Carved into one was the face of the Führer, flanked by shields of the Teutonic Knights. Beneath were the words "This war will not come to an end as the Jews imagine, with the extermination of the European-Aryan peoples, but that the result of this war will be the annihilation of Jewry. For the first time the old Jewish law will now be applied: an eye for an eye, a tooth for a tooth. The Führer, 30 January 1942." In the center, like an altar, was a bier of white marble, and on it, an oaken casket. Candles in brass stands were at its head and foot. Into its lid were carved intertwined leaves and swastikas. Set into it was a golden plate, and on it, the name "Adolf Hitler, 1889–1945," and the words, "Here I lie, until Germany calls me forth again!" At either side of the bier lay the remains of a man in an SS uniform with a rifle beside him. From the boots of each emerged the leg bones, with shards of rotting cloth. On the floor were two caps with the Death's Head insignia of the SS. Before the crypt lay four withered wreathes. The Director touched one with his foot.

"See comrades?" he said. "Four times Lenz returned here. And four times he left a wreath!"

"What is this place, Comrade?" said Breitbach.

"The death chamber of the Führer! *Here* is where he died! *He* was among that ragged party that made its way here on the night of April 30, 1945! Here Goebbels and the hero and these two SS men laid him out. And here he was to remain, like Barbarossa in his mountain, until Germany needed him again! Come! Let us put our torches in the brackets on the wall and open this box to see what lies within!"

Breitbach slipped the crowbar beneath the lid and pried it up. With Hans's help, he pushed it until it fell to the floor and split. They leaned forward to look inside. The light of the torches fell on a corpse, clad in a military tunic. Its teeth were a disgusting brownish-yellow mass, covered with fillings and bridges. On the rotting cloth where the chest had been was an Iron Cross, suspended on a rib. Strands of dark hair remained on the crown of the skull and, adhering to where the lips had once been, the few hairs of a mustache.

"Comrades, behold the Führer!"

"Comrade Director," said Hans, "How can this be? The Russians found the Führer's remains. I have read it many times!"

"So they thought! What they found was a pile of charred bones and a shattered skull with a few teeth! Goebbels' last little joke! It was a Russian prisoner of war—a man the same size and with much the same features as the real Führer. Goebbels kept him in a cell below the bunker, like an animal in a cage! Only the twisted little doctor and these lads here beneath us knew he existed! When they needed him, they brought him out and shot him through the head! And while these two SS-men held Eva Braun down, Goebbels himself forced cyanide down her throat. Then, while the real Führer skulked in the hidden cell, they carried the double and Eva Braun into the courtyard, wrapped in blankets, poured gasoline on them, and burned them to ash! The teeth of the supposed Führer were a clever forgery, comrade! Like so much else, a trick of the twisted little doctor! Hitler would never allow X-rays to be made, so no exact records existed. And months before, Goebbels had had duplicate bridgework made by the Führer's dentist and worked into the double's mouth. Then Goebbels had the dentist taken outside and shot!"

The Director took from the valise the leather-bound notebook and stood beneath one of the torches.

"Comrades, now I shall read you the final entry from Goebbels' secret journal. Hear what he says!" The Director stood beneath one of the torches and began to read.

"'1 May 1945. Magde and the children are already dead, and soon I will join them. But it is a joyous moment! I die knowing that some day Germany will honor the Führer and build him monuments. Our sacrifices have not been in vain! Late in the hours of last night, we returned to the most holy place in Germany for its final consecration. With us were the hero and two members of the Führer's bodyguard, his personal favorites. The Führer's spirit was strong, but his body was weak. Our hero helped him down the stairs—he would let no one else do it! He died the death of a soldier. The hero and I and the two brave lads gave him a last salute. Proudly we said the words that shall echo through time: 'Heil Hitler! Sieg heil!' The Führer was deeply moved! Then, because in his illness his hand had become unsteady, the hero helped him hold the barrel of the pistol to his heart and pull the trigger. A shot rang out—one era in history came to a close and another began!

"'We laid him in the tomb and placed the box with the sacred decree beneath his hand. It is the central document in the history of our race! We saluted once more and lifted the lid and put it on the coffin. Then, as the two brave lads presented arms, the hero shot each through the heart. We only learned their Christian names as we bid them farewell—Reinhardt and Heinrich! They will guard the Führer as long as he shall lie here! At the door, the hero and I parted. He knows his sacred task! And some day he will pass it on to a new hero, one who has likewise shed blood for Germany!'"

The Director closed the journal and stepped forward. Nearly concealed in the shadows of the crypt was an ebony box beneath the corpse's right hand. He reached in and removed it. Inlaid in its cover was the seal of the Siegfried League. He opened it. Inside was a rolled-up parchment, tied with a satin ribbon. The Director handed it to Hans. "Herr Doktor, read it aloud!"

Hans unrolled the scroll, and read.

"Berlin, the Reich's Chancellery, 18 January 1942. To Reichsführer Heinrich Himmler, Gestapo Headquarters, Prinz-Albrecht-Strasse. Top secret! I herewith command you, as Reichsführer of the SS, to take all measures and use all means to eradicate forever from Europe the plague of verminous Jews, unto the last man, woman, and child. Not one must be spared! Only through the total annihilation of Jewry can the German Reich be made safe! May Providence protect and hasten you in your historic task! Adolf Hitler, Führer of the German Volk."

The Director put the parchment back in the box and placed it by his valise.

"You knew what was here, Comrade Director?"

"Of course, Herr Doktor. I have known for many years. I knew, too, that the Siegfried League would someday return to life. Its mission was to guard the Führer's remains until Germans could again pay them tribute. Now that time is drawing near! Fascism is reemerging! It is capitalism in its purest form! It will conquer the world and rule for five generations, and then communism will sweep it away! That is the historical imperative. Communism can only triumph if fascism returns. History must repeat itself. Only then, after a time of struggle and revolution, will there at last be a just society. In the face of these forces, Comrade, none of us matters. We can only serve them blindly! If the Jews have to die, what difference should that make? They are a humane people. They will understand that their sacrifice serves to redeem mankind. That is their historic role! And now, Herr Doktor, we shall have a little ceremony." The Director knelt and pulled from the valise a plastic bag. From it he took the uniform of a colonel in State Security.

"Comrade Klug, put this on!" Hans looked over at Breitbach, who gave a little nod. Turning around, Hans removed his shirt and trousers, laid them on the floor, and put on the uniform. The Director had meanwhile taken two decorations, on ribbons, from the valise, which he put on the edge of the crypt. He stepped up to Breitbach, placed both his hands on Breitbach's shoulders, and looked him in the eye.

"Comrade," he said, "it is my honor to award you the Order of the Defender of the State! It is the highest decoration that the Ministry of State Security bestows! You have earned it! While the weak and the vacillating fell away, you held true to the old ideals! Nothing shook your faith! But more than that, you have been a friend to a friendless old man. Without you, this moment of victory would have never have come!" He took one of the medals and placed the ribbon around Breitbach's neck. Breitbach's chin quivered, and he wiped away a tear.

Then the Director turned to Hans. Hans snapped to attention. He placed the silk ribbon of the second medal around Hans's neck. "Comrade," he said, "I hearby decorate you as the Eternal Hero of World Socialism. I have created this order to be given to the discoverer of the Black Vault. You have won it! You will wear it for all time! You have played your role well, dear boy! You are the flower of German youth! You are the historical imperative made flesh. You and I will jolt history back into its forward path! Even if your name is lost, your spirit will live on forever."

Then he stepped back and said, "And now, comrades, it is time for us to fulfill our historic destinies." He took from the bag a pistol, raised it, and shot Breitbach through the chest. Breitbach fell first to his knees, then forward on his face, on the bones of one of the guards.

"Comrade Director, what have you done?"

"There never was a truer or more loyal Comrade than Comrade Breitbach. He deserves this honor."

"Honor? What honor?"

"Comrade Breitbach will guard the Red Hero, for all eternity."

"The Red Hero?"

"You, Comrade! The greatest hero Germany has produced! *You* will rest here. In a hundred years, or a thousand, when the tomb is uncovered, it is *you* they will find! In tune with the historic forces, it is the Red Hero who must rest in the tomb at the heart of Berlin. That will change history. That will form the spirit of the city! Germania will some day crumble into dust, and in its place there will arise the glorious socialist capital of all races and all peoples of the world, Marx-Engels-Stadt!"

"Marx-Engels-Stadt?"

"Yes, Comrade! Communism is Germany's destiny! It arose from German soil! It is the way Germany will at last rule the earth. Surely, Comrade, you recognize the historic necessity of what we do here! Yours is an important role in history. I shall remove these wretched bones and lay you, the Red Hero, in their place!"

With that, the Director stepped back and leveled the pistol at Hans's chest. Hans felt no fear. All that occurred to him was, "So this is how it ends." He felt free of everything—free of life, free of the past. He waited for a wave of nothingness to wash over him.

Instead, from behind him, came a woman's voice, shattering his thoughts. It spoke in Russian. "Quickly, Hans," it said, "stand aside!" He turned, stepped back, and at that moment a shot rang out from the door behind him, and then two more. At the first he felt a sting on his shoulder and when he put his hand there his fingers were wet with blood. Behind him the Director fell back against the tomb and slumped to the floor.

Slowly a figure stepped from the shadows and into the room. It was Sonja Davidovna. In the flickering light of the torches, he could see her hair sticking out at least twenty centimeters from her head.

"That man," she said, "is he dead?"

Hans looked down at the Director. There were two holes in his chest and another in his neck.

"Yes," he said.

"I'm sorry, my dearest Hans, that I had to nick you a little bit."

"You did that on purpose?"

"Well, you didn't step back quickly enough. What was I to do? Let him shoot you and then me as well?"

"Where did you get a pistol?"

"Where do you think? From you yourself! It was in that box you gave me."

"You opened it?"

"Of course. Did you expect otherwise? I want to know all about you. You won't tell me yourself, so I'm forced to resort to such measures. Besides, how am I going to defend you if I don't know who you are?"

"But how did you learn how to shoot?"

"In the Young Pioneers. When I was fourteen, they gave us military training. I won a medal. I was the best shot of all!"

"I feel a little weak, Sonja Davidovna."

"You do, do you? Some hero you are! It's barely a scratch! I suppose you're going to make a big fuss about it! Don't be such a big baby! I know somebody from our community, Dr. Mandelbaum, who lives nearby us—he was one of the finest surgeons in all Moscow! He will fix you up like new, no questions asked! Then you can come home, and Father and I will take care of you and do our best to keep you out of trouble! Not an easy task, from the looks of it. Now let us get you out of those stupid clothes, and let us leave this horrible place!"

Helping him to change, she used the shirt of the uniform to bind his wound. Then she leaned over and peered into the tomb.

"Do you know whose bones these are?" said Hans.

"Of course."

"What are we to do with them?"

"We'll think of something." Taking a kerchief from around her neck, she picked up the bones and put them into the plastic bag that had covered the uniform; as the last thing, she dropped in the skull. She slung it over her shoulder.

"Dearest Hans, if the authorities learn of your role in all this, will it mean difficulties for you?"

"Yes, a great many."

"What will happen?"

"I'll go to prison for the rest of my life."

"Then let us leave things just as they are." They started down the passageway.

"How did you get here?"

"In a car we borrowed from a countryman. The same one we took to the country that day. Didn't you see us drive by when you parked? It was only because that man went back to his taxi that I was able to find you at all!"

They passed the three doors and came to the stairs. Sonja Davidovna walked up ahead of him, the bag over her shoulder. At the top the professor was waiting.

"Herr Doktor!" he said. "Sonja wouldn't let me come down. I heard shots!"

"It was nothing, Father. The doctor has had a little mishap. But he'll be fine." And it was true that the flow of blood had stopped.

"Sonja Davidovna, I know that you are not telling me the truth! You are very brave but you are also a very bad young woman. What am I to do with you? Herr Doktor, perhaps in the future you will help me to restrain her impulses."

"I will try, Herr Professor." At this the man embraced him and kissed him on both cheeks.

"Father, you must never speak of this night. We will erase it from our memories."

"Yes, dearest Sonja."

They shut the door. Hans removed the key, put it back in its sheath, and dropped it in his pocket. They pulled the panel shut and turned the bolt. Sonja shined a light on it. It was impossible to see that it had ever been opened or that it existed at all.

They walked quickly down to the alley where Hans had seen a car disappear just as he arrived. The car was parked there. Sonja went around and opened the door for Hans while her father climbed into the back seat from the other side. He took that opportunity to say a word to her.

"Sonja, you are a good person and I love you more than I have ever loved anyone else. But please understand, I've done things I can never tell you about."

"Judging by what you get mixed up in, I'm sure of that! But perhaps you'd consider leaving that part of your life behind. Haven't you done enough to make it a better world? Now it's time to try something else for a while."

They drove toward home, turning onto the Mehringdamm and passing the Viktoria-Park, with its illuminated waterfall. Along the streets were little shops with signs in Turkish on them. Soon they were passing the Hermannplatz, then turning up the Kottbusser Damm and coming to the Paul-Lincke-Ufer, along the Landwehr Canal, where people were cleaning up after the outdoor market that was held there each Sunday. They pulled up behind a garbage truck with its Turkish crew, picking up the leavings of dozens of stalls, selling meat, fruit, and vegetables.

Sonja got out, taking the remains with her. "Hey there, brothers," she said, "do you have room for one more bag?" The men smiled and tipped their hats. One of them started the compactor and threw it in. And in a moment it had become part of the trash of a great city.